VALIANT
HIGH

DANIEL KIBBLESMITH | DEREK CHARM | DAVID BARON | SIMON BOWLAND

CONTENTS

5 **WELCOME TO VALIANT HIGH**
VALIANT HIGH #1

Writer: Daniel Kibblesmith
Artist: Derek Charm
Colorist: David Baron
Letterer: Simon Bowland
Cover Artists: David Lafuente with Brian Reber

29 **THE BIG TEST**
VALIANT HIGH #2

Writer: Daniel Kibblesmith
Artist: Derek Charm
Colorist: David Baron
Letterer: Simon Bowland
Cover Artists: David Lafuente with David Baron

53 **THE BIG GAME**
VALIANT HIGH #3

Writer: Daniel Kibblesmith
Artist: Derek Charm
Colorist: David Baron
Letterer: Simon Bowland
Cover Artists: David Lafuente with David Baron

Collection Cover Art: Derek Charm

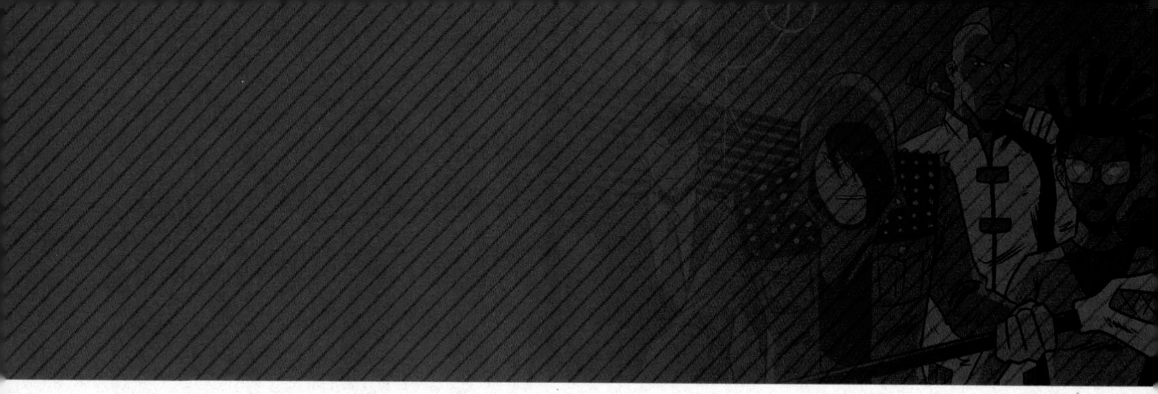

77 THE BIG DANCE
VALIANT HIGH #4

Writer: Daniel Kibblesmith
Artist: Derek Charm
Colorist: David Baron
Letterer: Simon Bowland
Cover Artists: David Lafuente with David Baron

101 GALLERY

Derek Charm
Sina Grace
David Lafuente
Irene Lee
Dan Parent

Assistant Editor: Benjamin Peterson
Editors: Lauren Hitzhusen and Warren Simons

VALIANT.

Dan Mintz
Chairman

Fred Pierce
Publisher

Walter Black
VP Operations

Atom! Freeman
Vice President of Sales

Joseph Illidge
Executive Editor

Robert Meyers
Editorial Director

Mel Caylo
Director of Marketing

Matthew Klein
Director of Sales

Travis Escarfullery
Director of Design & Production

Peter Stern
Director of International Publishing & Merchandising

Karl Bollers
Editor

Victoria McNally
Senior Marketing & Communications Manager

Jeff Walker
Production & Design Manager

Julia Walchuk
Sales Manager

Benjamin Peterson
David Menchel
Assistant Editors

Connor Hill
Sales Operations Coordinator

Ryan Stayton
Director of Special Projects

Ivan Cohen
Collection Editor

Steve Blackwell
Collection Designer

Rian Hughes/Device
Original Trade Dress & Book Design

Russ Brown
President, Consumer Products,
Promotions & Ad Sales

Caritza Berlioz
Licensing Coordinator

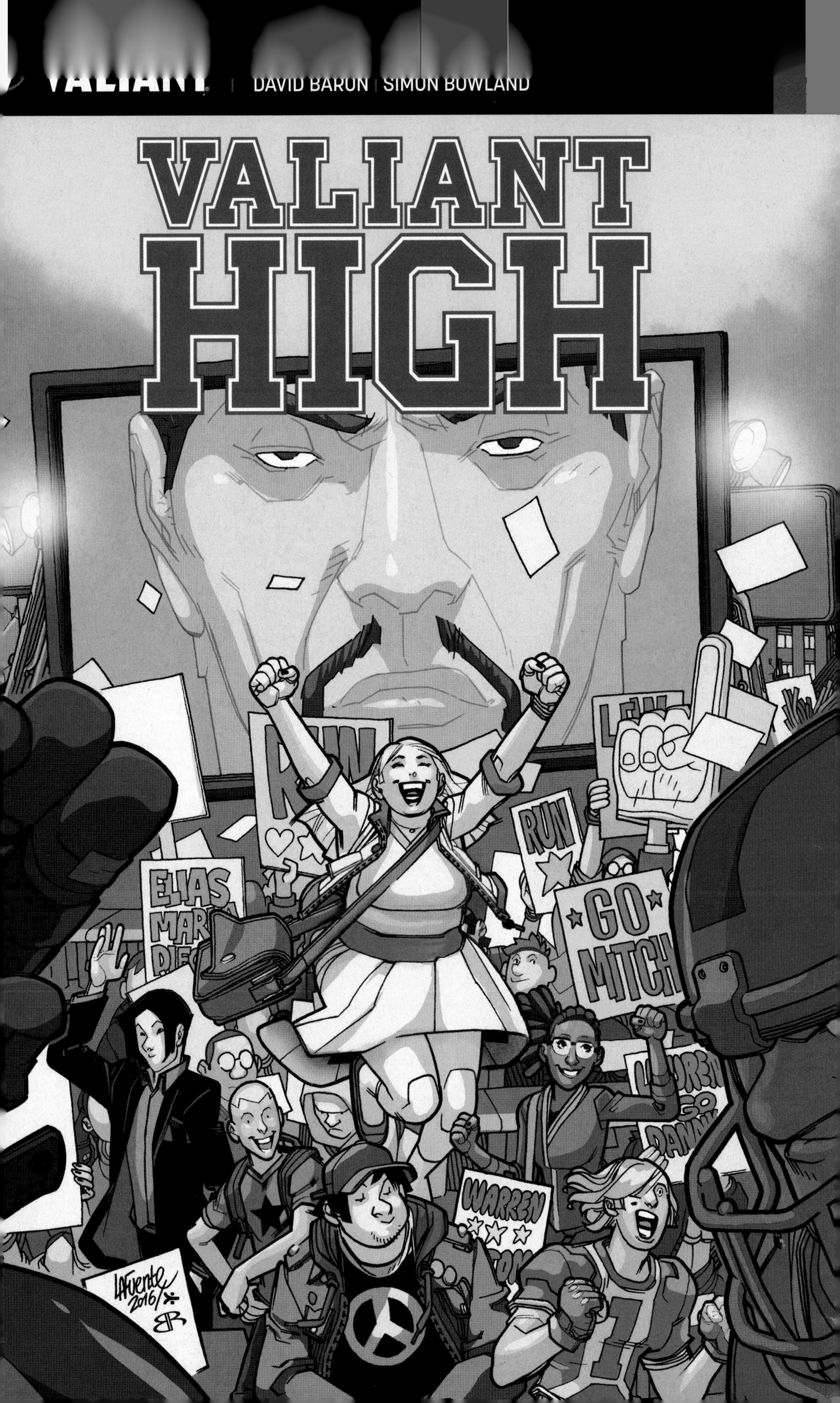
VALIANT
DAVID BARON
SIMON BOWLAND
VALIANT HIGH
RUN
RUN
ELIAS
GO MITCH
WARREN

VALIANT HIGH

CLASS OF 2018

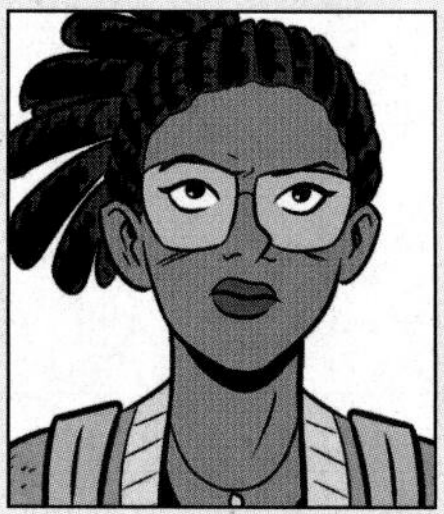

LIVEWIRE
AKA AMANDA McKEE, SOPHOMORE.
Talks to machines.
(it's easier than boys).

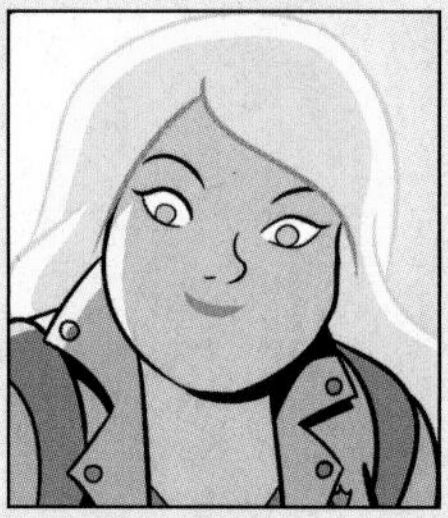

ZEPHYR
AKA FAITH HERBERT, SOPHOMORE.
Flies (can bring a +1). Geeks out.

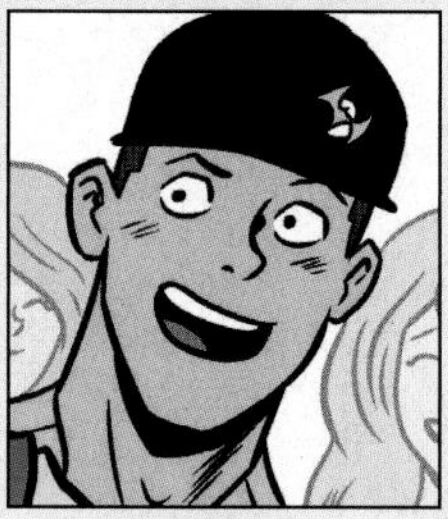

TORQUE
AKA JOHN TORKELSON, JUNIOR.
Star Quarterback. Acts like one.

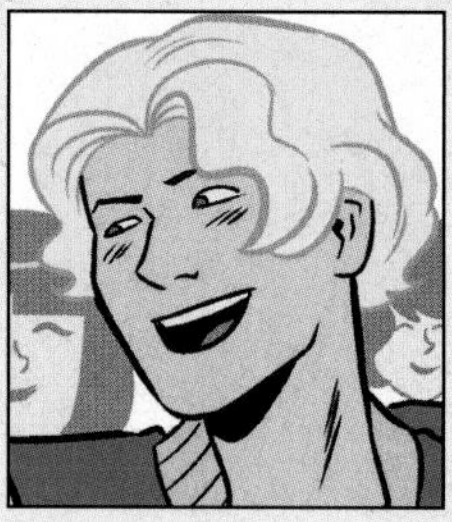

X-O
AKA ARIC DACIA, JUNIOR.
Star running back. King among boys.

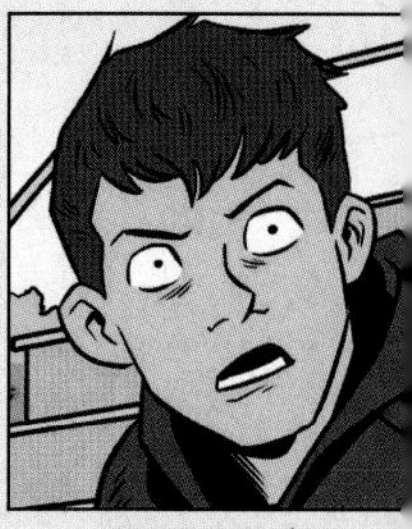

PETER STANCHEK
AKA NOT COOL ENOUGH
FOR A CODENAME, SOPHOMORE.
Brain Powers. (All of them).

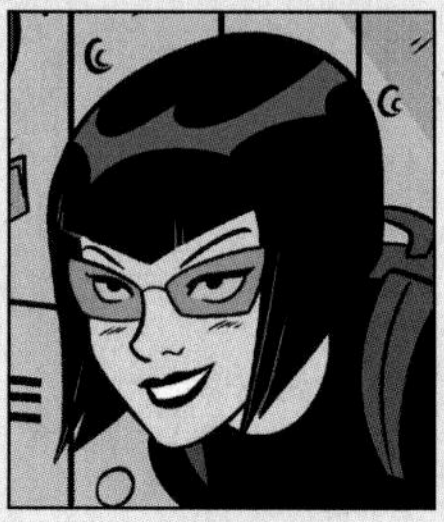

KRIS HATHAWAY
AKA TOO COOL FOR
CODENAMES, SOPHOMORE.
Mystery girl.

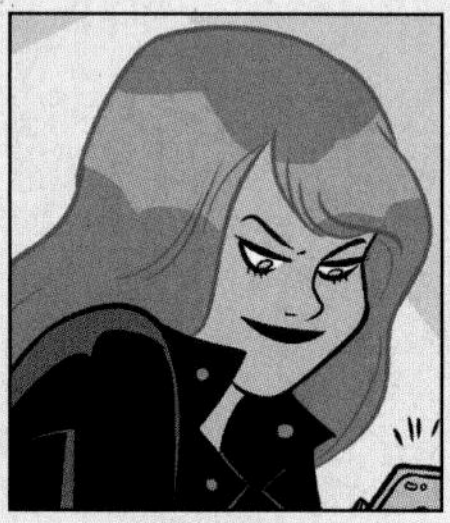

FLAMINGO
AKA CHARLENE DUPRE, SOPHOMORE.
Pyrokinetic. Hot 2 trot.

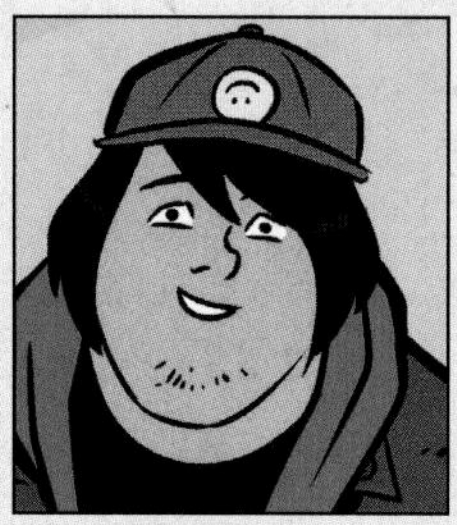

ARMSTRONG
AKA ARAM, SENIOR (POSSIBLY?).
Warrior poet.

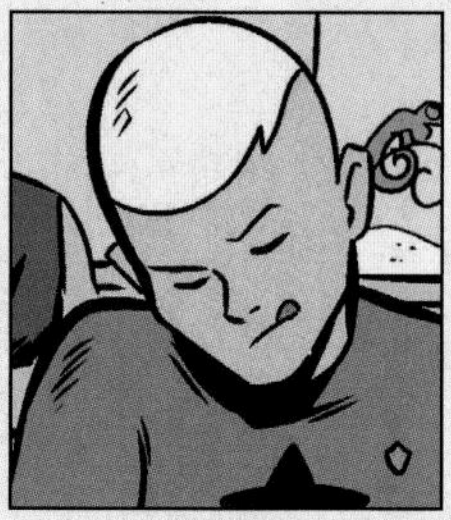

ARCHER
AKA OBADIAH ARCHER, FRESHMAN
(FORMERLY HOMESCHOOLED).
Quiet (too quiet?).

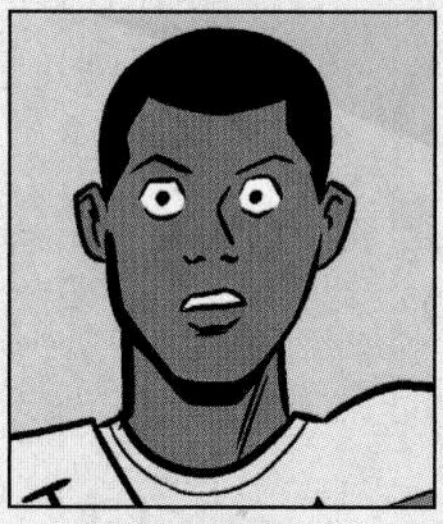

QUANTUM
AKA ERIC HENDERSON, SOPHOMORE.
Overachiever (in theory).

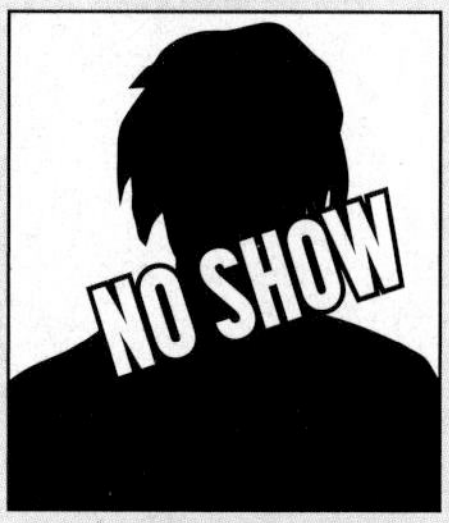
NO SHOW

WOODY
AKA WOODY (OF "QUANTUM AND" FAME),
SOPHOMORE.
Eric Henderson's brother (wiki it).

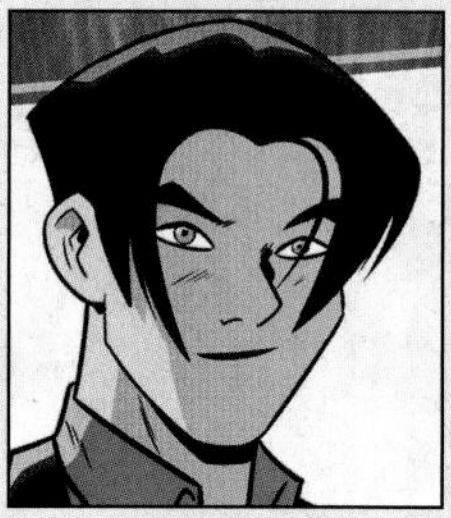

THE NEW KID
AKA COLIN KING, SOPHOMORE.
Powers: pulling off that suit.

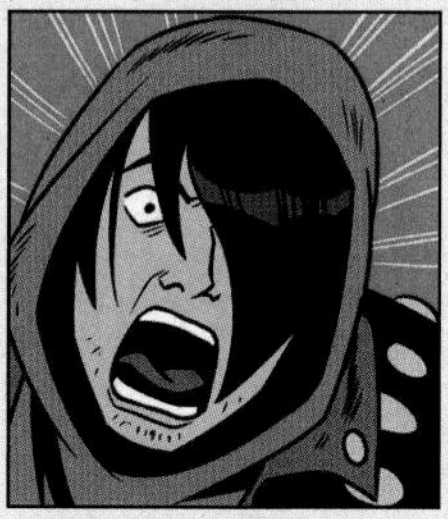

GILAD
AKA THE ETERNAL SOPHOMORE.
Stop asking him questions.

FACULTY ADVISORS

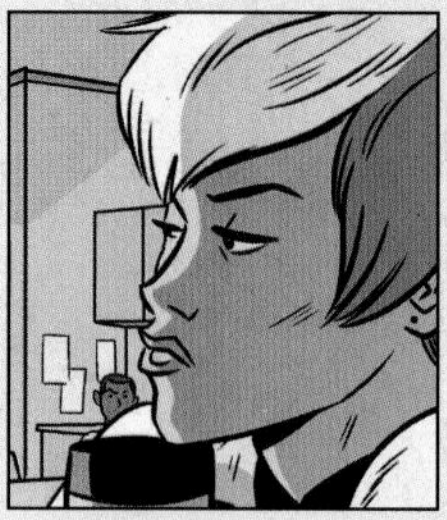

DR. MIRAGE, First-Period Biology
Professor of Life (and Afterlife -- shh).

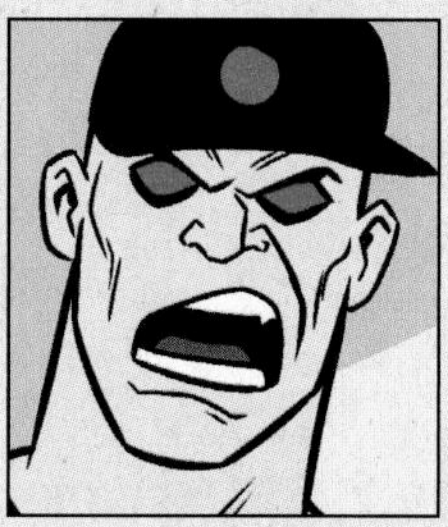

COACH BLOODSHOT, Gym Teacher
Ex-military (probably?),
default status: shouting.

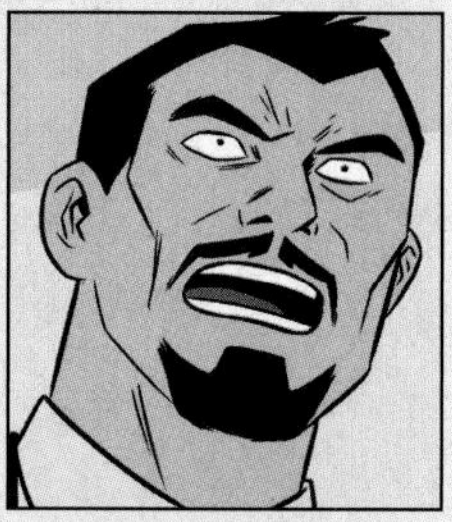

TOYO HARADA, Principal of Valiant High (and probably the universe)
Telepathic, telekinetic, teletcetera.

VALIANT

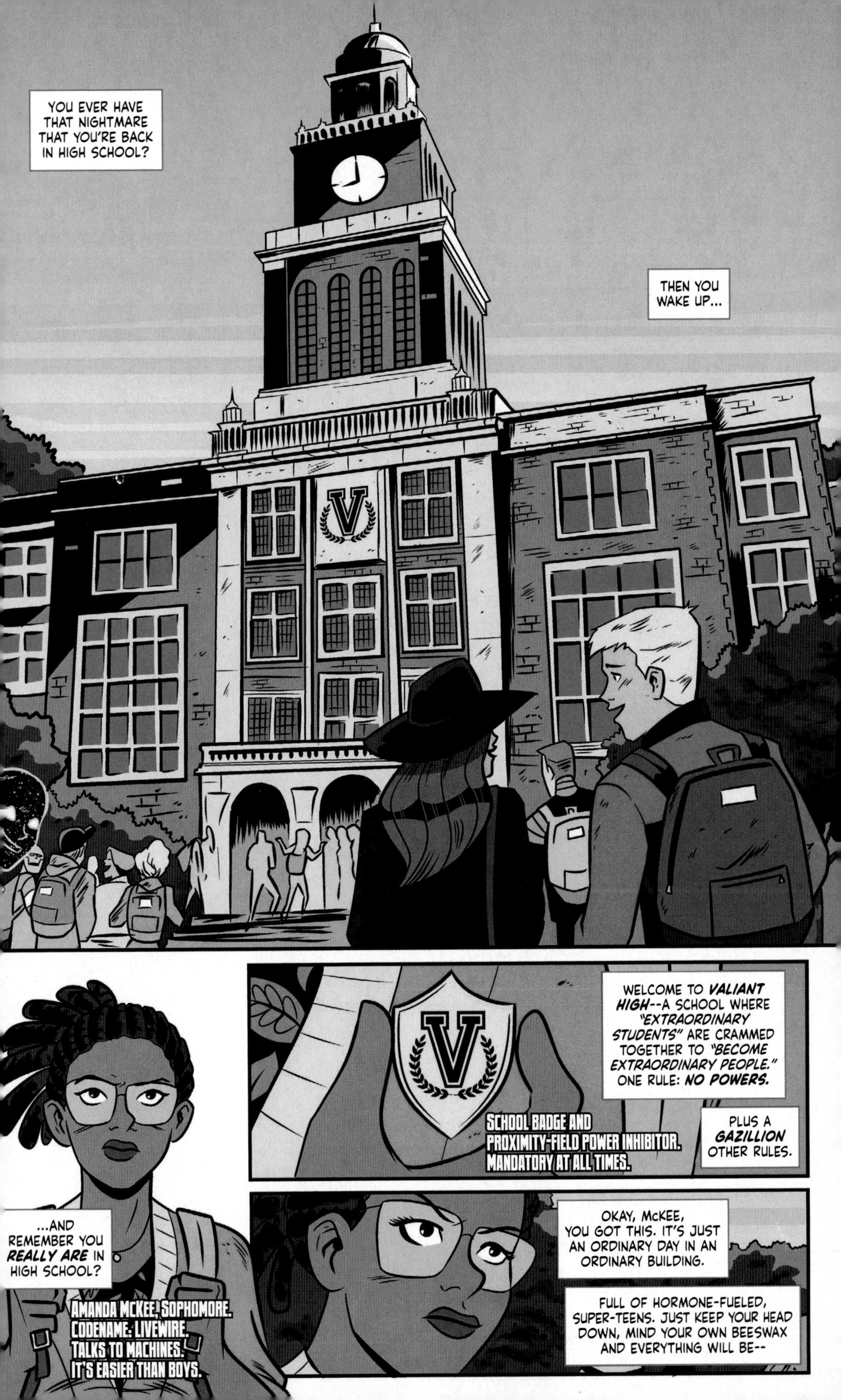
YOU EVER HAVE THAT NIGHTMARE THAT YOU'RE BACK IN HIGH SCHOOL?
THEN YOU WAKE UP...
...AND REMEMBER YOU *REALLY ARE* IN HIGH SCHOOL?
AMANDA McKEE, SOPHOMORE. CODENAME: LIVEWIRE. TALKS TO MACHINES. IT'S EASIER THAN BOYS.
WELCOME TO *VALIANT HIGH*--A SCHOOL WHERE *"EXTRAORDINARY STUDENTS"* ARE CRAMMED TOGETHER TO *"BECOME EXTRAORDINARY PEOPLE."* ONE RULE: ***NO POWERS.***
SCHOOL BADGE AND PROXIMITY-FIELD POWER INHIBITOR. MANDATORY AT ALL TIMES.
PLUS A ***GAZILLION*** OTHER RULES.
OKAY, McKEE, YOU GOT THIS. IT'S JUST AN ORDINARY DAY IN AN ORDINARY BUILDING.
FULL OF HORMONE-FUELED, SUPER-TEENS. JUST KEEP YOUR HEAD DOWN, MIND YOUR OWN BEESWAX AND EVERYTHING WILL BE--

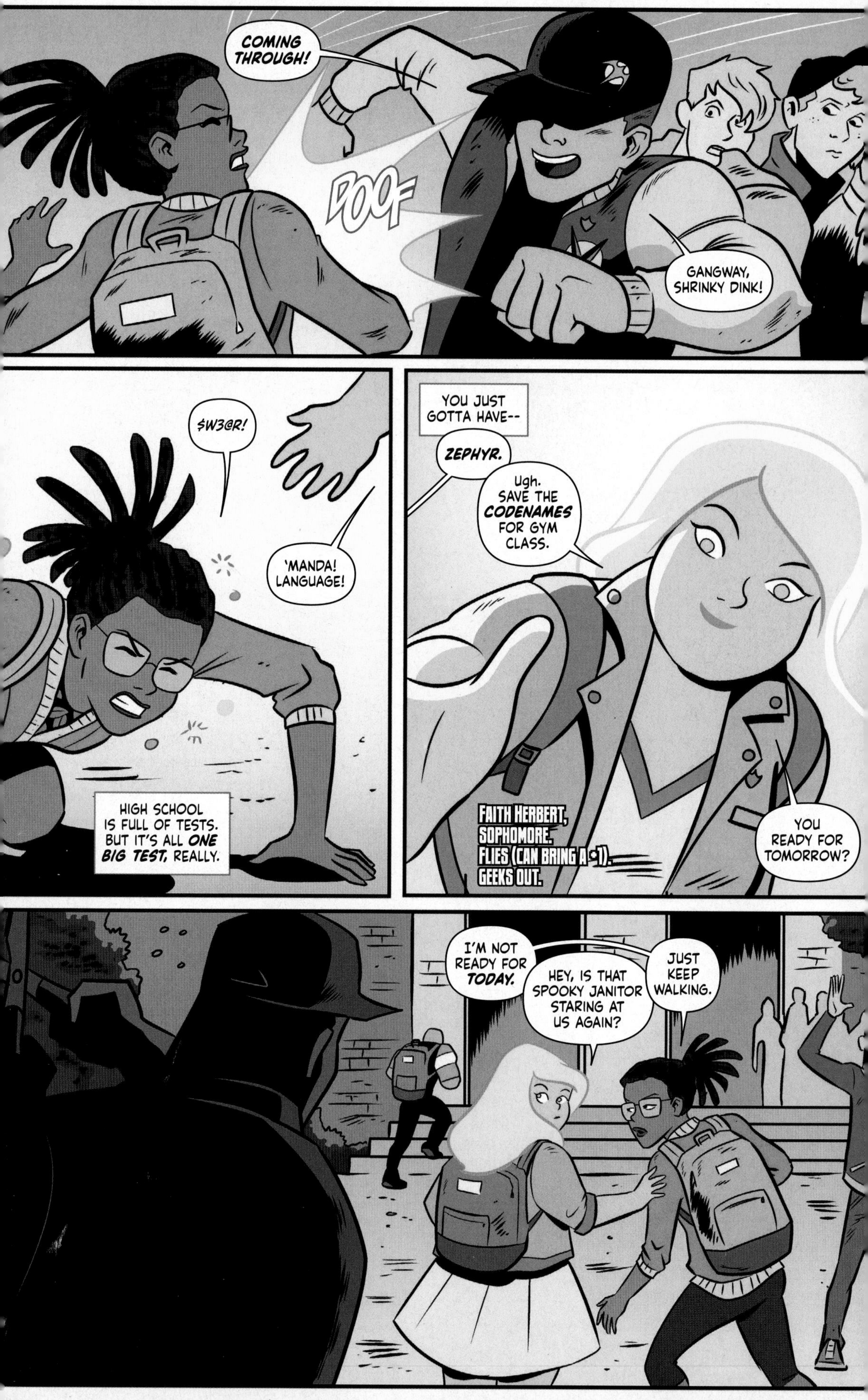
COMING THROUGH!
DOOF
GANGWAY, SHRINKY DINK!
$W3@R!
'MANDA! LANGUAGE!
HIGH SCHOOL IS FULL OF TESTS. BUT IT'S ALL ONE BIG TEST, REALLY.
YOU JUST GOTTA HAVE--
ZEPHYR.
Ugh. SAVE THE CODENAMES FOR GYM CLASS.
FAITH HERBERT, SOPHOMORE.
GEEKS OUT.
YOU READY FOR TOMORROW?
I'M NOT READY FOR TODAY.
HEY, IS THAT SPOOKY JANITOR STARING AT US AGAIN?
JUST KEEP WALKING.

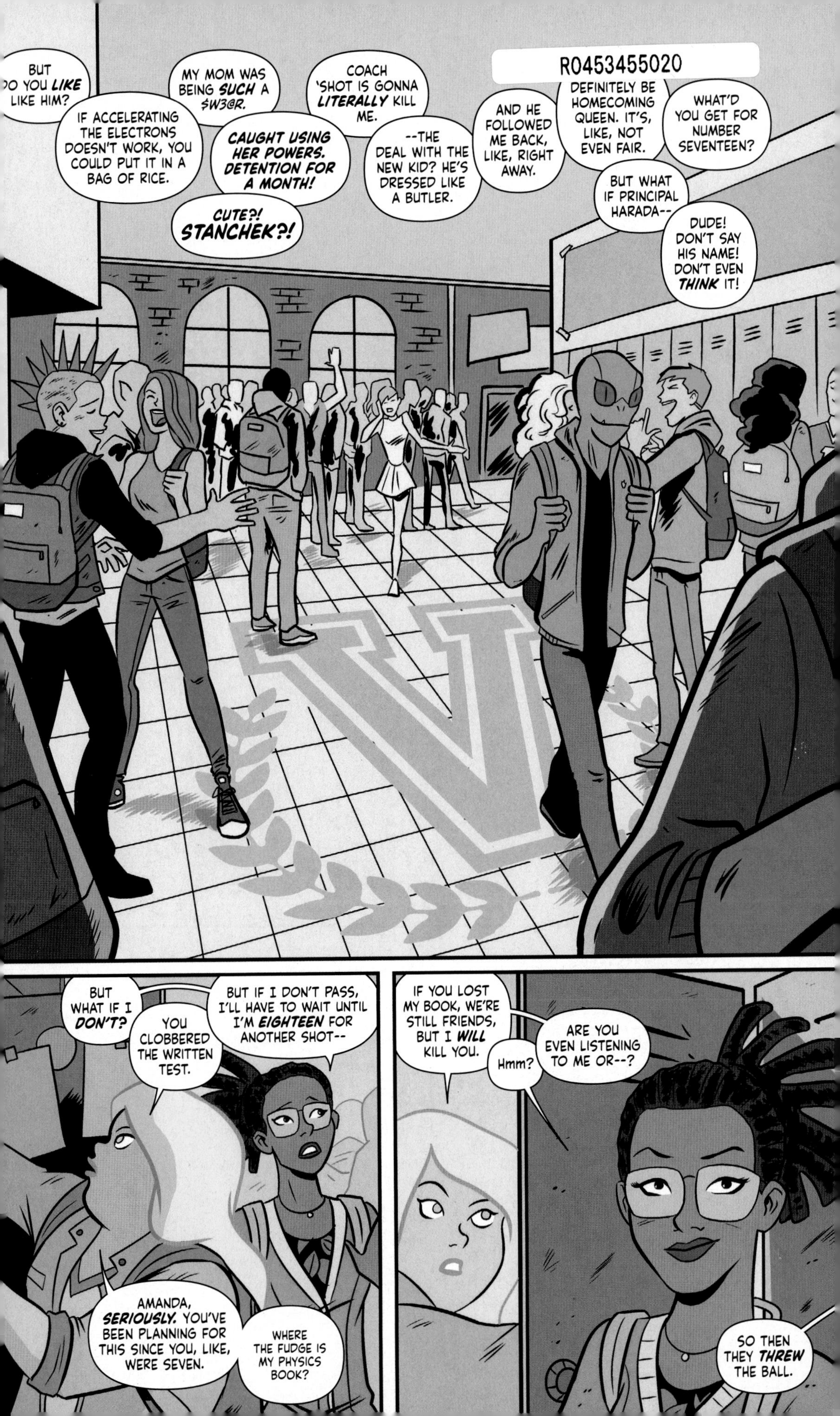
R0453455020
BUT DO YOU LIKE LIKE HIM?
IF ACCELERATING THE ELECTRONS DOESN'T WORK, YOU COULD PUT IT IN A BAG OF RICE.
MY MOM WAS BEING SUCH A $W3@R.
CAUGHT USING HER POWERS. DETENTION FOR A MONTH!
CUTE?! STANCHEK?!
COACH 'SHOT IS GONNA LITERALLY KILL ME.
--THE DEAL WITH THE NEW KID? HE'S DRESSED LIKE A BUTLER.
AND HE FOLLOWED ME BACK, LIKE, RIGHT AWAY.
DEFINITELY BE HOMECOMING QUEEN. IT'S, LIKE, NOT EVEN FAIR.
WHAT'D YOU GET FOR NUMBER SEVENTEEN?
BUT WHAT IF PRINCIPAL HARADA--
DUDE! DON'T SAY HIS NAME! DON'T EVEN THINK IT!
BUT WHAT IF I DON'T?
YOU CLOBBERED THE WRITTEN TEST.
BUT IF I DON'T PASS, I'LL HAVE TO WAIT UNTIL I'M EIGHTEEN FOR ANOTHER SHOT--
AMANDA, SERIOUSLY. YOU'VE BEEN PLANNING FOR THIS SINCE YOU, LIKE, WERE SEVEN.
WHERE THE FUDGE IS MY PHYSICS BOOK?
IF YOU LOST MY BOOK, WE'RE STILL FRIENDS, BUT I WILL KILL YOU.
Hmm?
ARE YOU EVEN LISTENING TO ME OR--?
SO THEN THEY THREW THE BALL.

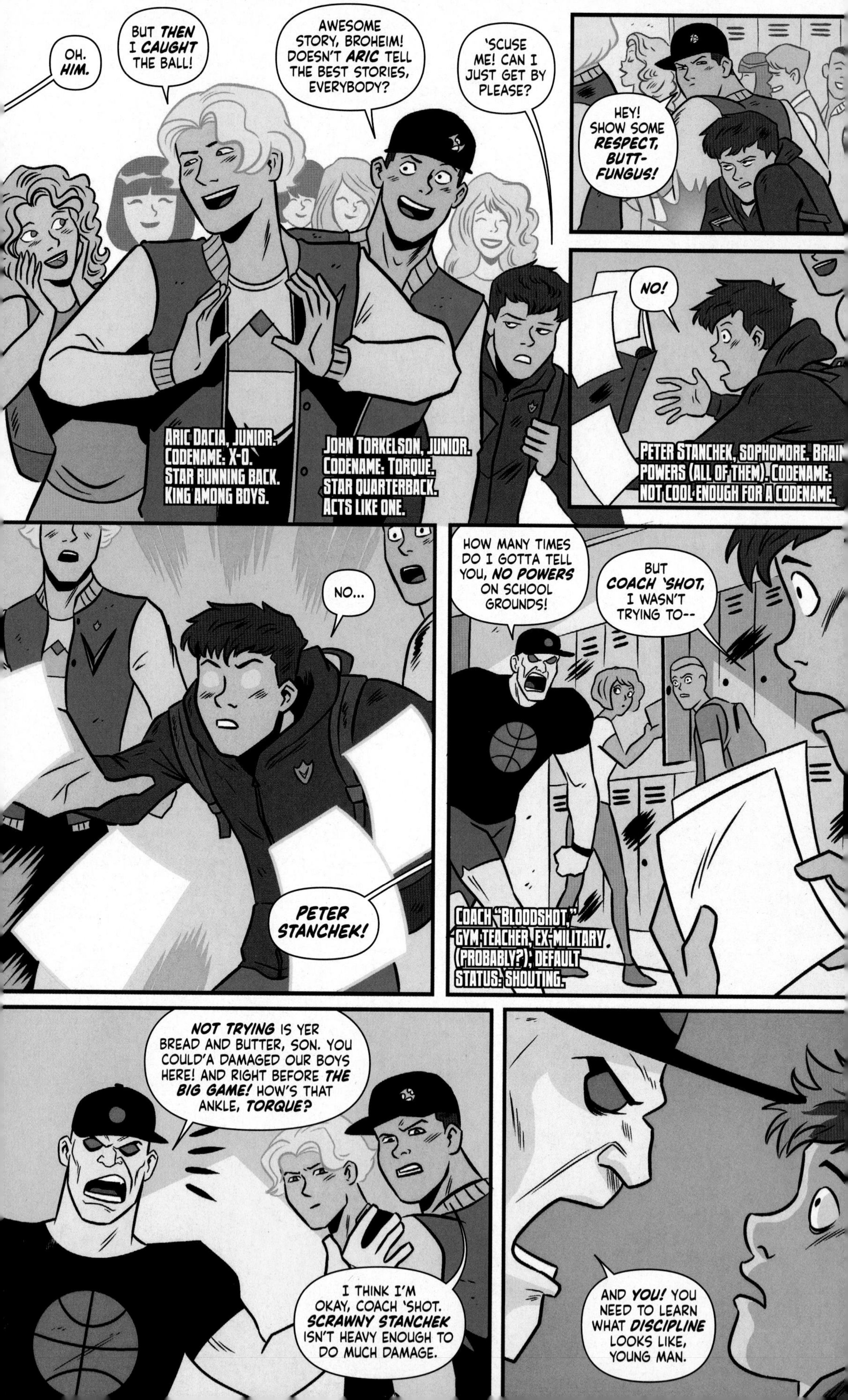
OH. HIM.
BUT THEN I CAUGHT THE BALL!
AWESOME STORY, BROHEIM! DOESN'T ARIC TELL THE BEST STORIES, EVERYBODY?
'SCUSE ME! CAN I JUST GET BY PLEASE?
ARIC DACIA, JUNIOR. CODENAME: X-O. STAR RUNNING BACK. KING AMONG BOYS.
JOHN TORKELSON, JUNIOR. CODENAME: TORQUE. STAR QUARTERBACK. ACTS LIKE ONE.
HEY! SHOW SOME RESPECT, BUTT-FUNGUS!
NO!
PETER STANCHEK, SOPHOMORE. BRAIN POWERS (ALL OF THEM). CODENAME: NOT COOL ENOUGH FOR A CODENAME.
NO...
PETER STANCHEK!
HOW MANY TIMES DO I GOTTA TELL YOU, NO POWERS ON SCHOOL GROUNDS!
BUT COACH 'SHOT, I WASN'T TRYING TO--
COACH "BLOODSHOT," GYM TEACHER, EX-MILITARY (PROBABLY?); DEFAULT STATUS: SHOUTING.
NOT TRYING IS YER BREAD AND BUTTER, SON. YOU COULD'A DAMAGED OUR BOYS HERE! AND RIGHT BEFORE THE BIG GAME! HOW'S THAT ANKLE, TORQUE?
I THINK I'M OKAY, COACH 'SHOT. SCRAWNY STANCHEK ISN'T HEAVY ENOUGH TO DO MUCH DAMAGE.
AND YOU! YOU NEED TO LEARN WHAT DISCIPLINE LOOKS LIKE, YOUNG MAN.

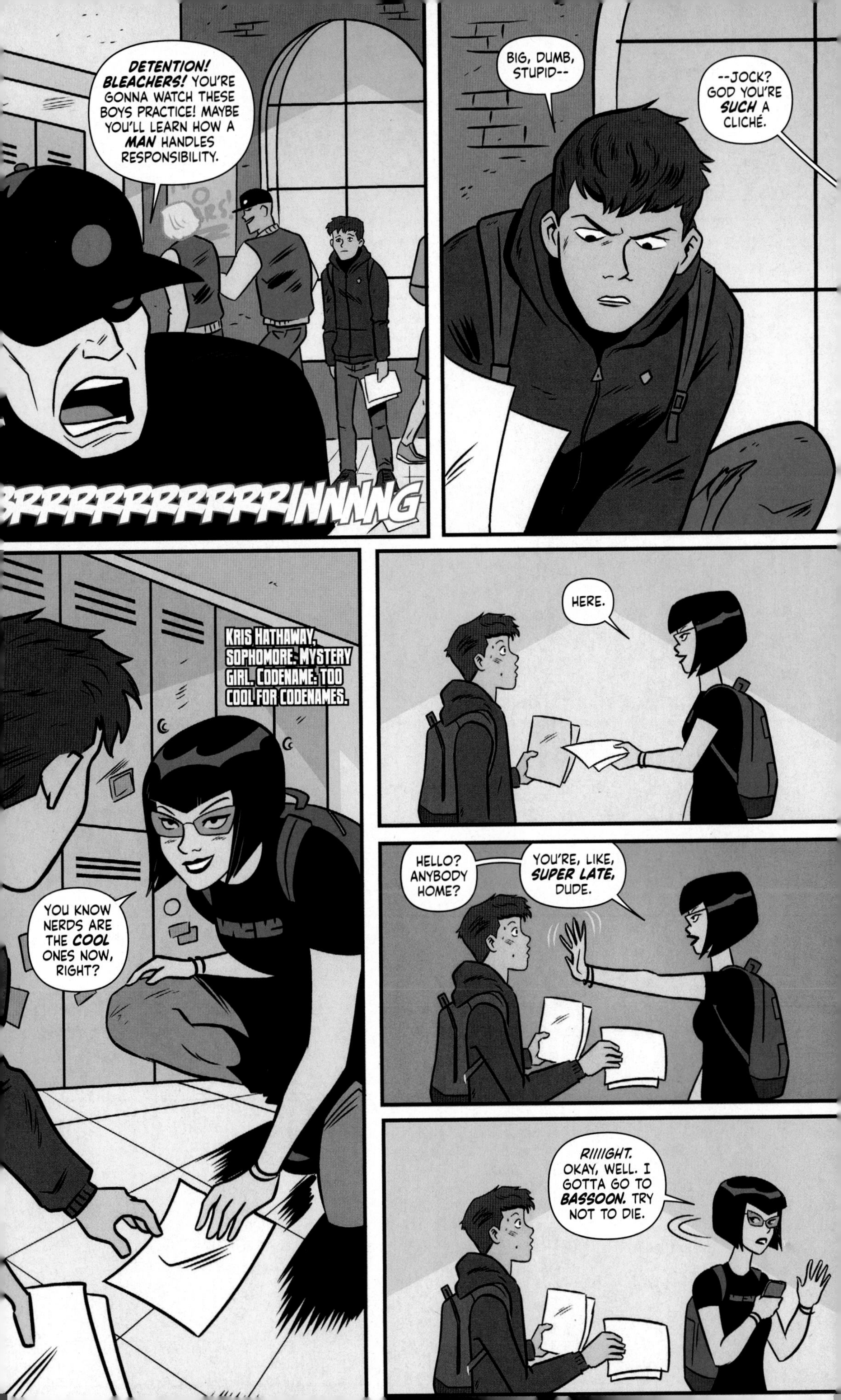

DETENTION! BLEACHERS! YOU'RE GONNA WATCH THESE BOYS PRACTICE! MAYBE YOU'LL LEARN HOW A MAN HANDLES RESPONSIBILITY.
BRRRRRRRRRRRRINNNNG
BIG, DUMB, STUPID--
--JOCK? GOD YOU'RE SUCH A CLICHÉ.
KRIS HATHAWAY, SOPHOMORE. MYSTERY GIRL. CODENAME: TOO COOL FOR CODENAMES.
YOU KNOW NERDS ARE THE COOL ONES NOW, RIGHT?
HERE.
HELLO? ANYBODY HOME?
YOU'RE, LIKE, SUPER LATE, DUDE.
RIIIIGHT. OKAY, WELL. I GOTTA GO TO BASSOON. TRY NOT TO DIE.

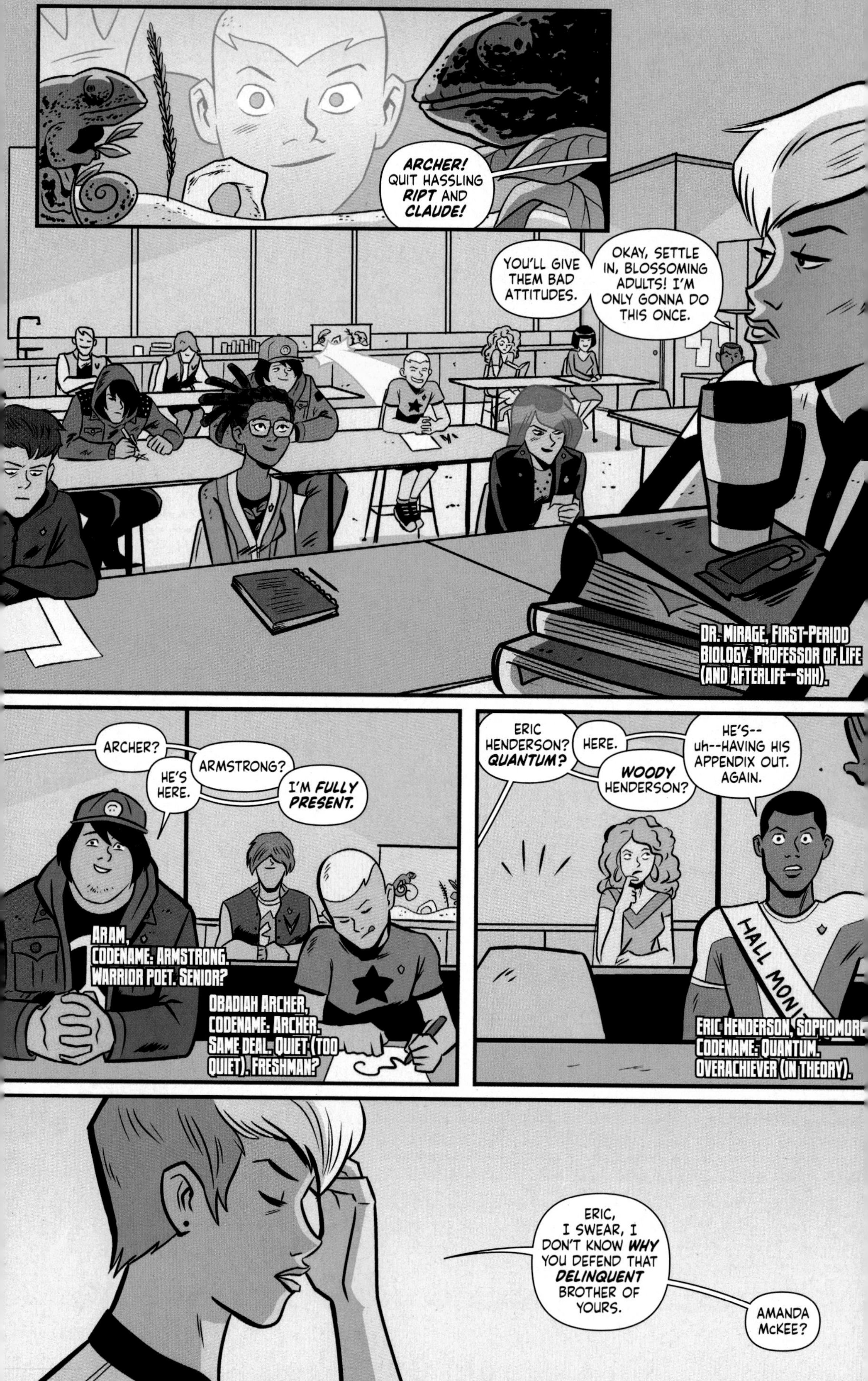
ARCHER! QUIT HASSLING RIPT AND CLAUDE!
OKAY, SETTLE IN, BLOSSOMING ADULTS! I'M ONLY GONNA DO THIS ONCE.
YOU'LL GIVE THEM BAD ATTITUDES.
DR. MIRAGE, FIRST-PERIOD BIOLOGY. PROFESSOR OF LIFE (AND AFTERLIFE--SHH).
ARCHER?
HE'S HERE.
ARMSTRONG?
I'M FULLY PRESENT.
ARAM, CODENAME: ARMSTRONG. WARRIOR POET. SENIOR?
OBADIAH ARCHER, CODENAME: ARCHER. SAME DEAL. QUIET (TOO QUIET). FRESHMAN?
ERIC HENDERSON? QUANTUM?
HERE.
WOODY HENDERSON?
HE'S-- uh--HAVING HIS APPENDIX OUT. AGAIN.
HALL MONI
ERIC HENDERSON, SOPHOMORE. CODENAME: QUANTUM. OVERACHIEVER (IN THEORY).
ERIC, I SWEAR, I DON'T KNOW WHY YOU DEFEND THAT DELINQUENT BROTHER OF YOURS.
AMANDA McKEE?

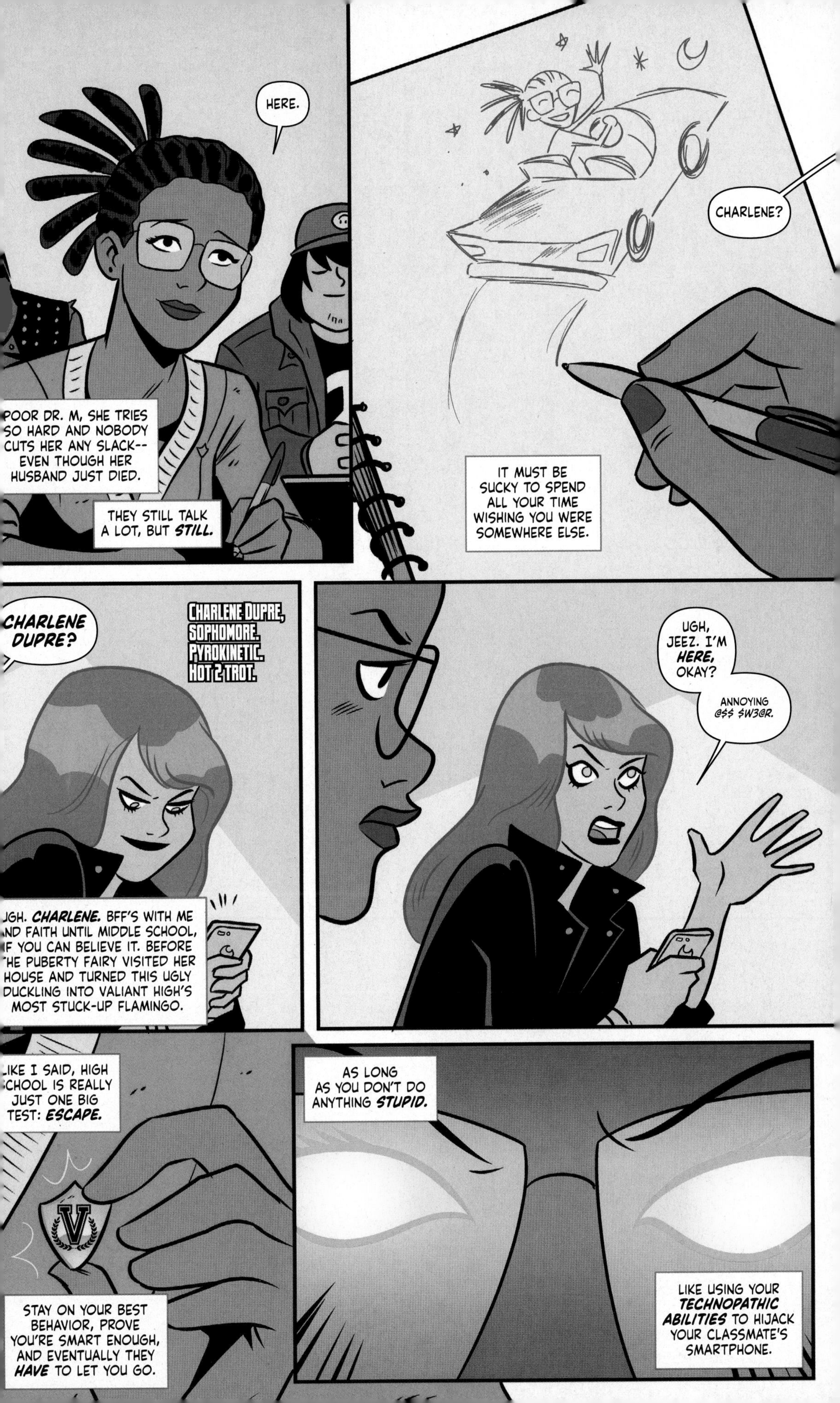
HERE.
POOR DR. M, SHE TRIES SO HARD AND NOBODY CUTS HER ANY SLACK-- EVEN THOUGH HER HUSBAND JUST DIED.
THEY STILL TALK A LOT, BUT STILL.
CHARLENE?
IT MUST BE SUCKY TO SPEND ALL YOUR TIME WISHING YOU WERE SOMEWHERE ELSE.
CHARLENE DUPRE?
CHARLENE DUPRE, SOPHOMORE. PYROKINETIC. HOT 2 TROT.
GH. CHARLENE. BFF'S WITH ME ND FAITH UNTIL MIDDLE SCHOOL, F YOU CAN BELIEVE IT. BEFORE HE PUBERTY FAIRY VISITED HER HOUSE AND TURNED THIS UGLY DUCKLING INTO VALIANT HIGH'S MOST STUCK-UP FLAMINGO.
UGH, JEEZ. I'M HERE, OKAY?
ANNOYING @$$ $W3@R.
LIKE I SAID, HIGH SCHOOL IS REALLY JUST ONE BIG TEST: ESCAPE.
V
STAY ON YOUR BEST BEHAVIOR, PROVE YOU'RE SMART ENOUGH, AND EVENTUALLY THEY HAVE TO LET YOU GO.
AS LONG AS YOU DON'T DO ANYTHING STUPID.
LIKE USING YOUR TECHNOPATHIC ABILITIES TO HIJACK YOUR CLASSMATE'S SMARTPHONE.

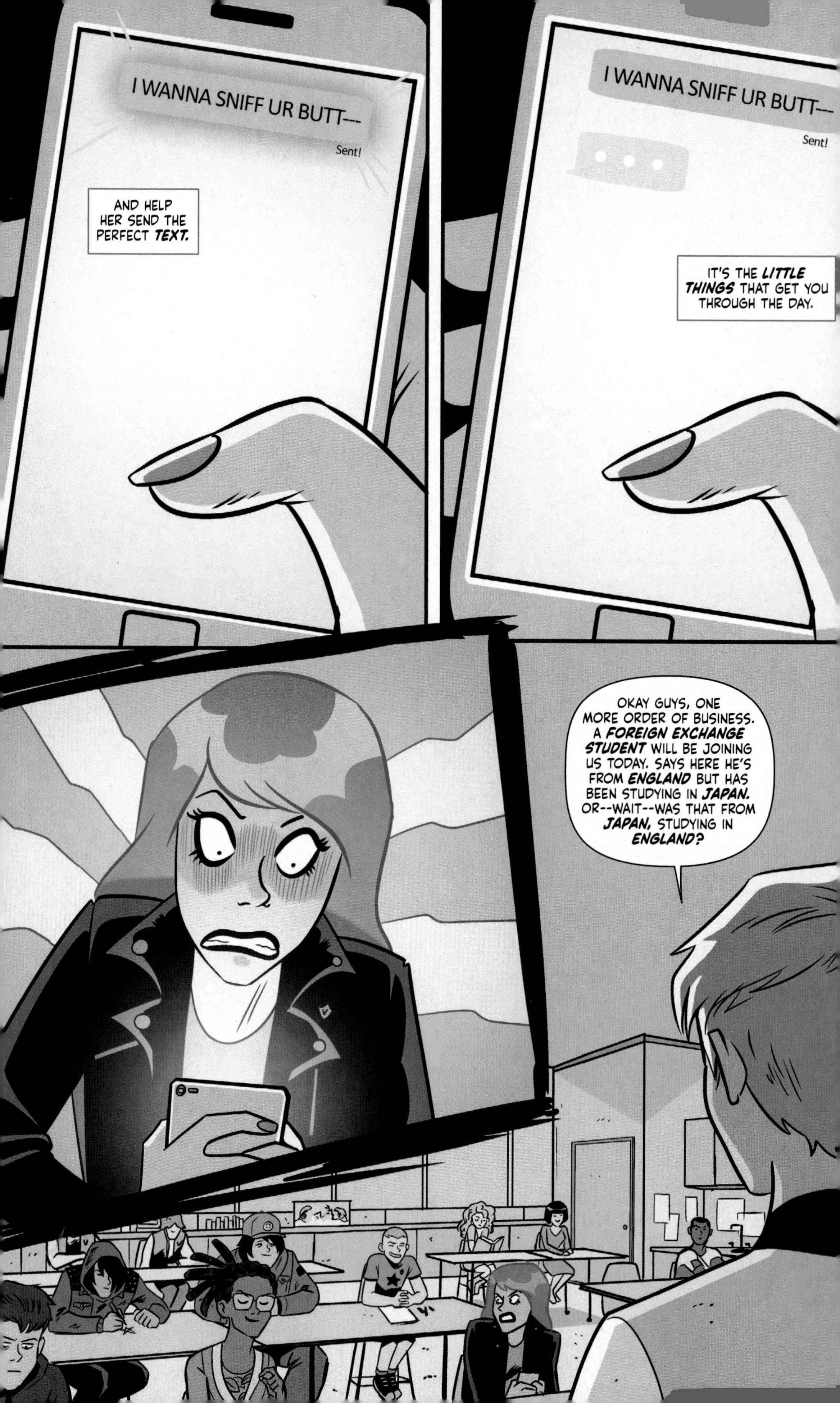
I WANNA SNIFF UR BUTT---
Sent!
AND HELP HER SEND THE PERFECT TEXT.
I WANNA SNIFF UR BUTT---
Sent!
...
IT'S THE LITTLE THINGS THAT GET YOU THROUGH THE DAY.
OKAY GUYS, ONE MORE ORDER OF BUSINESS. A FOREIGN EXCHANGE STUDENT WILL BE JOINING US TODAY. SAYS HERE HE'S FROM ENGLAND BUT HAS BEEN STUDYING IN JAPAN. OR--WAIT--WAS THAT FROM JAPAN, STUDYING IN ENGLAND?

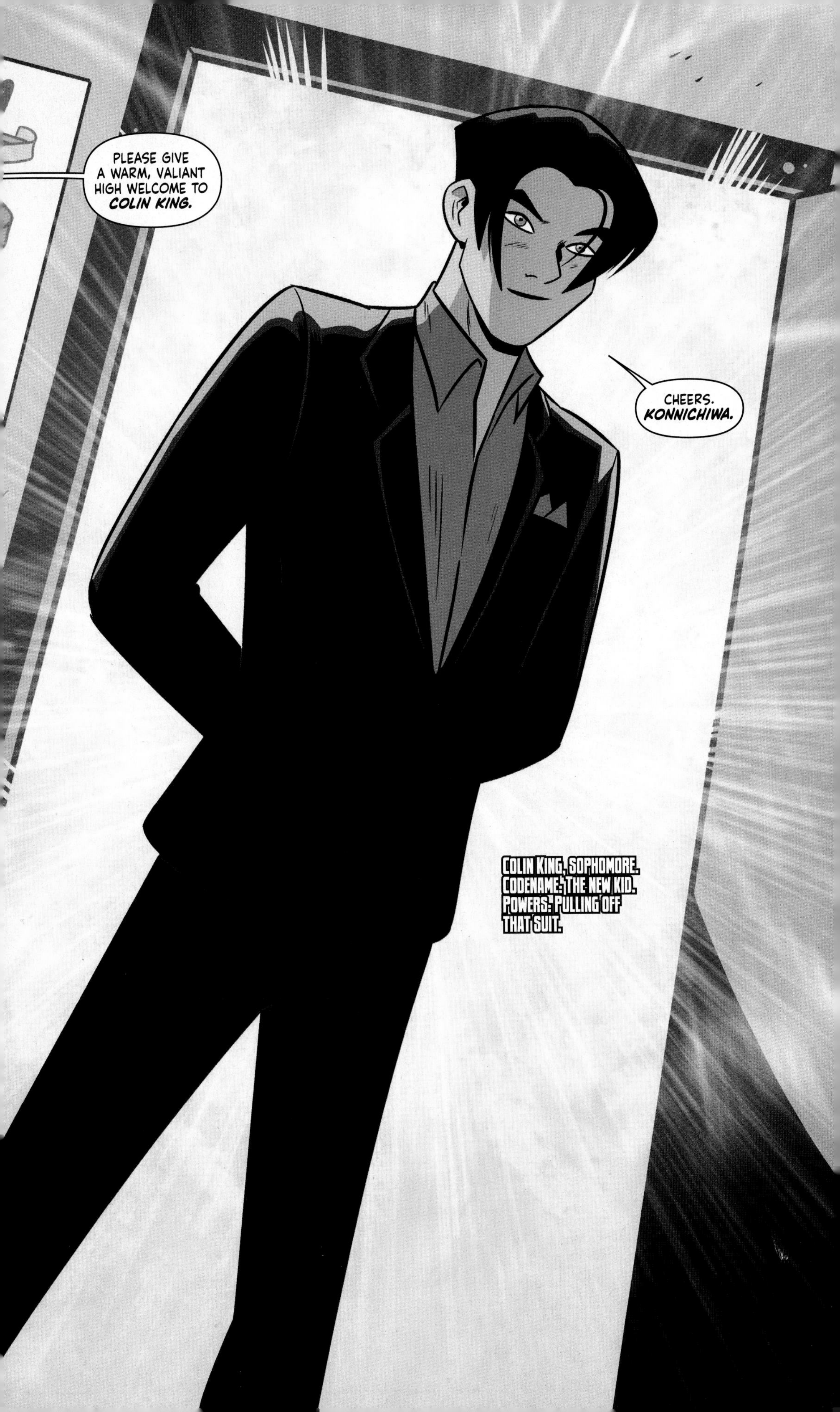
PLEASE GIVE A WARM, VALIANT HIGH WELCOME TO COLIN KING.
CHEERS. KONNICHIWA.
COLIN KING, SOPHOMORE. CODENAME: THE NEW KID. POWERS: PULLING OFF THAT SUIT.

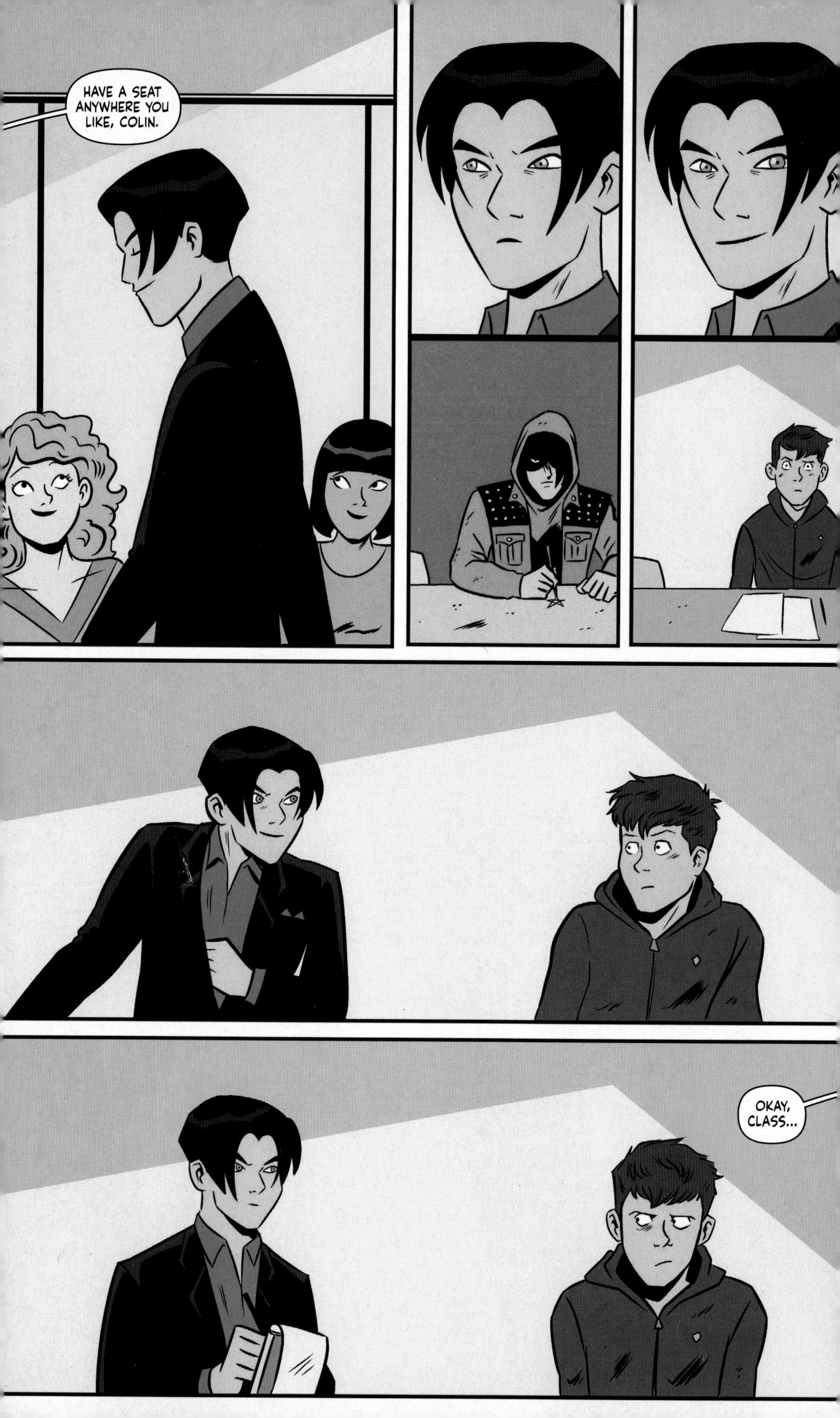
HAVE A SEAT ANYWHERE YOU LIKE, COLIN.
OKAY, CLASS...

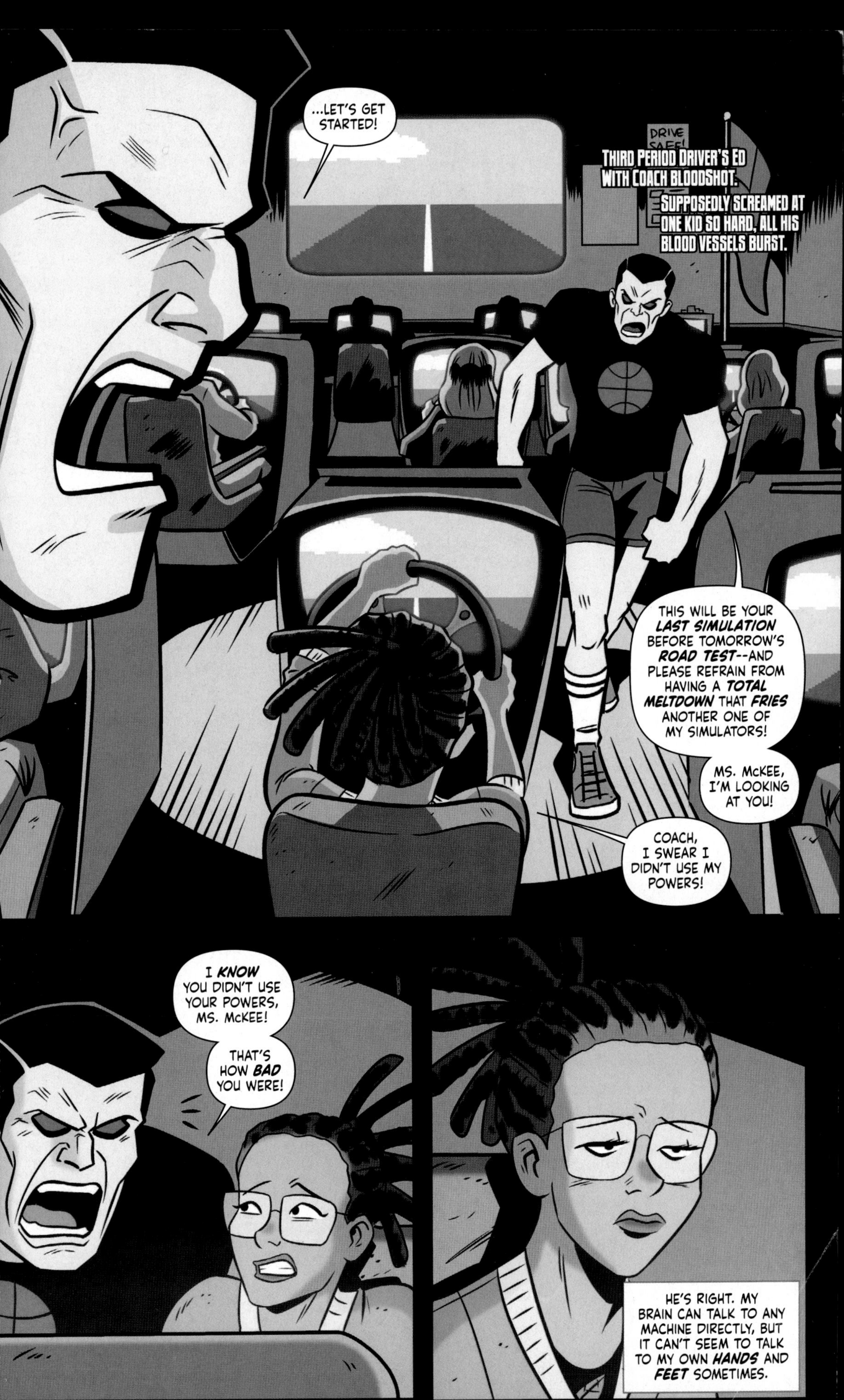
...LET'S GET STARTED!
DRIVE SAFE!
THIRD PERIOD DRIVER'S ED WITH COACH BLOODSHOT.
SUPPOSEDLY SCREAMED AT ONE KID SO HARD, ALL HIS BLOOD VESSELS BURST.
THIS WILL BE YOUR *LAST SIMULATION* BEFORE TOMORROW'S *ROAD TEST*--AND PLEASE REFRAIN FROM HAVING A *TOTAL MELTDOWN* THAT *FRIES* ANOTHER ONE OF MY SIMULATORS!
MS. McKEE, I'M LOOKING AT YOU!
COACH, I SWEAR I DIDN'T USE MY POWERS!
I *KNOW* YOU DIDN'T USE YOUR POWERS, MS. McKEE!
THAT'S HOW *BAD* YOU WERE!
HE'S RIGHT. MY BRAIN CAN TALK TO ANY MACHINE DIRECTLY, BUT IT CAN'T SEEM TO TALK TO MY OWN *HANDS* AND *FEET* SOMETIMES.

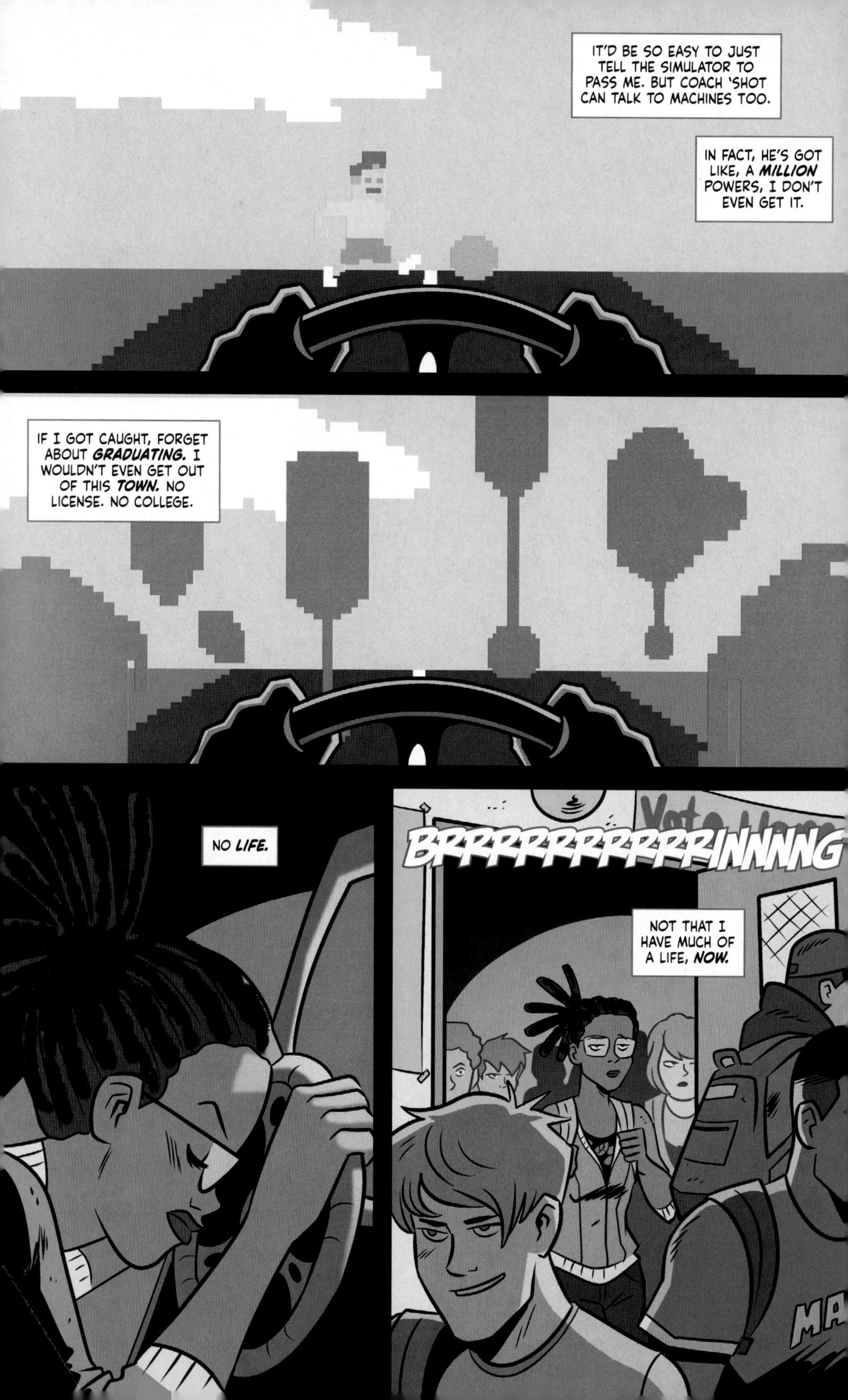

IT'D BE SO EASY TO JUST TELL THE SIMULATOR TO PASS ME. BUT COACH 'SHOT CAN TALK TO MACHINES TOO.
IN FACT, HE'S GOT LIKE, A *MILLION* POWERS, I DON'T EVEN GET IT.
IF I GOT CAUGHT, FORGET ABOUT *GRADUATING.* I WOULDN'T EVEN GET OUT OF THIS *TOWN.* NO LICENSE. NO COLLEGE.
NO *LIFE.*
BRRRRRRRRRRRRRINNNNG
NOT THAT I HAVE MUCH OF A LIFE, *NOW.*

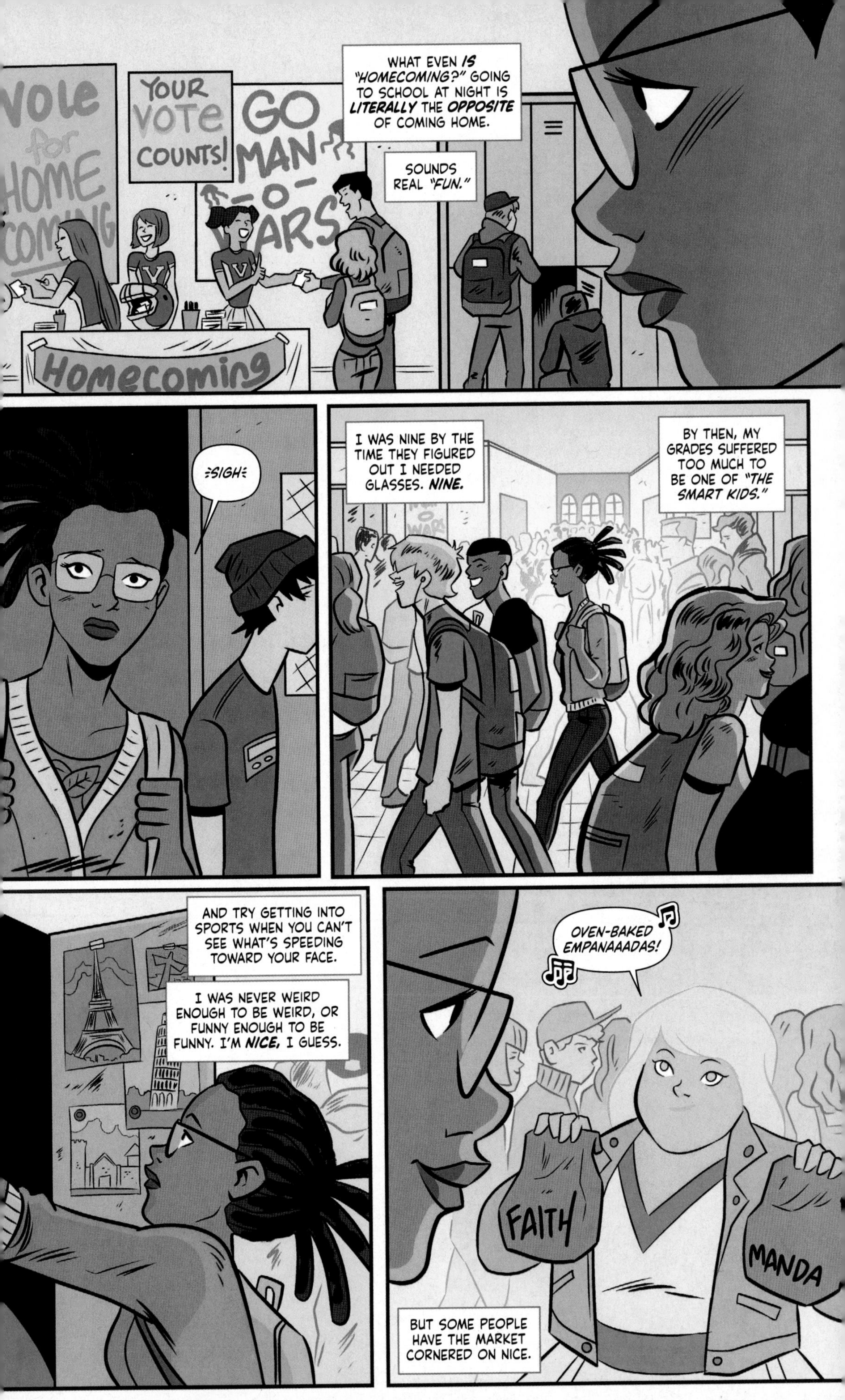
Vote for HOME COMING
YOUR VOTE COUNTS!
GO MAN-O-WARS
Homecoming
WHAT EVEN *IS* *"HOMECOMING?"* GOING TO SCHOOL AT NIGHT IS ***LITERALLY*** THE ***OPPOSITE*** OF COMING HOME.
SOUNDS REAL *"FUN."*
SIGH
I WAS NINE BY THE TIME THEY FIGURED OUT I NEEDED GLASSES. ***NINE.***
BY THEN, MY GRADES SUFFERED TOO MUCH TO BE ONE OF *"THE SMART KIDS."*
AND TRY GETTING INTO SPORTS WHEN YOU CAN'T SEE WHAT'S SPEEDING TOWARD YOUR FACE.
I WAS NEVER WEIRD ENOUGH TO BE WEIRD, OR FUNNY ENOUGH TO BE FUNNY. I'M ***NICE,*** I GUESS.
OVEN-BAKED EMPANAAADAS!
FAITH
MANDA
BUT SOME PEOPLE HAVE THE MARKET CORNERED ON NICE.

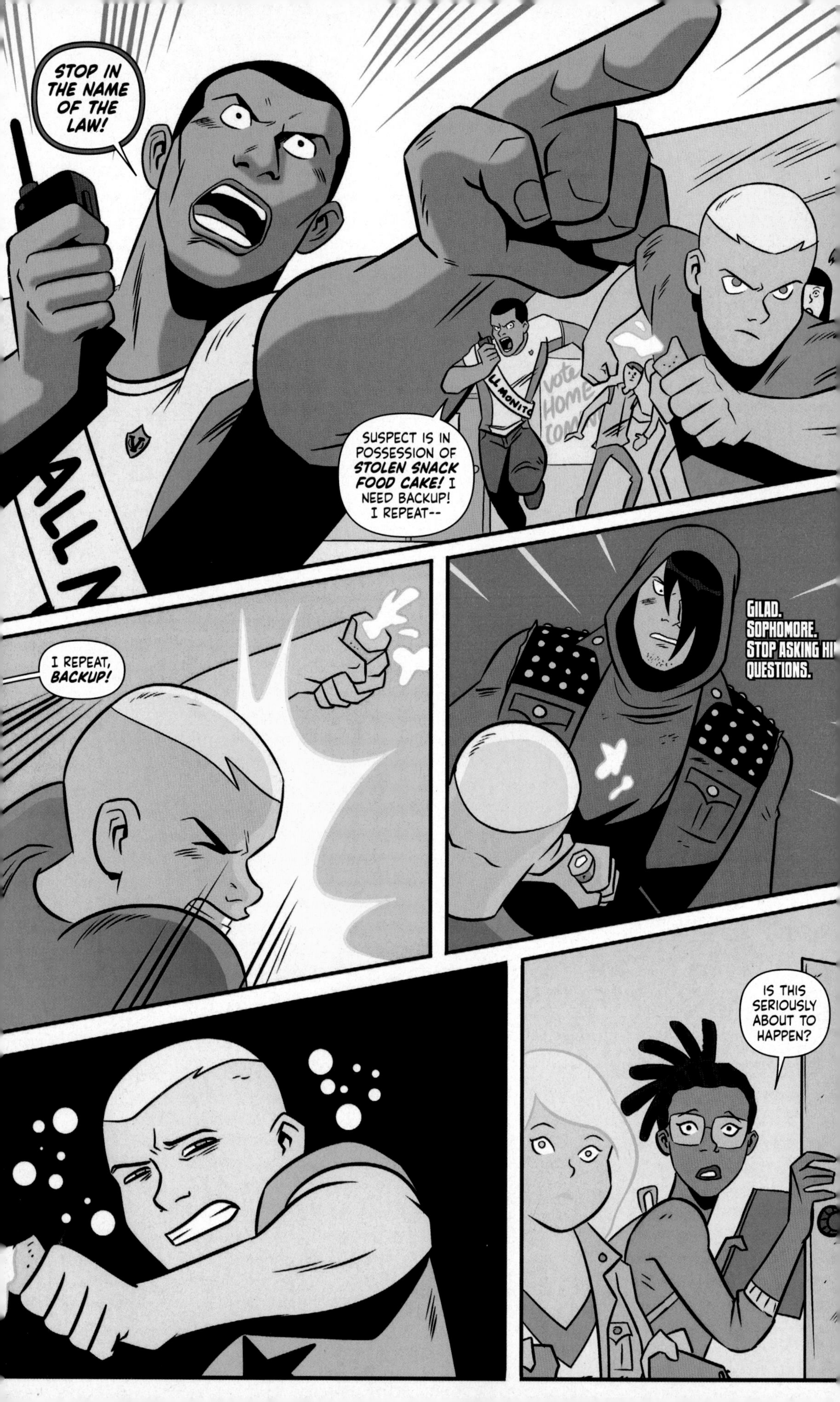
STOP IN THE NAME OF THE LAW!
SUSPECT IS IN POSSESSION OF *STOLEN SNACK FOOD CAKE!* I NEED BACKUP! I REPEAT--
I REPEAT, *BACKUP!*
GILAD. SOPHOMORE. STOP ASKING HI QUESTIONS.
IS THIS SERIOUSLY ABOUT TO HAPPEN?

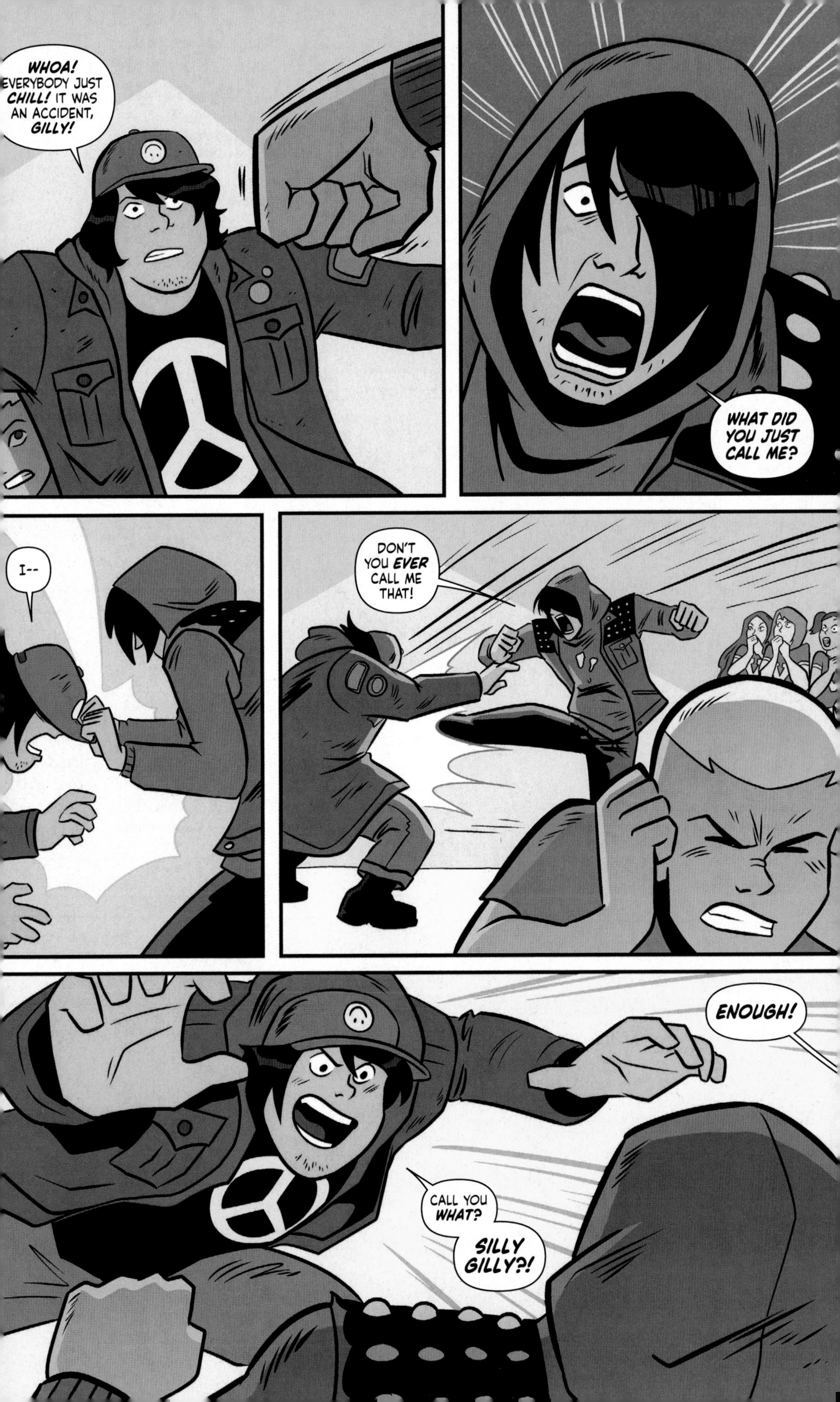
WHOA! EVERYBODY JUST CHILL! IT WAS AN ACCIDENT, GILLY!
WHAT DID YOU JUST CALL ME?
I--
DON'T YOU EVER CALL ME THAT!
ENOUGH!
CALL YOU WHAT?
SILLY GILLY?!

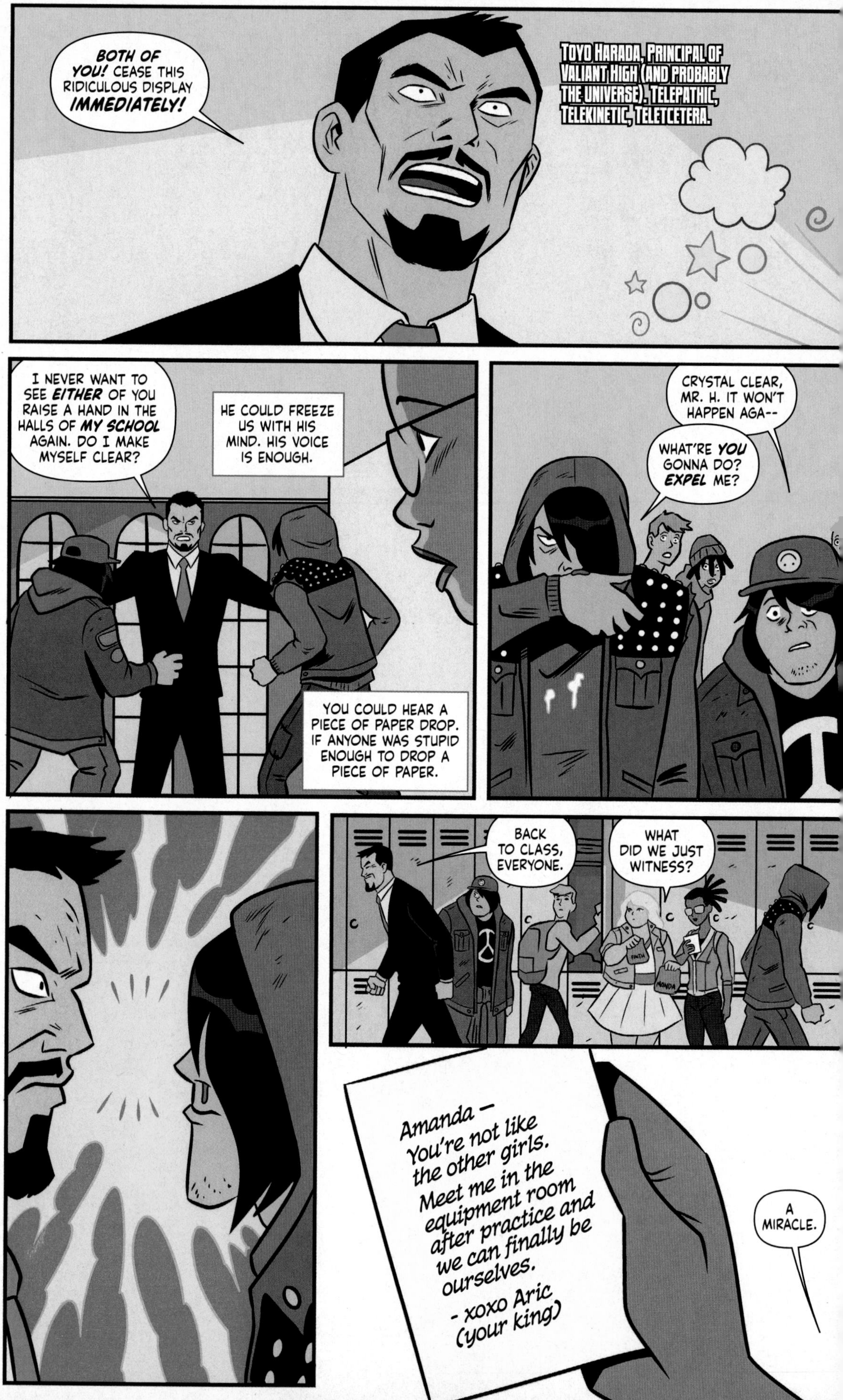
BOTH OF YOU! CEASE THIS RIDICULOUS DISPLAY IMMEDIATELY!
TOYO HARADA, PRINCIPAL OF VALIANT HIGH (AND PROBABLY THE UNIVERSE). TELEPATHIC, TELEKINETIC, TELETCETERA.
I NEVER WANT TO SEE EITHER OF YOU RAISE A HAND IN THE HALLS OF MY SCHOOL AGAIN. DO I MAKE MYSELF CLEAR?
HE COULD FREEZE US WITH HIS MIND. HIS VOICE IS ENOUGH.
YOU COULD HEAR A PIECE OF PAPER DROP. IF ANYONE WAS STUPID ENOUGH TO DROP A PIECE OF PAPER.
CRYSTAL CLEAR, MR. H. IT WON'T HAPPEN AGA--
WHAT'RE YOU GONNA DO? EXPEL ME?
BACK TO CLASS, EVERYONE.
WHAT DID WE JUST WITNESS?
Amanda – You're not like the other girls. Meet me in the equipment room after practice and we can finally be ourselves. - xoxo Aric (your king)
A MIRACLE.

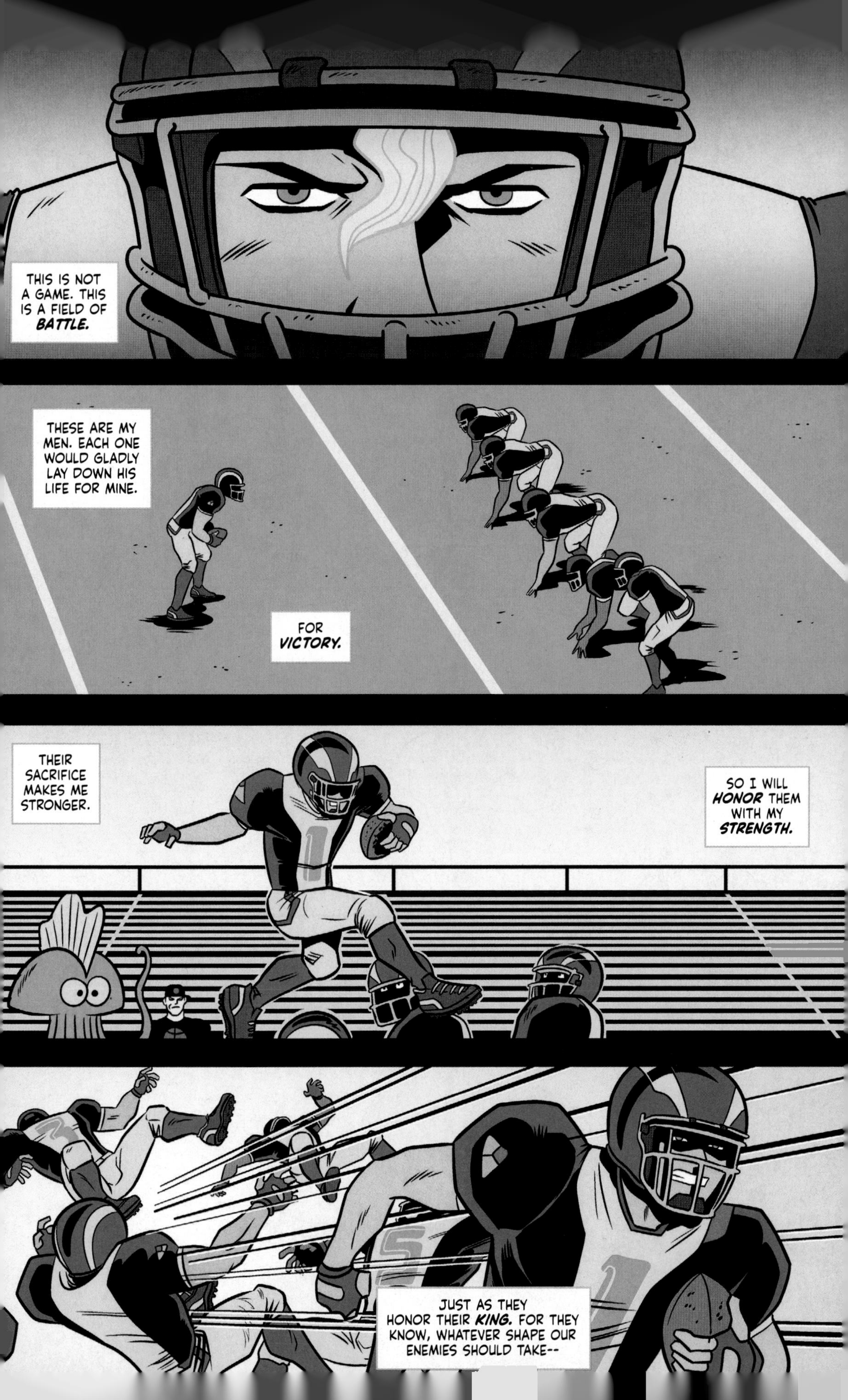
THIS IS NOT A GAME. THIS IS A FIELD OF ***BATTLE.***
THESE ARE MY MEN. EACH ONE WOULD GLADLY LAY DOWN HIS LIFE FOR MINE.
FOR ***VICTORY.***
THEIR SACRIFICE MAKES ME STRONGER.
SO I WILL ***HONOR*** THEM WITH MY ***STRENGTH.***
JUST AS THEY HONOR THEIR ***KING.*** FOR THEY KNOW, WHATEVER SHAPE OUR ENEMIES SHOULD TAKE--

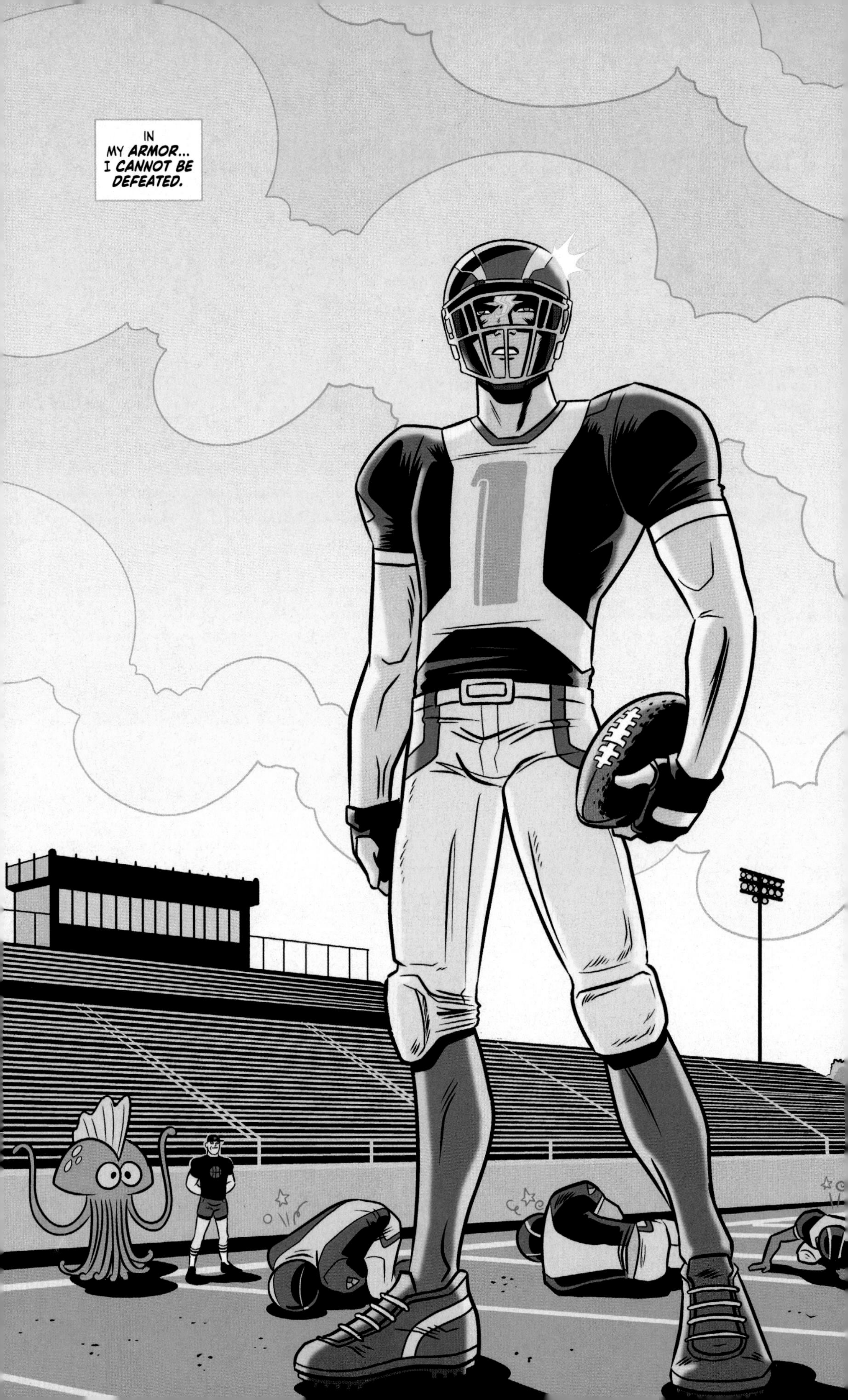
IN MY ARMOR... I CANNOT BE DEFEATED.

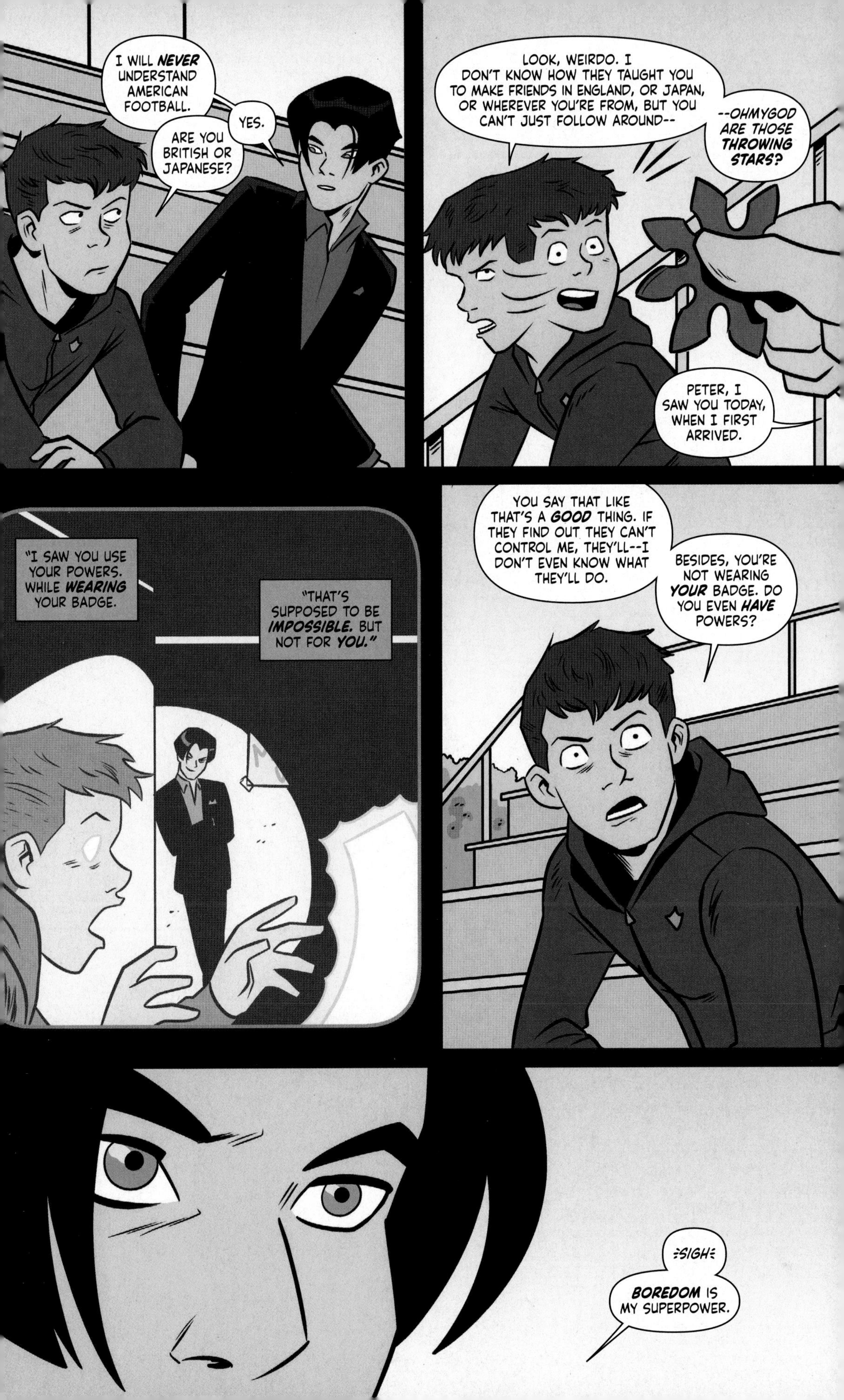
I WILL *NEVER* UNDERSTAND AMERICAN FOOTBALL.
ARE YOU BRITISH OR JAPANESE?
YES.
LOOK, WEIRDO. I DON'T KNOW HOW THEY TAUGHT YOU TO MAKE FRIENDS IN ENGLAND, OR JAPAN, OR WHEREVER YOU'RE FROM, BUT YOU CAN'T JUST FOLLOW AROUND--
--OHMYGOD ARE THOSE *THROWING STARS?*
PETER, I SAW YOU TODAY, WHEN I FIRST ARRIVED.
"I SAW YOU USE YOUR POWERS. WHILE *WEARING* YOUR BADGE.
"THAT'S SUPPOSED TO BE *IMPOSSIBLE.* BUT NOT FOR *YOU.*"
YOU SAY THAT LIKE THAT'S A *GOOD* THING. IF THEY FIND OUT THEY CAN'T CONTROL ME, THEY'LL--I DON'T EVEN KNOW WHAT THEY'LL DO.
BESIDES, YOU'RE NOT WEARING *YOUR* BADGE. DO YOU EVEN *HAVE* POWERS?
SIGH
BOREDOM IS MY SUPERPOWER.

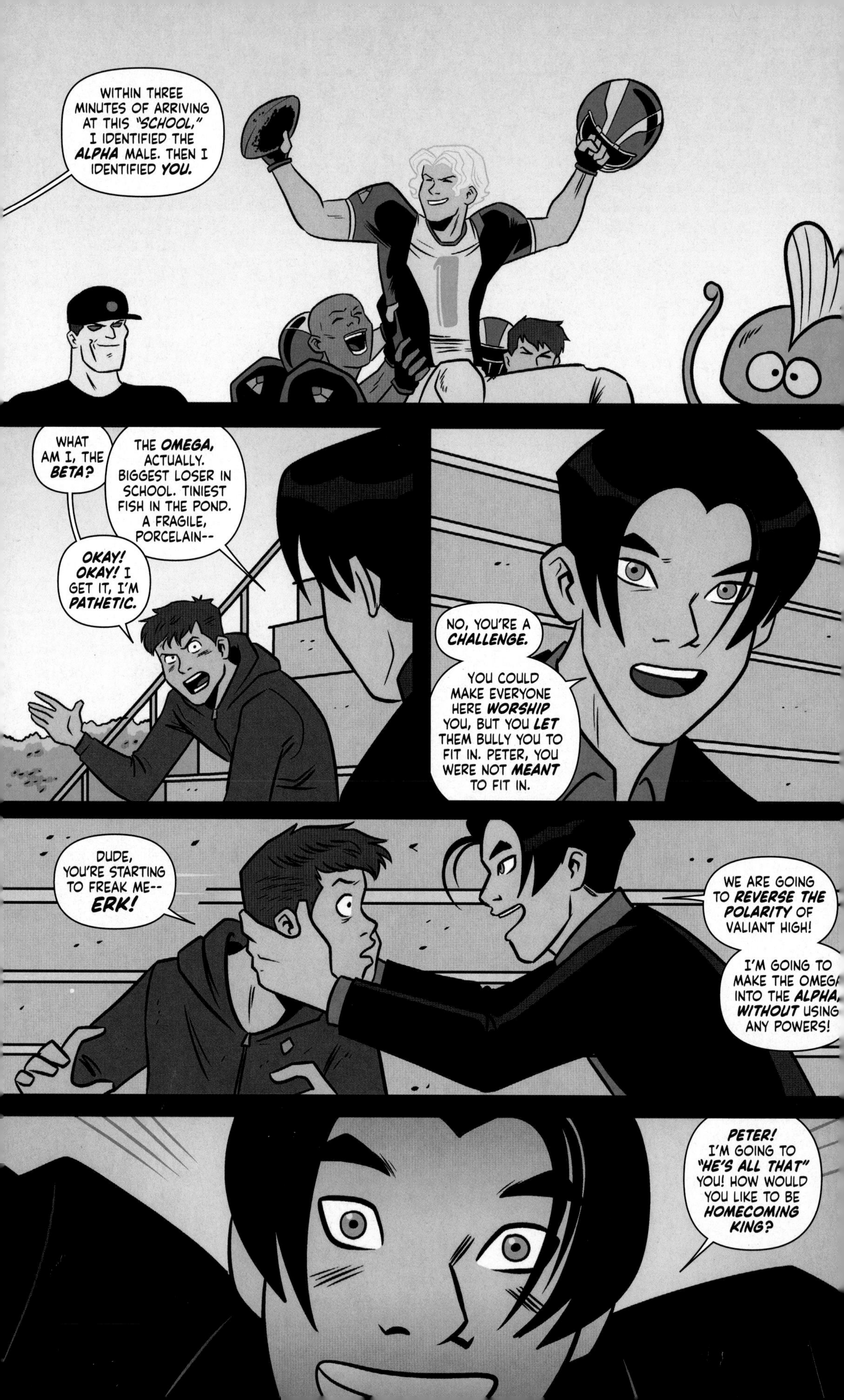

WITHIN THREE MINUTES OF ARRIVING AT THIS "SCHOOL," I IDENTIFIED THE ALPHA MALE. THEN I IDENTIFIED YOU.
WHAT AM I, THE BETA?
THE OMEGA, ACTUALLY. BIGGEST LOSER IN SCHOOL. TINIEST FISH IN THE POND. A FRAGILE, PORCELAIN--
OKAY! OKAY! I GET IT, I'M PATHETIC.
NO, YOU'RE A CHALLENGE.
YOU COULD MAKE EVERYONE HERE WORSHIP YOU, BUT YOU LET THEM BULLY YOU TO FIT IN. PETER, YOU WERE NOT MEANT TO FIT IN.
DUDE, YOU'RE STARTING TO FREAK ME-- ERK!
WE ARE GOING TO REVERSE THE POLARITY OF VALIANT HIGH!
I'M GOING TO MAKE THE OMEGA INTO THE ALPHA, WITHOUT USING ANY POWERS!
PETER! I'M GOING TO "HE'S ALL THAT" YOU! HOW WOULD YOU LIKE TO BE HOMECOMING KING?

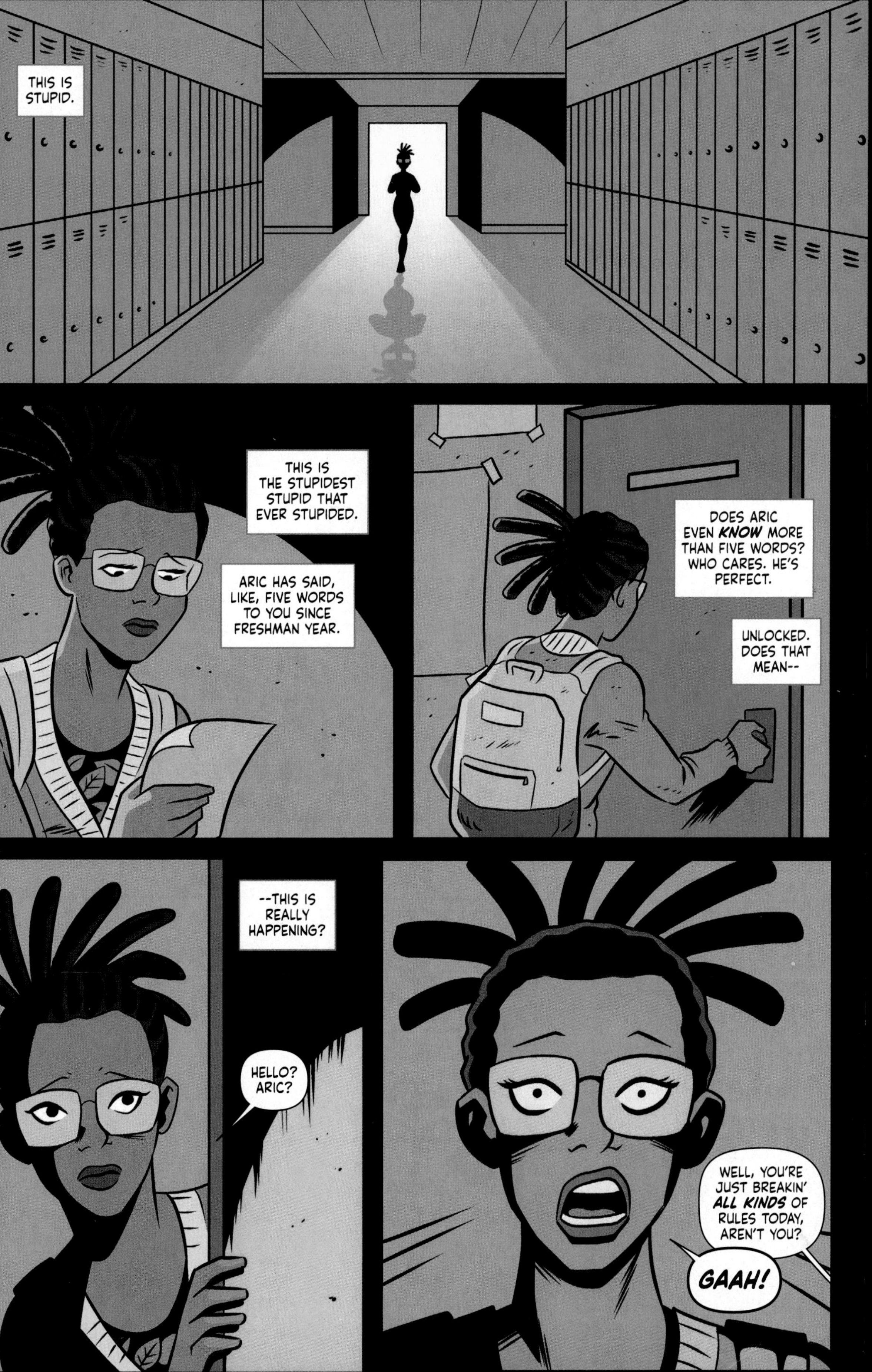
THIS IS STUPID.
THIS IS THE STUPIDEST STUPID THAT EVER STUPIDED.
ARIC HAS SAID, LIKE, FIVE WORDS TO YOU SINCE FRESHMAN YEAR.
DOES ARIC EVEN **KNOW** MORE THAN FIVE WORDS? WHO CARES. HE'S PERFECT.
UNLOCKED. DOES THAT MEAN--
--THIS IS REALLY HAPPENING?
HELLO? ARIC?
WELL, YOU'RE JUST BREAKIN' **ALL KINDS** OF RULES TODAY, AREN'T YOU?
GAAH!

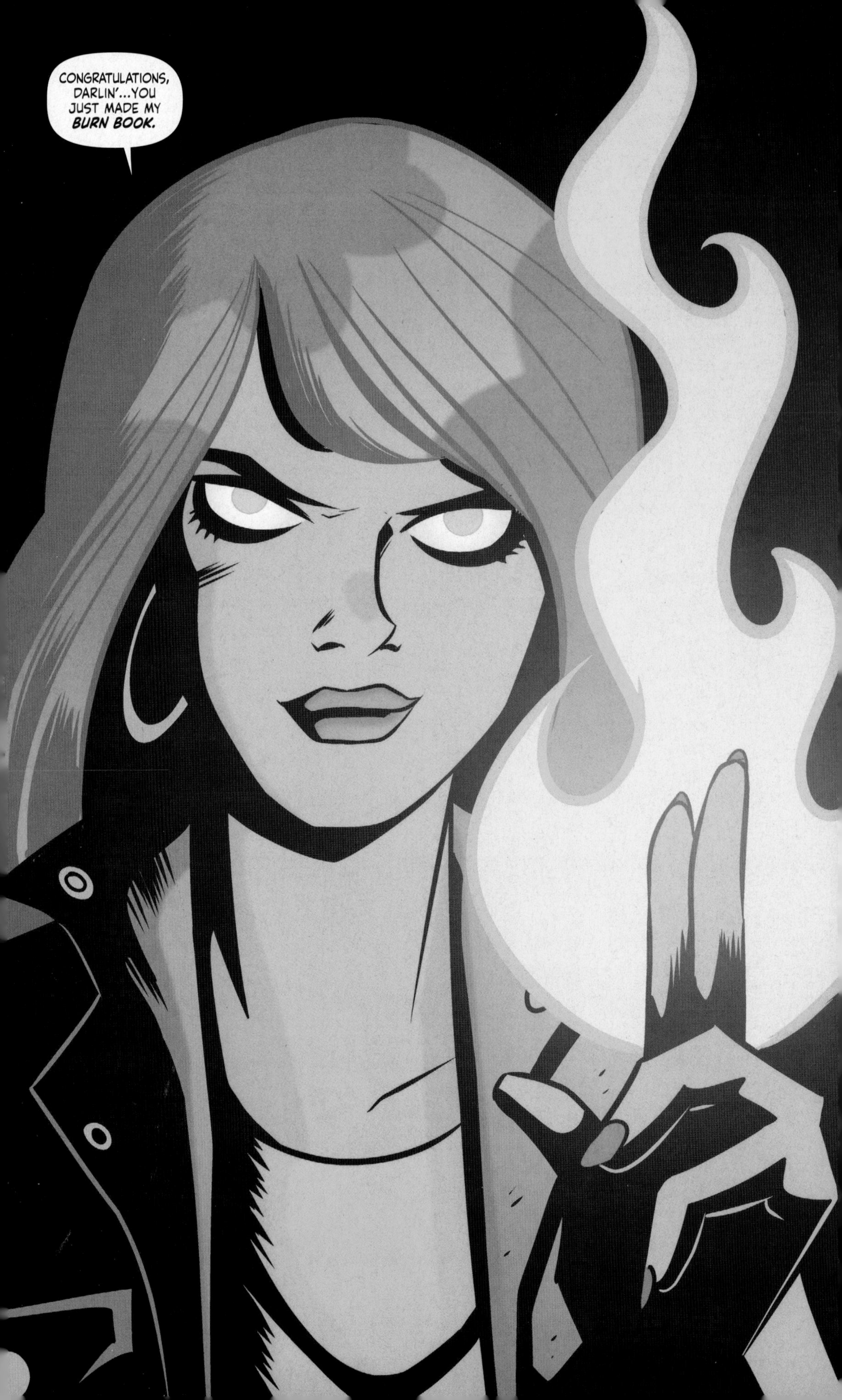
CONGRATULATIONS, DARLIN'...YOU JUST MADE MY ***BURN BOOK.***

VALIANT

DANIEL KIBBLESMITH | DEREK CHARM
DAVID BARON | SIMON BOWLAND

#2

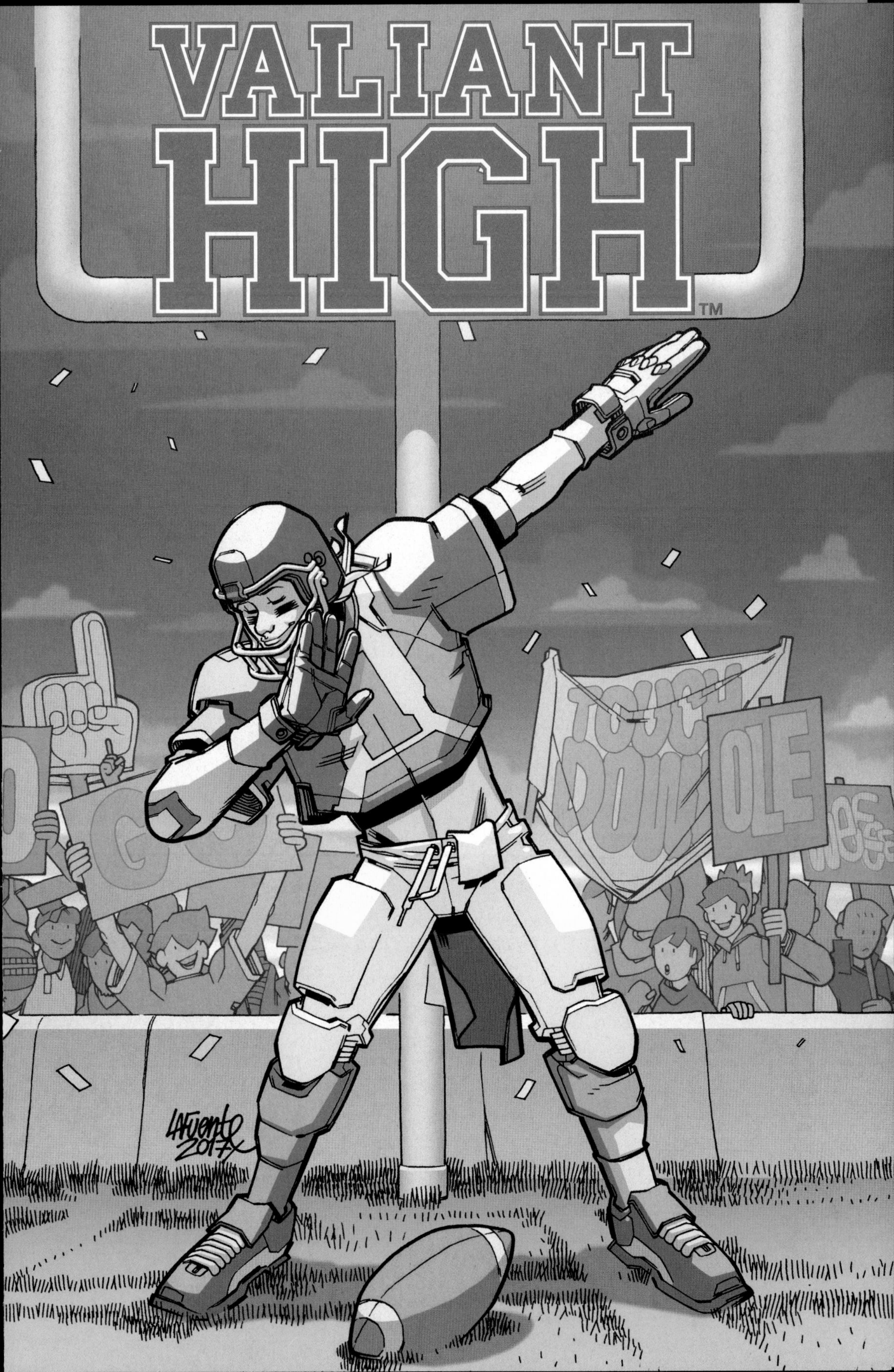
VALIANT
HIGH
TM
TOUCH
OLE
LAFUENTE 2017

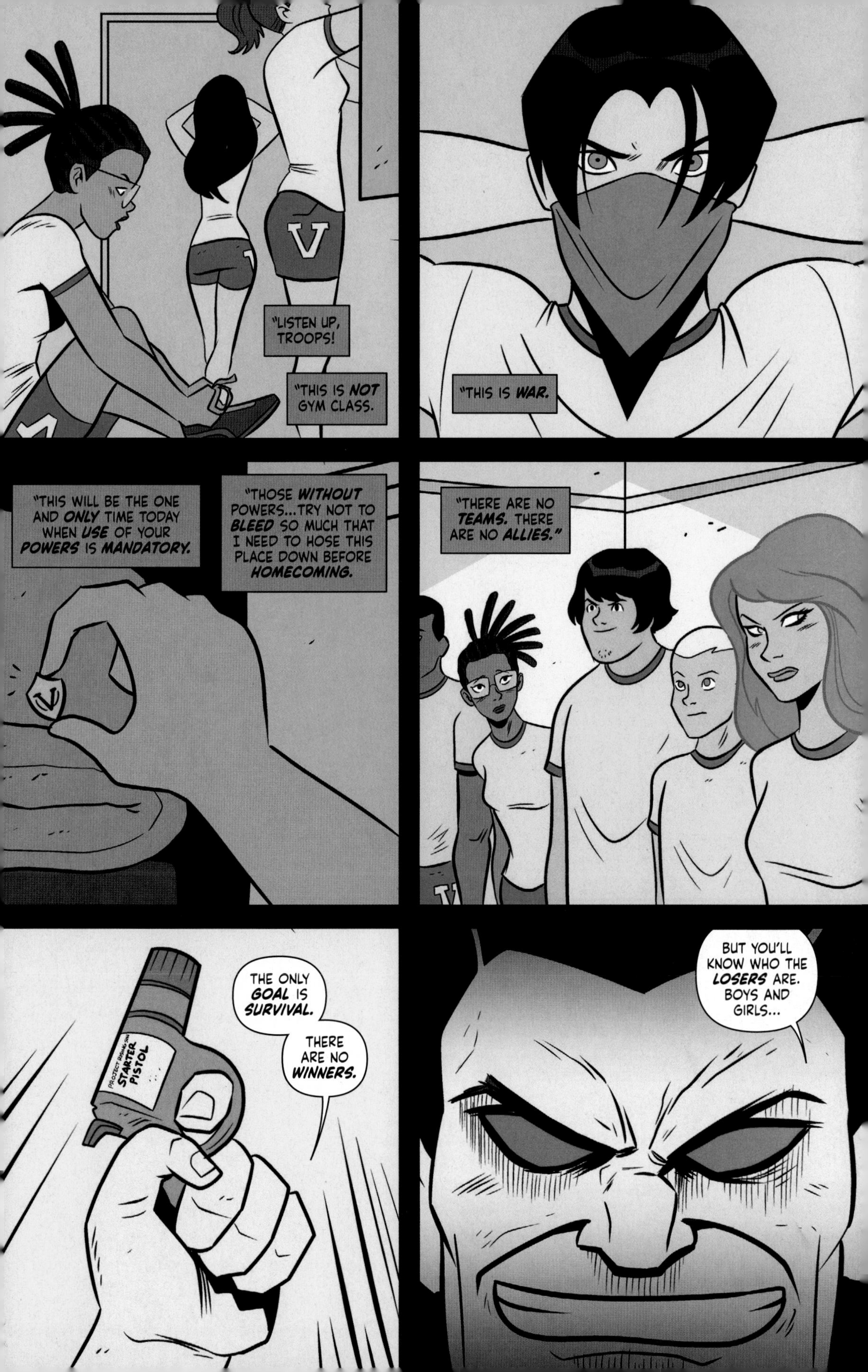
"LISTEN UP, TROOPS!
"THIS IS NOT GYM CLASS.
"THIS IS WAR.
"THIS WILL BE THE ONE AND ONLY TIME TODAY WHEN USE OF YOUR POWERS IS MANDATORY.
"THOSE WITHOUT POWERS...TRY NOT TO BLEED SO MUCH THAT I NEED TO HOSE THIS PLACE DOWN BEFORE HOMECOMING.
"THERE ARE NO TEAMS. THERE ARE NO ALLIES."
STARTER PISTOL
THE ONLY GOAL IS SURVIVAL.
THERE ARE NO WINNERS.
BUT YOU'LL KNOW WHO THE LOSERS ARE. BOYS AND GIRLS...

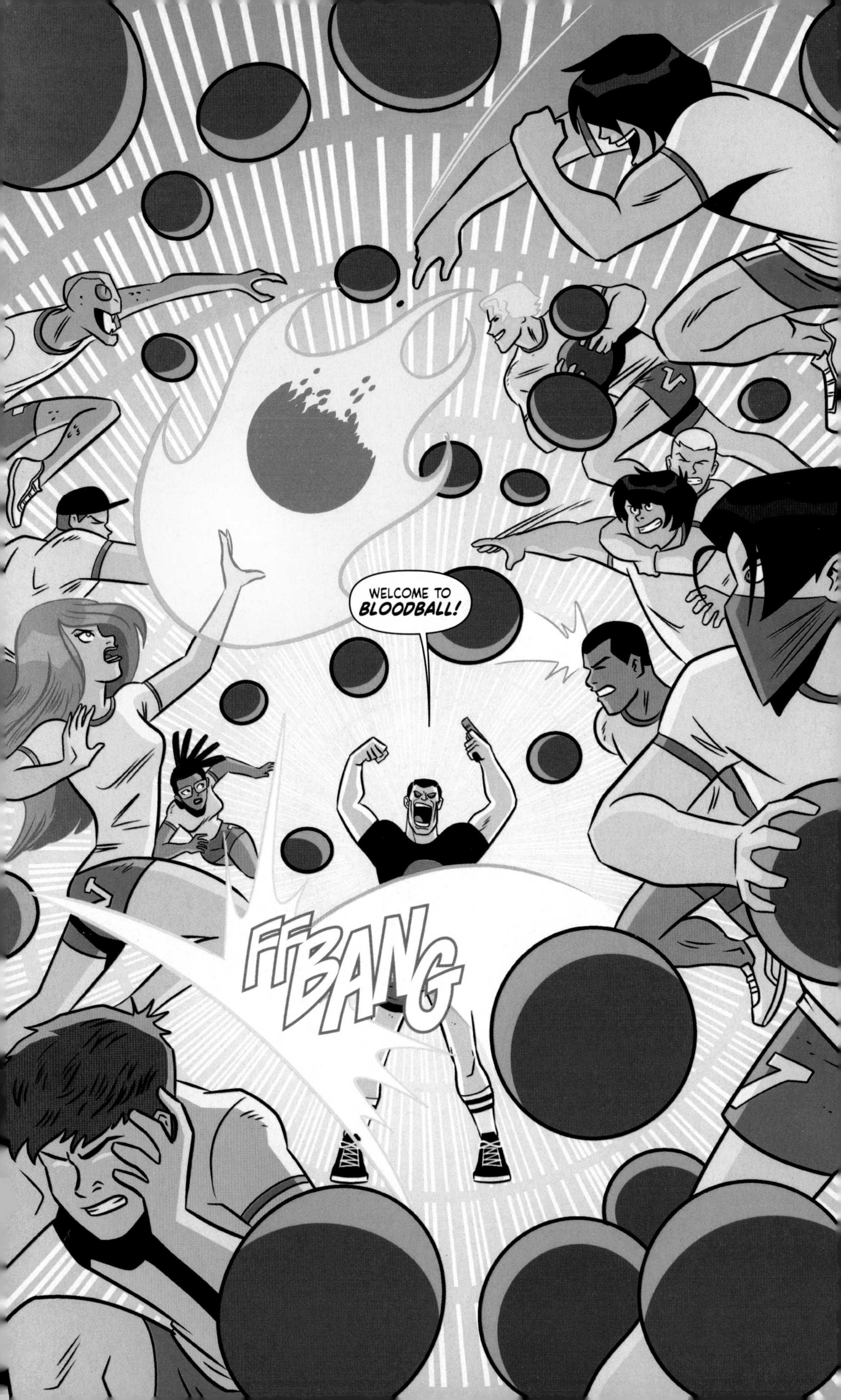
WELCOME TO BLOODBALL!
FFBANG

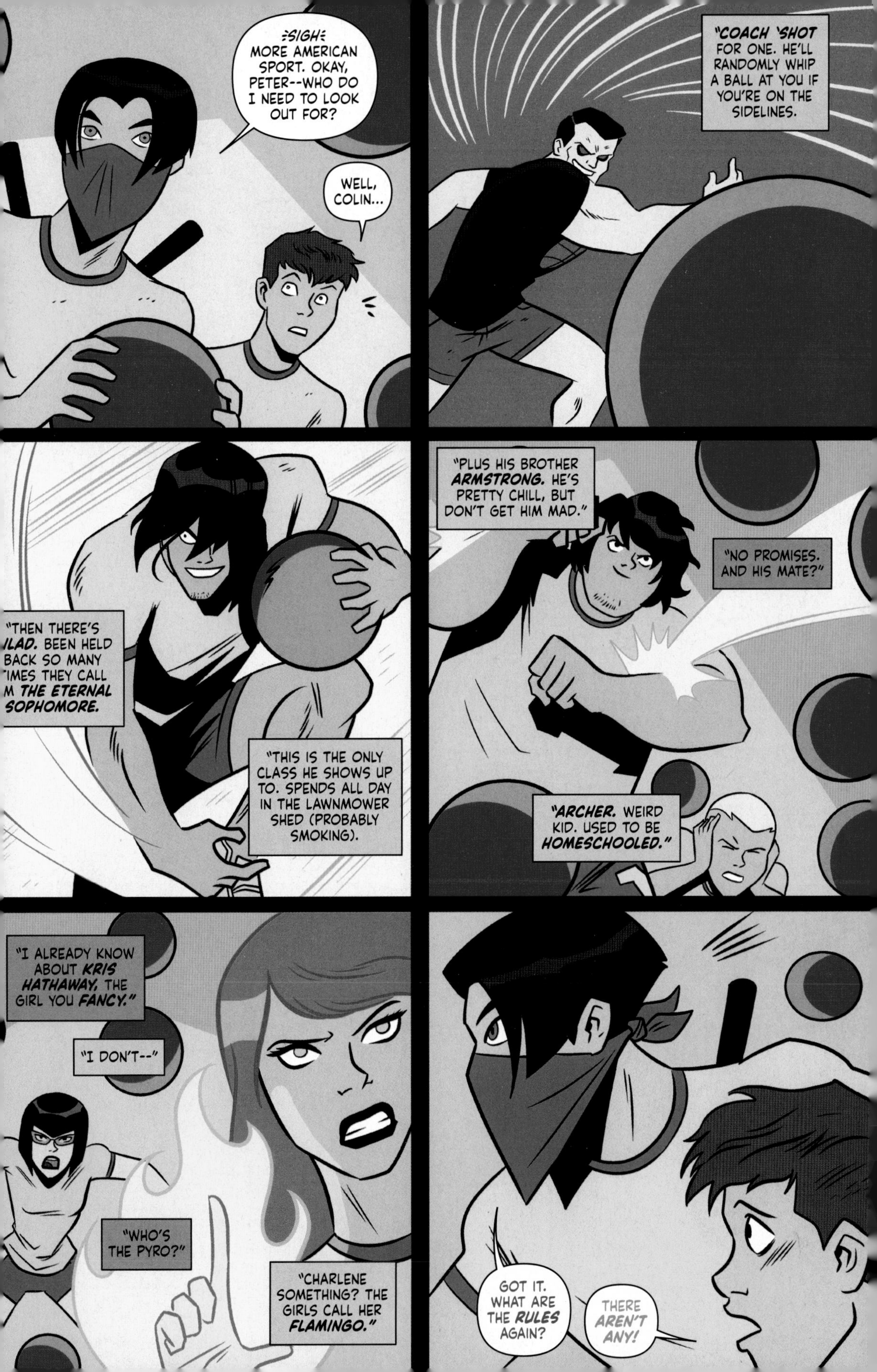

SIGH
MORE AMERICAN SPORT. OKAY, PETER--WHO DO I NEED TO LOOK OUT FOR?
WELL, COLIN...
"COACH 'SHOT FOR ONE. HE'LL RANDOMLY WHIP A BALL AT YOU IF YOU'RE ON THE SIDELINES.
"THEN THERE'S LAD. BEEN HELD BACK SO MANY TIMES THEY CALL M THE ETERNAL SOPHOMORE.
"THIS IS THE ONLY CLASS HE SHOWS UP TO. SPENDS ALL DAY IN THE LAWNMOWER SHED (PROBABLY SMOKING).
"PLUS HIS BROTHER ARMSTRONG. HE'S PRETTY CHILL, BUT DON'T GET HIM MAD."
"NO PROMISES. AND HIS MATE?"
"ARCHER. WEIRD KID. USED TO BE HOMESCHOOLED."
"I ALREADY KNOW ABOUT KRIS HATHAWAY, THE GIRL YOU FANCY."
"I DON'T--"
"WHO'S THE PYRO?"
"CHARLENE SOMETHING? THE GIRLS CALL HER FLAMINGO."
GOT IT. WHAT ARE THE RULES AGAIN?
THERE AREN'T ANY!

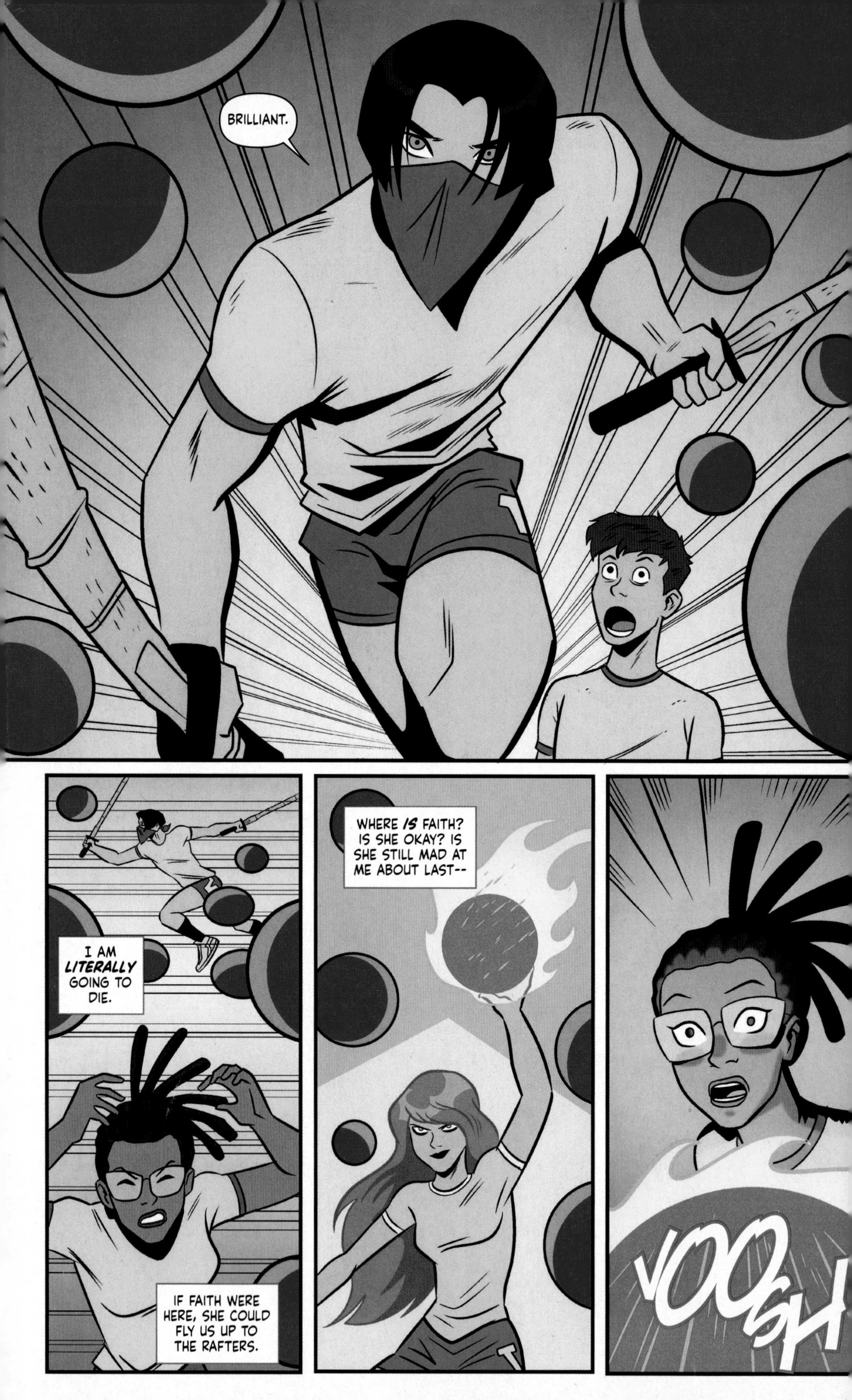
BRILLIANT.
I AM *LITERALLY* GOING TO DIE.
IF FAITH WERE HERE, SHE COULD FLY US UP TO THE RAFTERS.
WHERE *IS* FAITH? IS SHE OKAY? IS SHE STILL MAD AT ME ABOUT LAST--
VOOSH

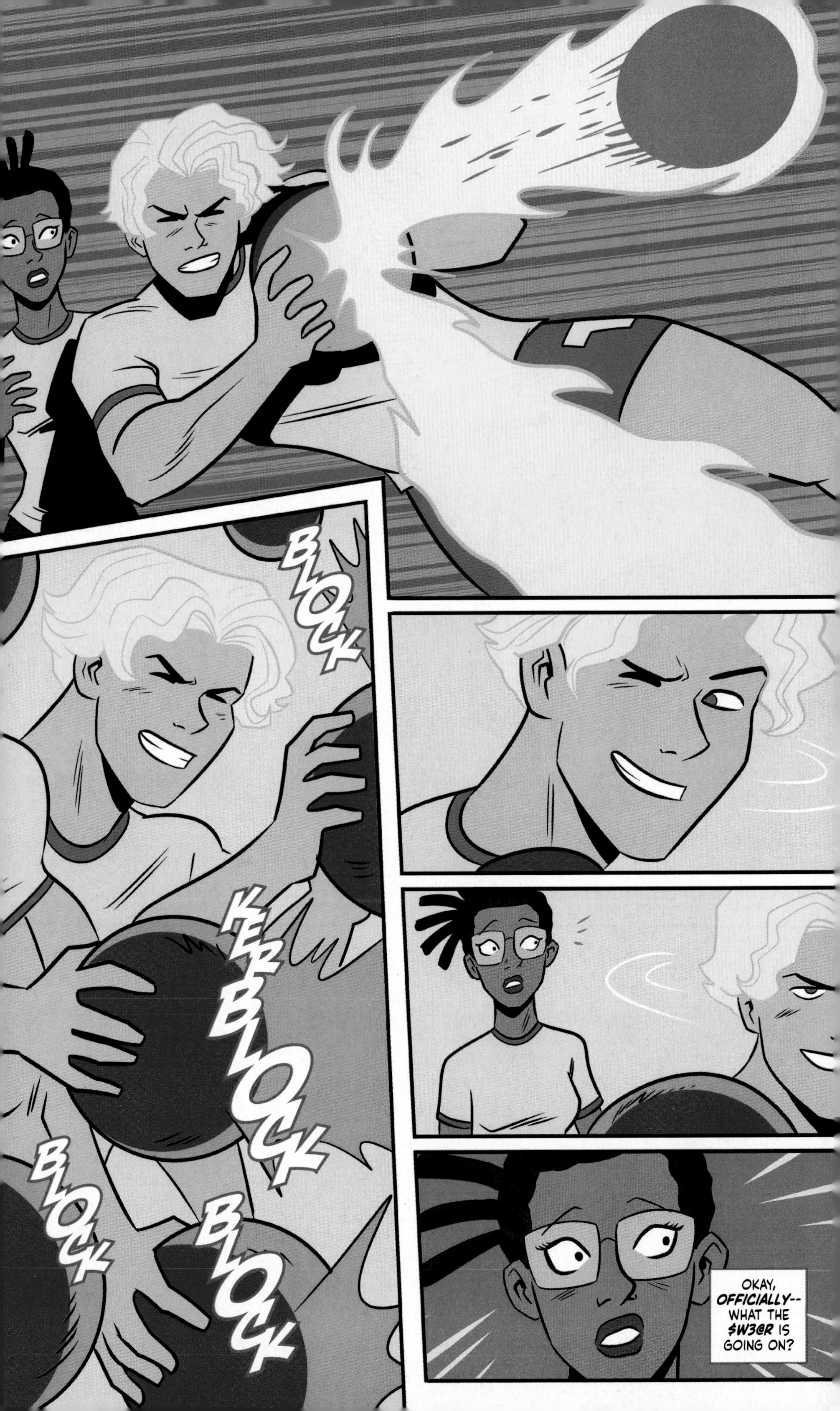
BLOCK
KERBLOCK
BLOCK
BLOCK
OKAY, OFFICIALLY-- WHAT THE $W3@R IS GOING ON?

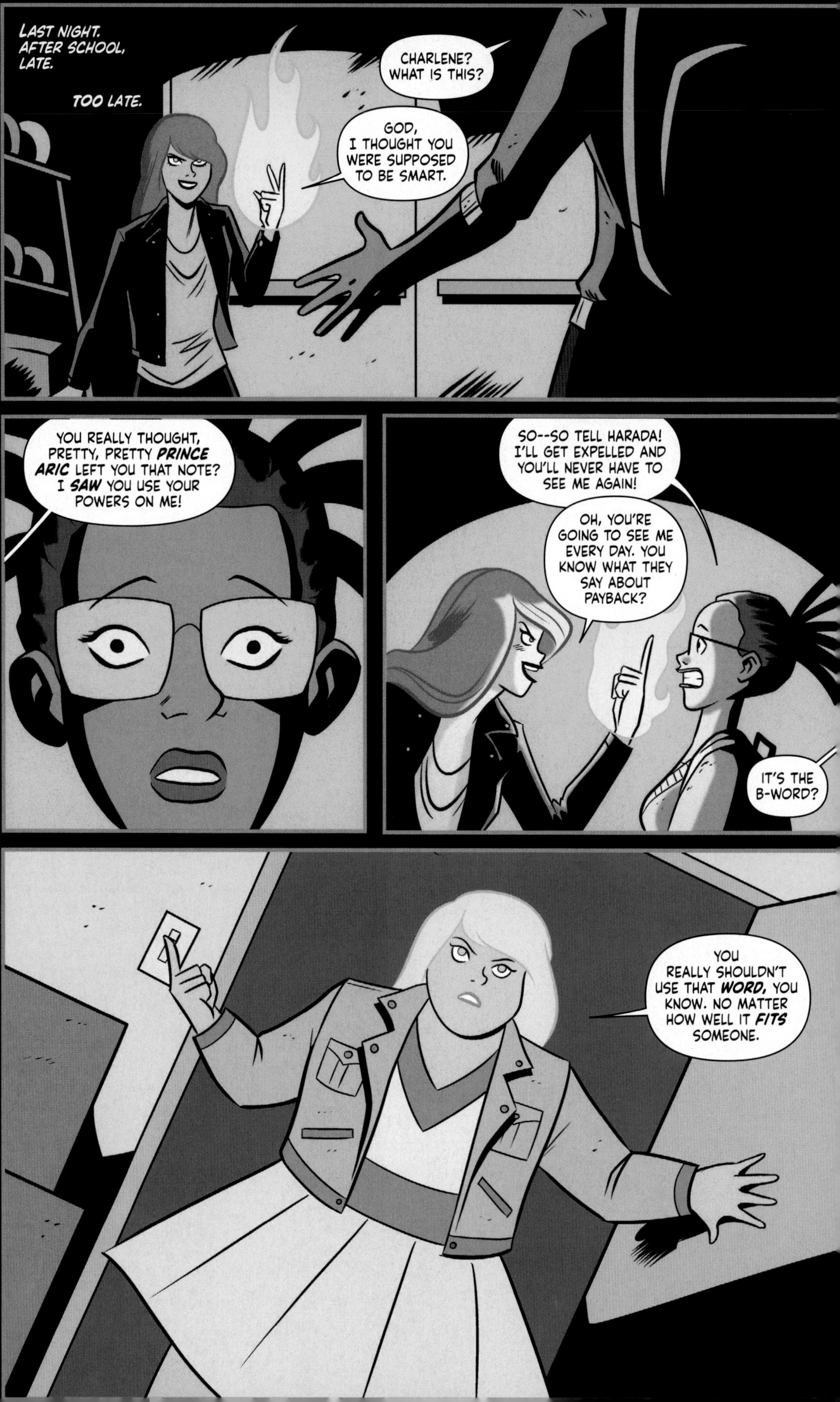
LAST NIGHT. AFTER SCHOOL, LATE.
TOO LATE.
CHARLENE? WHAT IS THIS?
GOD, I THOUGHT YOU WERE SUPPOSED TO BE SMART.
YOU REALLY THOUGHT, PRETTY, PRETTY PRINCE ARIC LEFT YOU THAT NOTE? I SAW YOU USE YOUR POWERS ON ME!
SO--SO TELL HARADA! I'LL GET EXPELLED AND YOU'LL NEVER HAVE TO SEE ME AGAIN!
OH, YOU'RE GOING TO SEE ME EVERY DAY. YOU KNOW WHAT THEY SAY ABOUT PAYBACK?
IT'S THE B-WORD?
YOU REALLY SHOULDN'T USE THAT WORD, YOU KNOW. NO MATTER HOW WELL IT FITS SOMEONE.

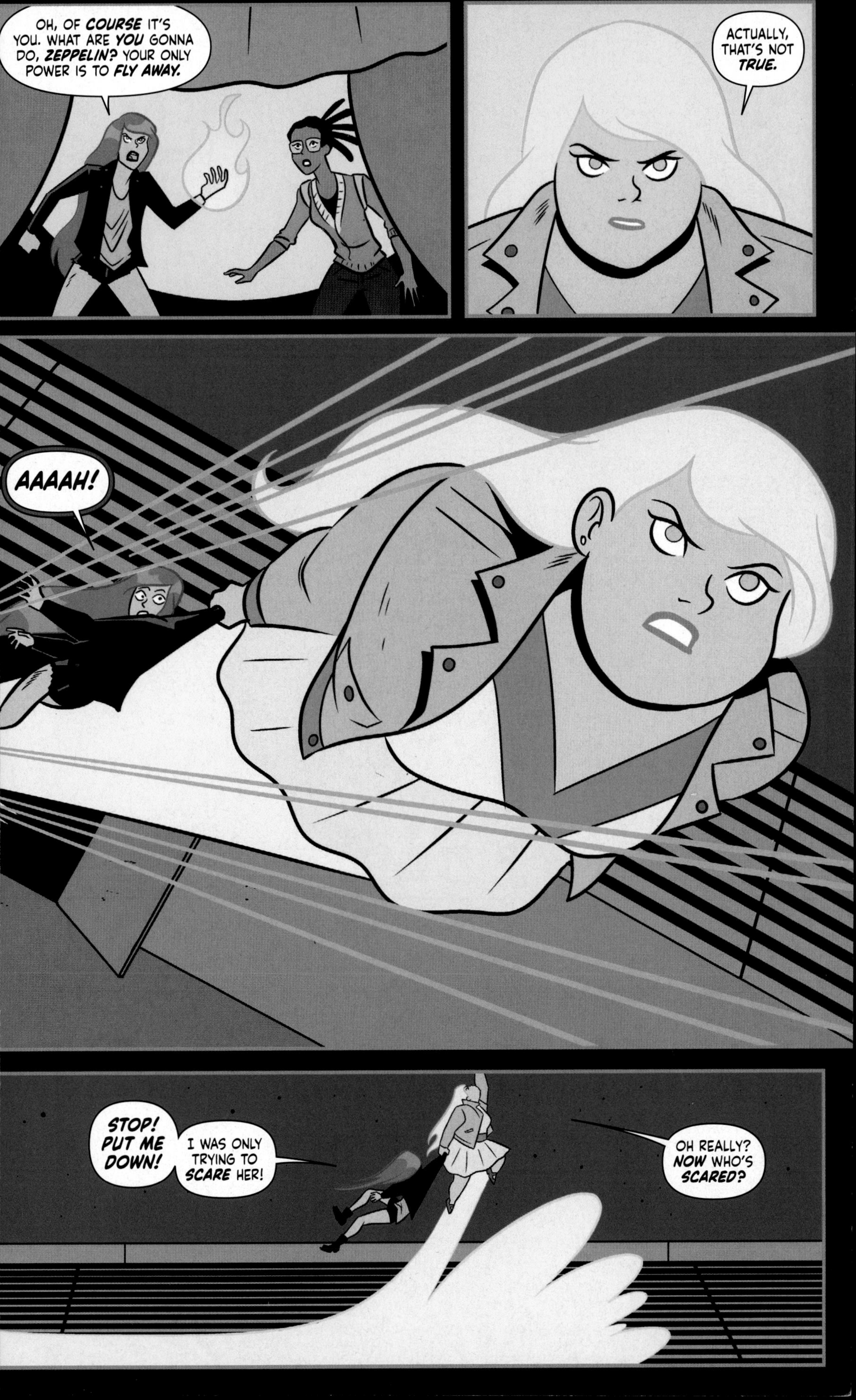
OH, OF **COURSE** IT'S YOU. WHAT ARE **YOU** GONNA DO, **ZEPPELIN?** YOUR ONLY POWER IS TO **FLY AWAY.**
ACTUALLY, THAT'S NOT **TRUE.**
AAAAH!
STOP! PUT ME DOWN!
I WAS ONLY TRYING TO **SCARE** HER!
OH REALLY? **NOW** WHO'S **SCARED?**

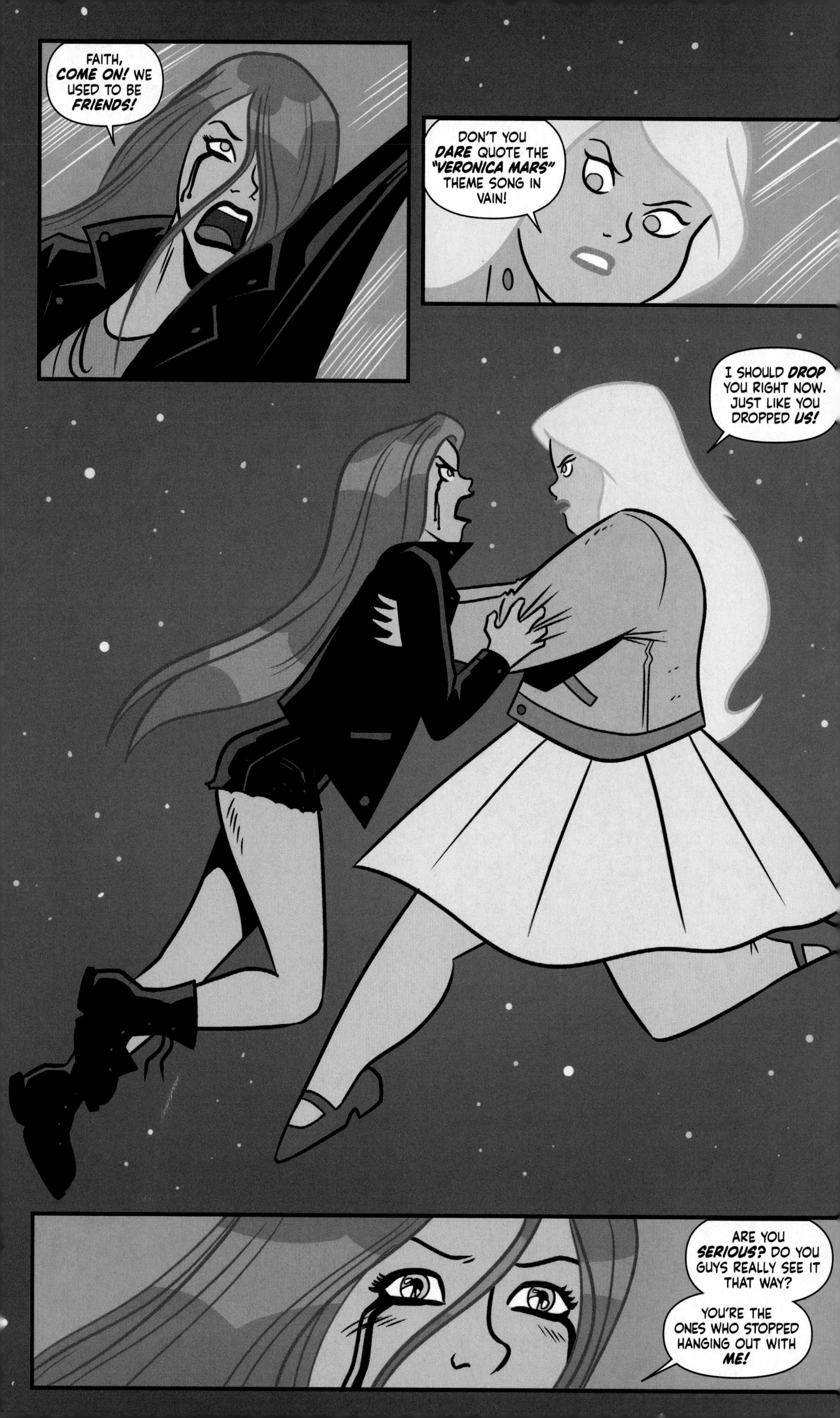
FAITH, COME ON! WE USED TO BE FRIENDS!
DON'T YOU DARE QUOTE THE "VERONICA MARS" THEME SONG IN VAIN!
I SHOULD DROP YOU RIGHT NOW. JUST LIKE YOU DROPPED US!
ARE YOU SERIOUS? DO YOU GUYS REALLY SEE IT THAT WAY?
YOU'RE THE ONES WHO STOPPED HANGING OUT WITH ME!

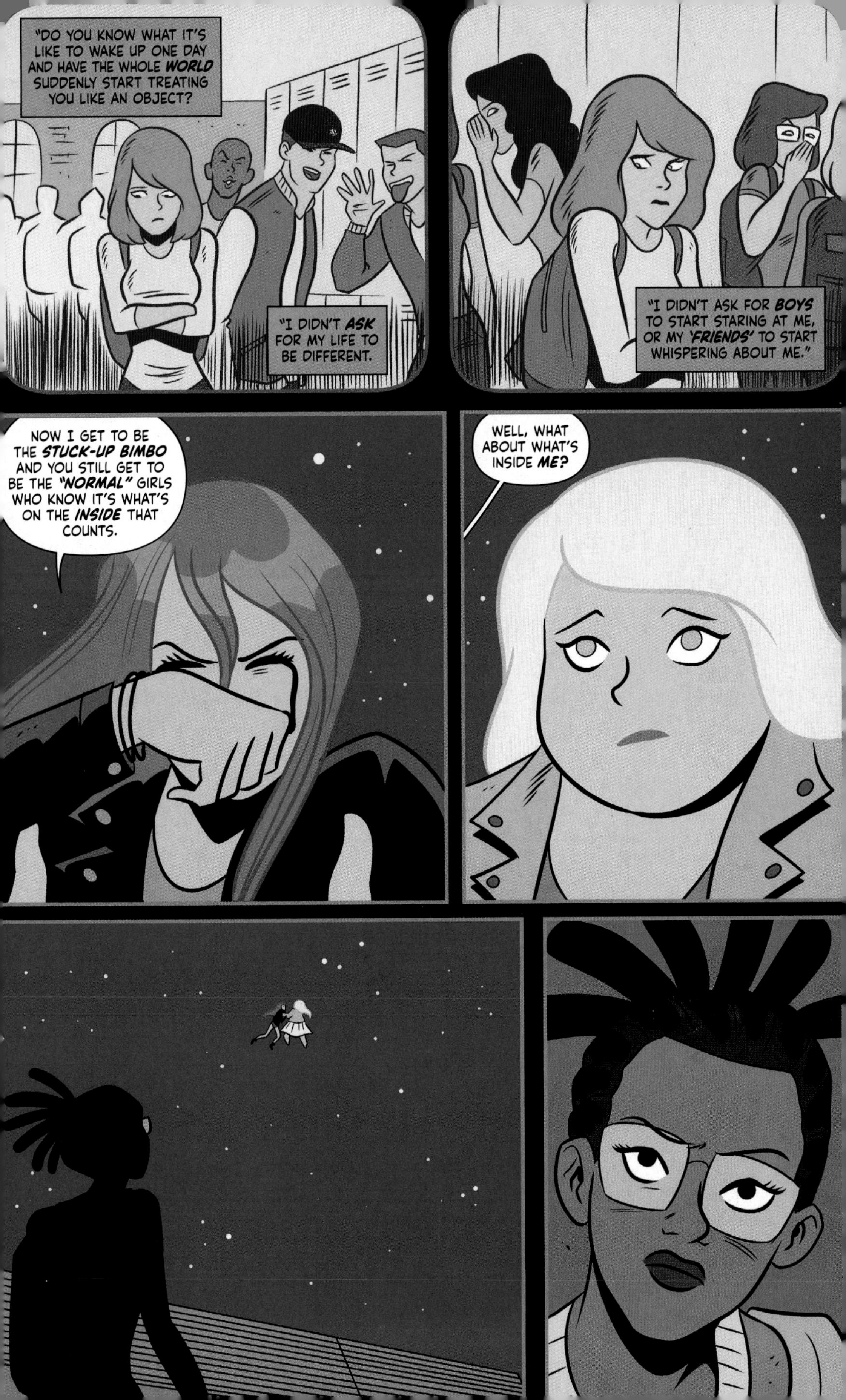

"DO YOU KNOW WHAT IT'S LIKE TO WAKE UP ONE DAY AND HAVE THE WHOLE WORLD SUDDENLY START TREATING YOU LIKE AN OBJECT?
"I DIDN'T ASK FOR MY LIFE TO BE DIFFERENT.
"I DIDN'T ASK FOR BOYS TO START STARING AT ME, OR MY 'FRIENDS' TO START WHISPERING ABOUT ME."
NOW I GET TO BE THE STUCK-UP BIMBO AND YOU STILL GET TO BE THE "NORMAL" GIRLS WHO KNOW IT'S WHAT'S ON THE INSIDE THAT COUNTS.
WELL, WHAT ABOUT WHAT'S INSIDE ME?

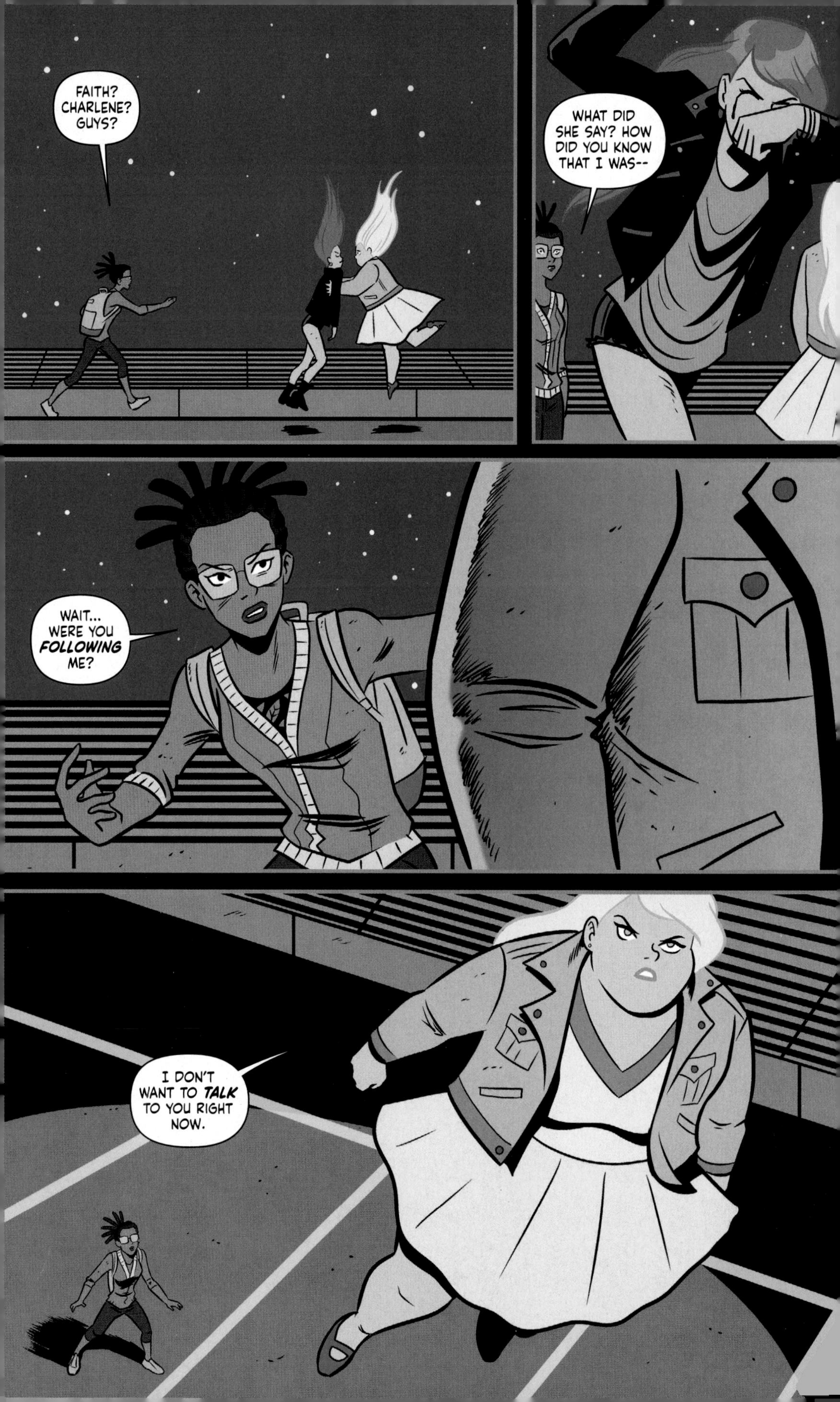
FAITH? CHARLENE? GUYS?
WHAT DID SHE SAY? HOW DID YOU KNOW THAT I WAS--
WAIT... WERE YOU *FOLLOWING* ME?
I DON'T WANT TO *TALK* TO YOU RIGHT NOW.

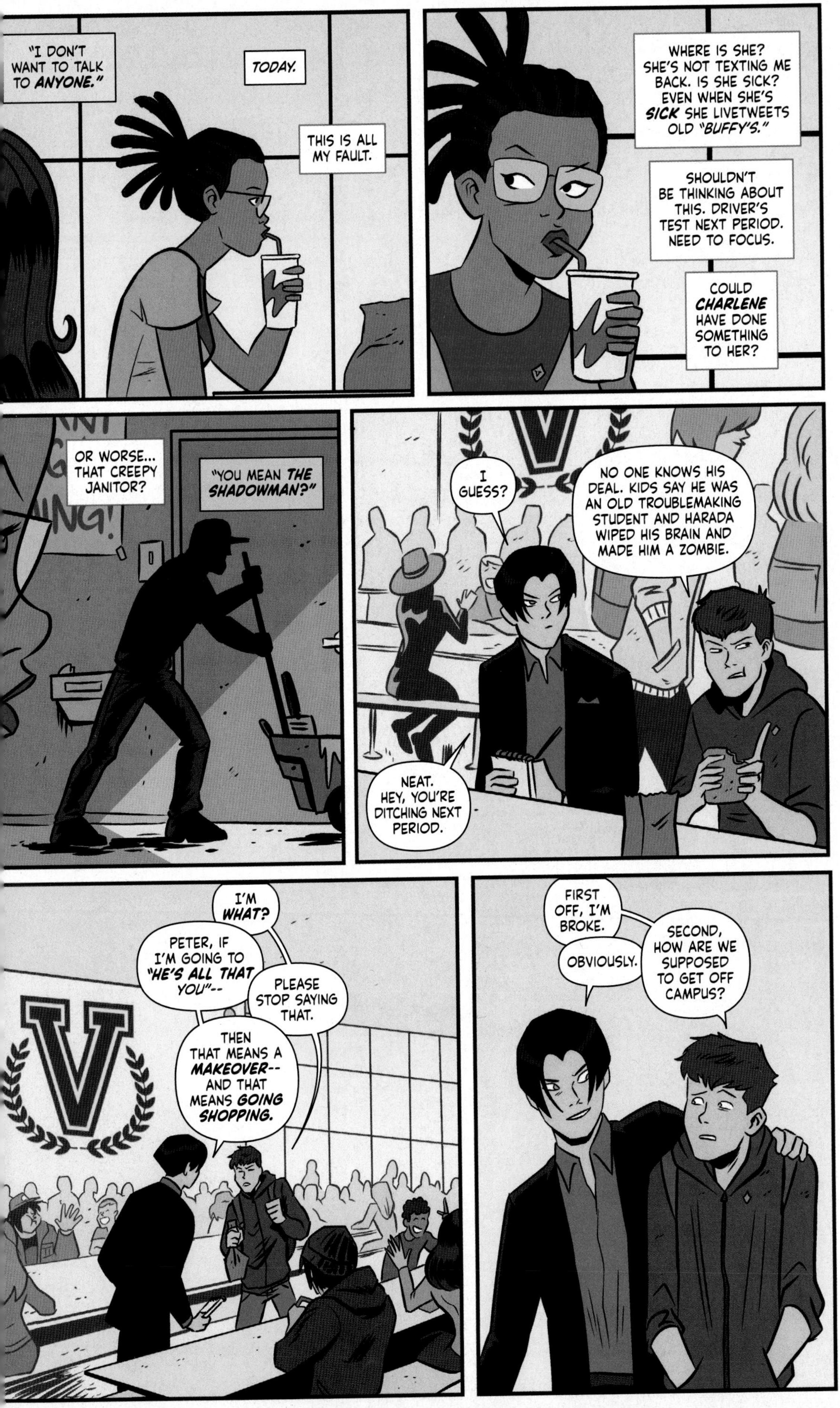
"I DON'T WANT TO TALK TO ANYONE."
TODAY.
THIS IS ALL MY FAULT.
WHERE IS SHE? SHE'S NOT TEXTING ME BACK. IS SHE SICK? EVEN WHEN SHE'S SICK SHE LIVETWEETS OLD "BUFFY'S."
SHOULDN'T BE THINKING ABOUT THIS. DRIVER'S TEST NEXT PERIOD. NEED TO FOCUS.
COULD CHARLENE HAVE DONE SOMETHING TO HER?
OR WORSE... THAT CREEPY JANITOR?
"YOU MEAN THE SHADOWMAN?"
I GUESS?
NO ONE KNOWS HIS DEAL. KIDS SAY HE WAS AN OLD TROUBLEMAKING STUDENT AND HARADA WIPED HIS BRAIN AND MADE HIM A ZOMBIE.
NEAT. HEY, YOU'RE DITCHING NEXT PERIOD.
I'M WHAT?
PETER, IF I'M GOING TO "HE'S ALL THAT YOU"--
PLEASE STOP SAYING THAT.
THEN THAT MEANS A MAKEOVER-- AND THAT MEANS GOING SHOPPING.
FIRST OFF, I'M BROKE.
OBVIOUSLY.
SECOND, HOW ARE WE SUPPOSED TO GET OFF CAMPUS?

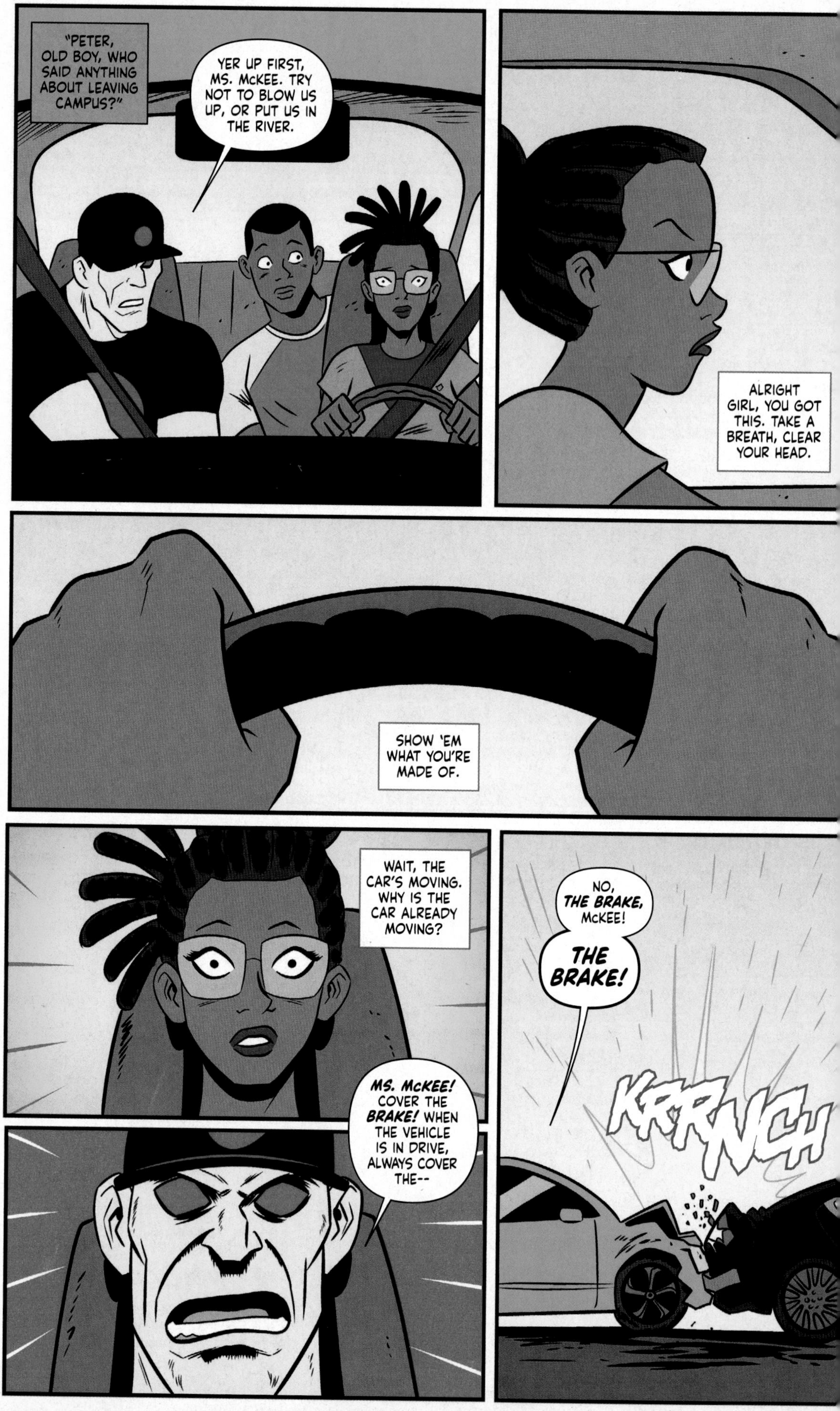
"PETER, OLD BOY, WHO SAID ANYTHING ABOUT LEAVING CAMPUS?"
YER UP FIRST, MS. McKEE. TRY NOT TO BLOW US UP, OR PUT US IN THE RIVER.
ALRIGHT GIRL, YOU GOT THIS. TAKE A BREATH, CLEAR YOUR HEAD.
SHOW 'EM WHAT YOU'RE MADE OF.
WAIT, THE CAR'S MOVING. WHY IS THE CAR ALREADY MOVING?
MS. McKEE! COVER THE BRAKE! WHEN THE VEHICLE IS IN DRIVE, ALWAYS COVER THE--
NO, THE BRAKE, McKEE!
THE BRAKE!
KRRNCH

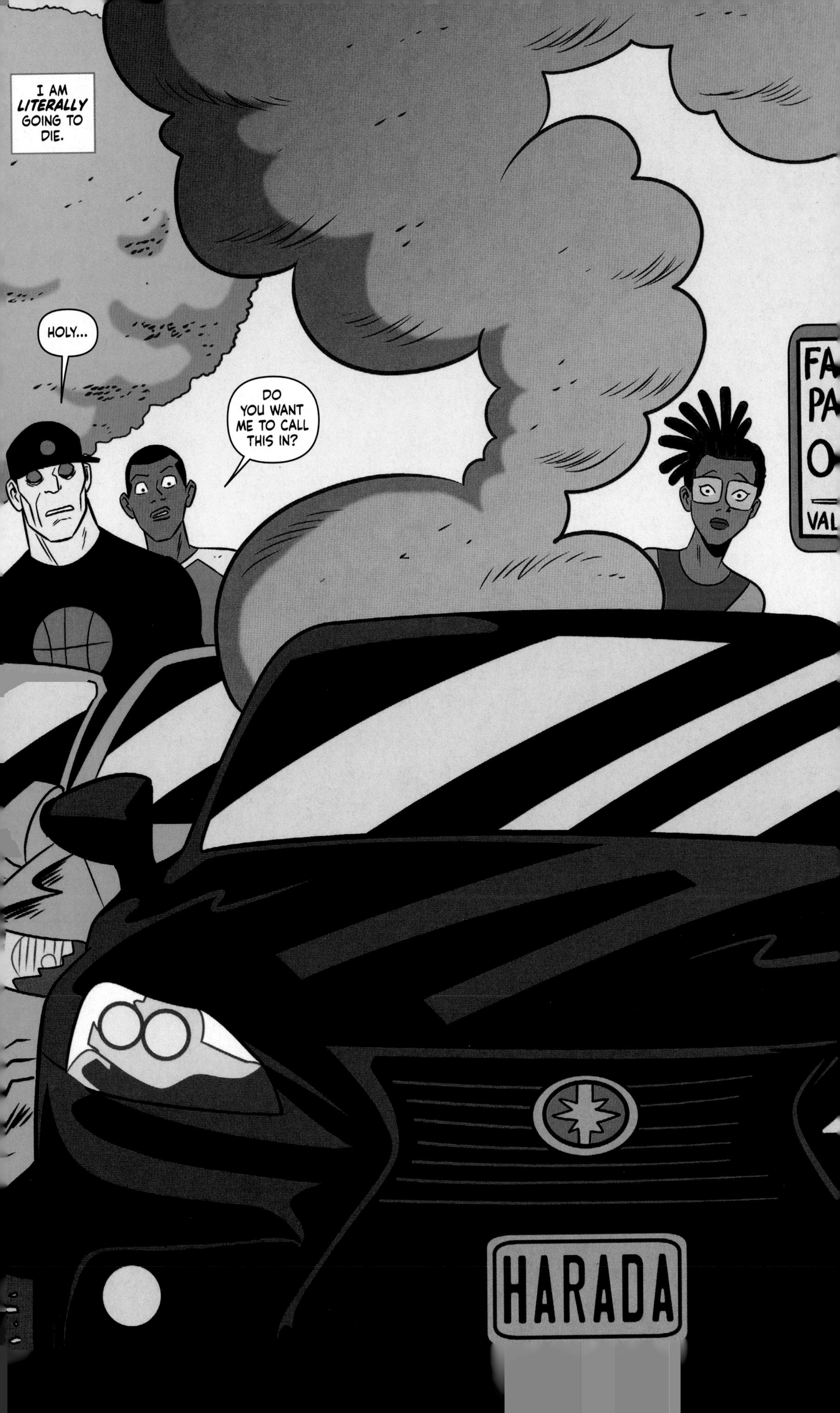
I AM *LITERALLY* GOING TO DIE.
HOLY...
DO YOU WANT ME TO CALL THIS IN?
HARADA

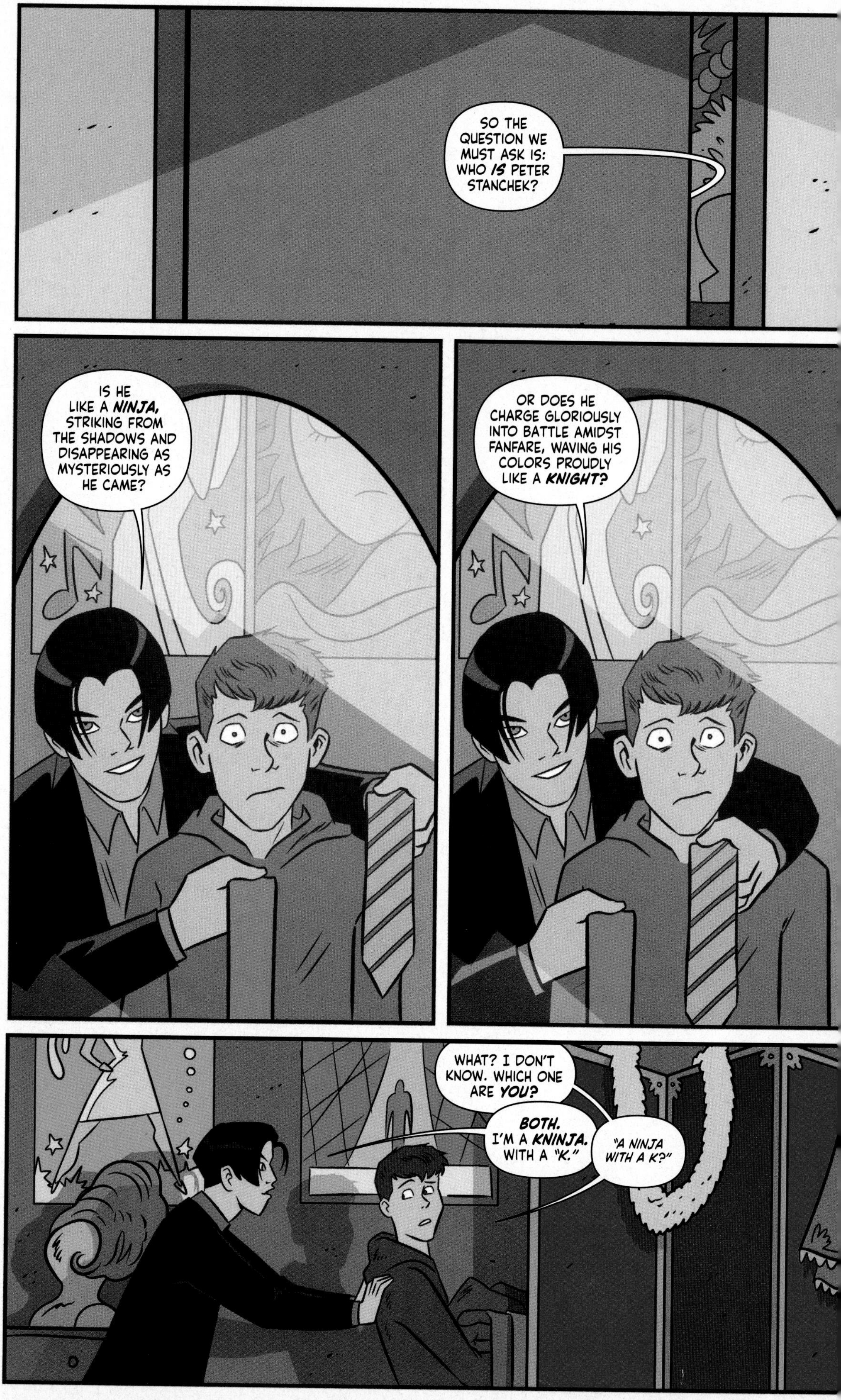
SO THE QUESTION WE MUST ASK IS: WHO *IS* PETER STANCHEK?
IS HE LIKE A *NINJA*, STRIKING FROM THE SHADOWS AND DISAPPEARING AS MYSTERIOUSLY AS HE CAME?
OR DOES HE CHARGE GLORIOUSLY INTO BATTLE AMIDST FANFARE, WAVING HIS COLORS PROUDLY LIKE A *KNIGHT?*
WHAT? I DON'T KNOW. WHICH ONE ARE *YOU?*
BOTH. I'M A *KNINJA.* WITH A "K."
"A NINJA WITH A K?"

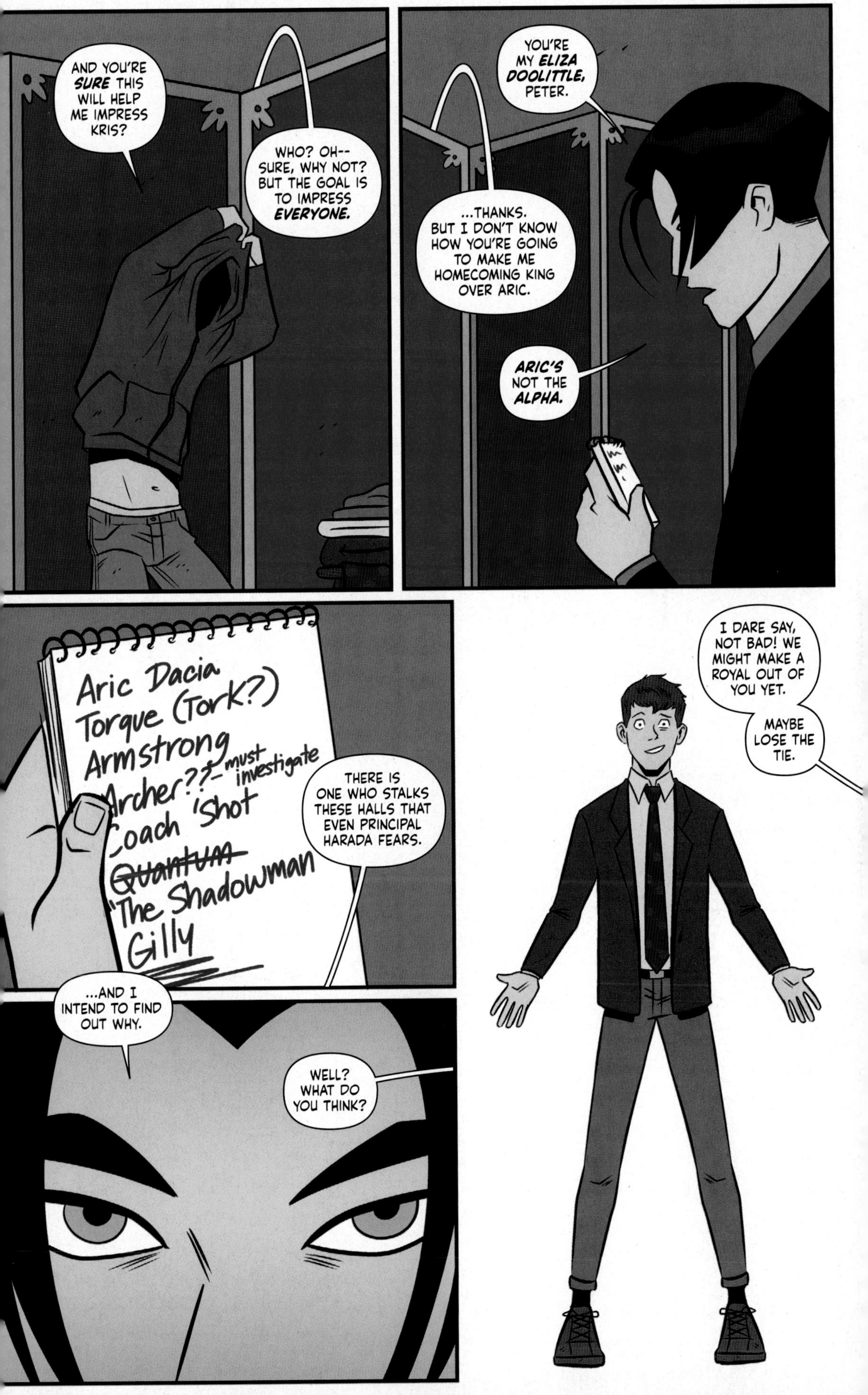
AND YOU'RE SURE THIS WILL HELP ME IMPRESS KRIS?
WHO? OH-- SURE, WHY NOT? BUT THE GOAL IS TO IMPRESS EVERYONE.
YOU'RE MY ELIZA DOOLITTLE, PETER.
...THANKS. BUT I DON'T KNOW HOW YOU'RE GOING TO MAKE ME HOMECOMING KING OVER ARIC.
ARIC'S NOT THE ALPHA.
Aric Dacia
Torque (Tork?)
Armstrong
Archer?? - must investigate
Coach 'Shot
Quantum
'The Shadowman
Gilly
THERE IS ONE WHO STALKS THESE HALLS THAT EVEN PRINCIPAL HARADA FEARS.
...AND I INTEND TO FIND OUT WHY.
WELL? WHAT DO YOU THINK?
I DARE SAY, NOT BAD! WE MIGHT MAKE A ROYAL OUT OF YOU YET.
MAYBE LOSE THE TIE.

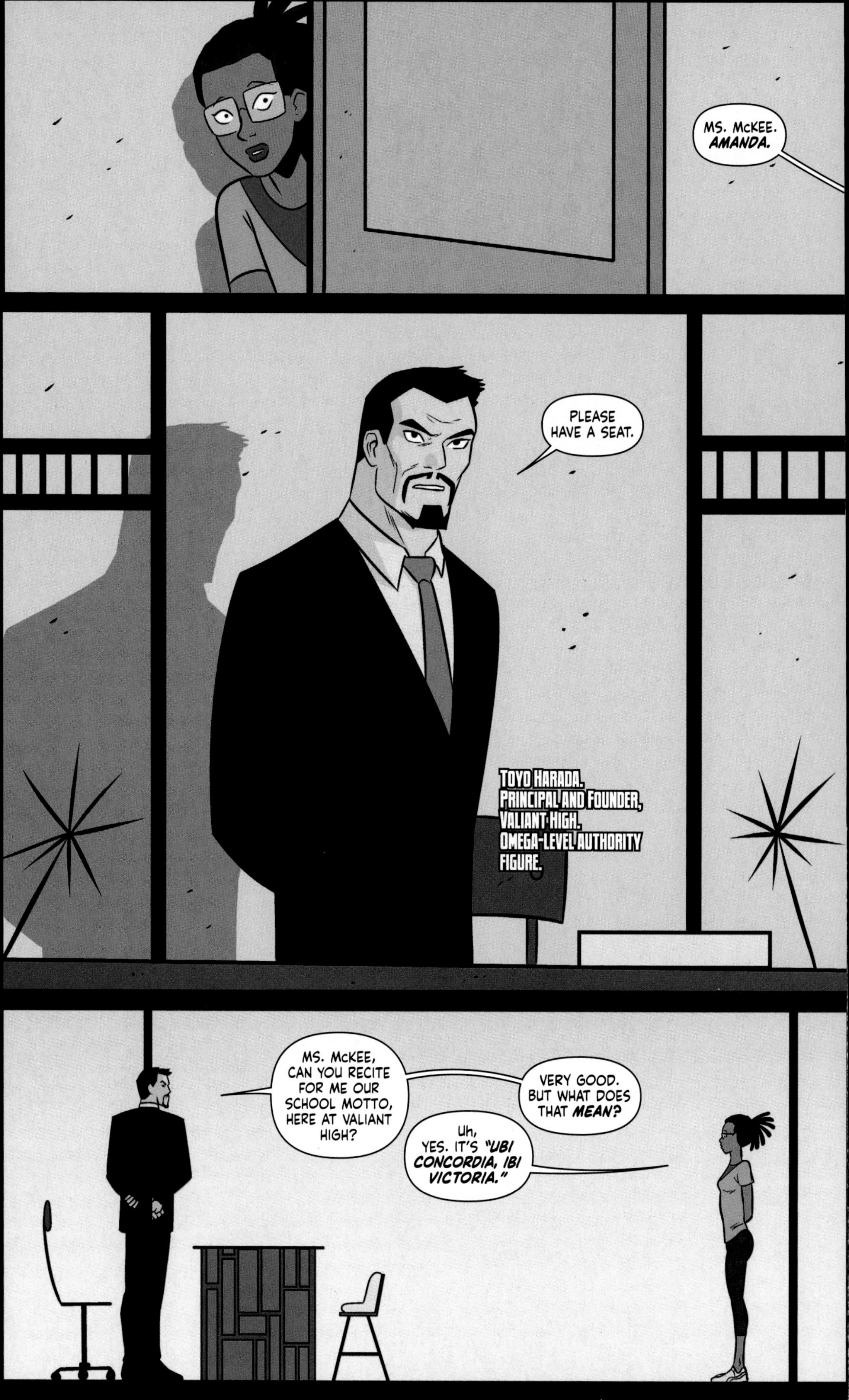
MS. McKEE. AMANDA.
PLEASE HAVE A SEAT.
TOYO HARADA. PRINCIPAL AND FOUNDER, VALIANT HIGH. OMEGA-LEVEL AUTHORITY FIGURE.
MS. McKEE, CAN YOU RECITE FOR ME OUR SCHOOL MOTTO, HERE AT VALIANT HIGH?
Uh, YES. IT'S "UBI CONCORDIA, IBI VICTORIA."
VERY GOOD. BUT WHAT DOES THAT MEAN?

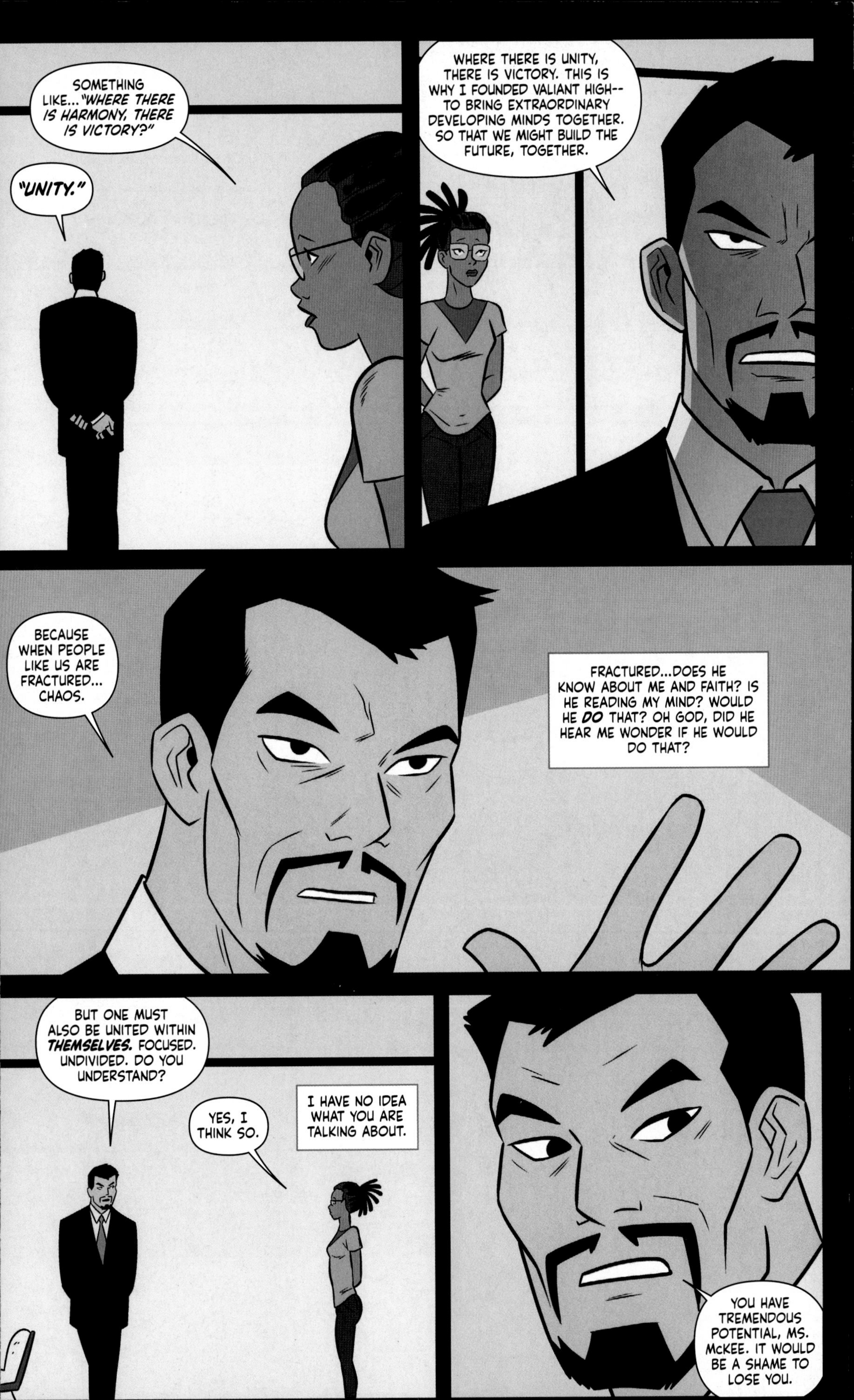
SOMETHING LIKE... "WHERE THERE IS HARMONY, THERE IS VICTORY?"
"UNITY."
WHERE THERE IS UNITY, THERE IS VICTORY. THIS IS WHY I FOUNDED VALIANT HIGH--TO BRING EXTRAORDINARY DEVELOPING MINDS TOGETHER. SO THAT WE MIGHT BUILD THE FUTURE, TOGETHER.
BECAUSE WHEN PEOPLE LIKE US ARE FRACTURED... CHAOS.
FRACTURED...DOES HE KNOW ABOUT ME AND FAITH? IS HE READING MY MIND? WOULD HE DO THAT? OH GOD, DID HE HEAR ME WONDER IF HE WOULD DO THAT?
BUT ONE MUST ALSO BE UNITED WITHIN THEMSELVES. FOCUSED. UNDIVIDED. DO YOU UNDERSTAND?
YES, I THINK SO.
I HAVE NO IDEA WHAT YOU ARE TALKING ABOUT.
YOU HAVE TREMENDOUS POTENTIAL, MS. McKEE. IT WOULD BE A SHAME TO LOSE YOU.

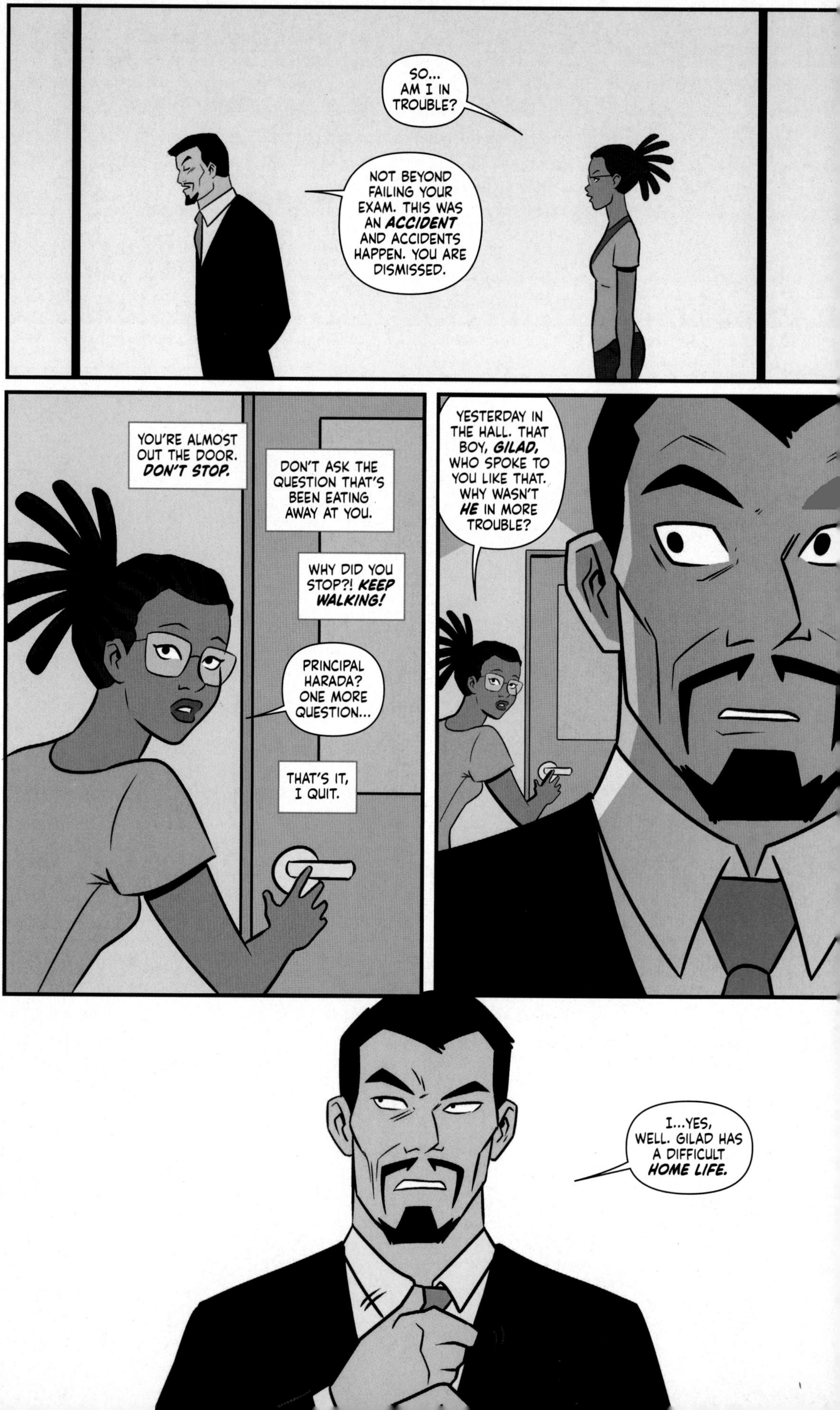
SO... AM I IN TROUBLE?
NOT BEYOND FAILING YOUR EXAM. THIS WAS AN *ACCIDENT* AND ACCIDENTS HAPPEN. YOU ARE DISMISSED.
YOU'RE ALMOST OUT THE DOOR. *DON'T STOP.*
DON'T ASK THE QUESTION THAT'S BEEN EATING AWAY AT YOU.
WHY DID YOU STOP?! *KEEP WALKING!*
PRINCIPAL HARADA? ONE MORE QUESTION...
THAT'S IT, I QUIT.
YESTERDAY IN THE HALL. THAT BOY, *GILAD,* WHO SPOKE TO YOU LIKE THAT. WHY WASN'T *HE* IN MORE TROUBLE?
I...YES, WELL. GILAD HAS A DIFFICULT *HOME LIFE.*

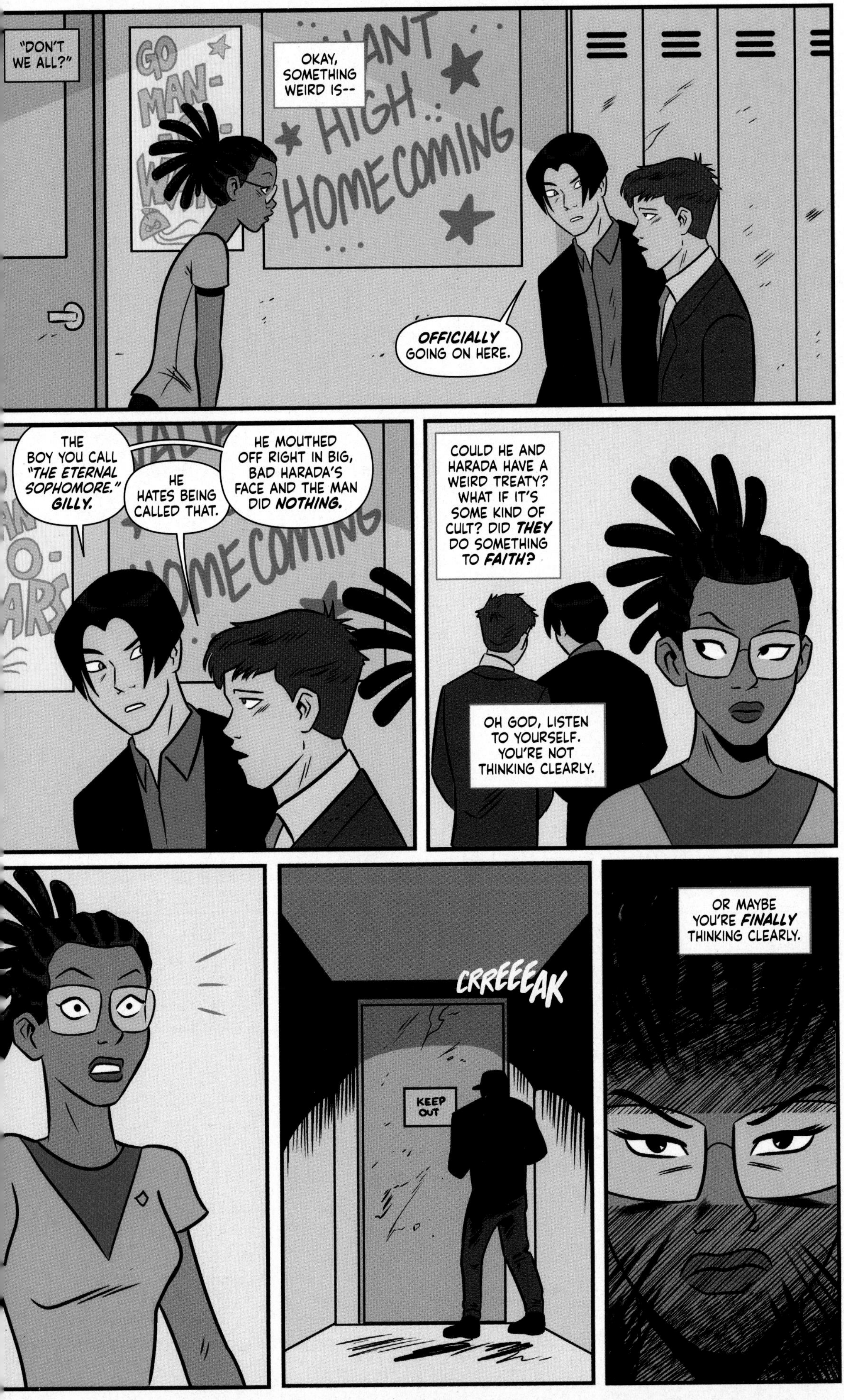
"DON'T WE ALL?"
OKAY, SOMETHING WEIRD IS--
OFFICIALLY GOING ON HERE.
HIGH HOMECOMING
THE BOY YOU CALL *"THE ETERNAL SOPHOMORE." GILLY.*
HE HATES BEING CALLED THAT.
HE MOUTHED OFF RIGHT IN BIG, BAD HARADA'S FACE AND THE MAN DID *NOTHING.*
COULD HE AND HARADA HAVE A WEIRD TREATY? WHAT IF IT'S SOME KIND OF CULT? DID *THEY* DO SOMETHING TO *FAITH?*
OH GOD, LISTEN TO YOURSELF. YOU'RE NOT THINKING CLEARLY.
CRREEEAK
KEEP OUT
OR MAYBE YOU'RE *FINALLY* THINKING CLEARLY.

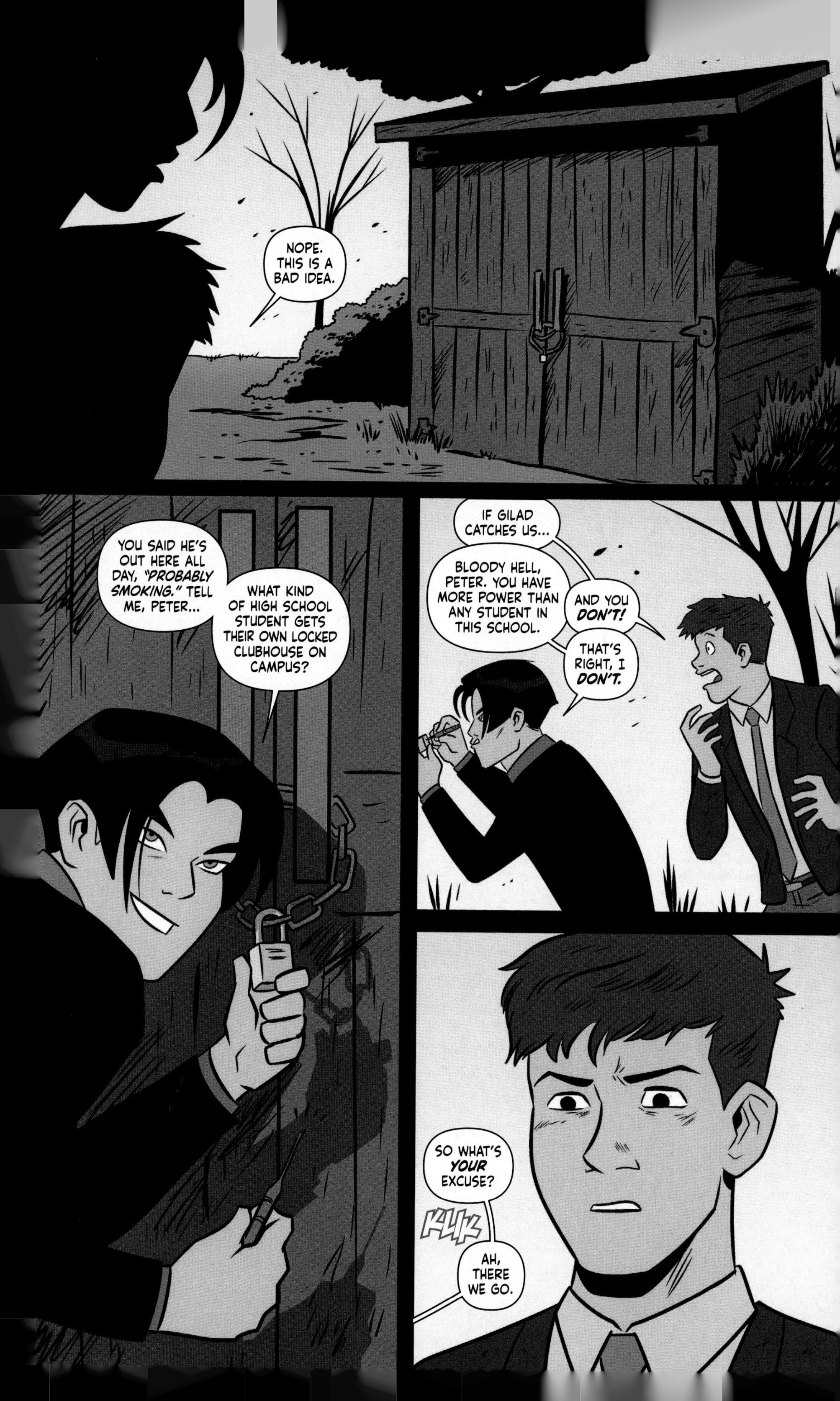
NOPE. THIS IS A BAD IDEA.
YOU SAID HE'S OUT HERE ALL DAY, *"PROBABLY SMOKING."* TELL ME, PETER...
WHAT KIND OF HIGH SCHOOL STUDENT GETS THEIR OWN LOCKED CLUBHOUSE ON CAMPUS?
IF GILAD CATCHES US...
BLOODY HELL, PETER. YOU HAVE MORE POWER THAN ANY STUDENT IN THIS SCHOOL.
AND YOU *DON'T!*
THAT'S RIGHT, I *DON'T.*
SO WHAT'S *YOUR* EXCUSE?
KLIK
AH, THERE WE GO.

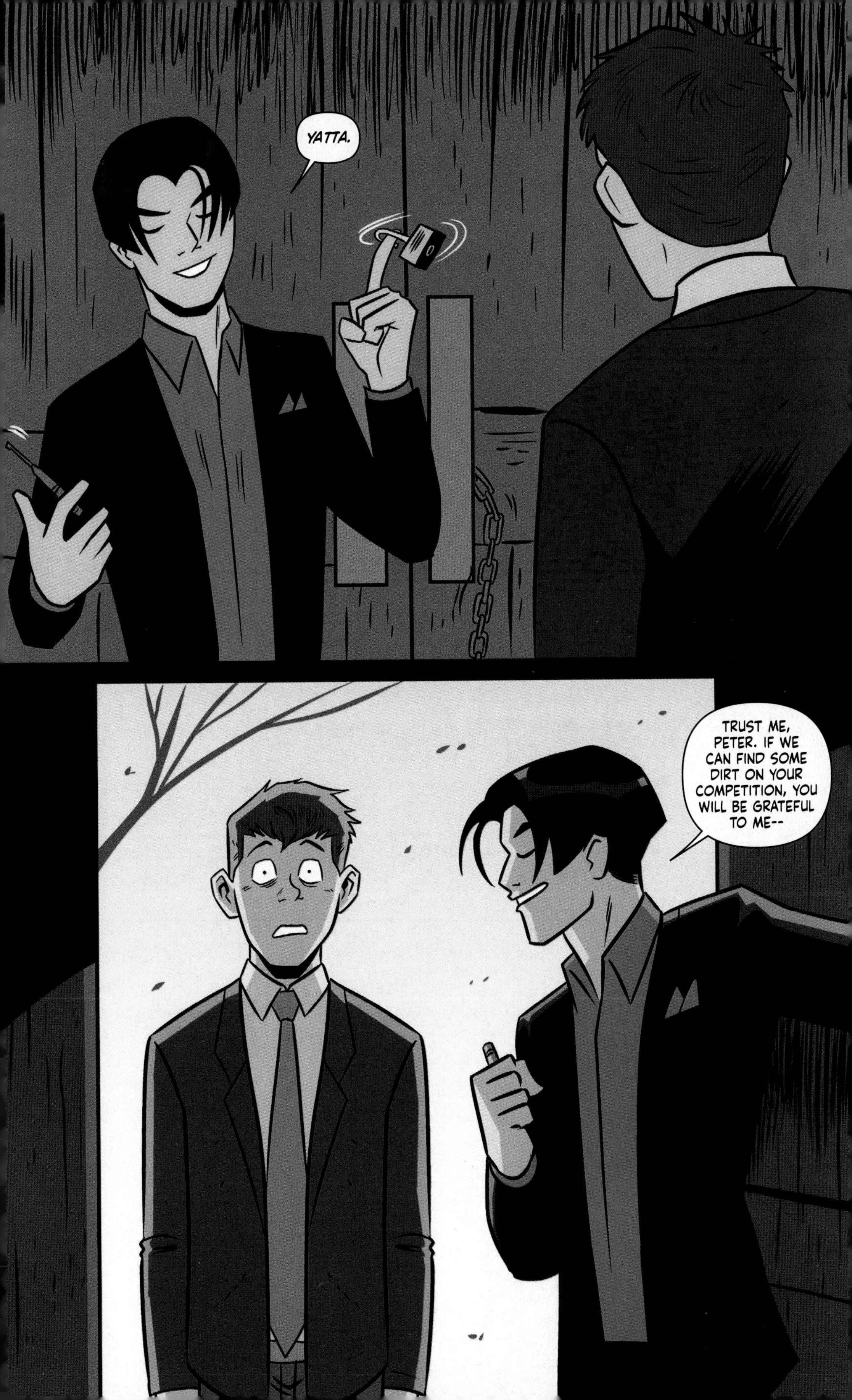
YATTA.
TRUST ME, PETER. IF WE CAN FIND SOME DIRT ON YOUR COMPETITION, YOU WILL BE GRATEFUL TO ME--

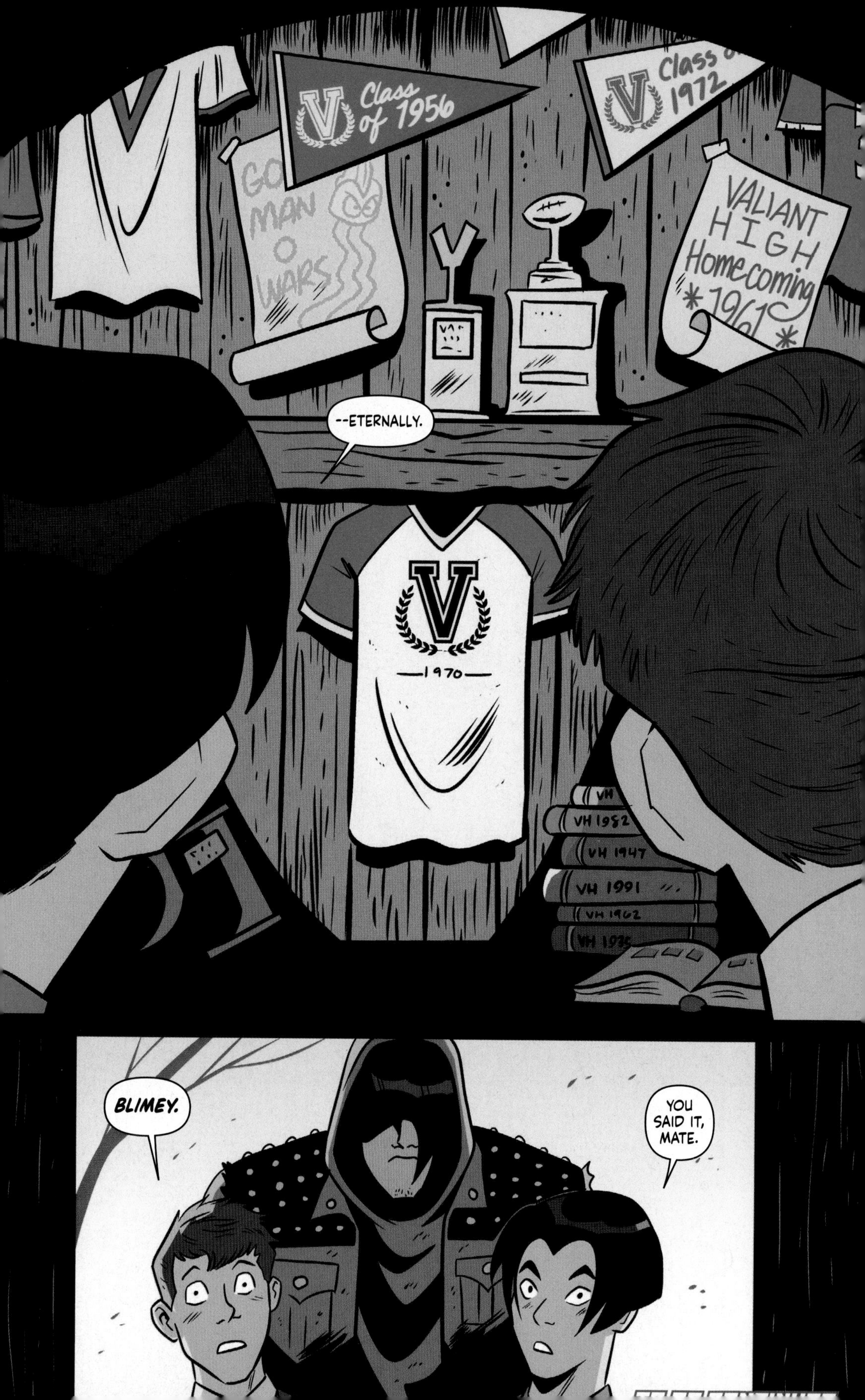

Class of 1956
Class of 1972
GO MAN O WARS
VALIANT HIGH Homecoming 1961
--ETERNALLY.
1970
VH 1982
VH 1947
VH 1991
VH 1962
BLIMEY.
YOU SAID IT, MATE.

VALIANT

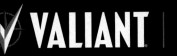

DANIEL KIBBLESMITH | DEREK CHARM
DAVID BARON | SIMON BOWLAND

#3

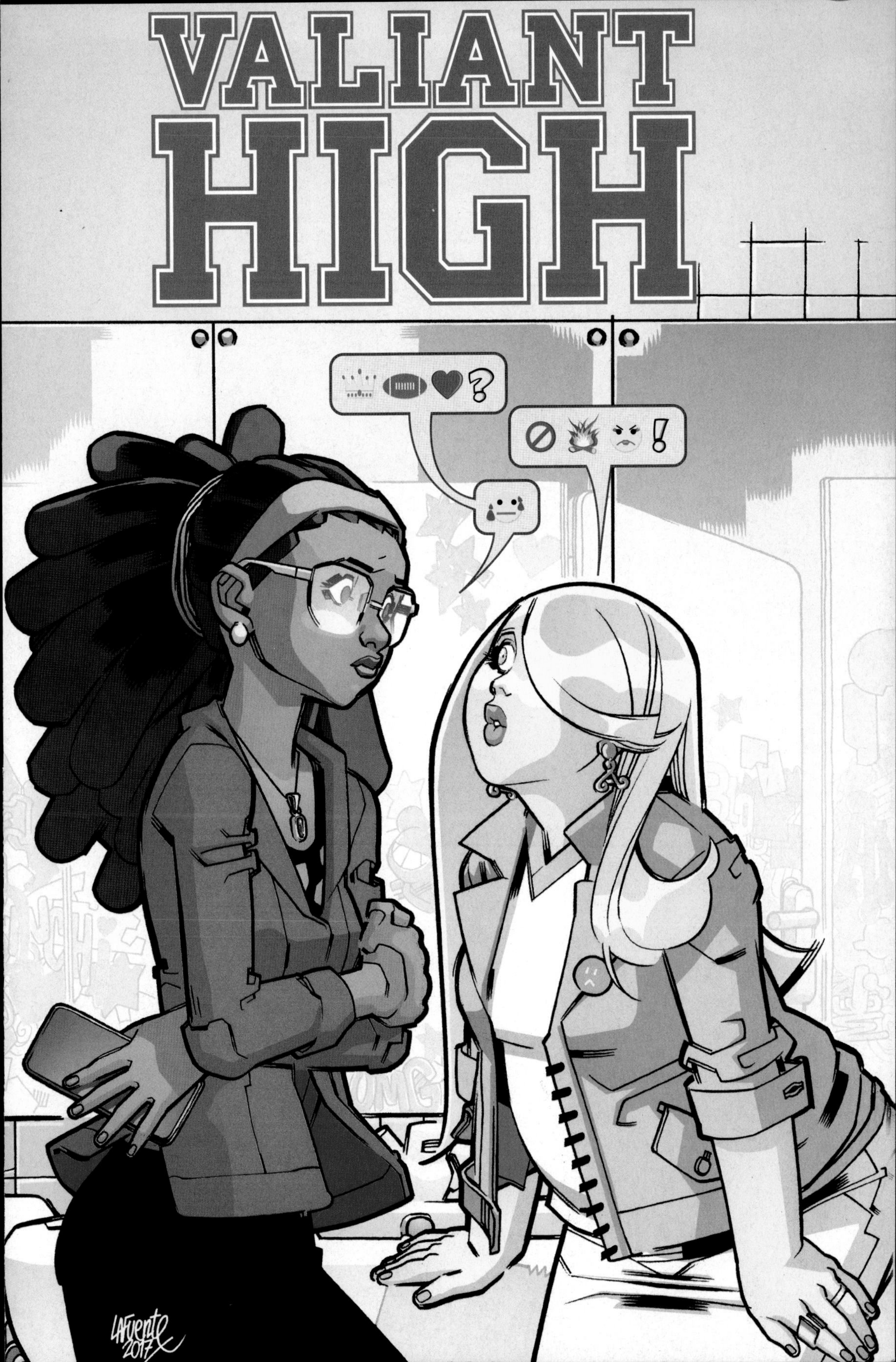
VALIANT HIGH

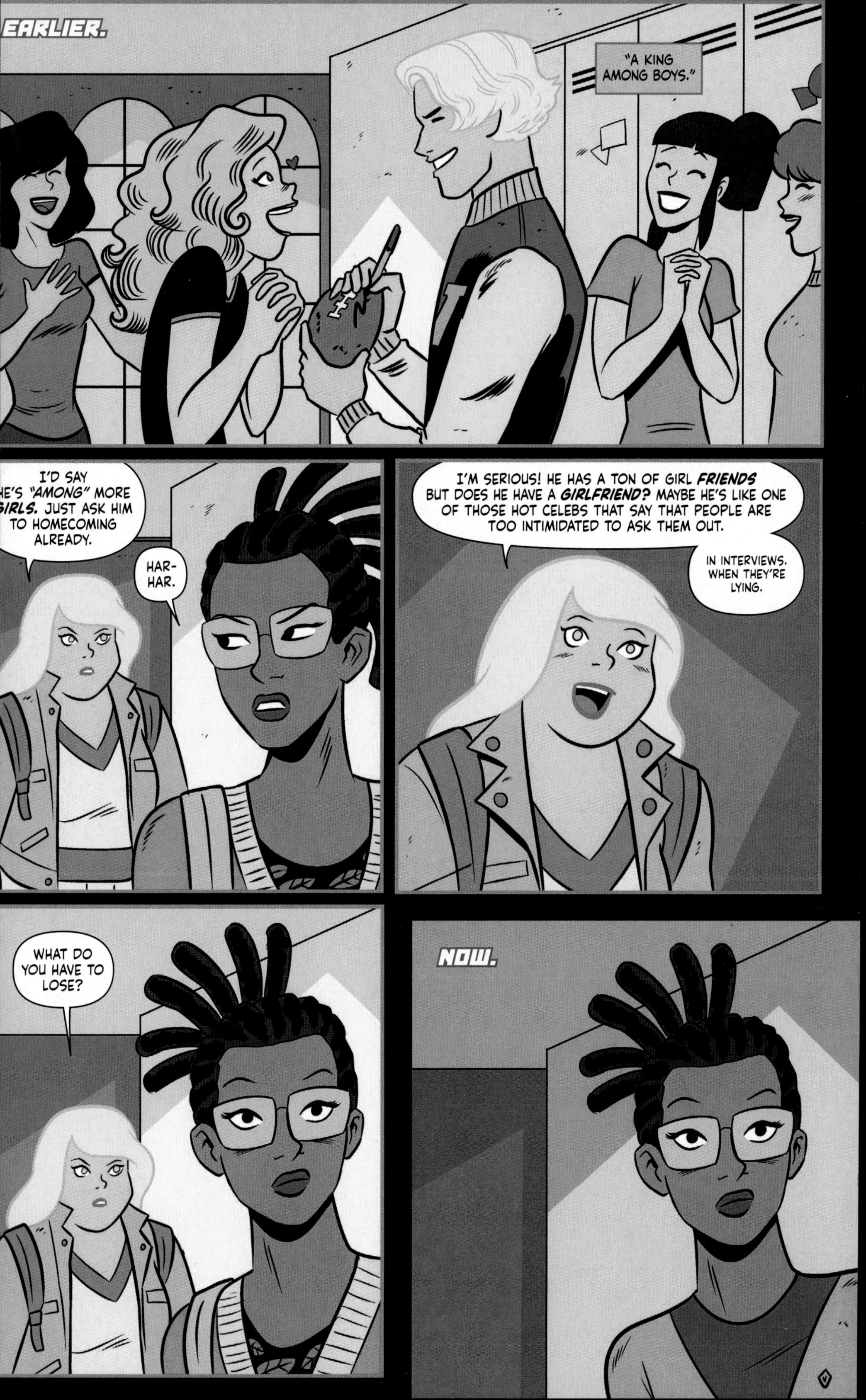
EARLIER.
"A KING AMONG BOYS."
I'D SAY E'S "AMONG" MORE IRLS. JUST ASK HIM TO HOMECOMING ALREADY.
HAR-HAR.
I'M SERIOUS! HE HAS A TON OF GIRL FRIENDS BUT DOES HE HAVE A GIRLFRIEND? MAYBE HE'S LIKE ONE OF THOSE HOT CELEBS THAT SAY THAT PEOPLE ARE TOO INTIMIDATED TO ASK THEM OUT.
IN INTERVIEWS. WHEN THEY'RE LYING.
WHAT DO YOU HAVE TO LOSE?
NOW.

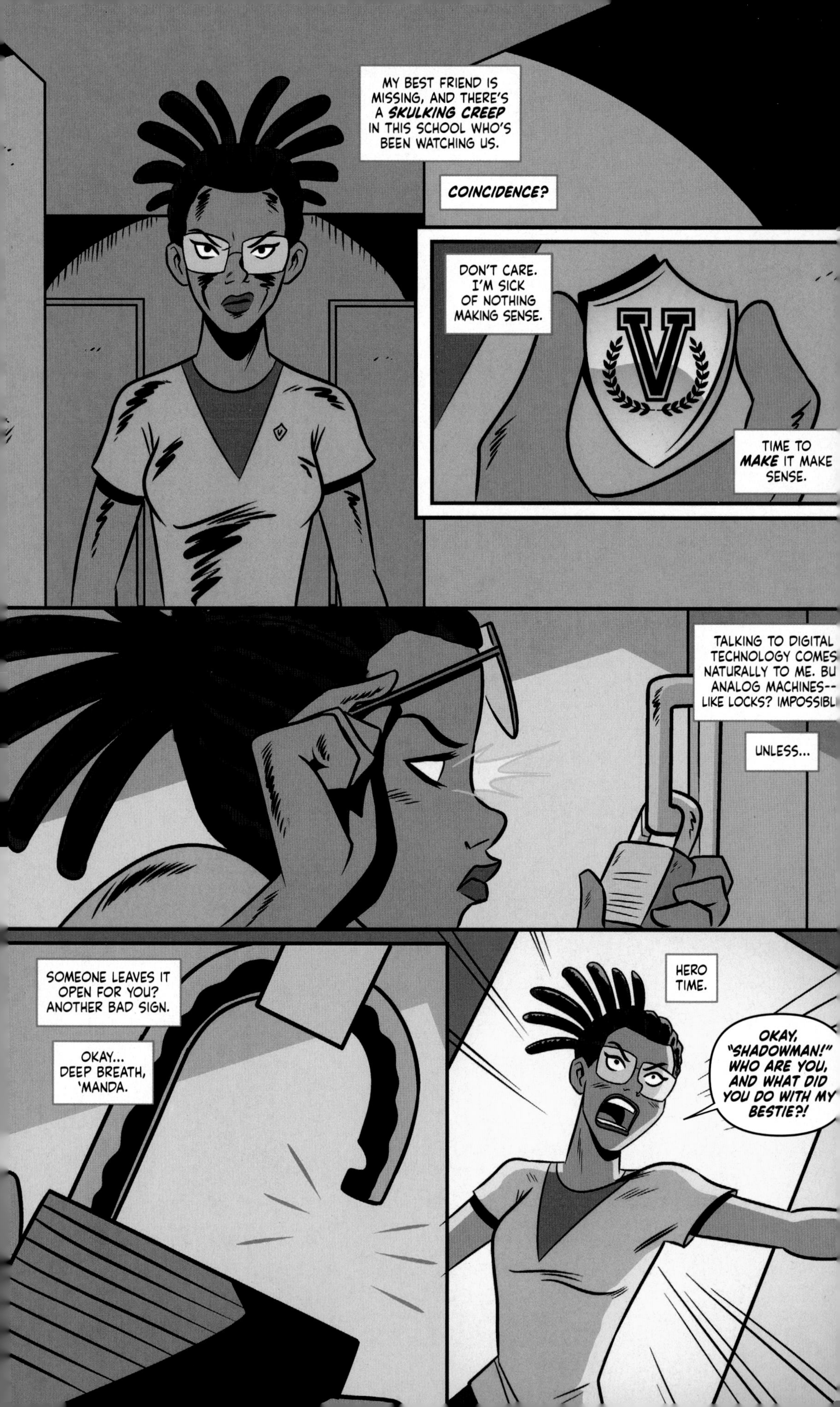

MY BEST FRIEND IS MISSING, AND THERE'S A SKULKING CREEP IN THIS SCHOOL WHO'S BEEN WATCHING US.
COINCIDENCE?
DON'T CARE. I'M SICK OF NOTHING MAKING SENSE.
TIME TO MAKE IT MAKE SENSE.
TALKING TO DIGITAL TECHNOLOGY COMES NATURALLY TO ME. BU ANALOG MACHINES-- LIKE LOCKS? IMPOSSIBL
UNLESS...
SOMEONE LEAVES IT OPEN FOR YOU? ANOTHER BAD SIGN.
OKAY... DEEP BREATH, 'MANDA.
HERO TIME.
OKAY, "SHADOWMAN!" WHO ARE YOU, AND WHAT DID YOU DO WITH MY BESTIE?!

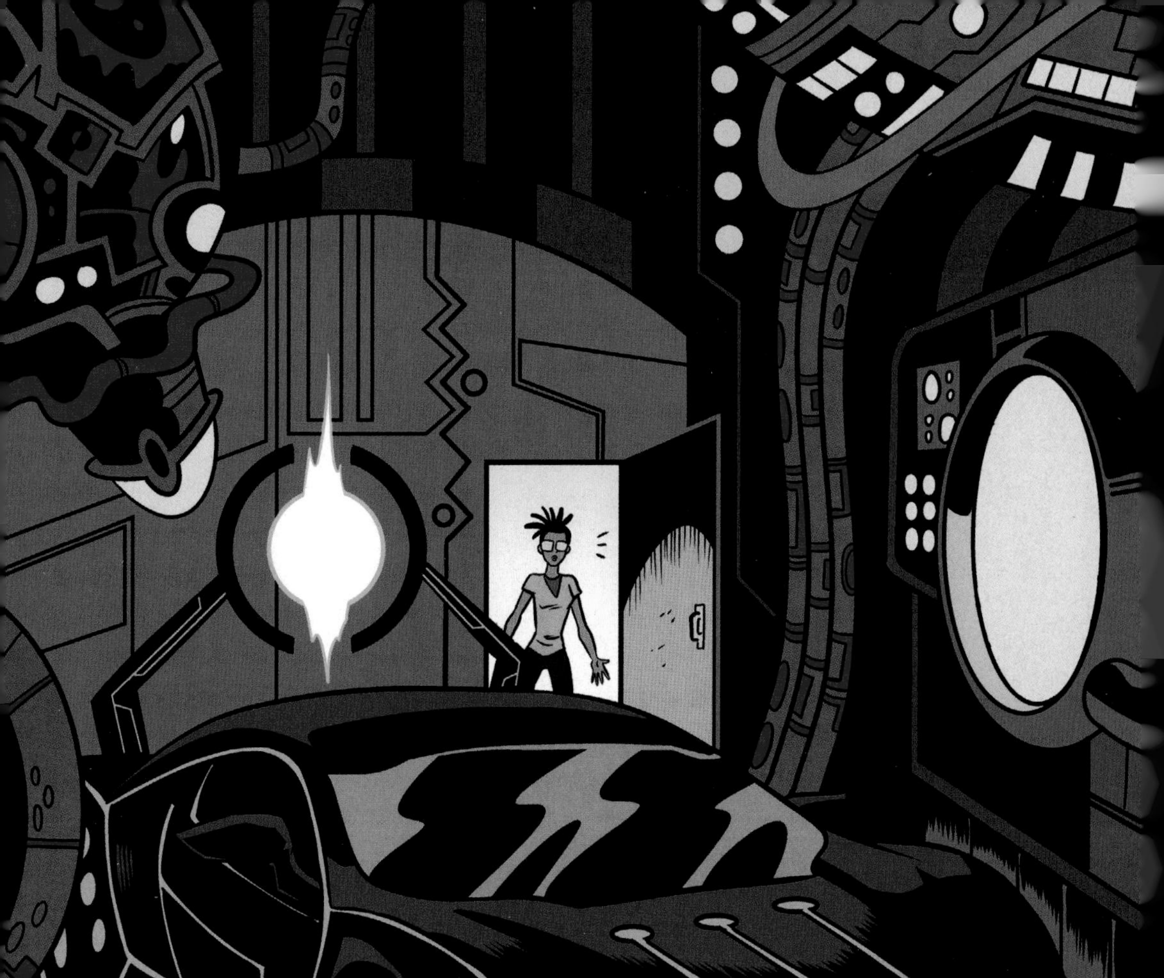
GIN-GR

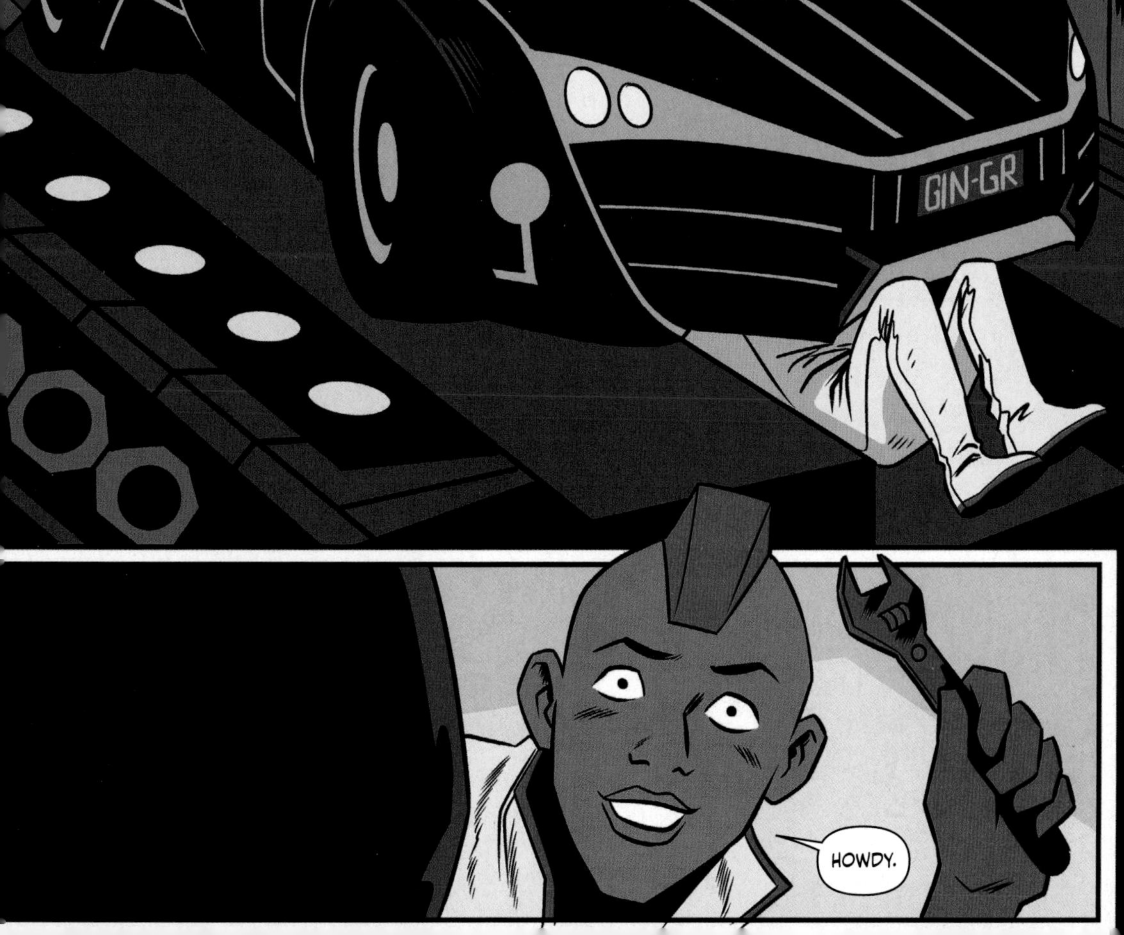
HOWDY.

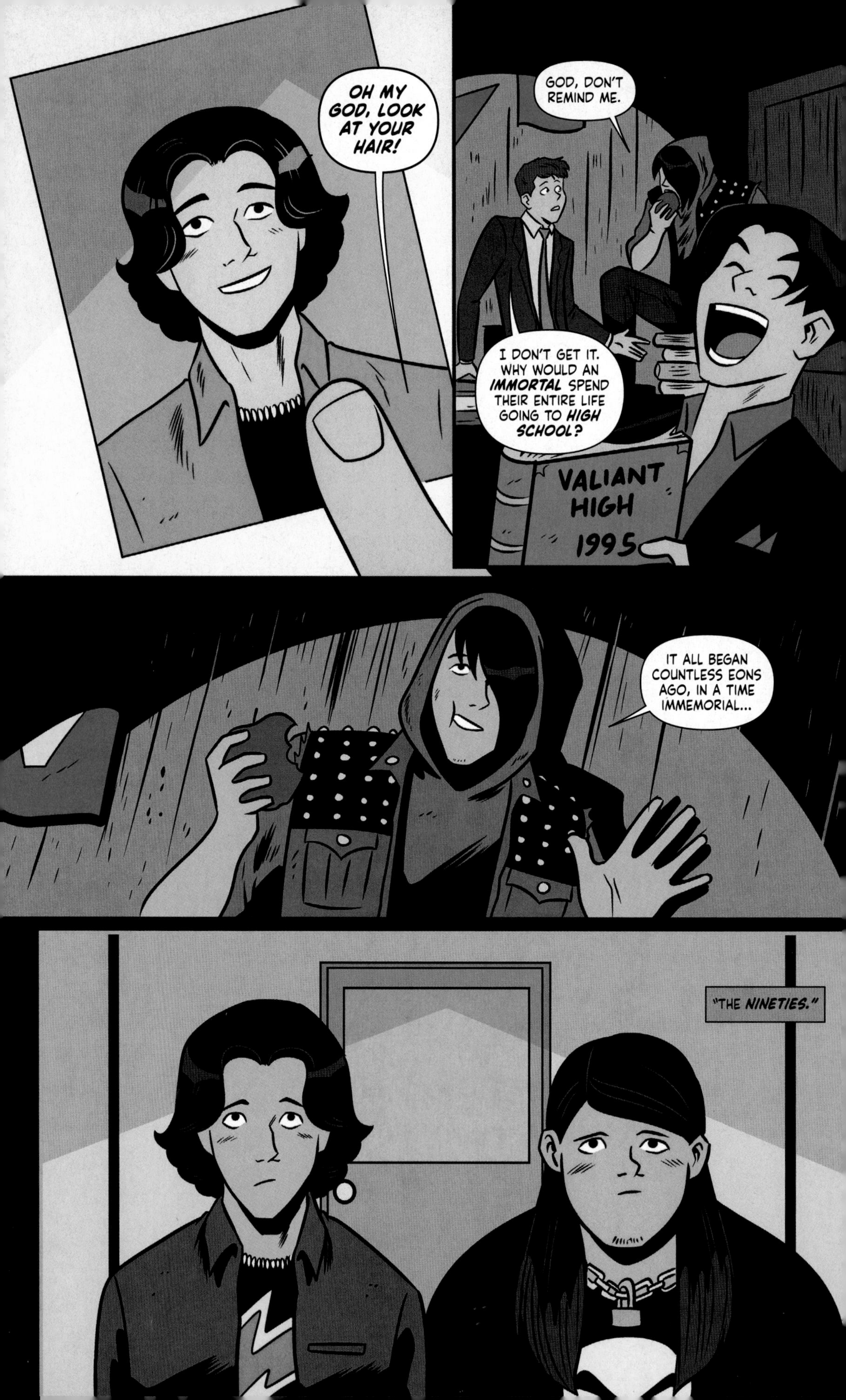
OH MY GOD, LOOK AT YOUR HAIR!
GOD, DON'T REMIND ME.
I DON'T GET IT. WHY WOULD AN IMMORTAL SPEND THEIR ENTIRE LIFE GOING TO HIGH SCHOOL?
VALIANT HIGH 1995
IT ALL BEGAN COUNTLESS EONS AGO, IN A TIME IMMEMORIAL...
"THE NINETIES."

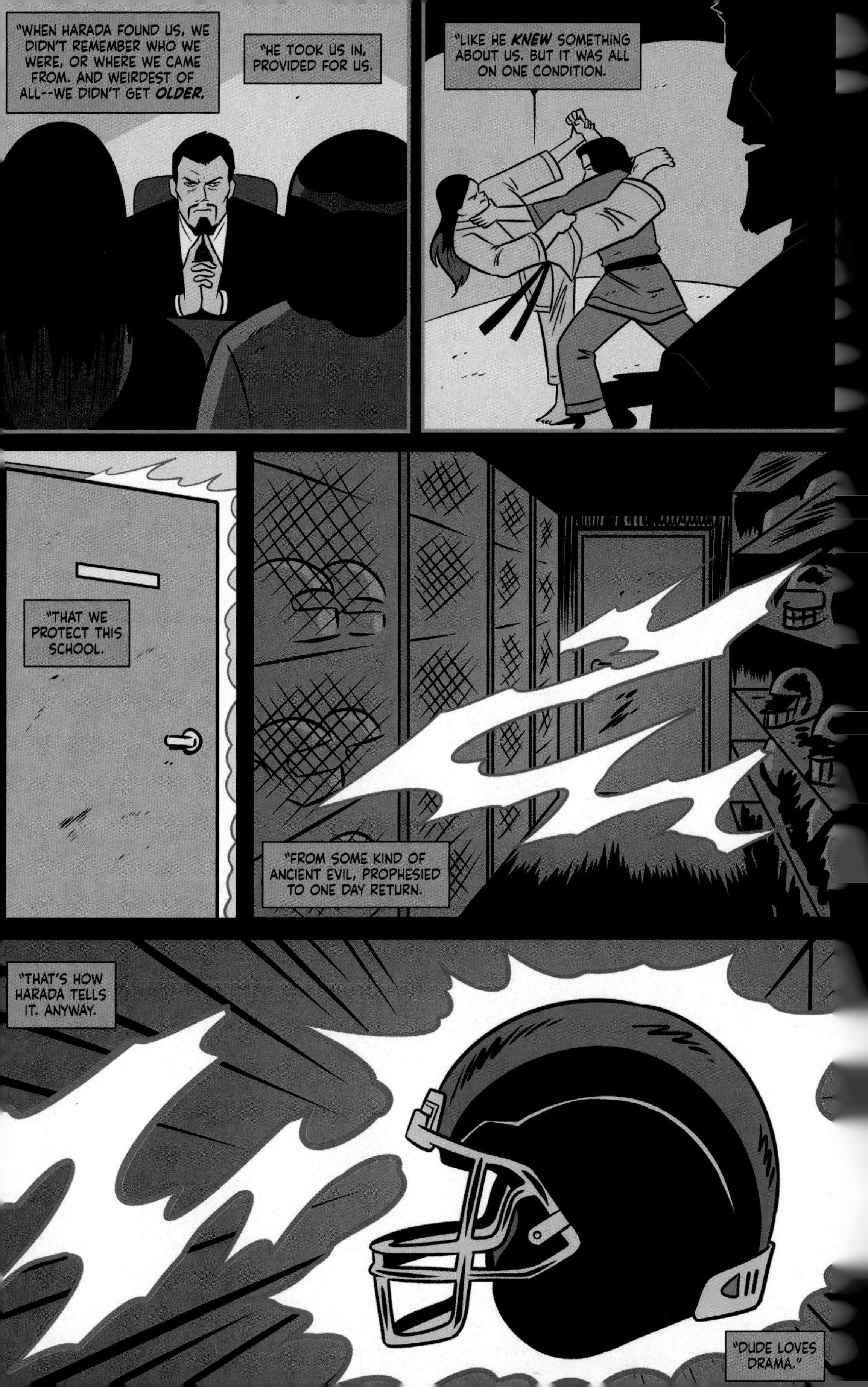
"WHEN HARADA FOUND US, WE DIDN'T REMEMBER WHO WE WERE, OR WHERE WE CAME FROM. AND WEIRDEST OF ALL--WE DIDN'T GET *OLDER*.
"HE TOOK US IN, PROVIDED FOR US.
"LIKE HE *KNEW* SOMETHING ABOUT US. BUT IT WAS ALL ON ONE CONDITION.
"THAT WE PROTECT THIS SCHOOL.
"FROM SOME KIND OF ANCIENT EVIL, PROPHESIED TO ONE DAY RETURN.
"THAT'S HOW HARADA TELLS IT. ANYWAY.
"DUDE LOVES DRAMA."

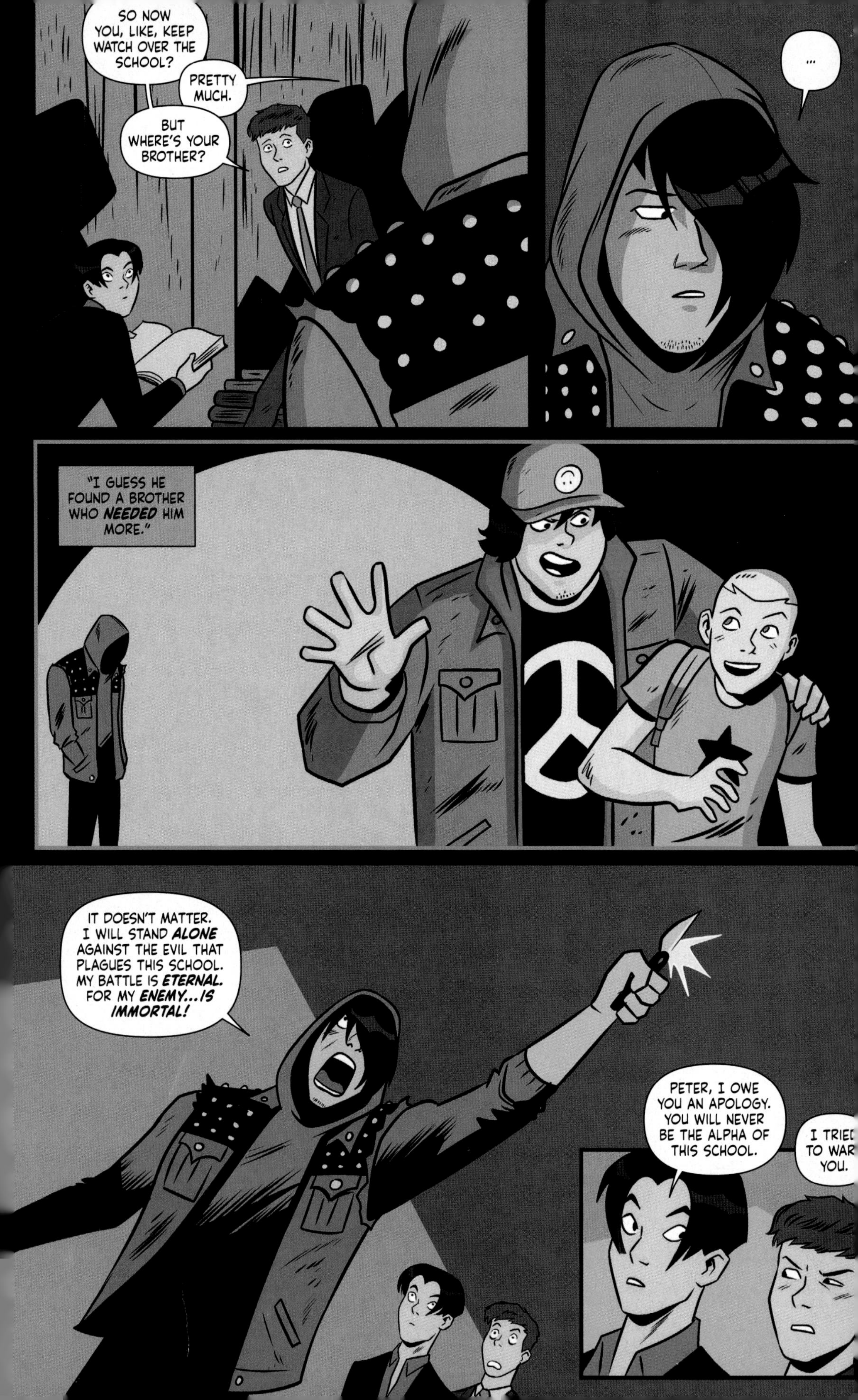
SO NOW YOU, LIKE, KEEP WATCH OVER THE SCHOOL?
PRETTY MUCH.
BUT WHERE'S YOUR BROTHER?
...
"I GUESS HE FOUND A BROTHER WHO NEEDED HIM MORE."
IT DOESN'T MATTER. I WILL STAND ALONE AGAINST THE EVIL THAT PLAGUES THIS SCHOOL. MY BATTLE IS ETERNAL. FOR MY ENEMY...IS IMMORTAL!
PETER, I OWE YOU AN APOLOGY. YOU WILL NEVER BE THE ALPHA OF THIS SCHOOL.

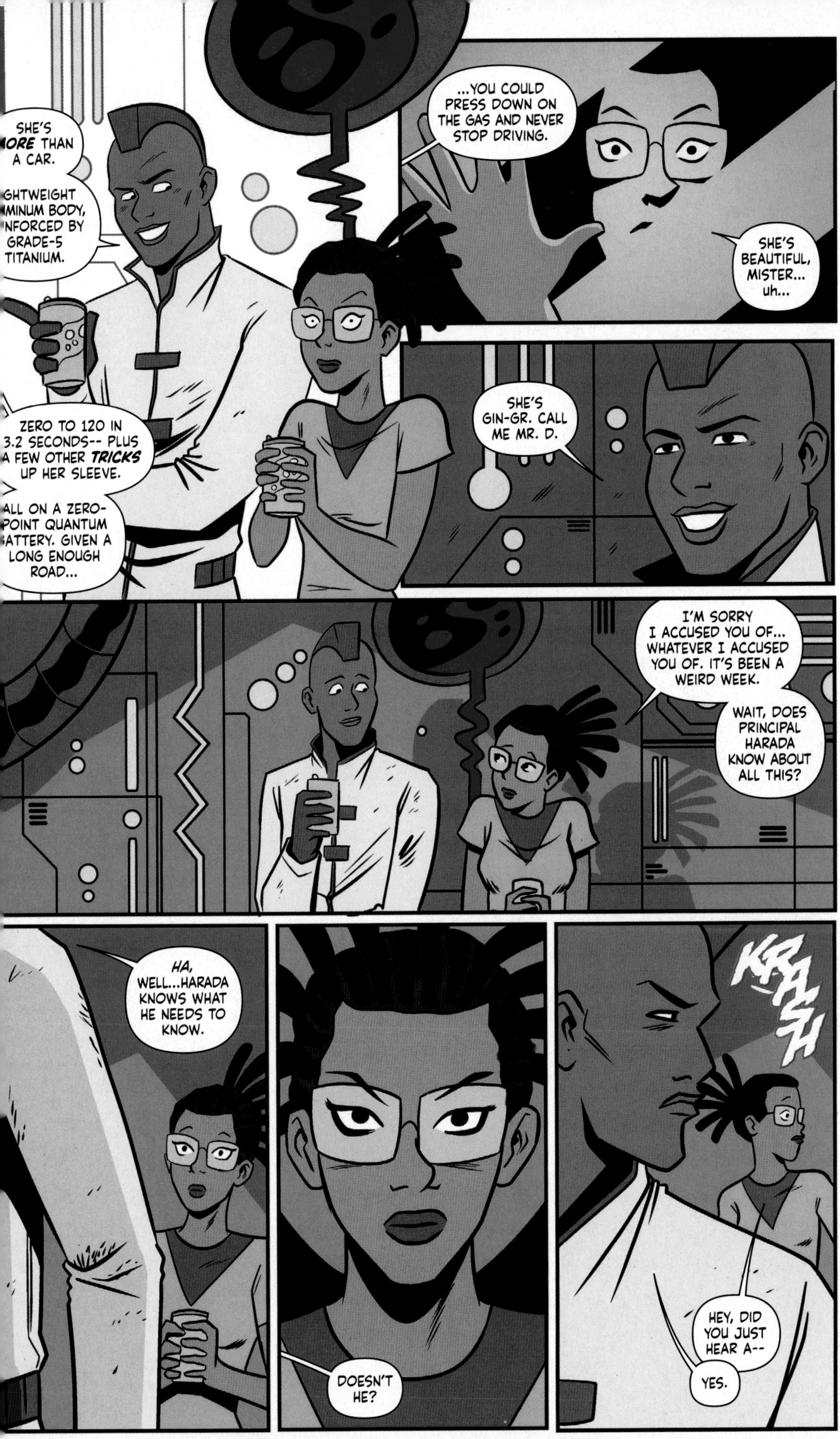

SHE'S ORE THAN A CAR.
GHTWEIGHT MINUM BODY, NFORCED BY GRADE-5 TITANIUM.
ZERO TO 120 IN 3.2 SECONDS-- PLUS A FEW OTHER *TRICKS* UP HER SLEEVE.
ALL ON A ZERO-POINT QUANTUM ATTERY. GIVEN A LONG ENOUGH ROAD...
...YOU COULD PRESS DOWN ON THE GAS AND NEVER STOP DRIVING.
SHE'S BEAUTIFUL, MISTER... uh...
SHE'S GIN-GR. CALL ME MR. D.
I'M SORRY I ACCUSED YOU OF... WHATEVER I ACCUSED YOU OF. IT'S BEEN A WEIRD WEEK.
WAIT, DOES PRINCIPAL HARADA KNOW ABOUT ALL THIS?
HA, WELL...HARADA KNOWS WHAT HE NEEDS TO KNOW.
DOESN'T HE?
KRASH
HEY, DID YOU JUST HEAR A--
YES.

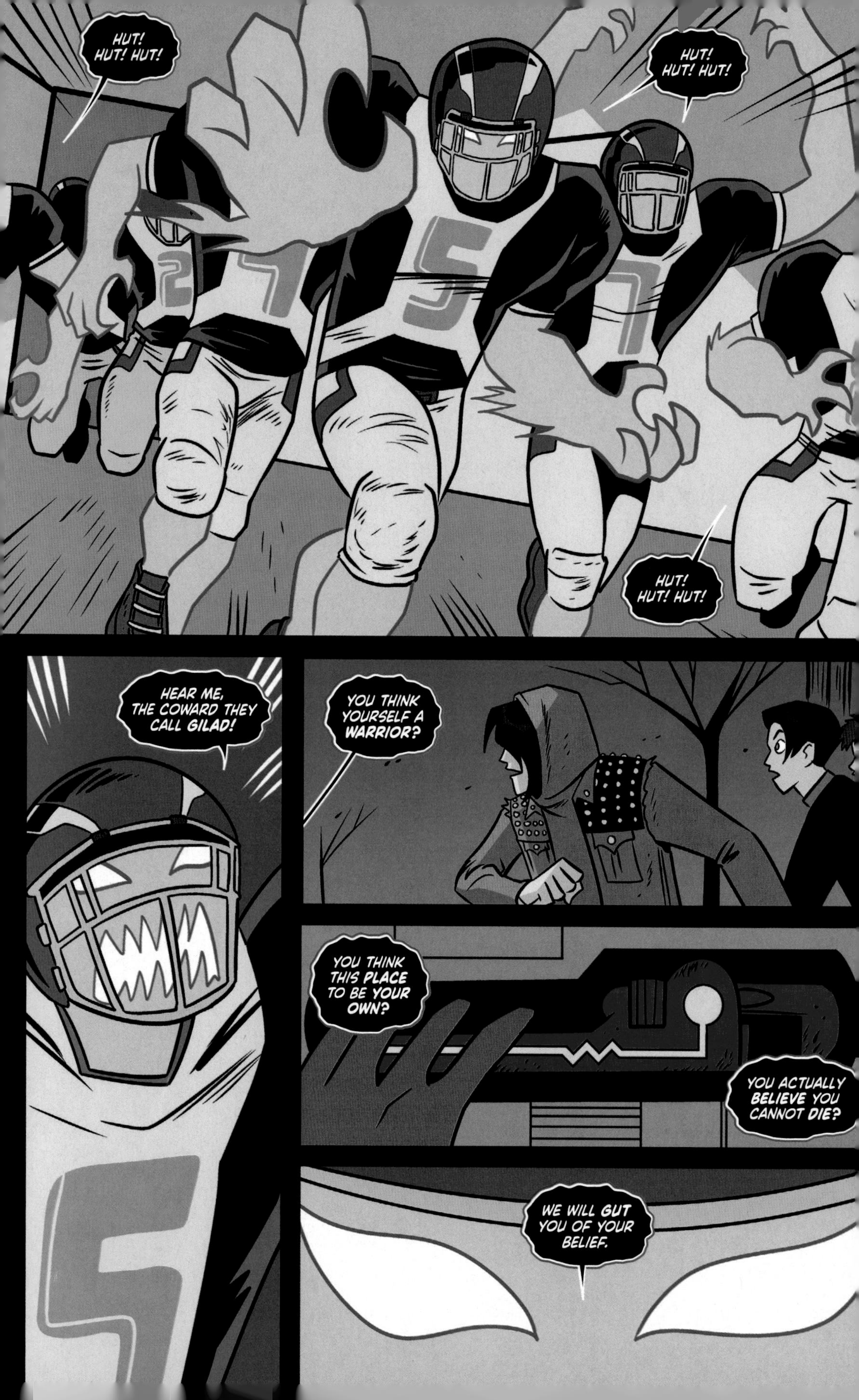
HUT! HUT! HUT!
HUT! HUT! HUT!
HUT! HUT! HUT!
HEAR ME, THE COWARD THEY CALL GILAD!
YOU THINK YOURSELF A WARRIOR?
YOU THINK THIS PLACE TO BE YOUR OWN?
YOU ACTUALLY BELIEVE YOU CANNOT DIE?
WE WILL GUT YOU OF YOUR BELIEF.

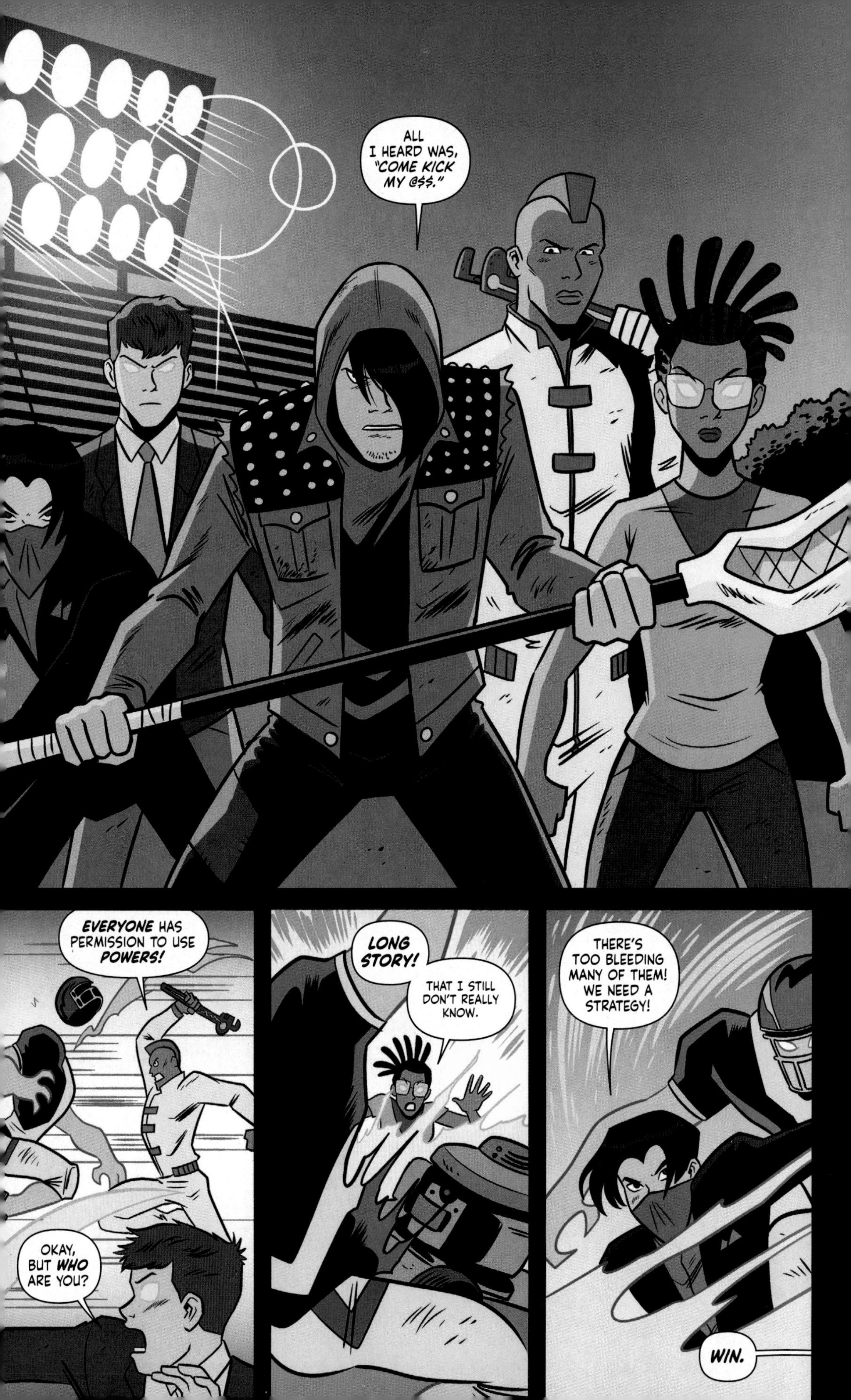
ALL I HEARD WAS, "COME KICK MY @$$."
EVERYONE HAS PERMISSION TO USE POWERS!
OKAY, BUT WHO ARE YOU?
LONG STORY!
THAT I STILL DON'T REALLY KNOW.
THERE'S TOO BLEEDING MANY OF THEM! WE NEED A STRATEGY!
WIN.

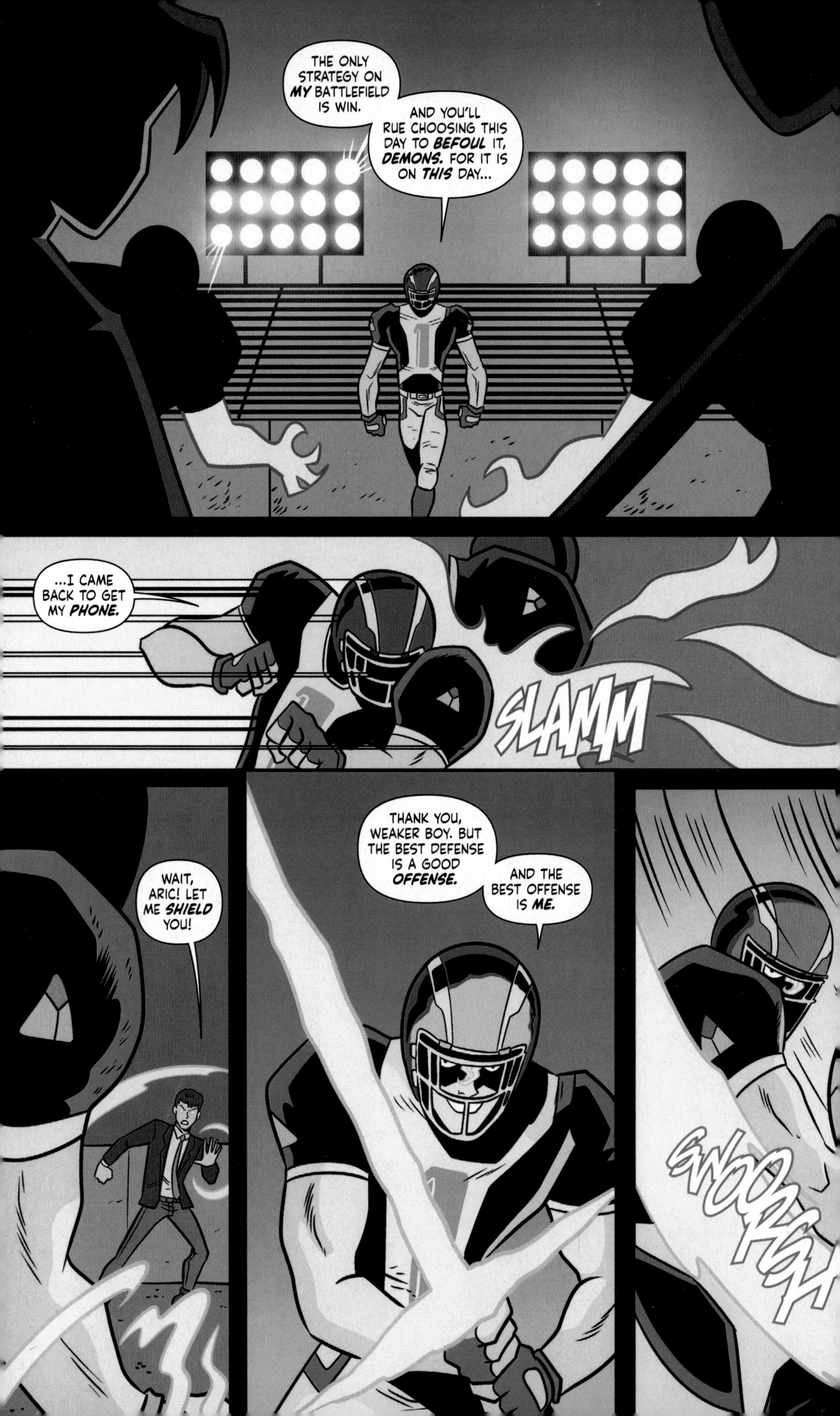
THE ONLY STRATEGY ON ***MY*** BATTLEFIELD IS WIN.
AND YOU'LL RUE CHOOSING THIS DAY TO ***BEFOUL*** IT, ***DEMONS.*** FOR IT IS ON ***THIS*** DAY...
...I CAME BACK TO GET MY ***PHONE.***
SLAMM
WAIT, ARIC! LET ME ***SHIELD*** YOU!
THANK YOU, WEAKER BOY. BUT THE BEST DEFENSE IS A GOOD ***OFFENSE.***
AND THE BEST OFFENSE IS ***ME.***

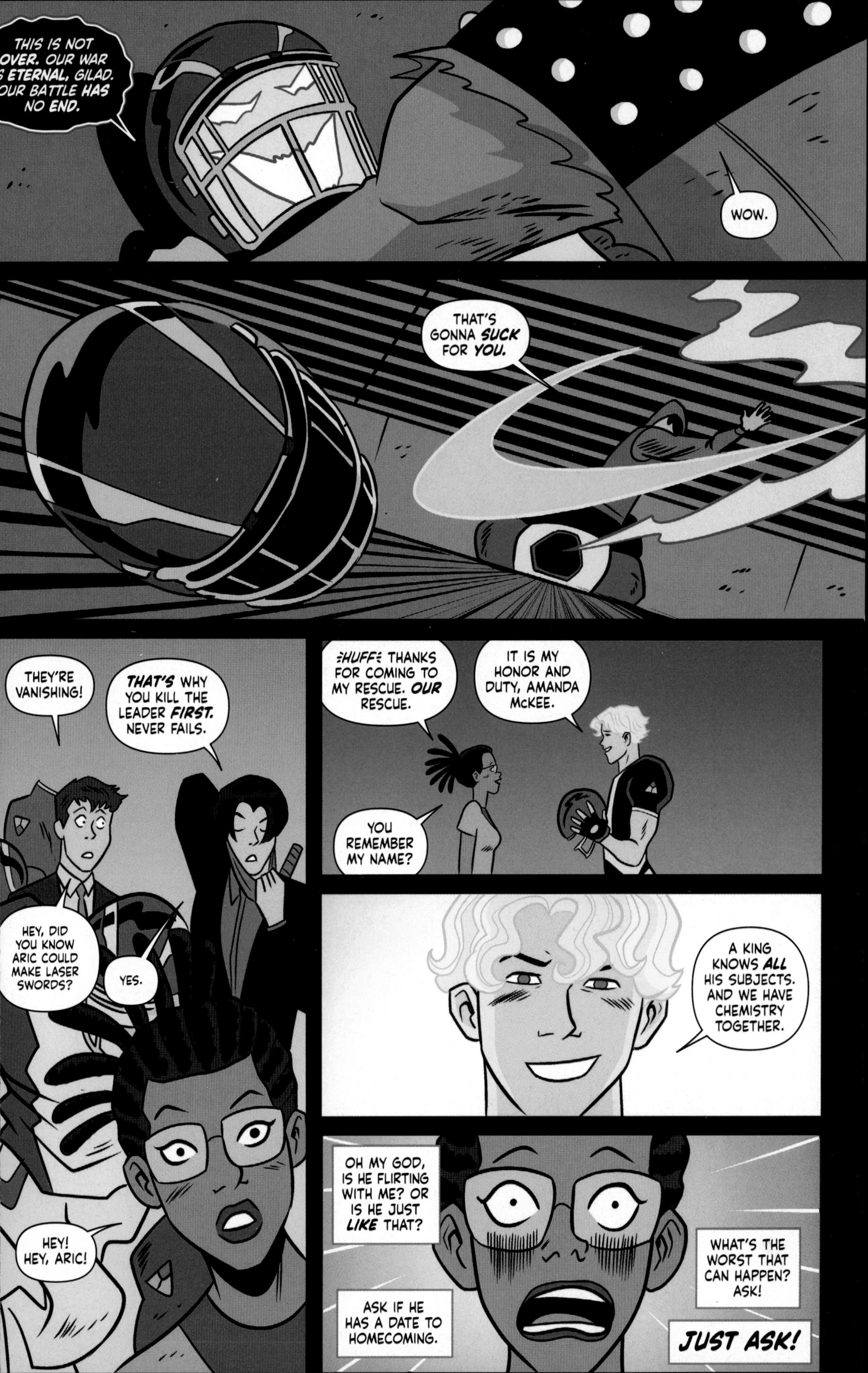
THIS IS NOT OVER. OUR WAR IS ETERNAL, GILAD. OUR BATTLE HAS NO END.
WOW.
THAT'S GONNA SUCK FOR YOU.
THEY'RE VANISHING!
THAT'S WHY YOU KILL THE LEADER FIRST. NEVER FAILS.
HEY, DID YOU KNOW ARIC COULD MAKE LASER SWORDS?
YES.
HEY! HEY, ARIC!
=HUFF= THANKS FOR COMING TO MY RESCUE. OUR RESCUE.
IT IS MY HONOR AND DUTY, AMANDA McKEE.
YOU REMEMBER MY NAME?
A KING KNOWS ALL HIS SUBJECTS. AND WE HAVE CHEMISTRY TOGETHER.
OH MY GOD, IS HE FLIRTING WITH ME? OR IS HE JUST LIKE THAT?
WHAT'S THE WORST THAT CAN HAPPEN? ASK!
ASK IF HE HAS A DATE TO HOMECOMING.
JUST ASK!

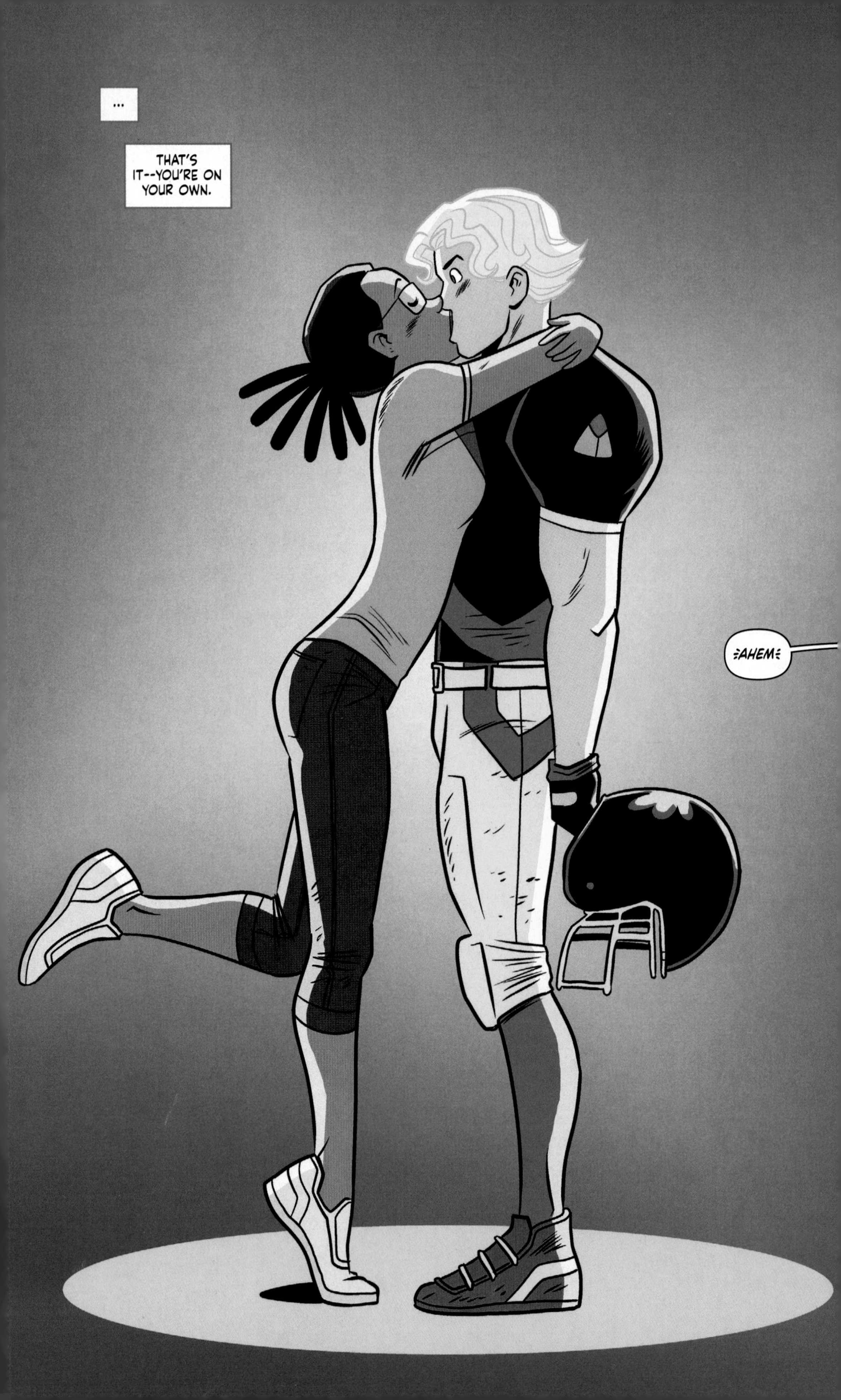
...
THAT'S IT--YOU'RE ON YOUR OWN.
AHEM

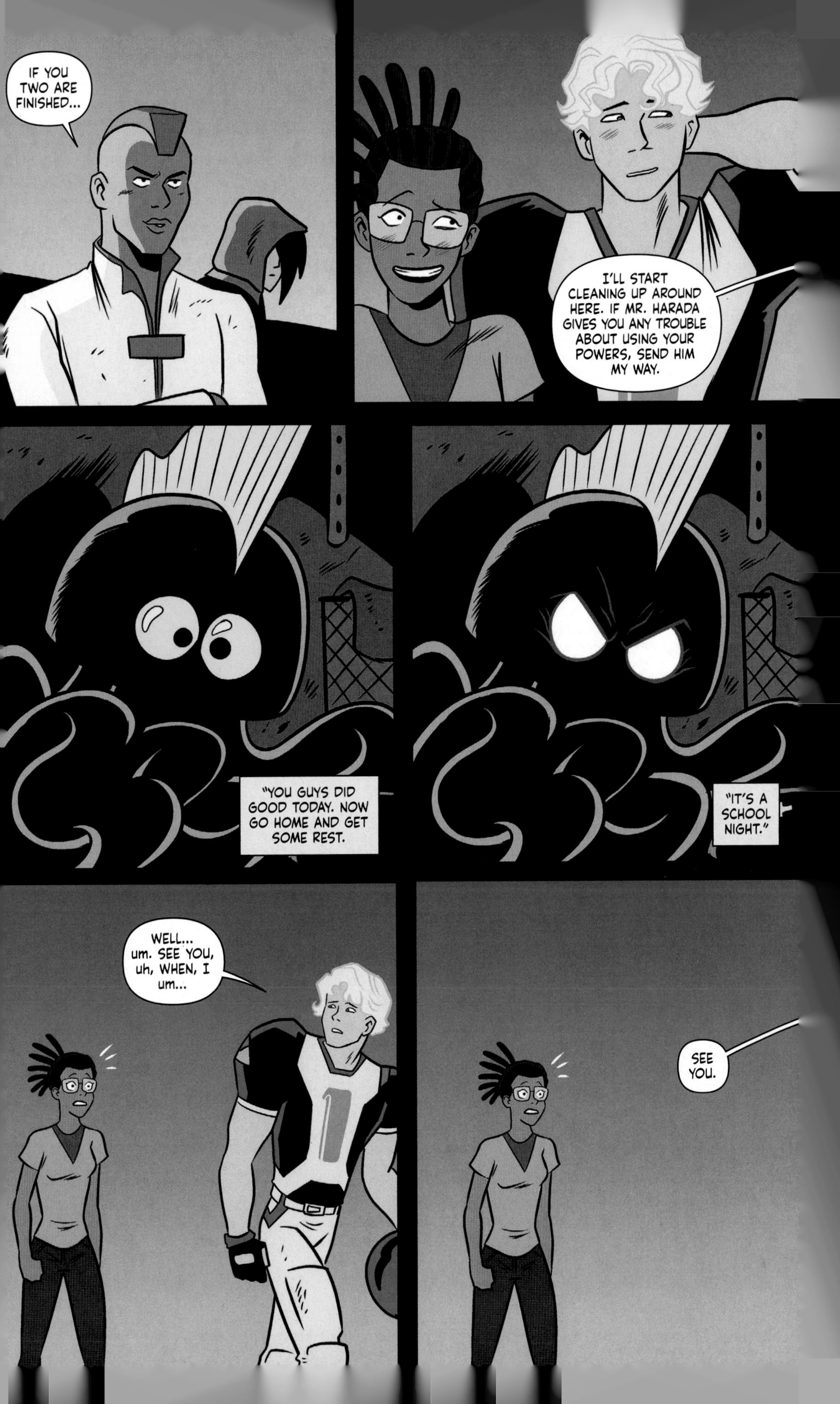
IF YOU TWO ARE FINISHED...
I'LL START CLEANING UP AROUND HERE. IF MR. HARADA GIVES YOU ANY TROUBLE ABOUT USING YOUR POWERS, SEND HIM MY WAY.
"YOU GUYS DID GOOD TODAY. NOW GO HOME AND GET SOME REST.
"IT'S A SCHOOL NIGHT."
WELL... um. SEE YOU, uh, WHEN, I um...
SEE YOU.

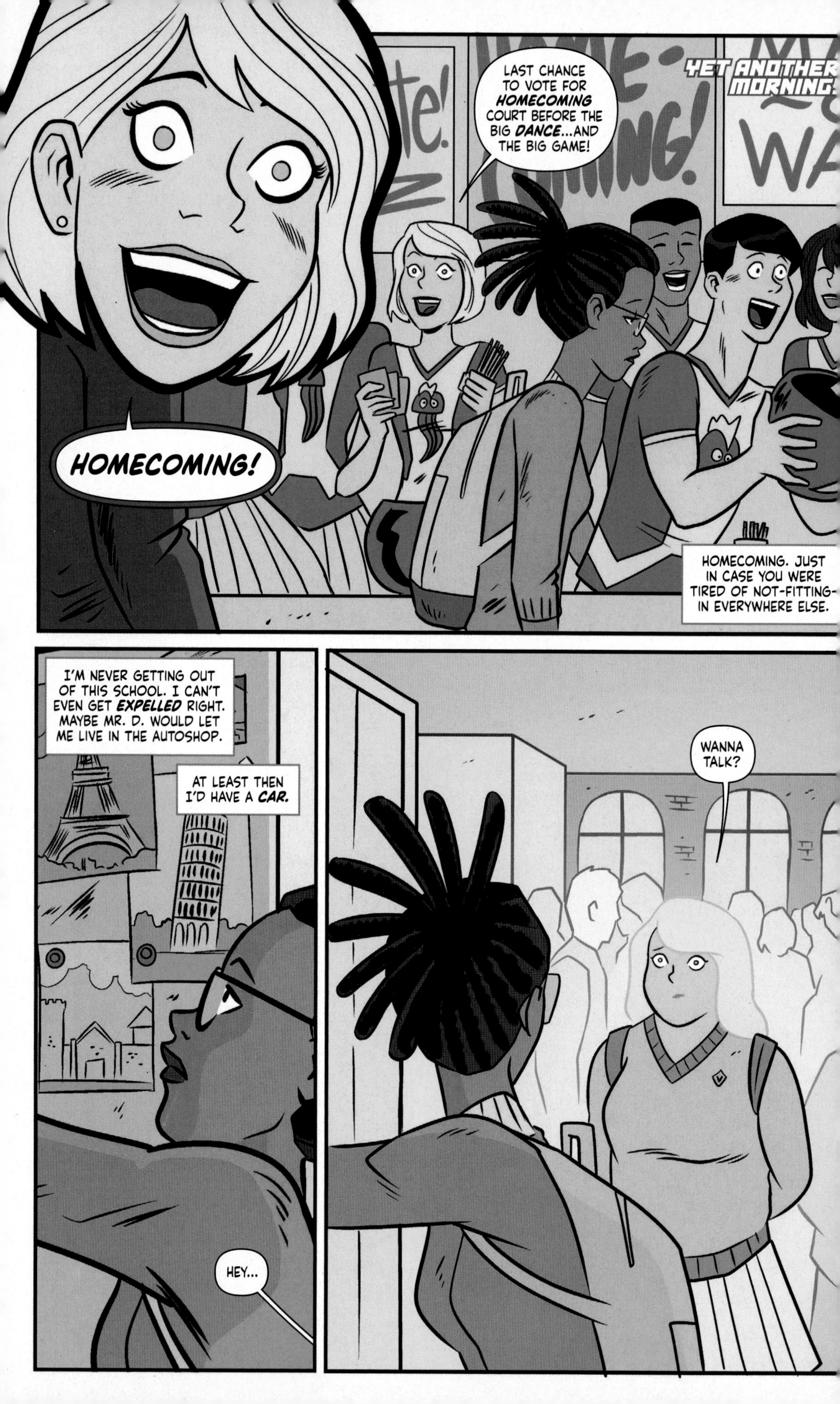
YET ANOTHER MORNING.
LAST CHANCE TO VOTE FOR HOMECOMING COURT BEFORE THE BIG DANCE...AND THE BIG GAME!
HOMECOMING!
HOMECOMING. JUST IN CASE YOU WERE TIRED OF NOT-FITTING-IN EVERYWHERE ELSE.
I'M NEVER GETTING OUT OF THIS SCHOOL. I CAN'T EVEN GET EXPELLED RIGHT. MAYBE MR. D. WOULD LET ME LIVE IN THE AUTOSHOP.
AT LEAST THEN I'D HAVE A CAR.
HEY...
WANNA TALK?

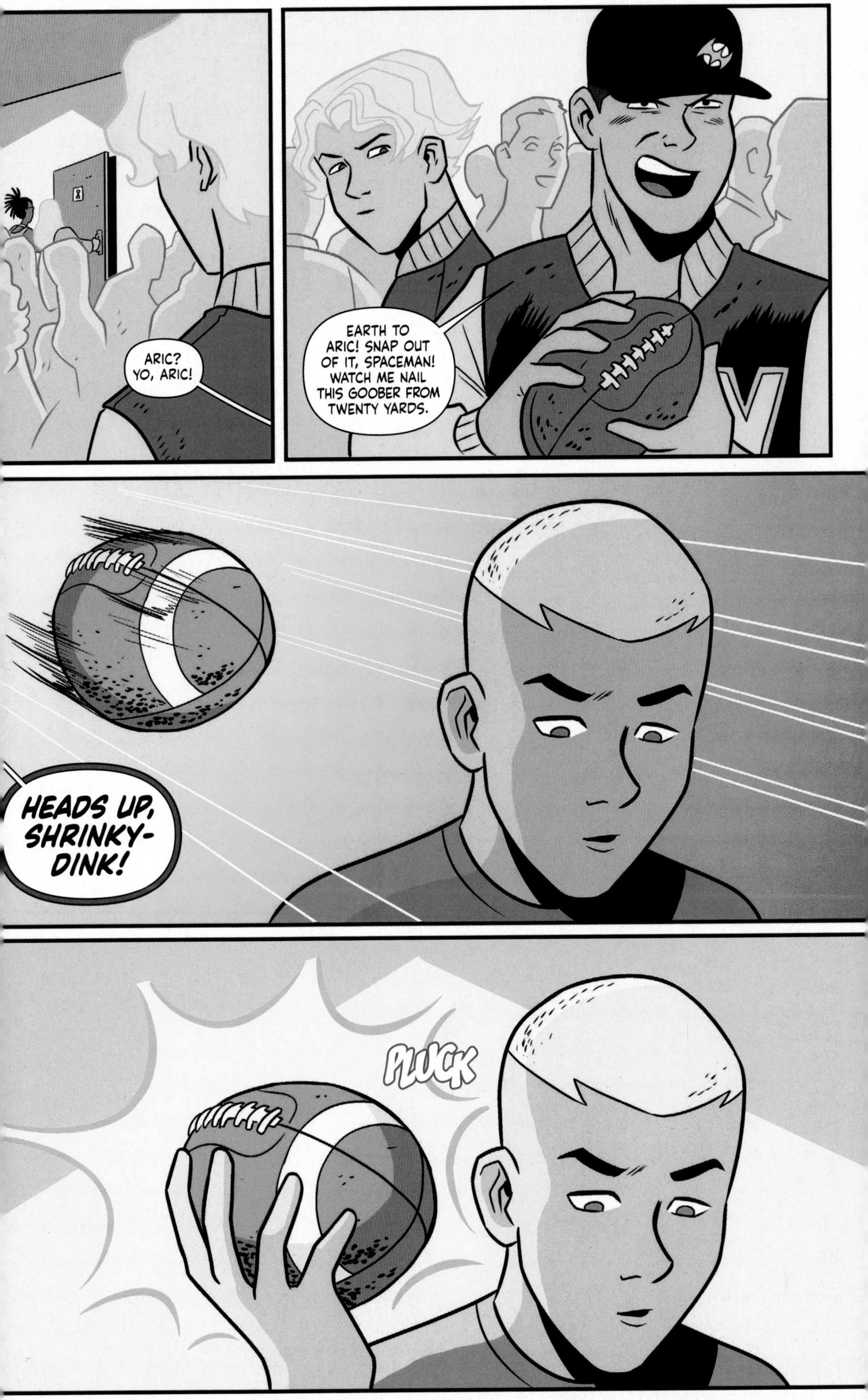
ARIC? YO, ARIC!
EARTH TO ARIC! SNAP OUT OF IT, SPACEMAN! WATCH ME NAIL THIS GOOBER FROM TWENTY YARDS.
HEADS UP, SHRINKY-DINK!
PLUCK

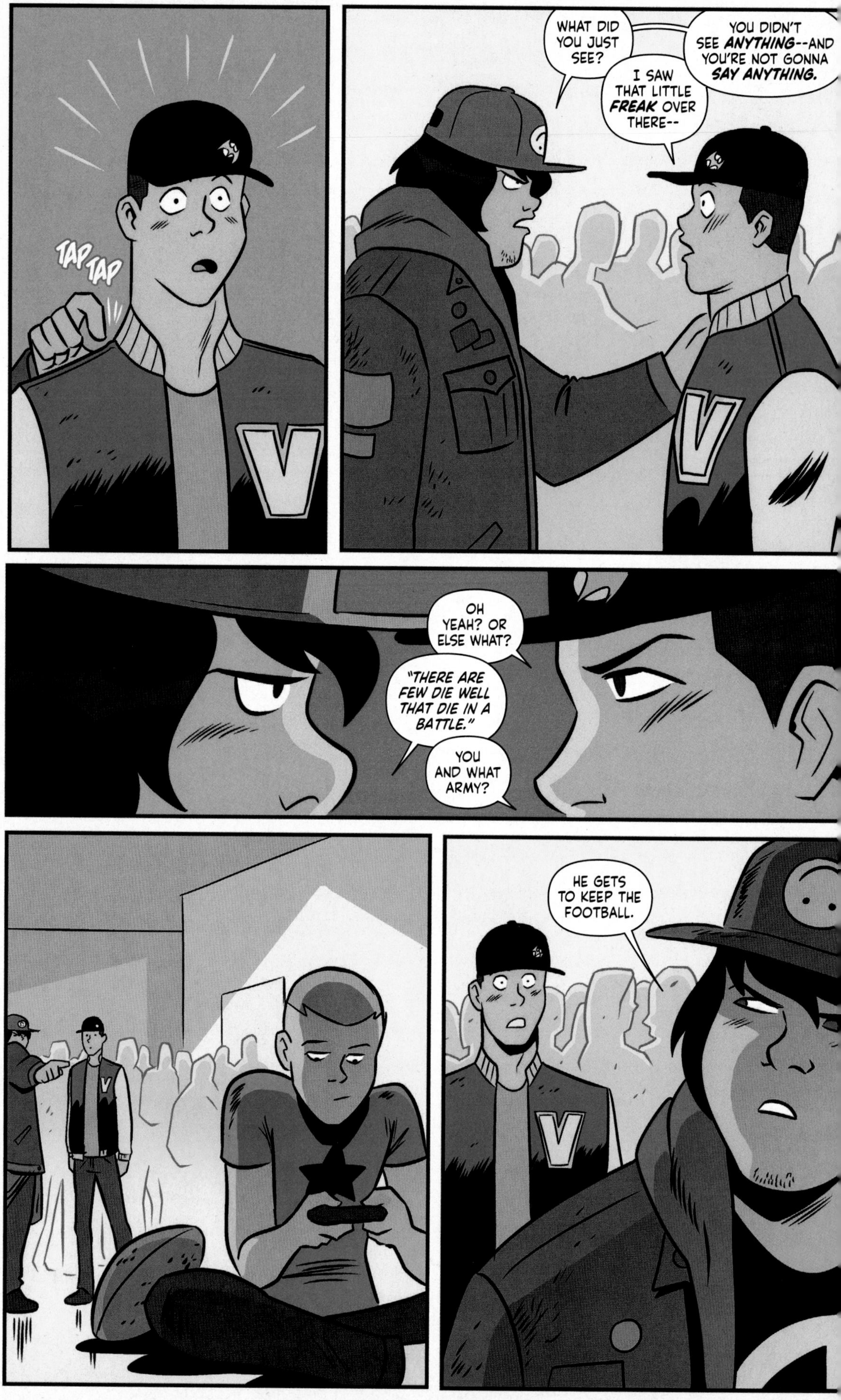

TAP TAP
WHAT DID YOU JUST SEE?
I SAW THAT LITTLE FREAK OVER THERE--
YOU DIDN'T SEE ANYTHING--AND YOU'RE NOT GONNA SAY ANYTHING.
OH YEAH? OR ELSE WHAT?
"THERE ARE FEW DIE WELL THAT DIE IN A BATTLE."
YOU AND WHAT ARMY?
HE GETS TO KEEP THE FOOTBALL.

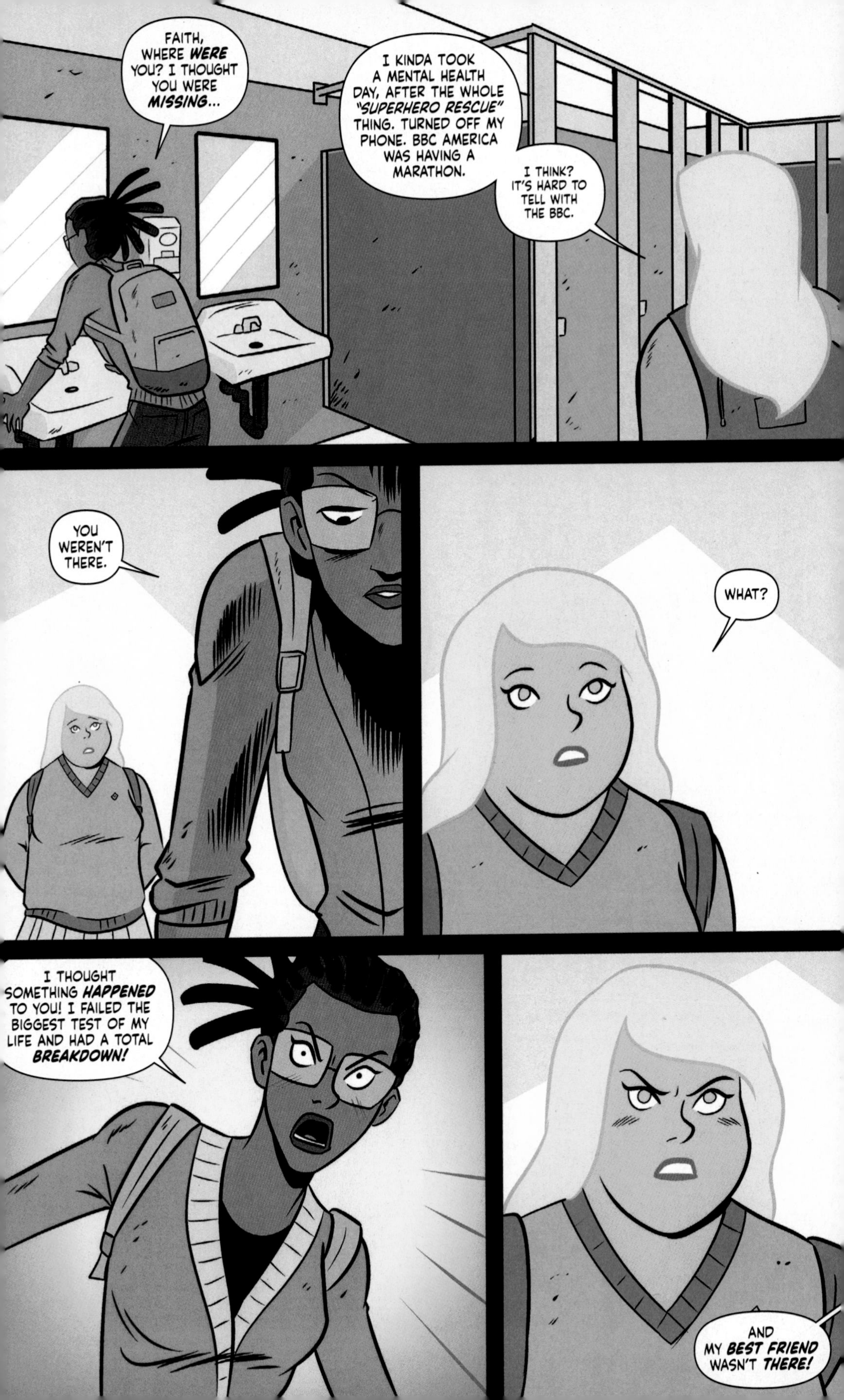
FAITH, WHERE WERE YOU? I THOUGHT YOU WERE MISSING...
I KINDA TOOK A MENTAL HEALTH DAY, AFTER THE WHOLE "SUPERHERO RESCUE" THING. TURNED OFF MY PHONE. BBC AMERICA WAS HAVING A MARATHON.
I THINK? IT'S HARD TO TELL WITH THE BBC.
YOU WEREN'T THERE.
WHAT?
I THOUGHT SOMETHING HAPPENED TO YOU! I FAILED THE BIGGEST TEST OF MY LIFE AND HAD A TOTAL BREAKDOWN!
AND MY BEST FRIEND WASN'T THERE!

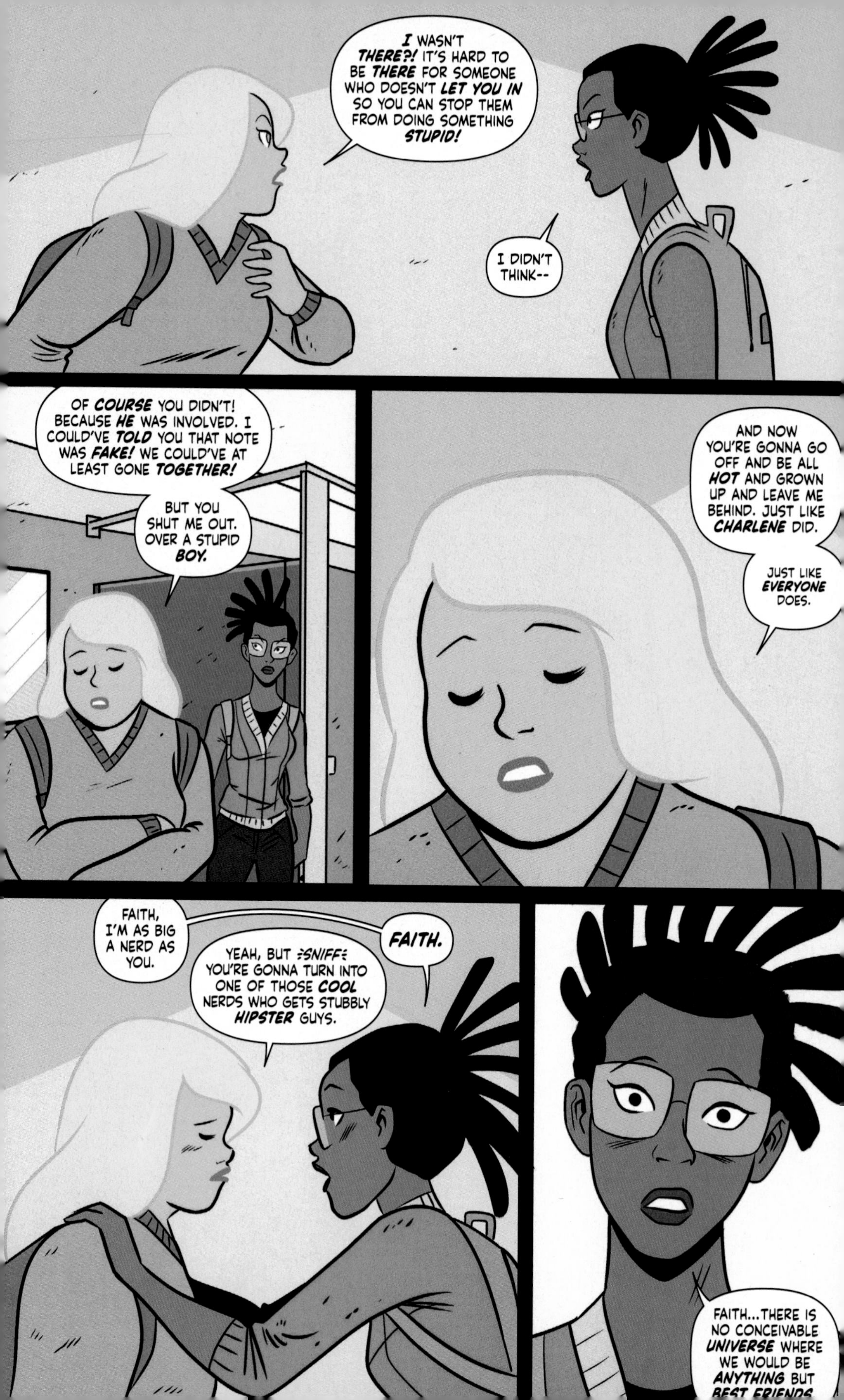
I WASN'T THERE?! IT'S HARD TO BE THERE FOR SOMEONE WHO DOESN'T LET YOU IN SO YOU CAN STOP THEM FROM DOING SOMETHING STUPID!
I DIDN'T THINK--
OF COURSE YOU DIDN'T! BECAUSE HE WAS INVOLVED. I COULD'VE TOLD YOU THAT NOTE WAS FAKE! WE COULD'VE AT LEAST GONE TOGETHER!
BUT YOU SHUT ME OUT. OVER A STUPID BOY.
AND NOW YOU'RE GONNA GO OFF AND BE ALL HOT AND GROWN UP AND LEAVE ME BEHIND. JUST LIKE CHARLENE DID.
JUST LIKE EVERYONE DOES.
FAITH, I'M AS BIG A NERD AS YOU.
YEAH, BUT SNIFF YOU'RE GONNA TURN INTO ONE OF THOSE COOL NERDS WHO GETS STUBBLY HIPSTER GUYS.
FAITH.
FAITH...THERE IS NO CONCEIVABLE UNIVERSE WHERE WE WOULD BE ANYTHING BUT

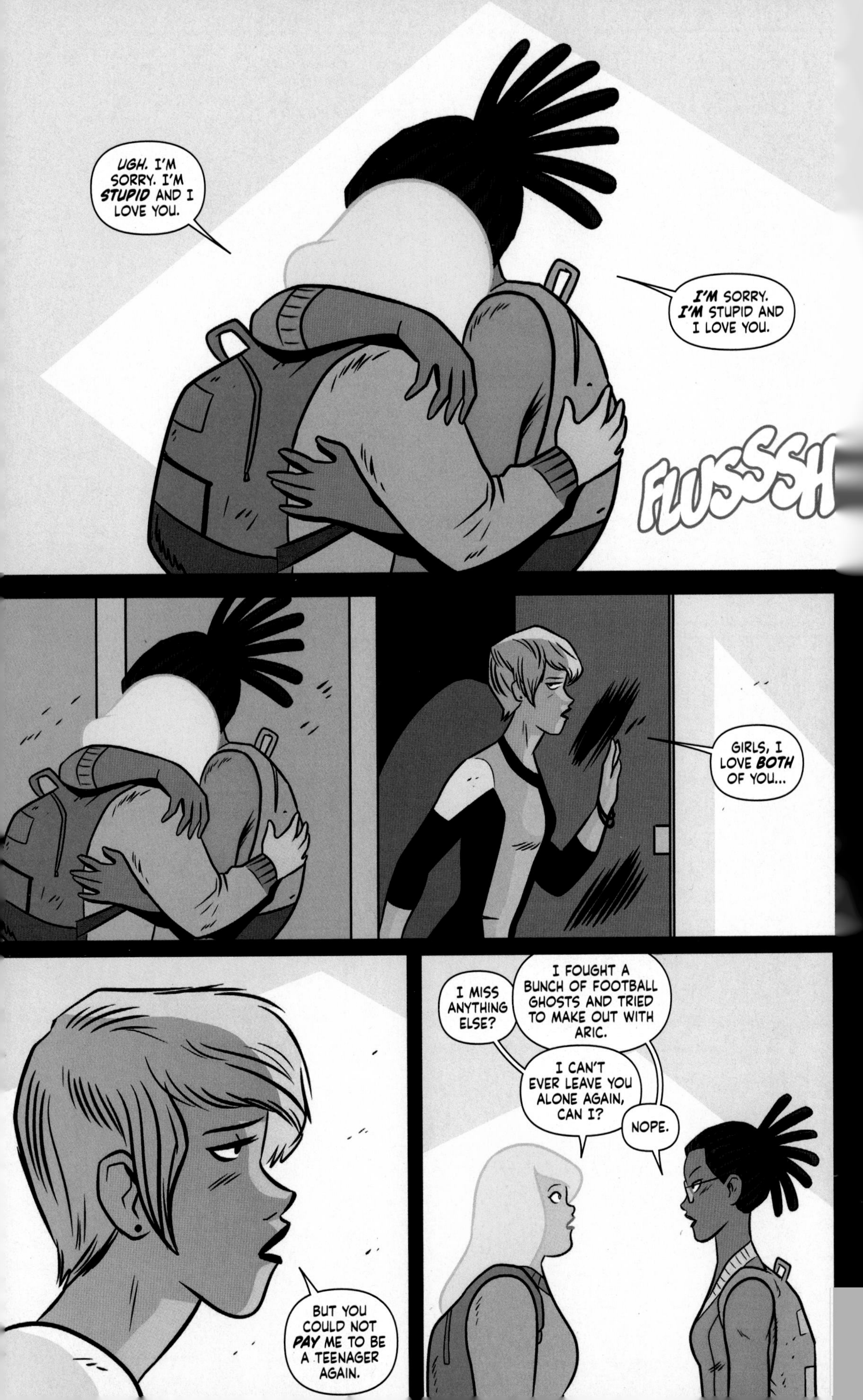
UGH. I'M SORRY. I'M STUPID AND I LOVE YOU.
I'M SORRY. I'M STUPID AND I LOVE YOU.
FLUSSSH
GIRLS, I LOVE BOTH OF YOU...
BUT YOU COULD NOT PAY ME TO BE A TEENAGER AGAIN.
I MISS ANYTHING ELSE?
I FOUGHT A BUNCH OF FOOTBALL GHOSTS AND TRIED TO MAKE OUT WITH ARIC.
I CAN'T EVER LEAVE YOU ALONE AGAIN, CAN I?
NOPE.

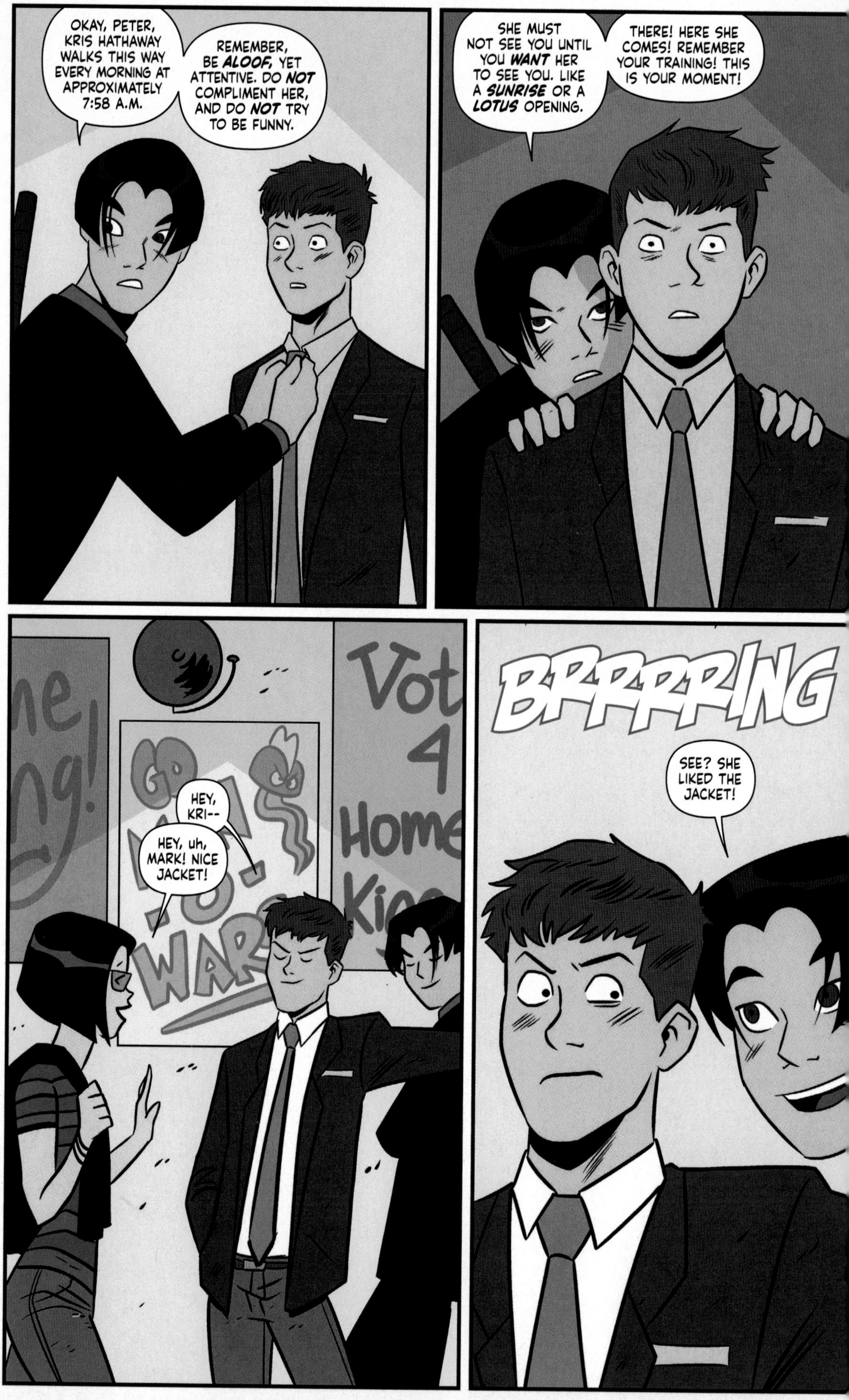
OKAY, PETER, KRIS HATHAWAY WALKS THIS WAY EVERY MORNING AT APPROXIMATELY 7:58 A.M.
REMEMBER, BE ALOOF, YET ATTENTIVE. DO NOT COMPLIMENT HER, AND DO NOT TRY TO BE FUNNY.
SHE MUST NOT SEE YOU UNTIL YOU WANT HER TO SEE YOU. LIKE A SUNRISE OR A LOTUS OPENING.
THERE! HERE SHE COMES! REMEMBER YOUR TRAINING! THIS IS YOUR MOMENT!
Vot 4 Home Kin
HEY, KRI--
HEY, uh, MARK! NICE JACKET!
BRRRRING
SEE? SHE LIKED THE JACKET!

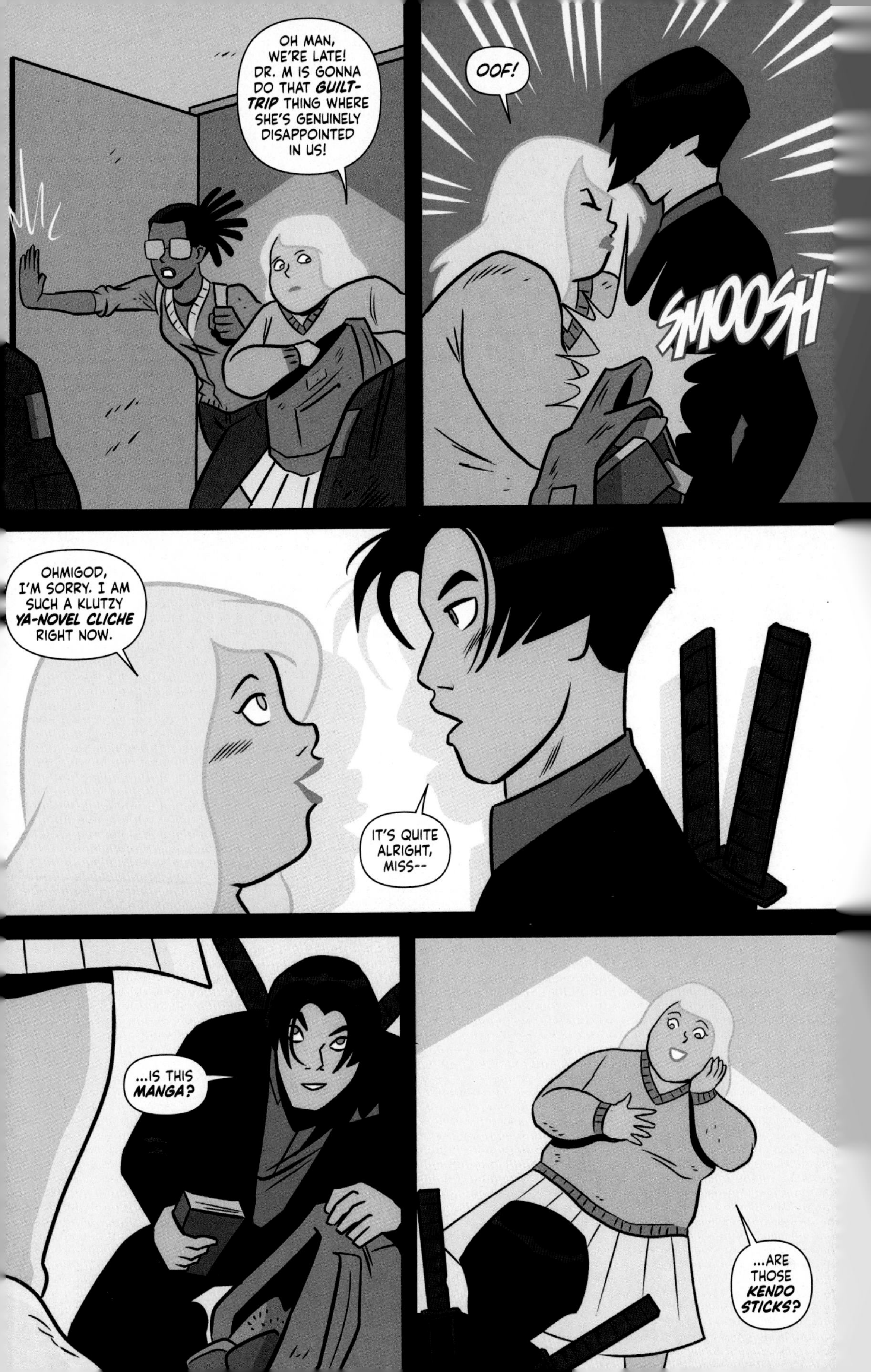
OH MAN, WE'RE LATE! DR. M IS GONNA DO THAT GUILT-TRIP THING WHERE SHE'S GENUINELY DISAPPOINTED IN US!
OOF!
SMOOSH
OHMIGOD, I'M SORRY. I AM SUCH A KLUTZY YA-NOVEL CLICHE RIGHT NOW.
IT'S QUITE ALRIGHT, MISS--
...IS THIS MANGA?
...ARE THOSE KENDO STICKS?

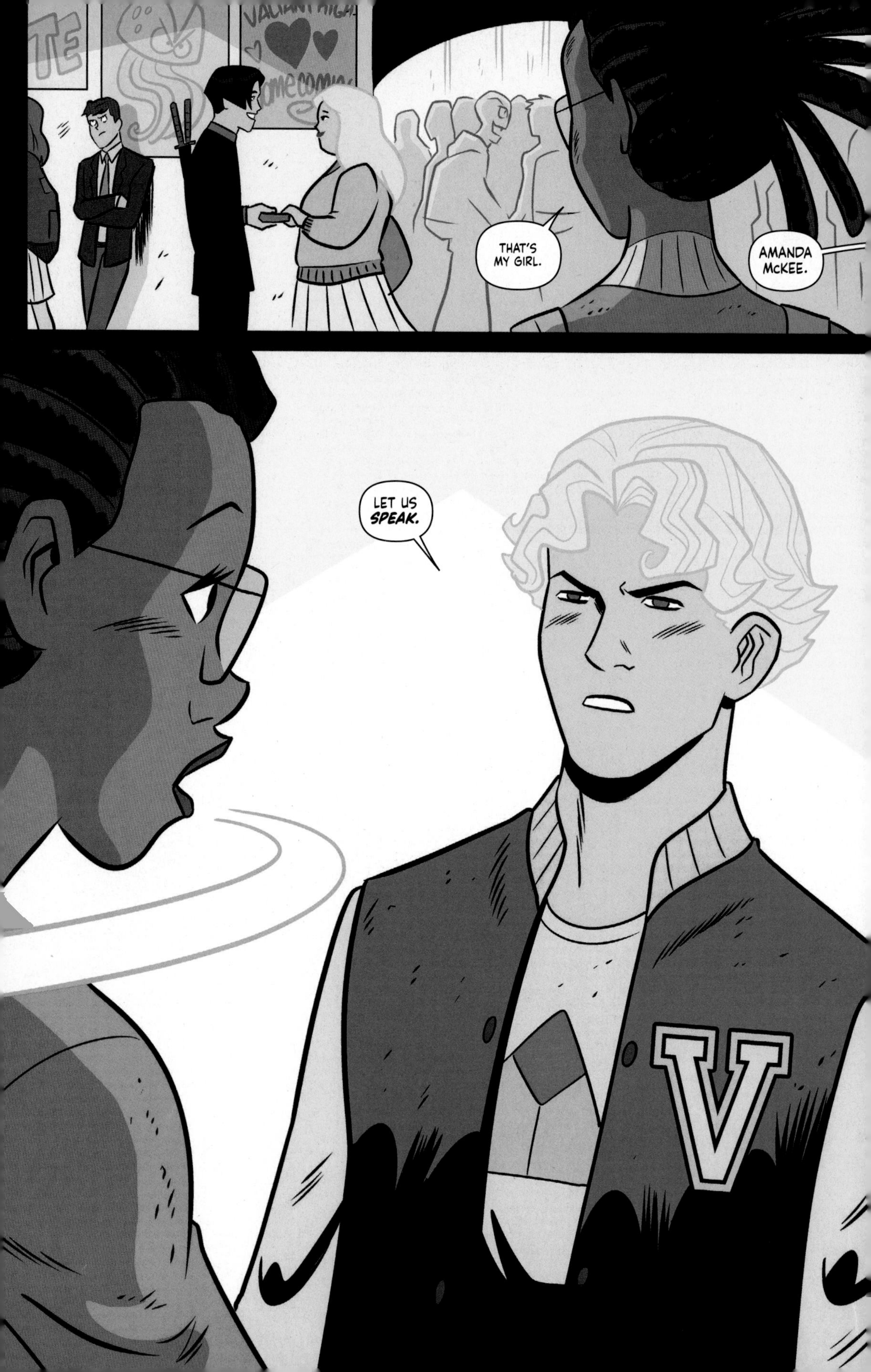
VALIANT HIGH
Homecoming
THAT'S MY GIRL.
AMANDA McKEE.
LET US SPEAK.

VALIANT

DANIEL KIBBLESMITH | DEREK CHARM
DAVID BARON | SIMON BOWLAND

#4

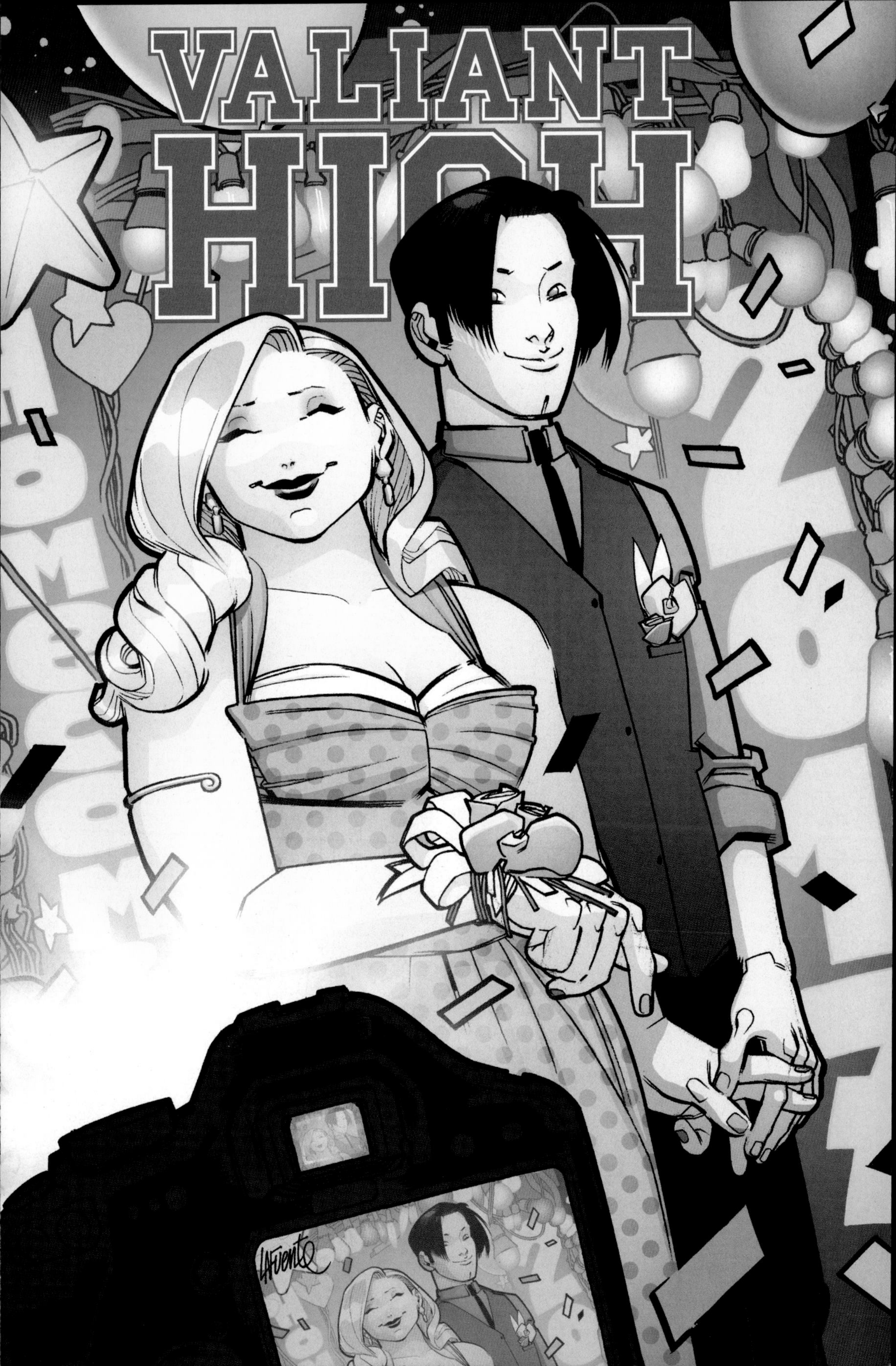
VALIANT HIGH

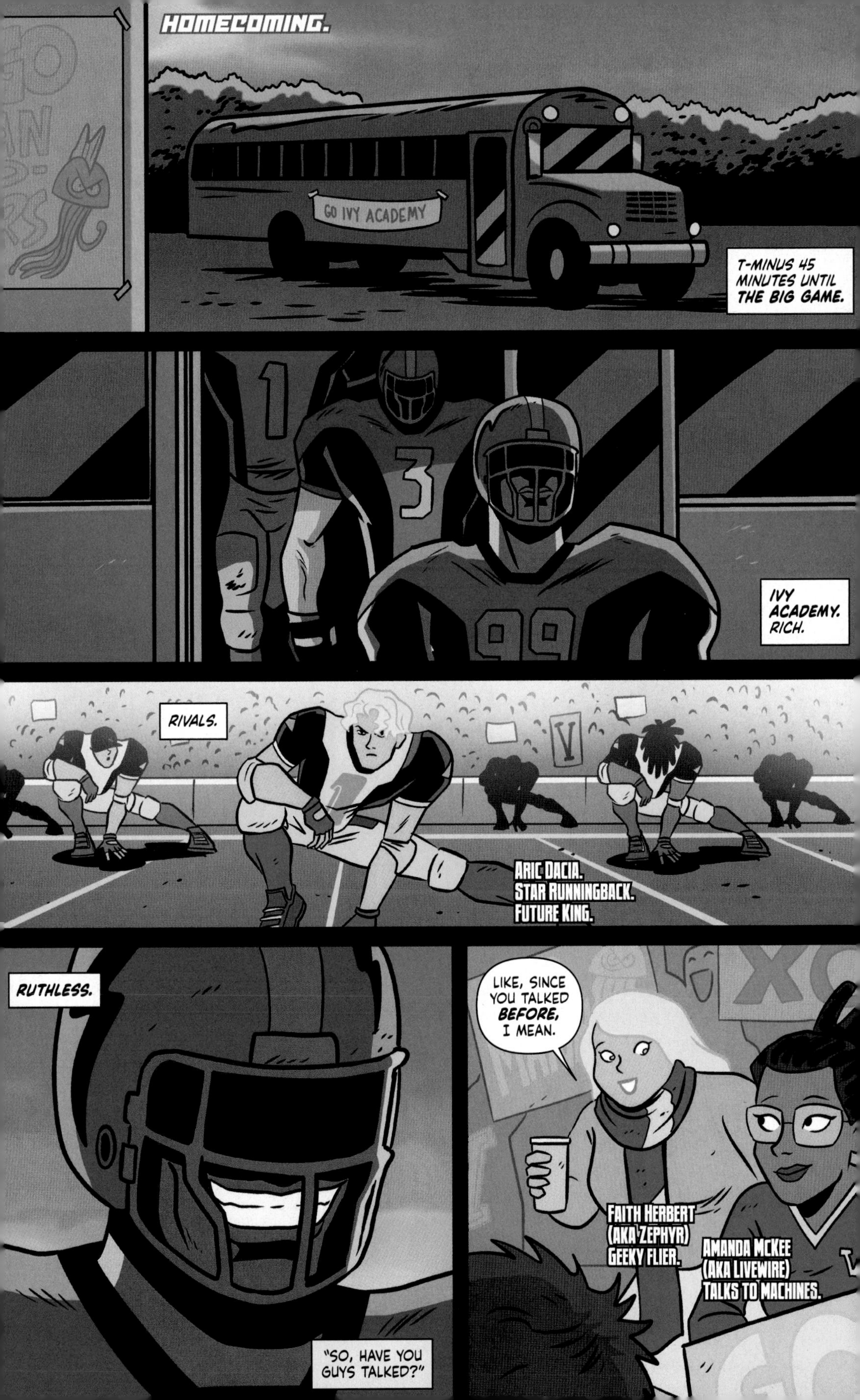
HOMECOMING.
GO IVY ACADEMY
T-MINUS 45 MINUTES UNTIL THE BIG GAME.
IVY ACADEMY. RICH.
RIVALS.
ARIC DACIA. STAR RUNNINGBACK. FUTURE KING.
RUTHLESS.
"SO, HAVE YOU GUYS TALKED?"
LIKE, SINCE YOU TALKED BEFORE, I MEAN.
FAITH HERBERT (AKA ZEPHYR) GEEKY FLIER.
AMANDA MCKEE (AKA LIVEWIRE) TALKS TO MACHINES.

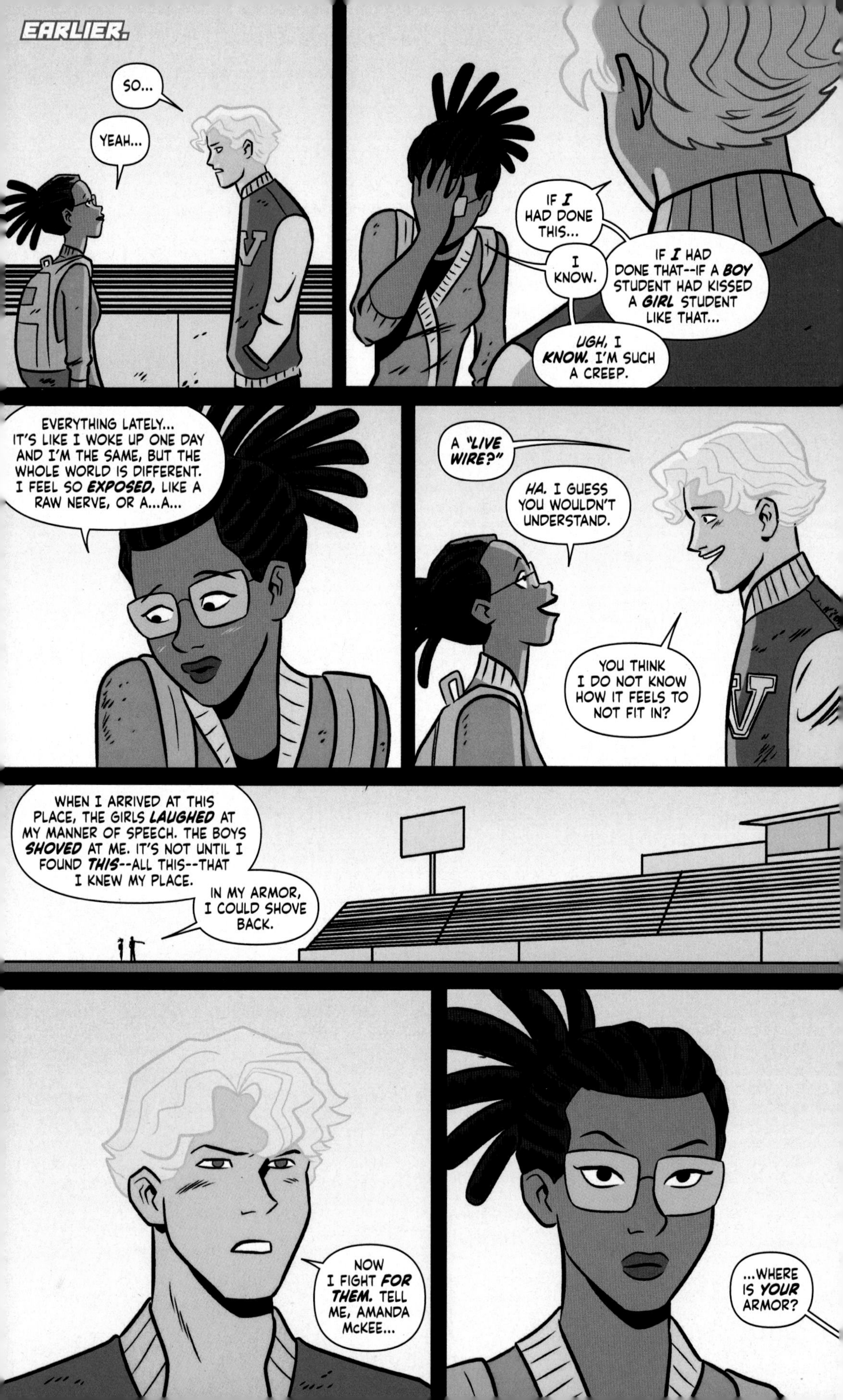
EARLIER.
SO...
YEAH...
IF I HAD DONE THIS...
I KNOW.
IF I HAD DONE THAT--IF A BOY STUDENT HAD KISSED A GIRL STUDENT LIKE THAT...
UGH, I KNOW. I'M SUCH A CREEP.
EVERYTHING LATELY... IT'S LIKE I WOKE UP ONE DAY AND I'M THE SAME, BUT THE WHOLE WORLD IS DIFFERENT. I FEEL SO EXPOSED, LIKE A RAW NERVE, OR A...A...
A "LIVE WIRE?"
HA. I GUESS YOU WOULDN'T UNDERSTAND.
YOU THINK I DO NOT KNOW HOW IT FEELS TO NOT FIT IN?
WHEN I ARRIVED AT THIS PLACE, THE GIRLS LAUGHED AT MY MANNER OF SPEECH. THE BOYS SHOVED AT ME. IT'S NOT UNTIL I FOUND THIS--ALL THIS--THAT I KNEW MY PLACE.
IN MY ARMOR, I COULD SHOVE BACK.
NOW I FIGHT FOR THEM. TELL ME, AMANDA McKEE...
...WHERE IS YOUR ARMOR?

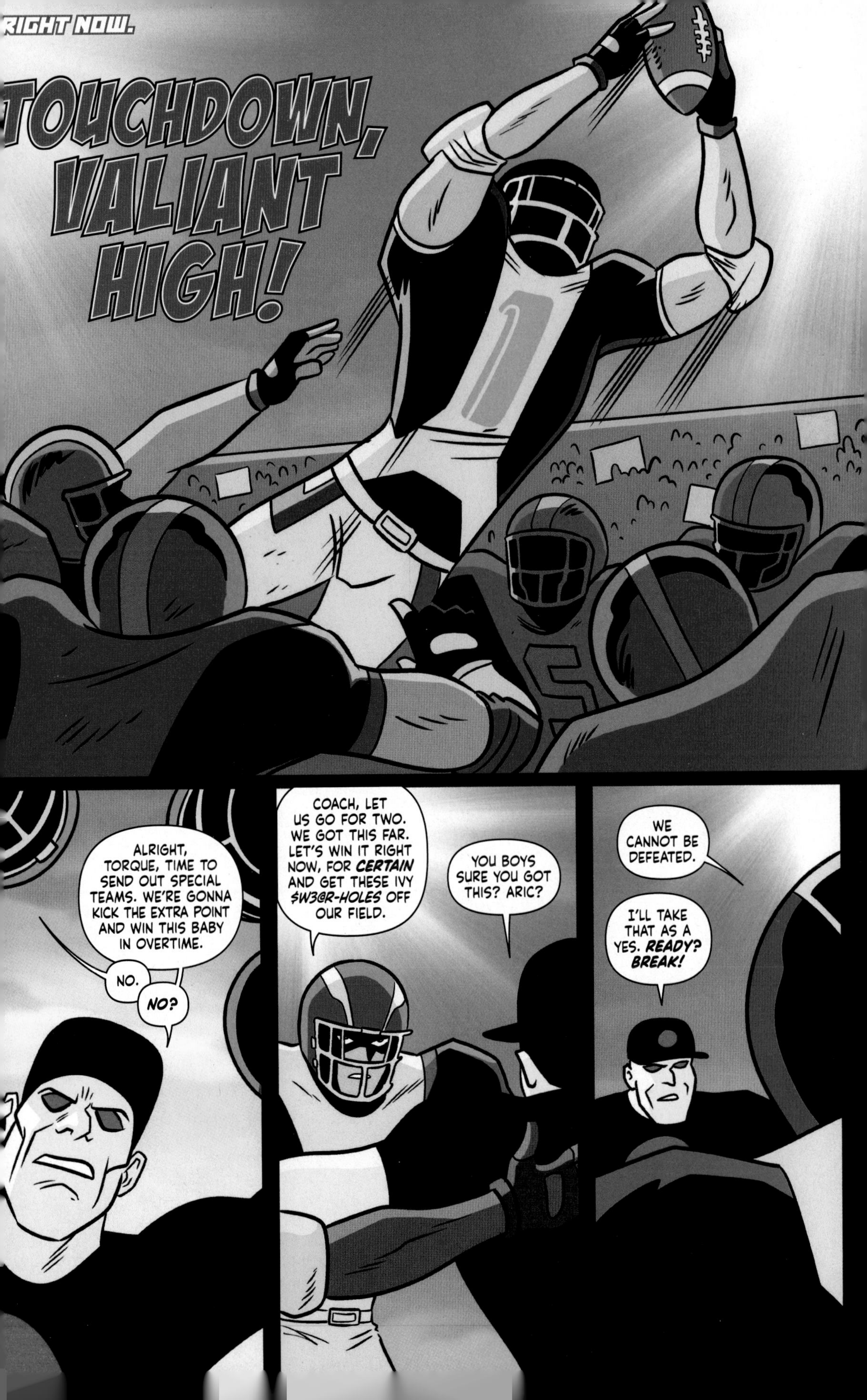
RIGHT NOW.
TOUCHDOWN, VALIANT HIGH!
ALRIGHT, TORQUE, TIME TO SEND OUT SPECIAL TEAMS. WE'RE GONNA KICK THE EXTRA POINT AND WIN THIS BABY IN OVERTIME.
NO.
NO?
COACH, LET US GO FOR TWO. WE GOT THIS FAR. LET'S WIN IT RIGHT NOW, FOR CERTAIN AND GET THESE IVY $W3@R-HOLES OFF OUR FIELD.
YOU BOYS SURE YOU GOT THIS? ARIC?
WE CANNOT BE DEFEATED.
I'LL TAKE THAT AS A YES. READY? BREAK!

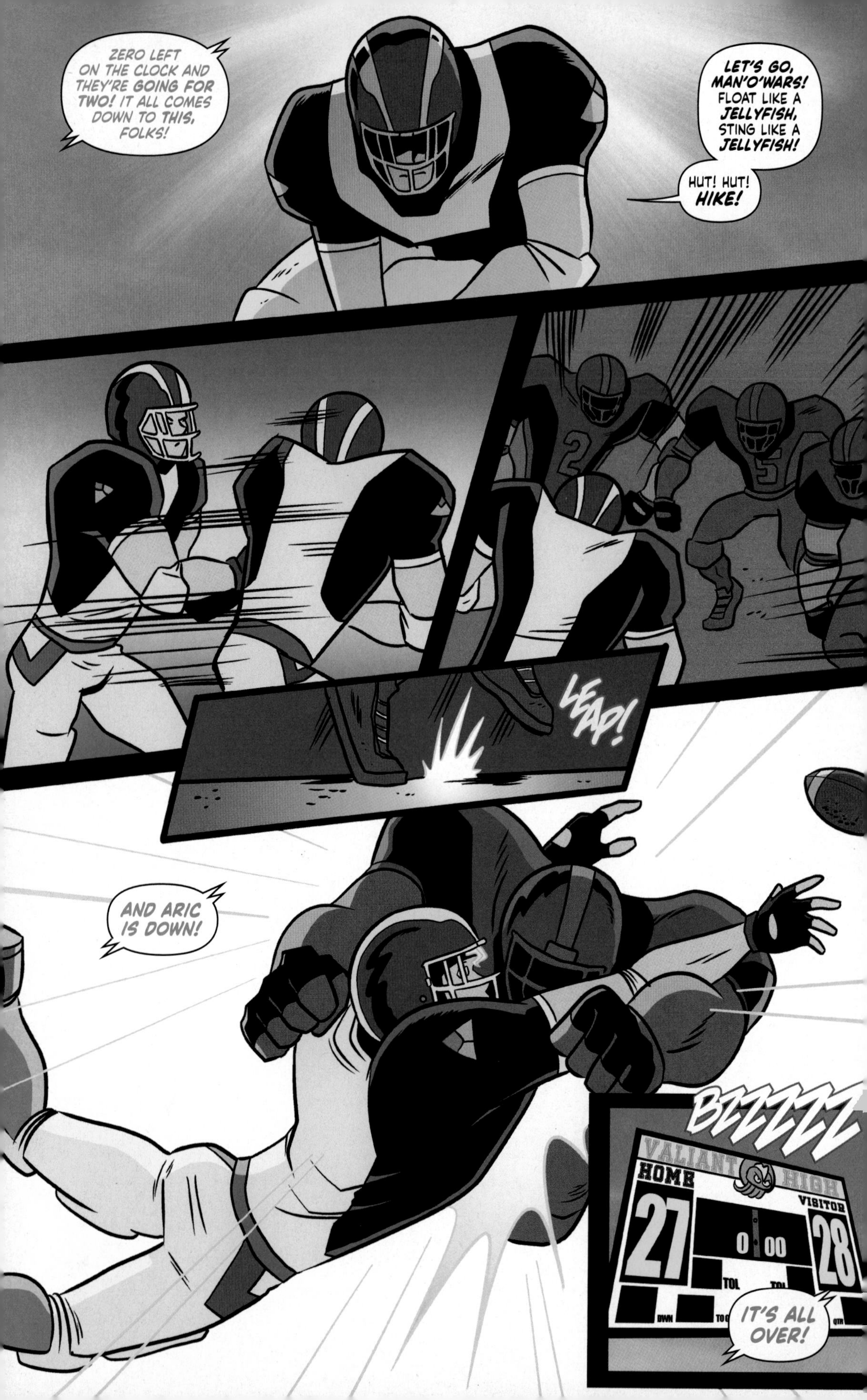
ZERO LEFT ON THE CLOCK AND THEY'RE GOING FOR TWO! IT ALL COMES DOWN TO THIS, FOLKS!
LET'S GO, MAN'O'WARS! FLOAT LIKE A JELLYFISH, STING LIKE A JELLYFISH!
HUT! HUT! HIKE!
LEAP!
AND ARIC IS DOWN!
BZZZZZ
VALIANT HIGH
HOME
VISITOR
27
0 00
28
IT'S ALL OVER!

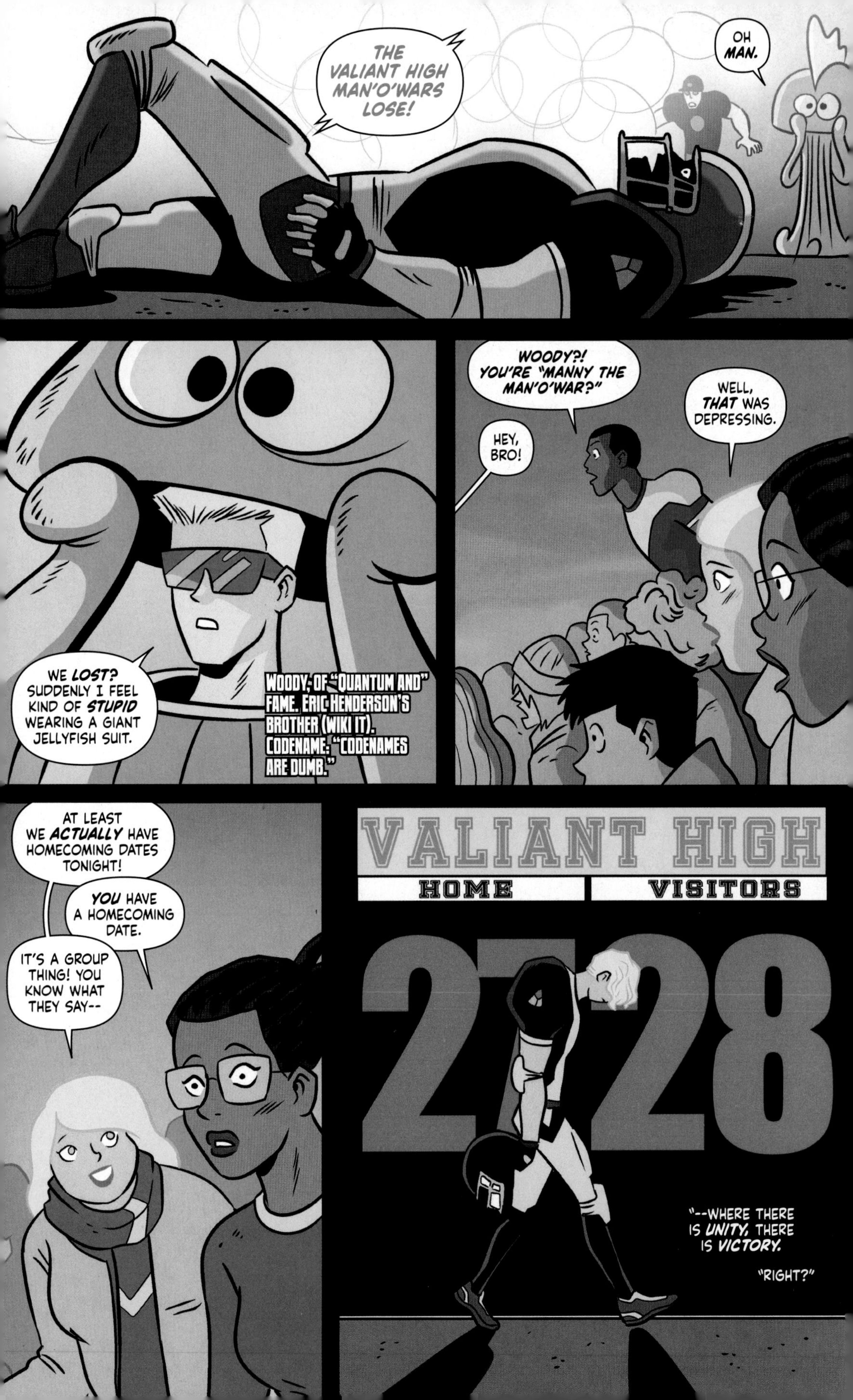
THE VALIANT HIGH MAN'O'WARS LOSE!
OH MAN.
WE LOST? SUDDENLY I FEEL KIND OF STUPID WEARING A GIANT JELLYFISH SUIT.
WOODY, OF "QUANTUM AND" FAME. ERIC HENDERSON'S BROTHER (WIKI IT). CODENAME: "CODENAMES ARE DUMB."
WOODY?! YOU'RE "MANNY THE MAN'O'WAR?"
HEY, BRO!
WELL, THAT WAS DEPRESSING.
AT LEAST WE ACTUALLY HAVE HOMECOMING DATES TONIGHT!
YOU HAVE A HOMECOMING DATE.
IT'S A GROUP THING! YOU KNOW WHAT THEY SAY--
VALIANT HIGH
HOME
VISITORS
2
28
"--WHERE THERE IS UNITY, THERE IS VICTORY.
"RIGHT?"

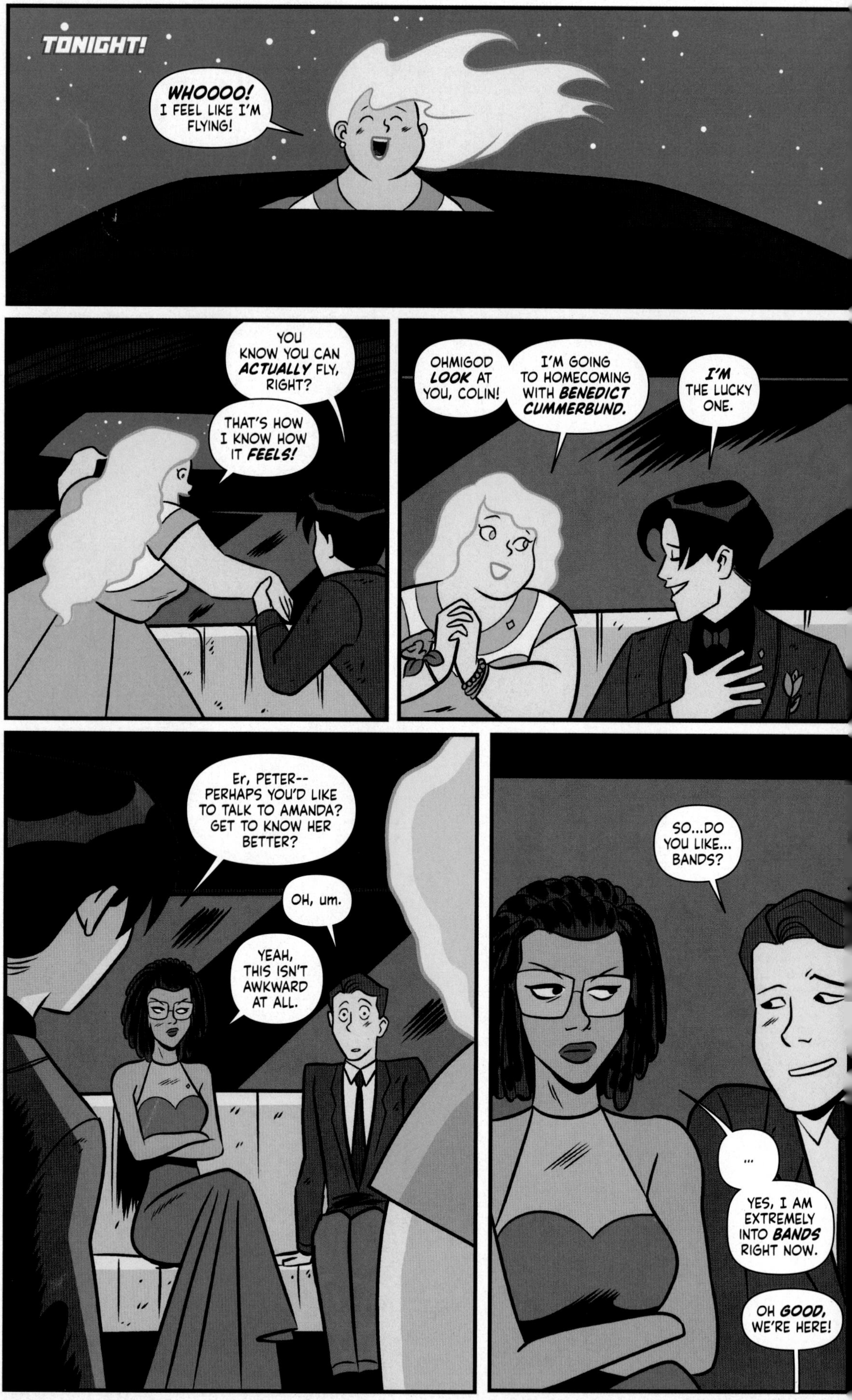
TONIGHT!
WHOOOO! I FEEL LIKE I'M FLYING!
YOU KNOW YOU CAN ACTUALLY FLY, RIGHT?
THAT'S HOW I KNOW HOW IT FEELS!
OHMIGOD LOOK AT YOU, COLIN!
I'M GOING TO HOMECOMING WITH BENEDICT CUMMERBUND.
I'M THE LUCKY ONE.
Er, PETER-- PERHAPS YOU'D LIKE TO TALK TO AMANDA? GET TO KNOW HER BETTER?
OH, um.
YEAH, THIS ISN'T AWKWARD AT ALL.
SO...DO YOU LIKE... BANDS?
...
YES, I AM EXTREMELY INTO BANDS RIGHT NOW.
OH GOOD, WE'RE HERE!

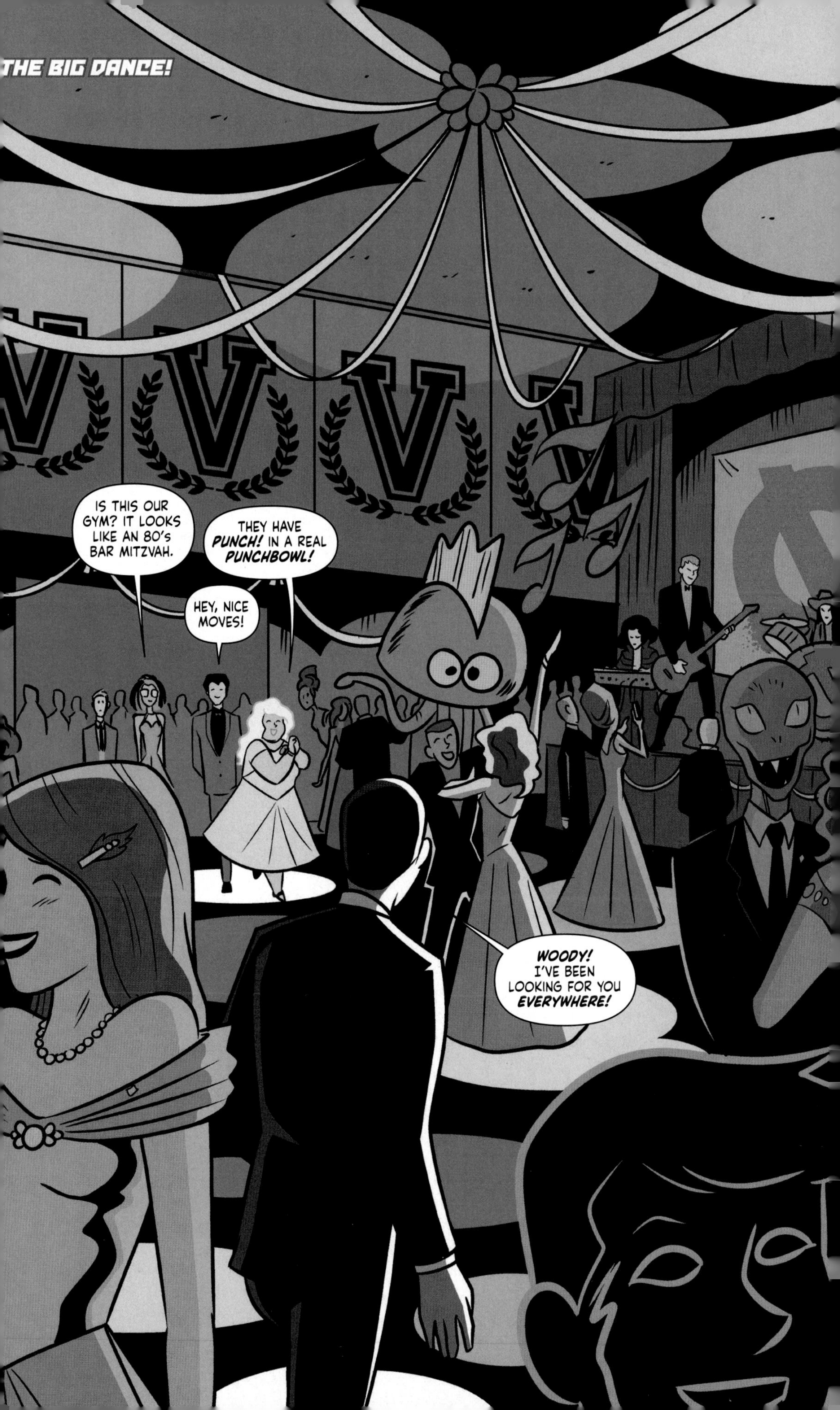
THE BIG DANCE!
IS THIS OUR GYM? IT LOOKS LIKE AN 80's BAR MITZVAH.
HEY, NICE MOVES!
THEY HAVE PUNCH! IN A REAL PUNCHBOWL!
WOODY! I'VE BEEN LOOKING FOR YOU EVERYWHERE!

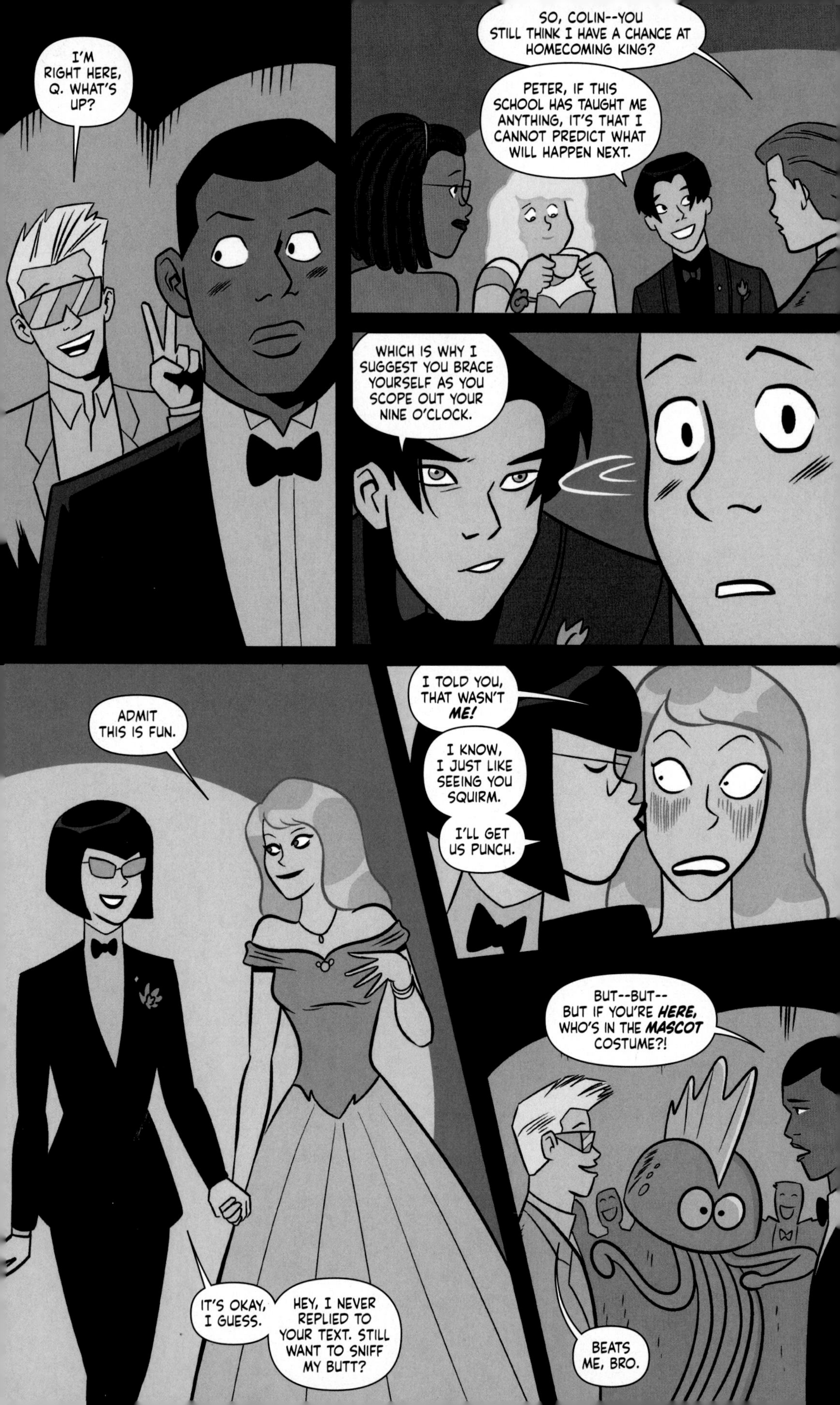
I'M RIGHT HERE, Q. WHAT'S UP?
SO, COLIN--YOU STILL THINK I HAVE A CHANCE AT HOMECOMING KING?
PETER, IF THIS SCHOOL HAS TAUGHT ME ANYTHING, IT'S THAT I CANNOT PREDICT WHAT WILL HAPPEN NEXT.
WHICH IS WHY I SUGGEST YOU BRACE YOURSELF AS YOU SCOPE OUT YOUR NINE O'CLOCK.
ADMIT THIS IS FUN.
IT'S OKAY, I GUESS.
HEY, I NEVER REPLIED TO YOUR TEXT. STILL WANT TO SNIFF MY BUTT?
I TOLD YOU, THAT WASN'T *ME!*
I KNOW, I JUST LIKE SEEING YOU SQUIRM.
I'LL GET US PUNCH.
BUT--BUT-- BUT IF YOU'RE *HERE,* WHO'S IN THE *MASCOT* COSTUME?!
BEATS ME, BRO.

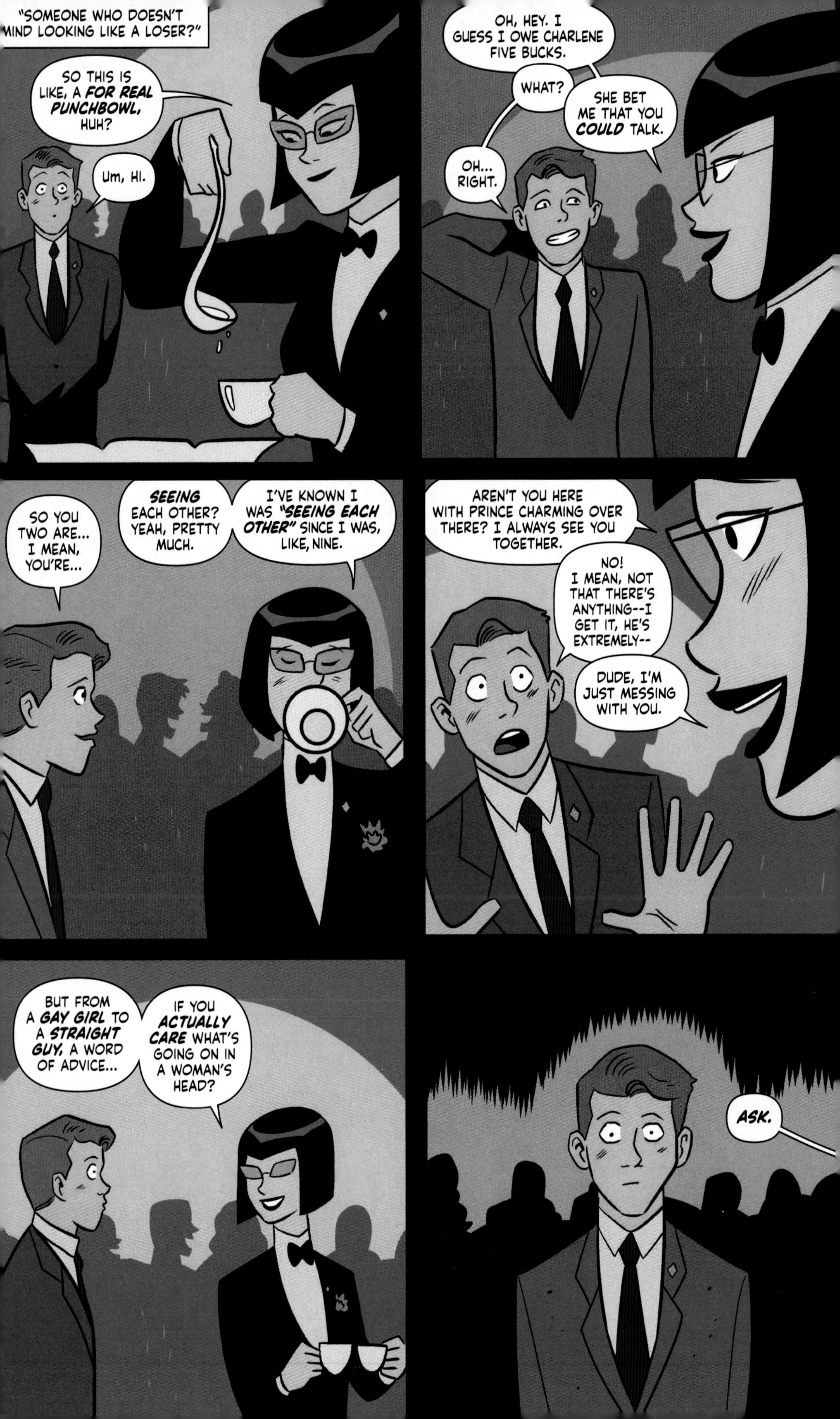
"SOMEONE WHO DOESN'T MIND LOOKING LIKE A LOSER?"
SO THIS IS LIKE, A FOR REAL PUNCHBOWL, HUH?
Um, HI.
OH, HEY. I GUESS I OWE CHARLENE FIVE BUCKS.
WHAT?
SHE BET ME THAT YOU COULD TALK.
OH... RIGHT.
SO YOU TWO ARE... I MEAN, YOU'RE...
SEEING EACH OTHER? YEAH, PRETTY MUCH.
I'VE KNOWN I WAS "SEEING EACH OTHER" SINCE I WAS, LIKE, NINE.
AREN'T YOU HERE WITH PRINCE CHARMING OVER THERE? I ALWAYS SEE YOU TOGETHER.
NO! I MEAN, NOT THAT THERE'S ANYTHING--I GET IT, HE'S EXTREMELY--
DUDE, I'M JUST MESSING WITH YOU.
BUT FROM A GAY GIRL TO A STRAIGHT GUY, A WORD OF ADVICE...
IF YOU ACTUALLY CARE WHAT'S GOING ON IN A WOMAN'S HEAD?
ASK.

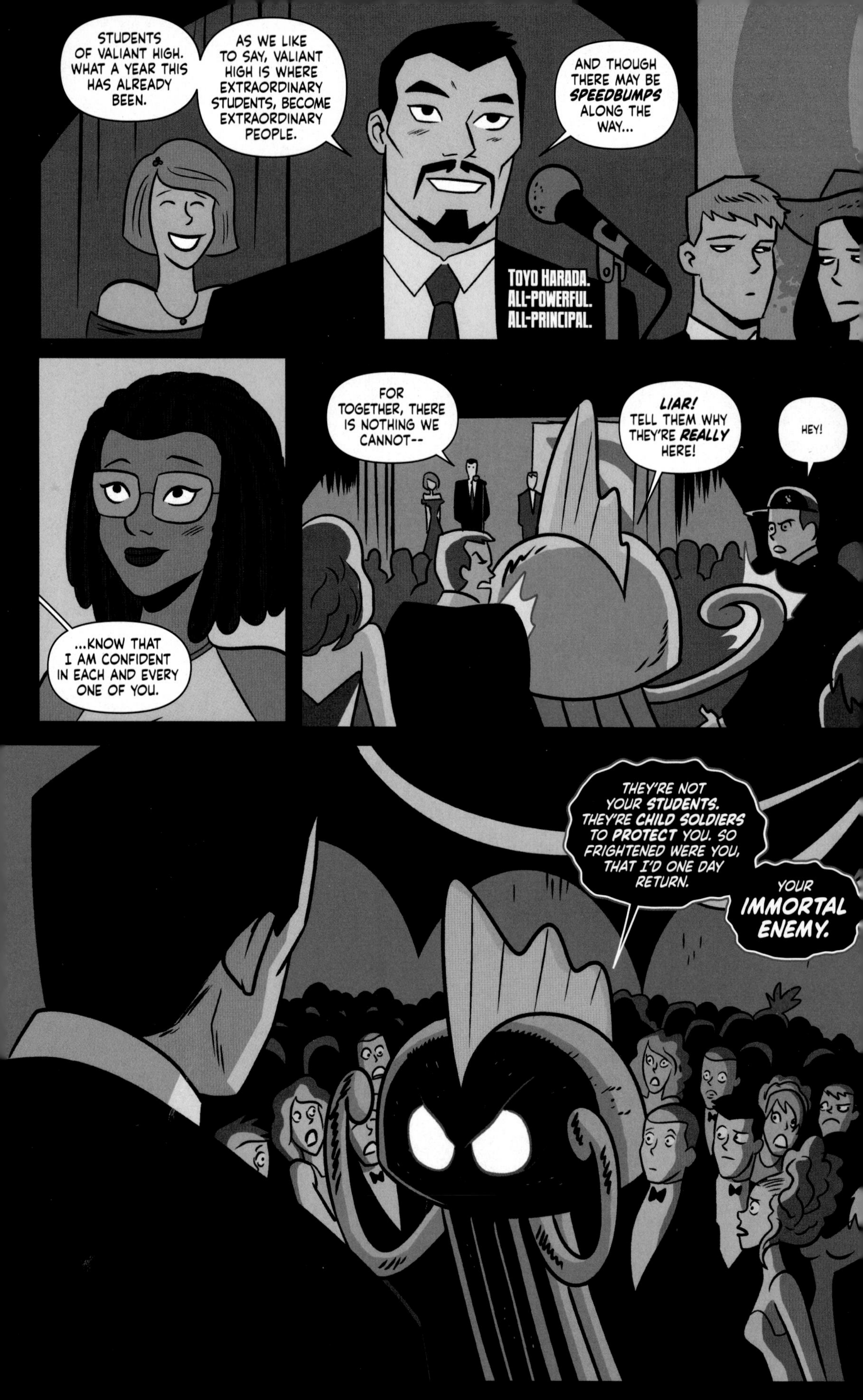

STUDENTS OF VALIANT HIGH. WHAT A YEAR THIS HAS ALREADY BEEN.
AS WE LIKE TO SAY, VALIANT HIGH IS WHERE EXTRAORDINARY STUDENTS, BECOME EXTRAORDINARY PEOPLE.
AND THOUGH THERE MAY BE SPEEDBUMPS ALONG THE WAY...
TOYO HARADA. ALL-POWERFUL. ALL-PRINCIPAL.
...KNOW THAT I AM CONFIDENT IN EACH AND EVERY ONE OF YOU.
FOR TOGETHER, THERE IS NOTHING WE CANNOT--
LIAR! TELL THEM WHY THEY'RE REALLY HERE!
HEY!
THEY'RE NOT YOUR STUDENTS. THEY'RE CHILD SOLDIERS TO PROTECT YOU. SO FRIGHTENED WERE YOU, THAT I'D ONE DAY RETURN.
YOUR IMMORTAL ENEMY.

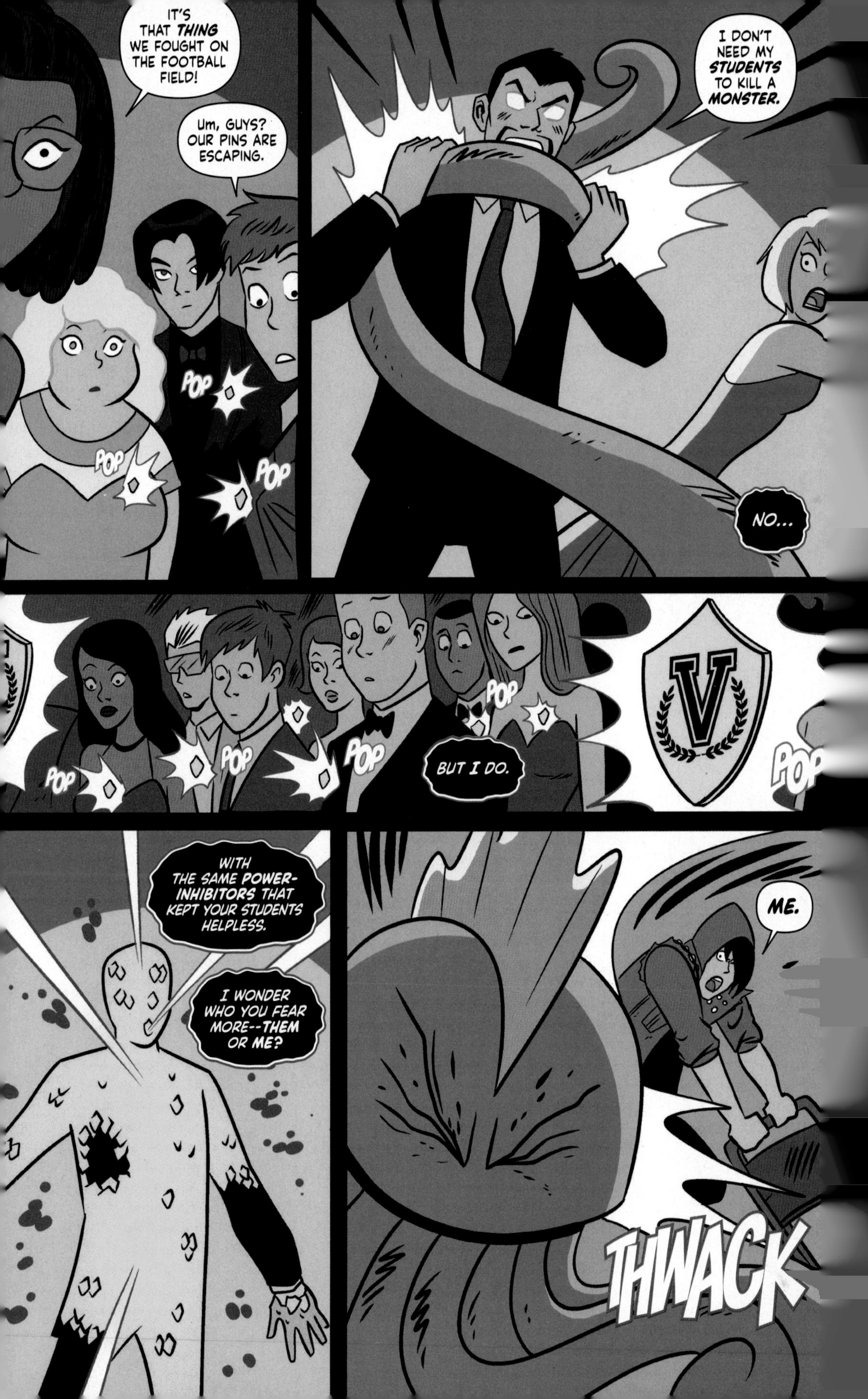
IT'S THAT THING WE FOUGHT ON THE FOOTBALL FIELD!
Um, GUYS? OUR PINS ARE ESCAPING.
POP
POP
POP
I DON'T NEED MY STUDENTS TO KILL A MONSTER.
NO...
POP
POP
POP
POP
BUT I DO.
POP
WITH THE SAME POWER-INHIBITORS THAT KEPT YOUR STUDENTS HELPLESS.
I WONDER WHO YOU FEAR MORE--THEM OR ME?
ME.
THWACK

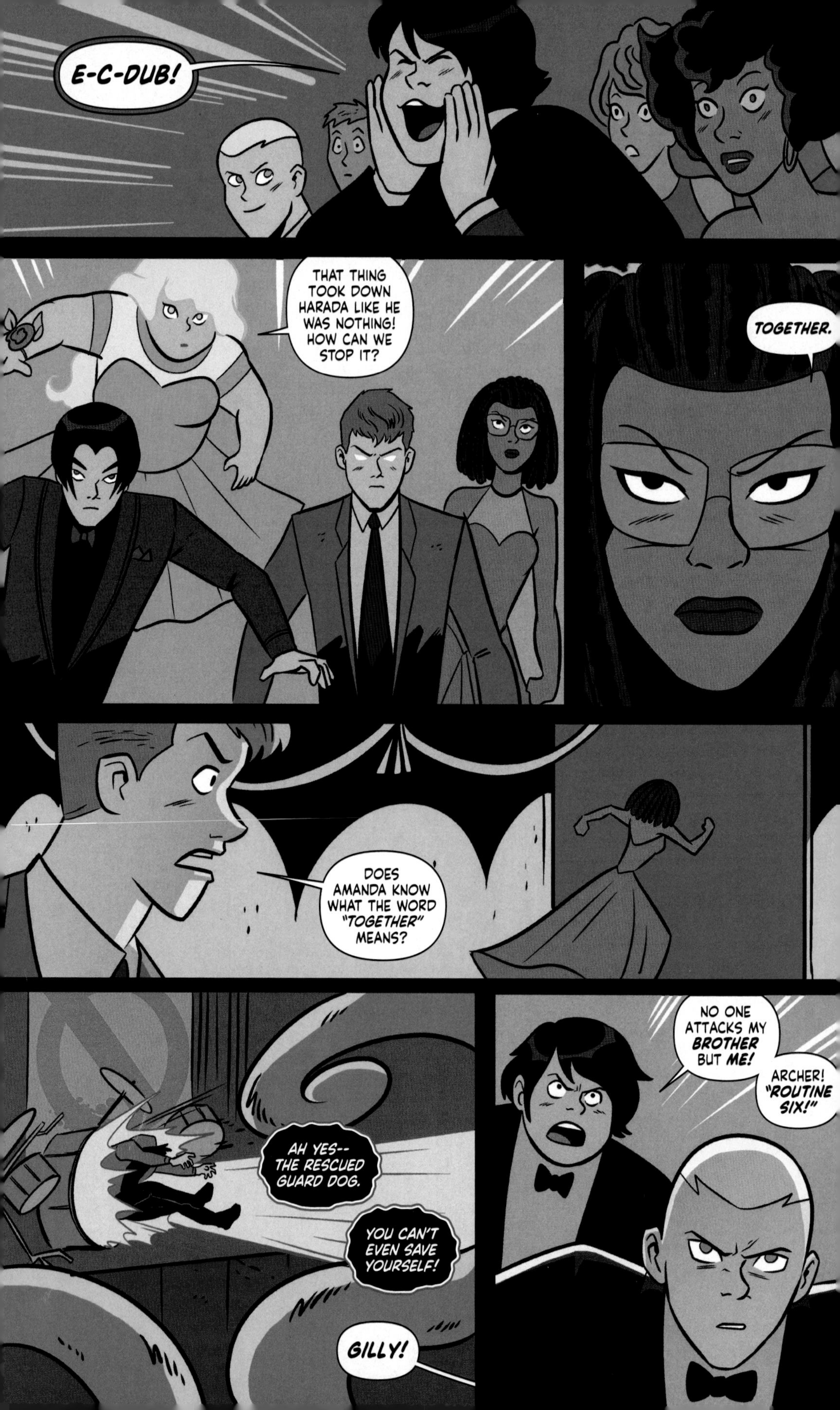
E-C-DUB!
THAT THING TOOK DOWN HARADA LIKE HE WAS NOTHING! HOW CAN WE STOP IT?
TOGETHER.
DOES AMANDA KNOW WHAT THE WORD "TOGETHER" MEANS?
AH YES-- THE RESCUED GUARD DOG.
YOU CAN'T EVEN SAVE YOURSELF!
GILLY!
NO ONE ATTACKS MY BROTHER BUT ME!
ARCHER! "ROUTINE SIX!"

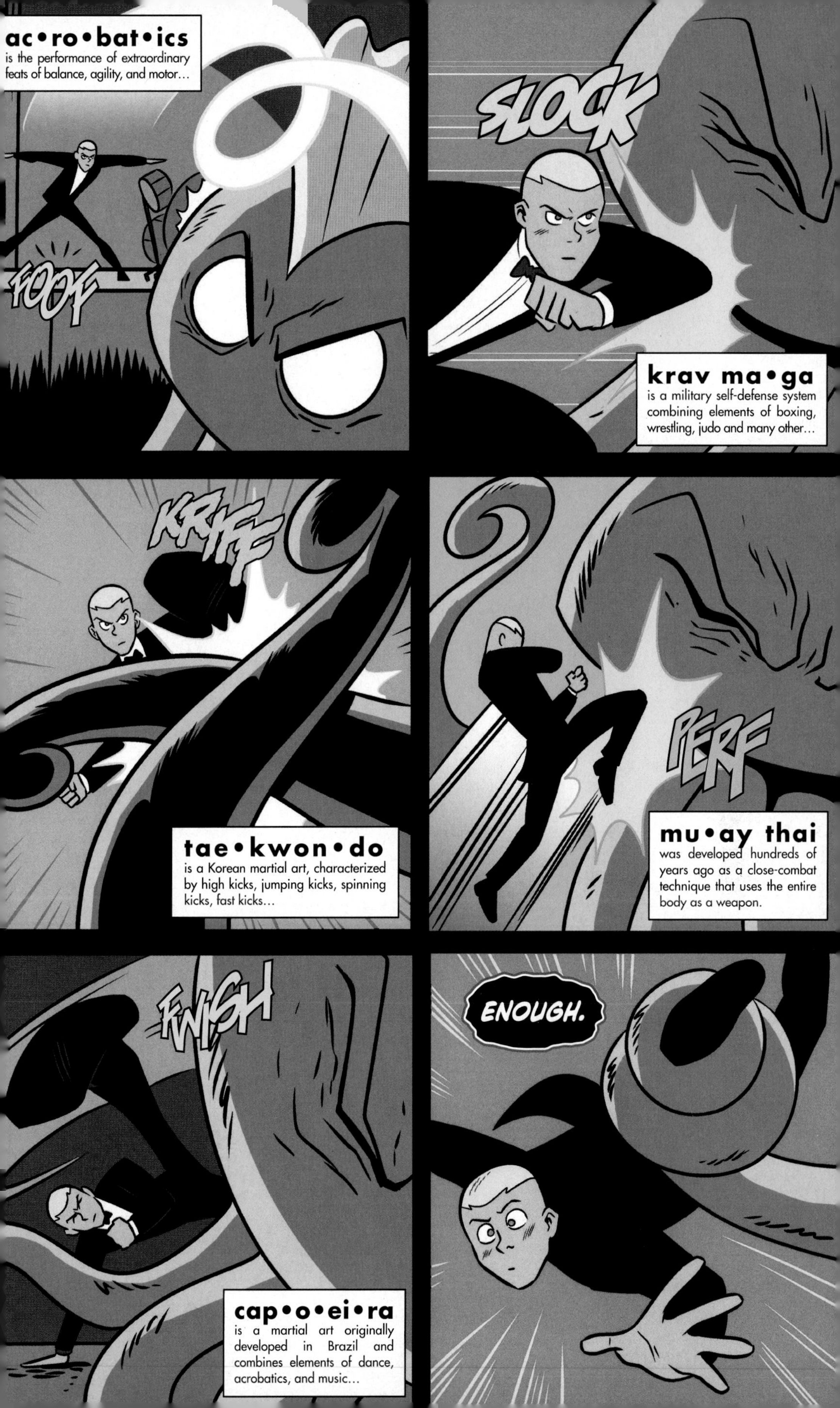

ac•ro•bat•ics
is the performance of extraordinary feats of balance, agility, and motor…
FOOF
SLOCK
krav ma•ga
is a military self-defense system combining elements of boxing, wrestling, judo and many other…
KRIFF
tae•kwon•do
is a Korean martial art, characterized by high kicks, jumping kicks, spinning kicks, fast kicks…
PERF
mu•ay thai
was developed hundreds of years ago as a close-combat technique that uses the entire body as a weapon.
FWISH
cap•o•ei•ra
is a martial art originally developed in Brazil and combines elements of dance, acrobatics, and music…
ENOUGH.

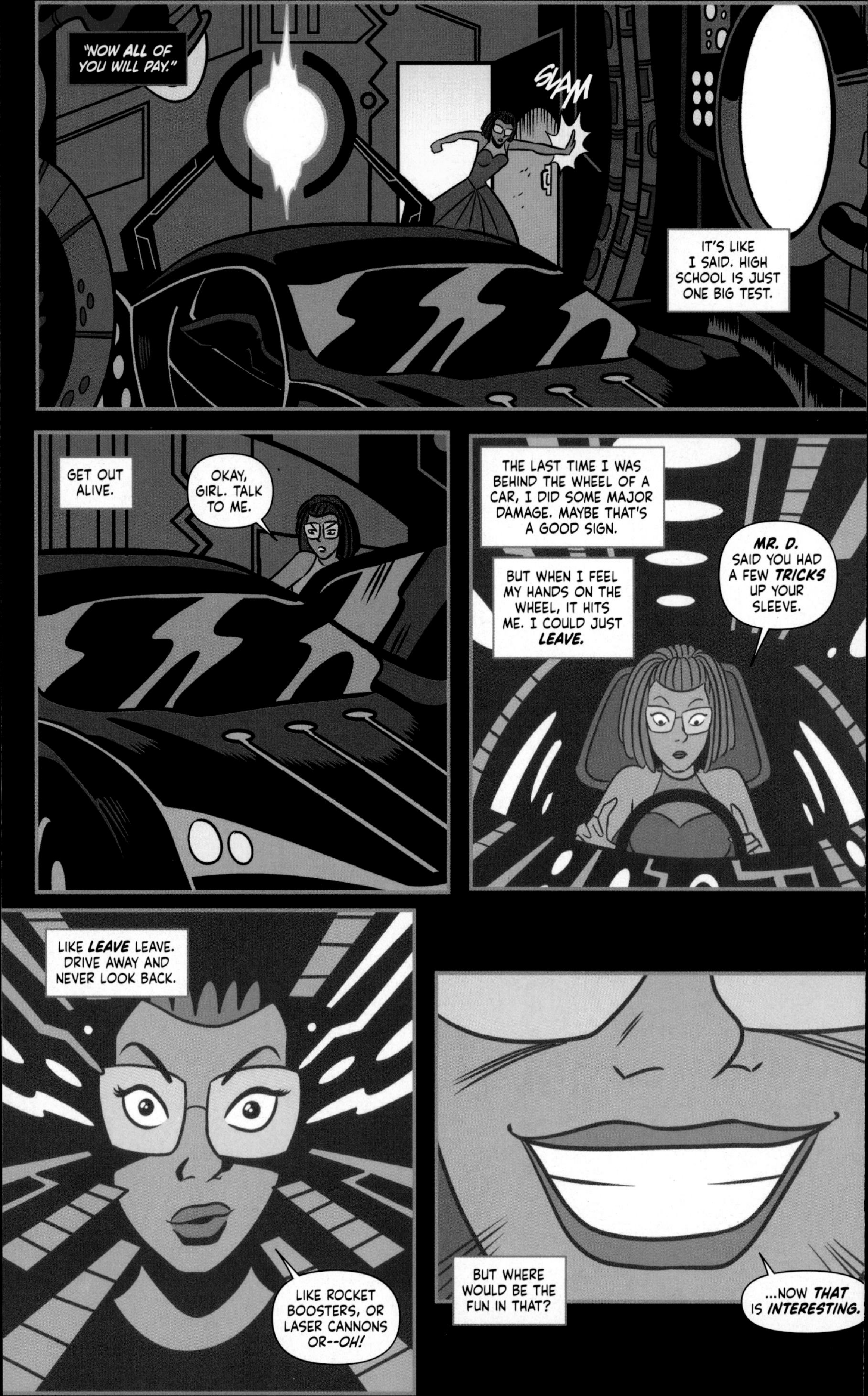
"NOW ALL OF YOU WILL PAY."
SLAM
IT'S LIKE I SAID. HIGH SCHOOL IS JUST ONE BIG TEST.
GET OUT ALIVE.
OKAY, GIRL. TALK TO ME.
THE LAST TIME I WAS BEHIND THE WHEEL OF A CAR, I DID SOME MAJOR DAMAGE. MAYBE THAT'S A GOOD SIGN.
BUT WHEN I FEEL MY HANDS ON THE WHEEL, IT HITS ME. I COULD JUST LEAVE.
MR. D. SAID YOU HAD A FEW TRICKS UP YOUR SLEEVE.
LIKE LEAVE LEAVE. DRIVE AWAY AND NEVER LOOK BACK.
LIKE ROCKET BOOSTERS, OR LASER CANNONS OR--OH!
BUT WHERE WOULD BE THE FUN IN THAT?
...NOW THAT IS INTERESTING.

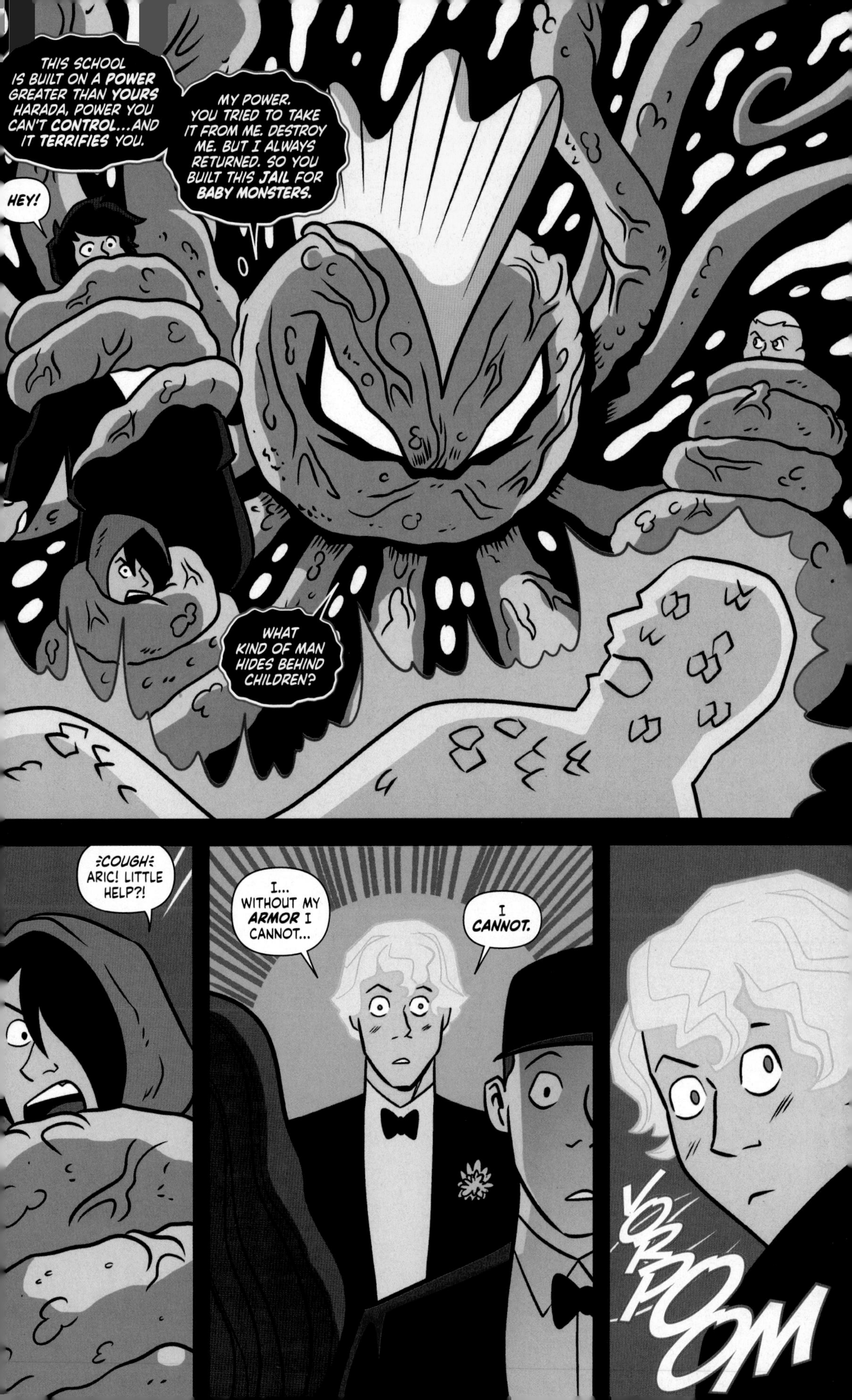
THIS SCHOOL IS BUILT ON A POWER GREATER THAN YOURS HARADA, POWER YOU CAN'T CONTROL...AND IT TERRIFIES YOU.
MY POWER. YOU TRIED TO TAKE IT FROM ME. DESTROY ME. BUT I ALWAYS RETURNED. SO YOU BUILT THIS JAIL FOR BABY MONSTERS.
HEY!
WHAT KIND OF MAN HIDES BEHIND CHILDREN?
COUGH ARIC! LITTLE HELP?!
I... WITHOUT MY ARMOR I CANNOT...
I CANNOT.
VOOOOM

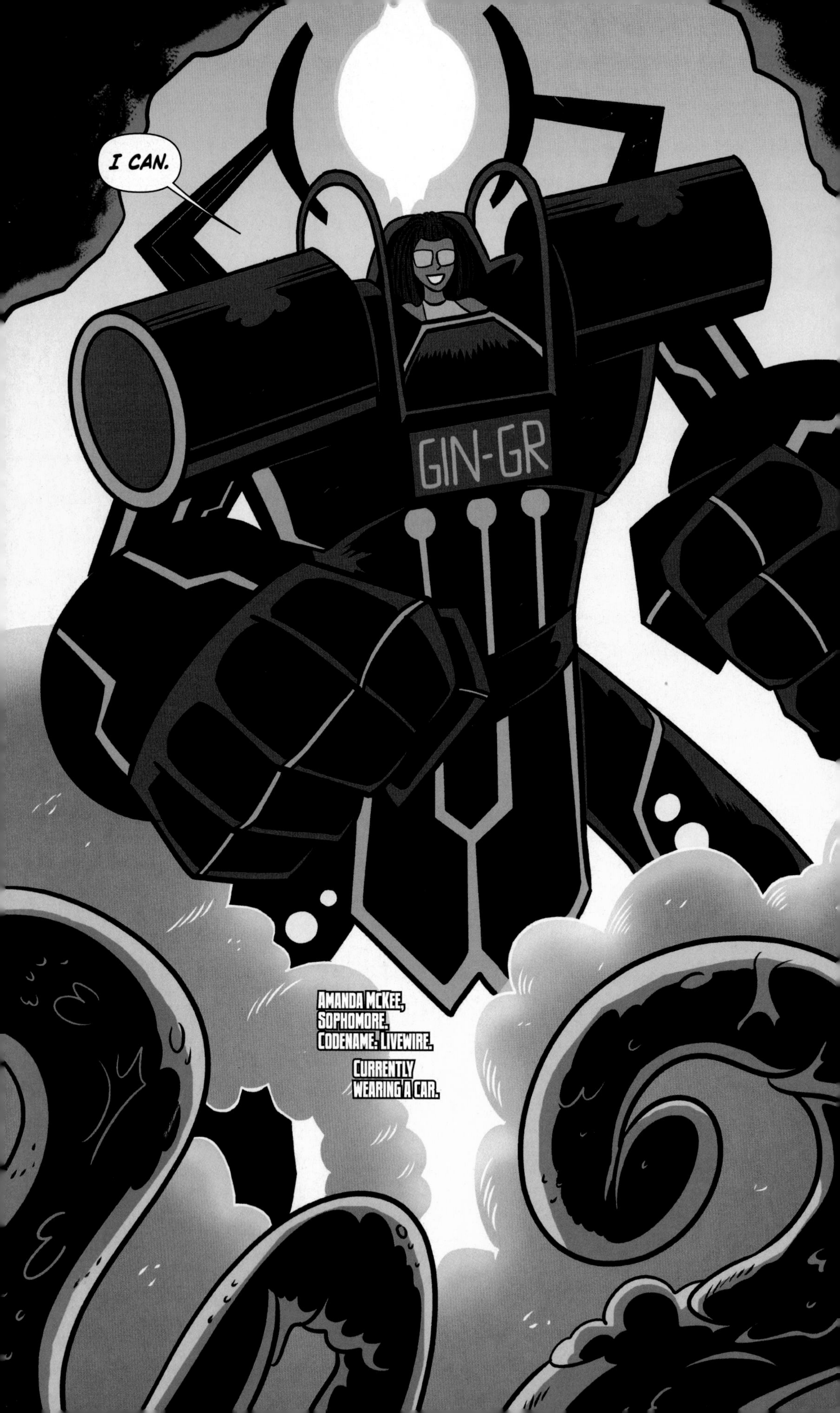
I CAN.
GIN-GR
AMANDA MCKEE, SOPHOMORE. CODENAME: LIVEWIRE.
CURRENTLY WEARING A CAR.

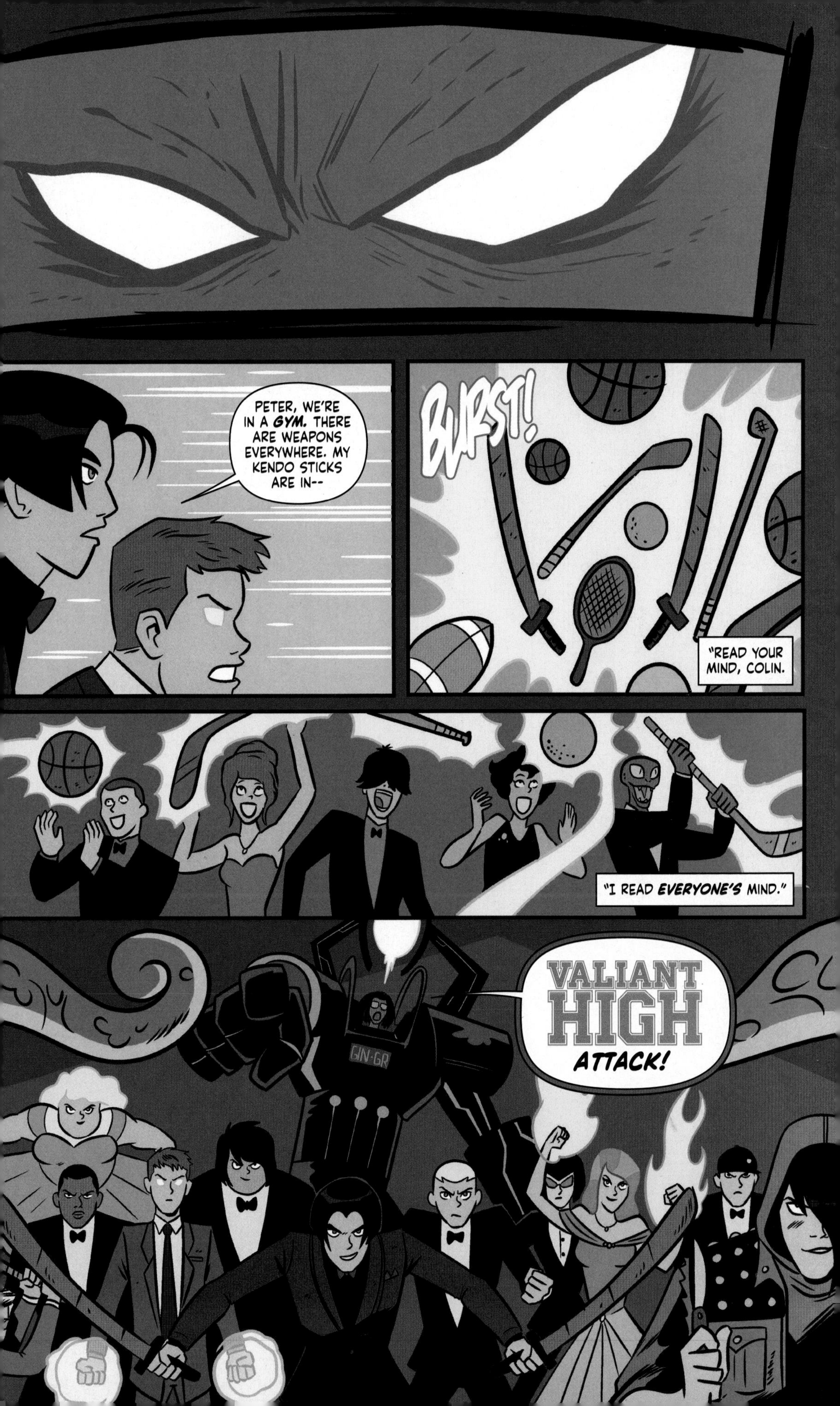
PETER, WE'RE IN A GYM. THERE ARE WEAPONS EVERYWHERE. MY KENDO STICKS ARE IN--
BURST!
"READ YOUR MIND, COLIN.
"I READ EVERYONE'S MIND."
VALIANT HIGH ATTACK!
GIN-GR

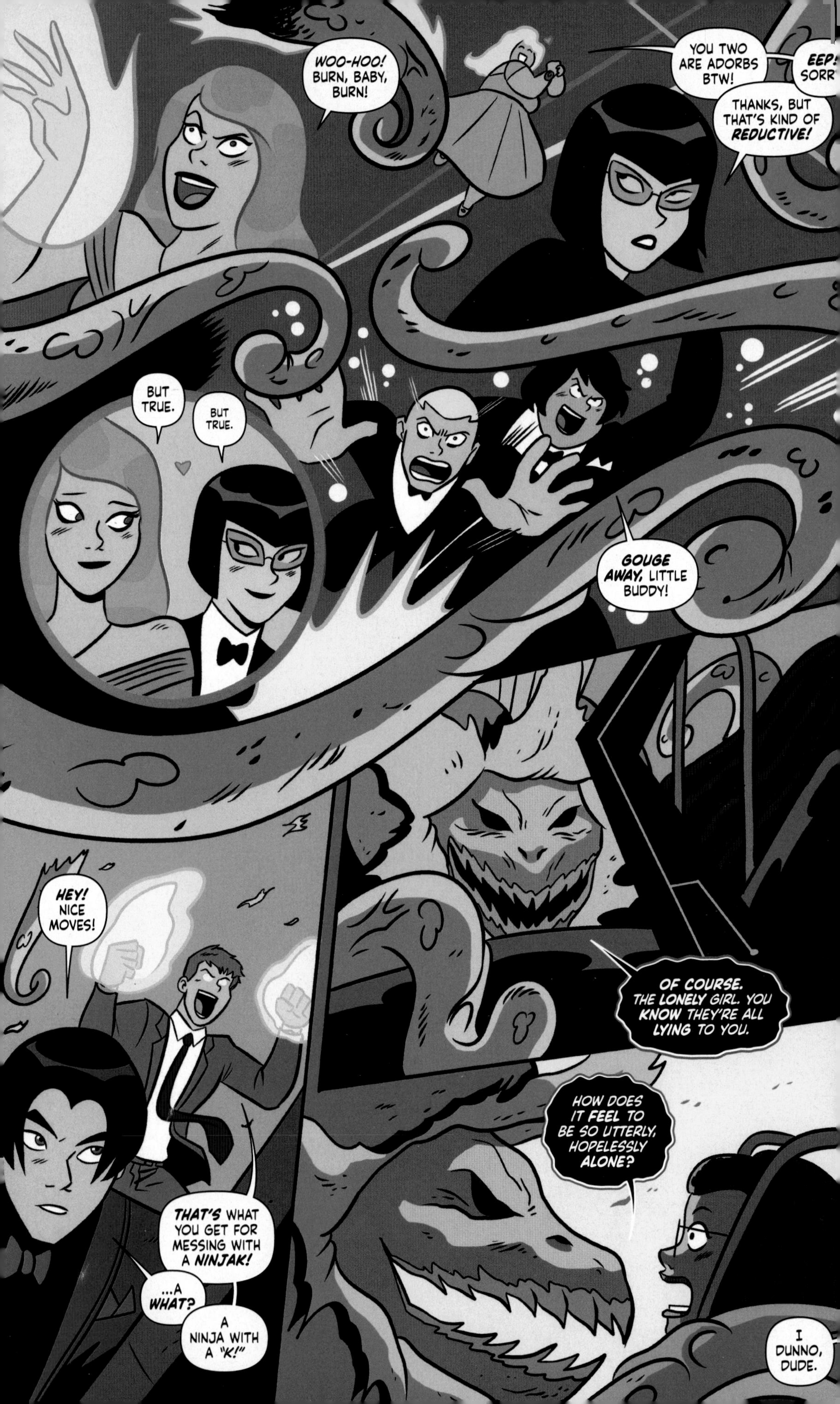
WOO-HOO! BURN, BABY, BURN!
YOU TWO ARE ADORBS BTW!
EEP! SORR
THANKS, BUT THAT'S KIND OF REDUCTIVE!
BUT TRUE.
BUT TRUE.
GOUGE AWAY, LITTLE BUDDY!
HEY! NICE MOVES!
OF COURSE. THE LONELY GIRL. YOU KNOW THEY'RE ALL LYING TO YOU.
HOW DOES IT FEEL TO BE SO UTTERLY, HOPELESSLY ALONE?
THAT'S WHAT YOU GET FOR MESSING WITH A NINJAK!
...A WHAT?
A NINJA WITH A "K!"
I DUNNO, DUDE.

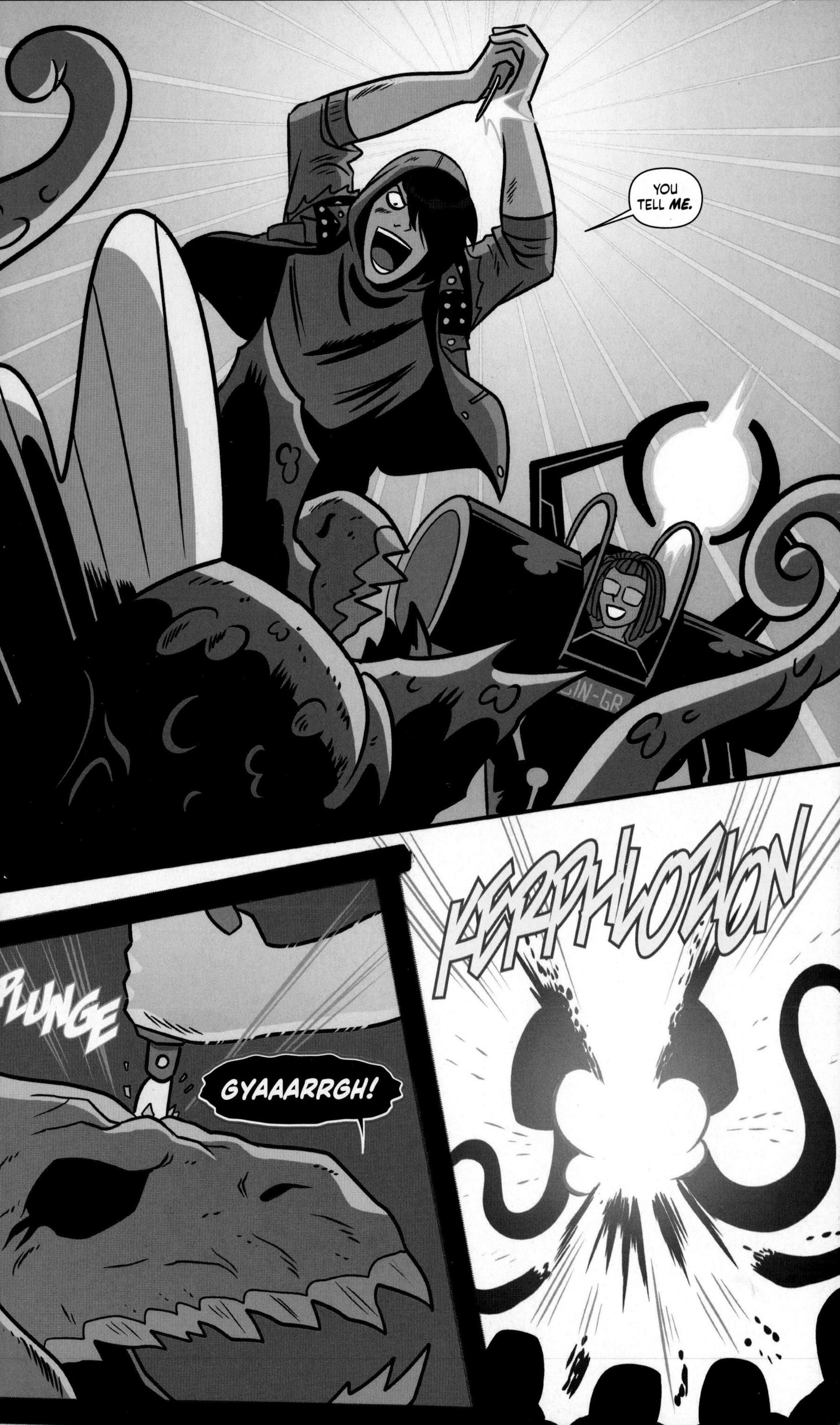
YOU TELL ME.
PLUNGE
GYAAARRGH!
KERPHLOOON

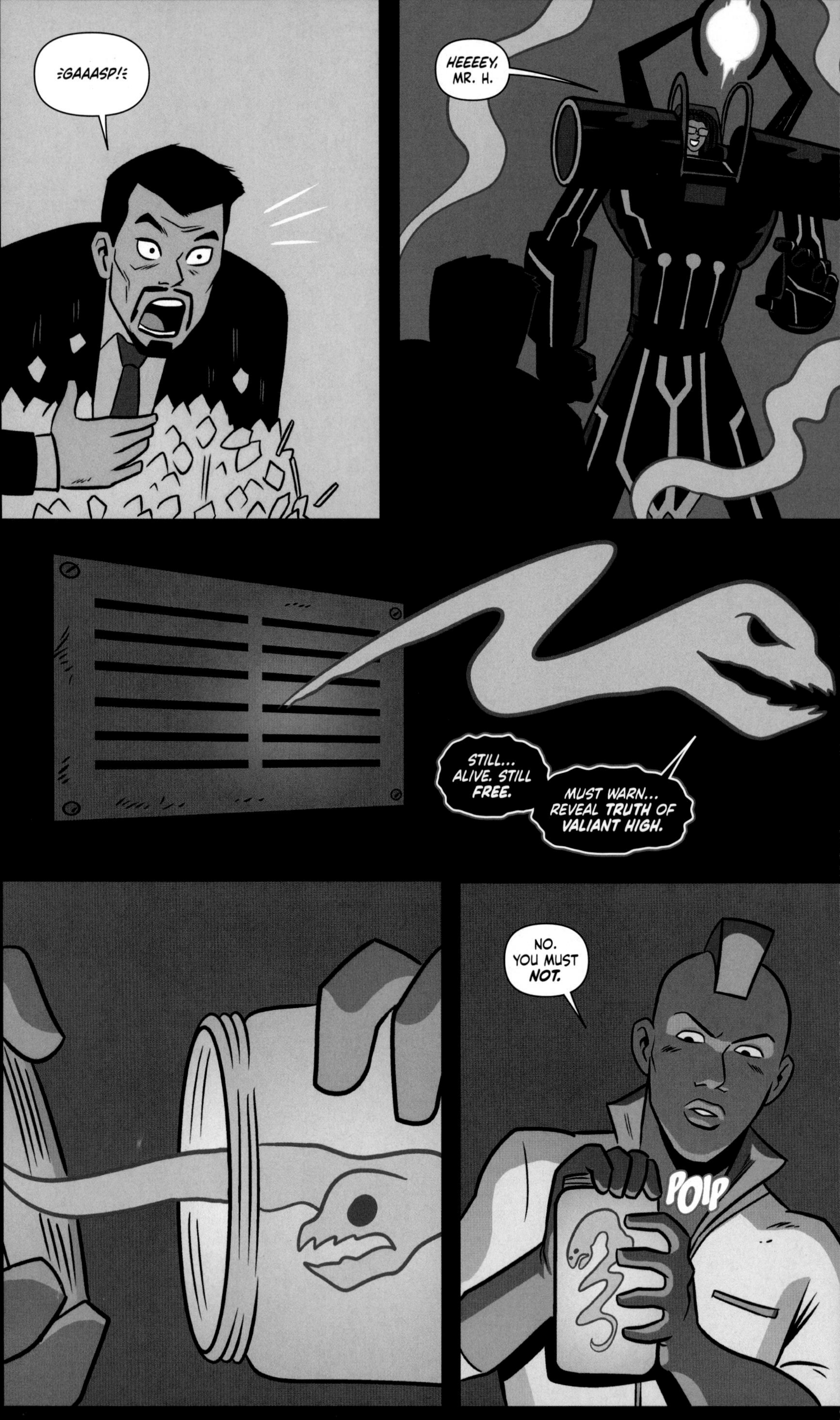
GAAASP!
HEEEEY, MR. H.
STILL... ALIVE. STILL FREE.
MUST WARN... REVEAL TRUTH OF VALIANT HIGH.
NO. YOU MUST NOT.
POIP

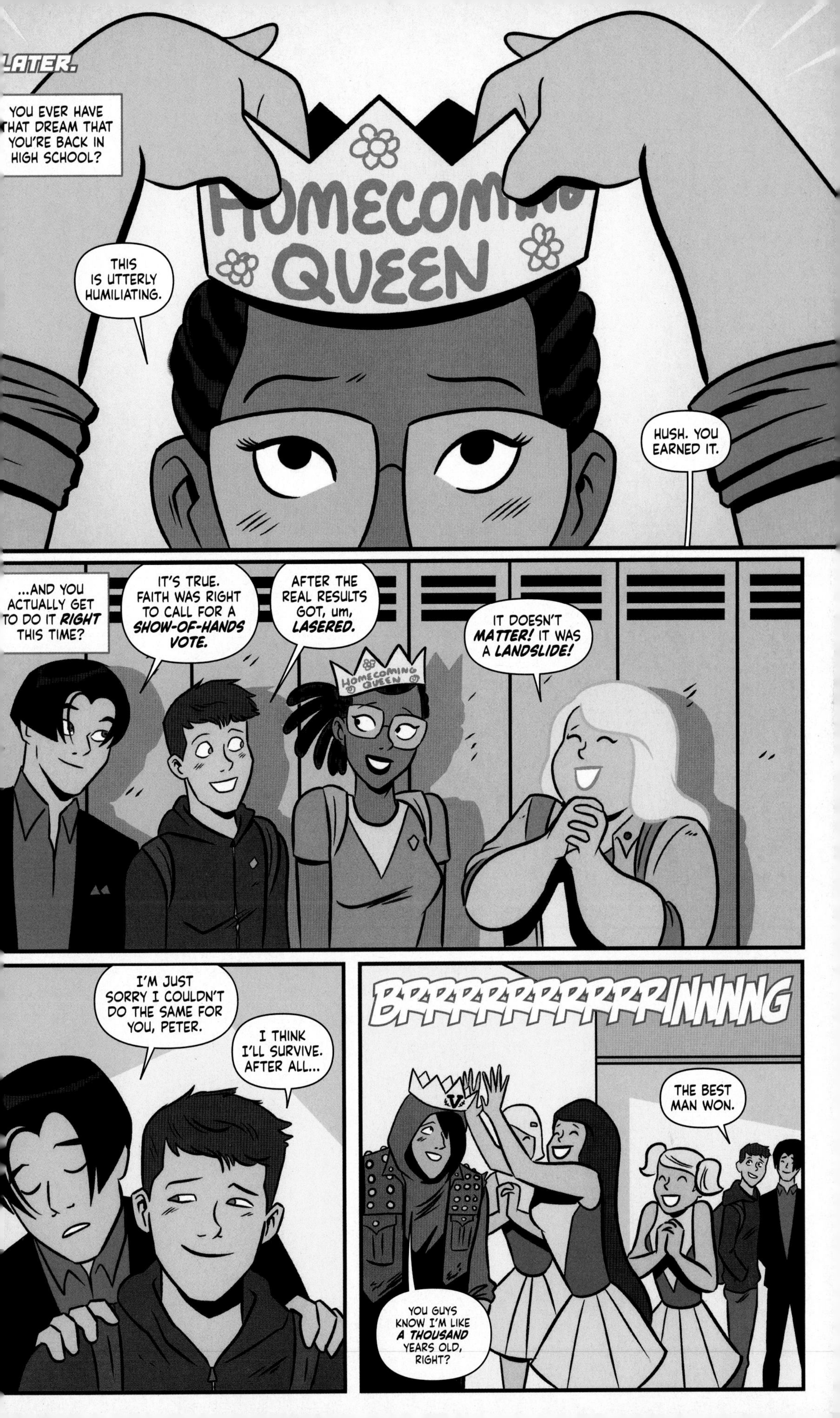
LATER.
YOU EVER HAVE THAT DREAM THAT YOU'RE BACK IN HIGH SCHOOL?
HOMECOMING QUEEN
THIS IS UTTERLY HUMILIATING.
HUSH. YOU EARNED IT.
...AND YOU ACTUALLY GET TO DO IT RIGHT THIS TIME?
IT'S TRUE. FAITH WAS RIGHT TO CALL FOR A SHOW-OF-HANDS VOTE.
AFTER THE REAL RESULTS GOT, um, LASERED.
IT DOESN'T MATTER! IT WAS A LANDSLIDE!
HOMECOMING QUEEN
I'M JUST SORRY I COULDN'T DO THE SAME FOR YOU, PETER.
I THINK I'LL SURVIVE. AFTER ALL...
BRRRRRRRRRRRRRINNNNG
THE BEST MAN WON.
YOU GUYS KNOW I'M LIKE A THOUSAND YEARS OLD, RIGHT?

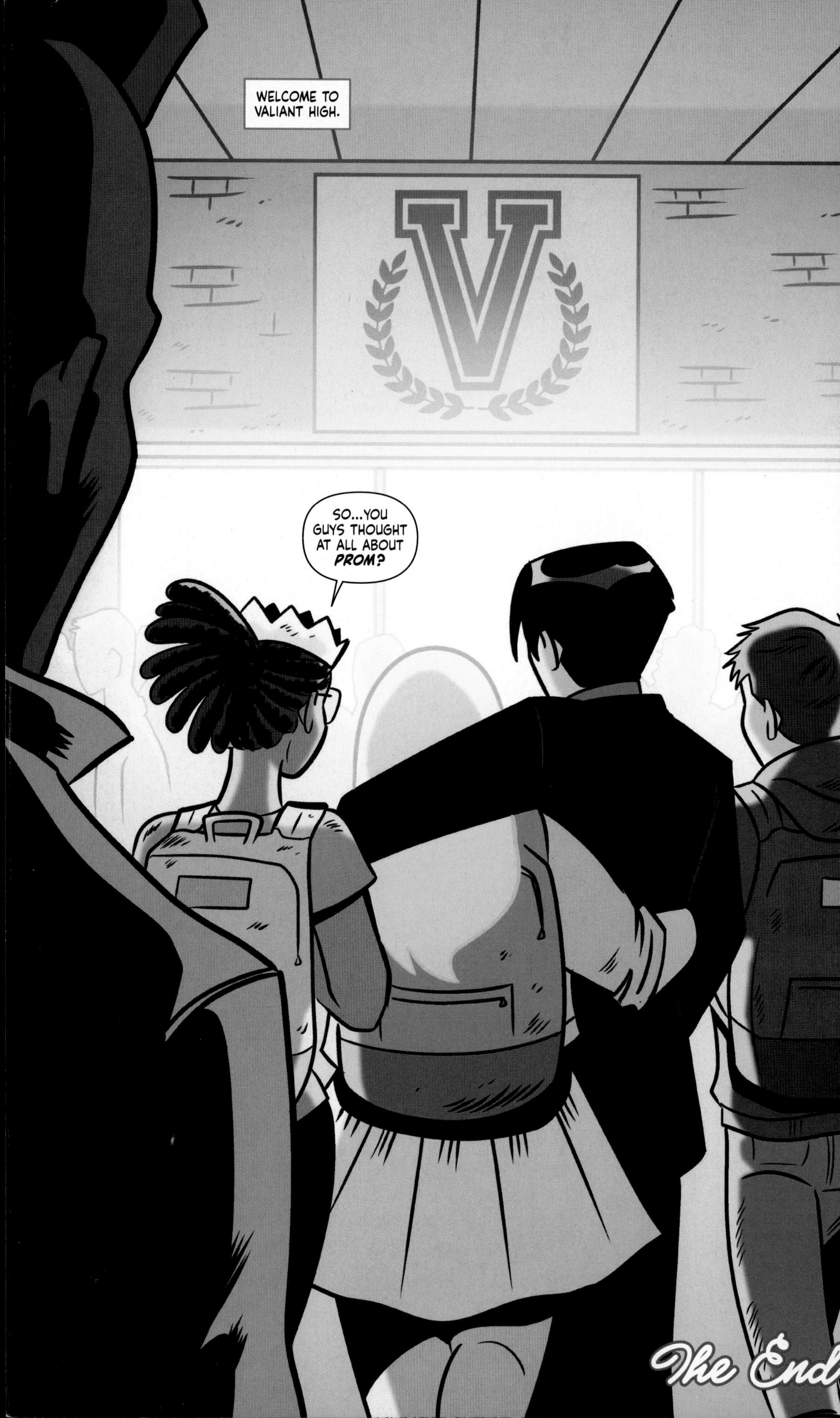
WELCOME TO VALIANT HIGH.
SO...YOU GUYS THOUGHT AT ALL ABOUT *PROM?*
The End

GALLERY

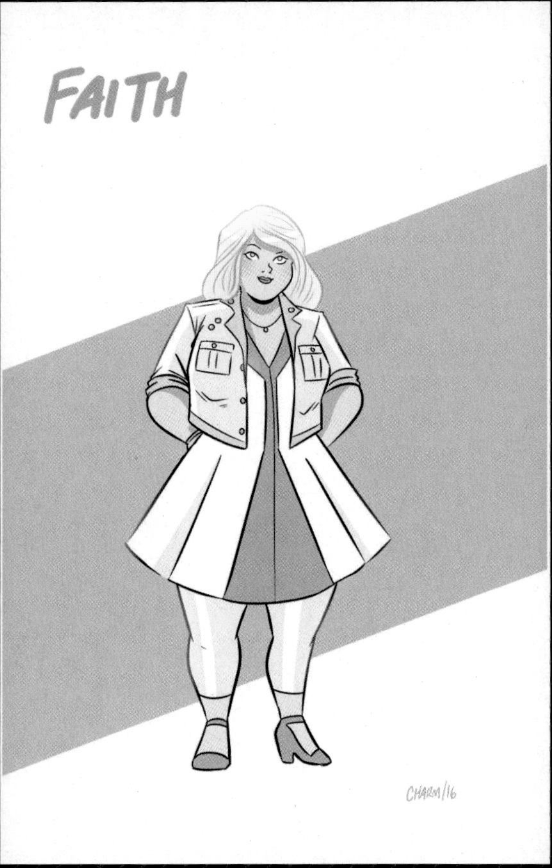
FAITH
CHARM/16

FAITH
Character design by DEREK CHARM

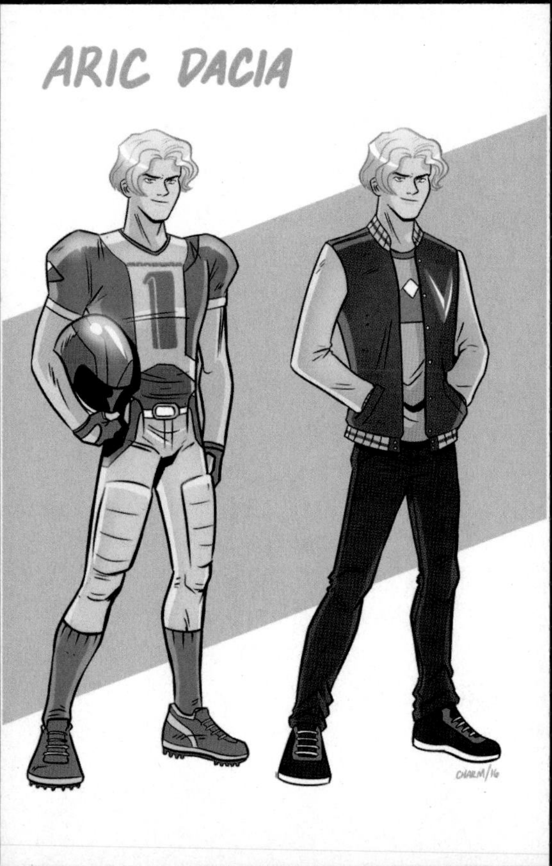
ARIC DACIA
CHARM/16

ARIC DACIA
Character designs by DEREK CHARM

COLIN KING
Character designs by DEREK CHARM

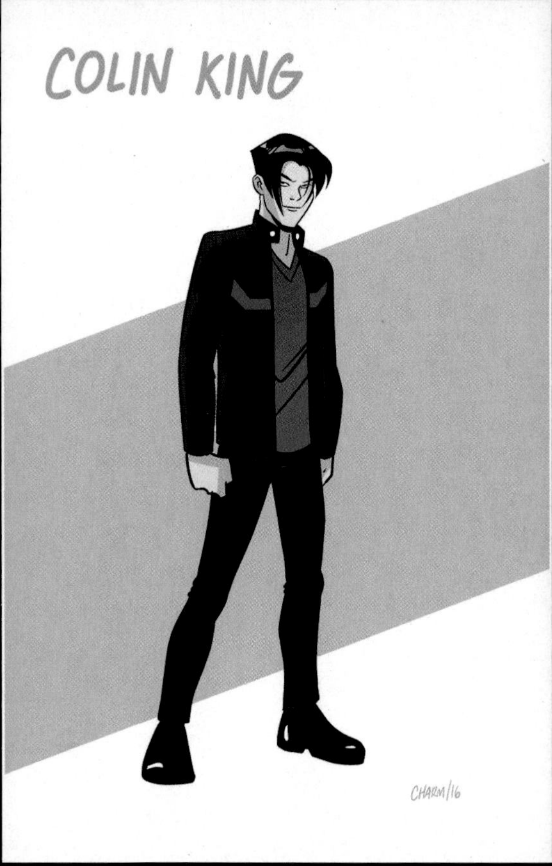
COLIN KING
CHARM/16

PETER STANCHEK
Character design by DEREK CHARM

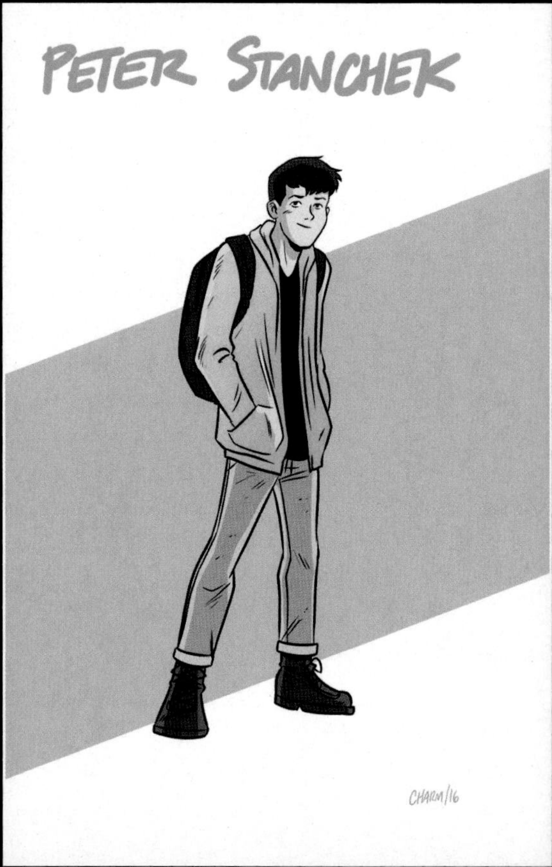
PETER STANCHEK
CHARM/16

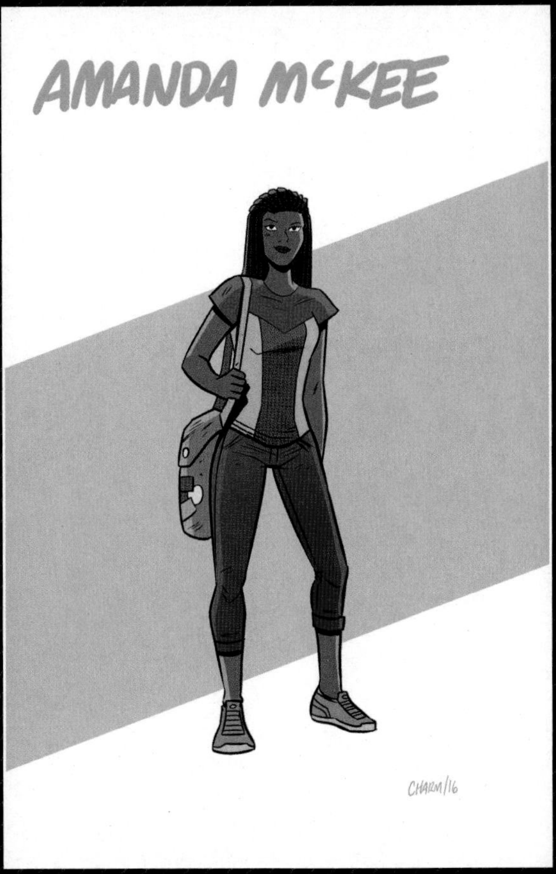
AMANDA McKEE
CHARM/16

AMANDA MCKEE
Character design by DEREK CHARM

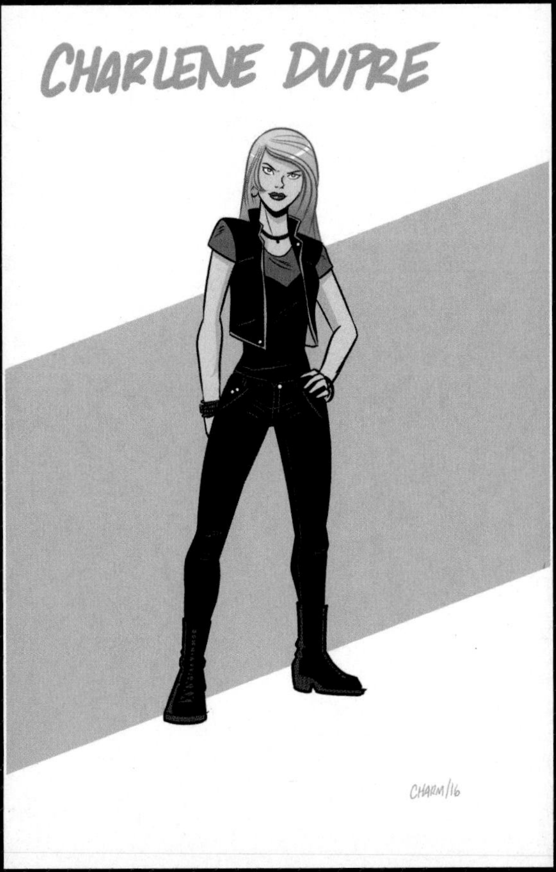
CHARLENE DUPRE
CHARM/16

CHARLENE DUPRE
Character design by DEREK CHARM

VALIANT HIGH #1 COVER
Art by DAVID LAFUENTE

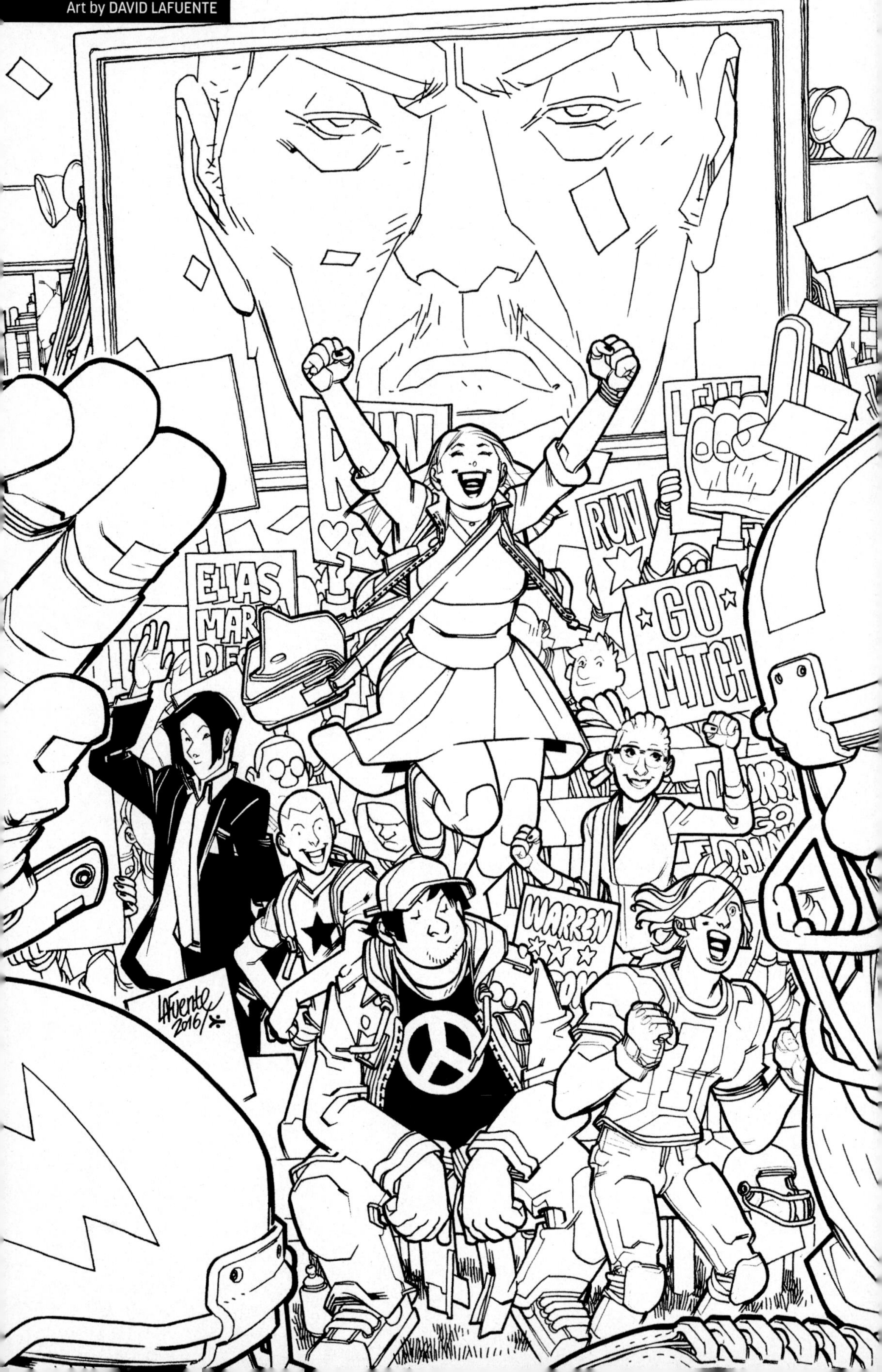
RUN
ELIAS
RUN
GO MITCH
WARREN
LAFUENTE 2016

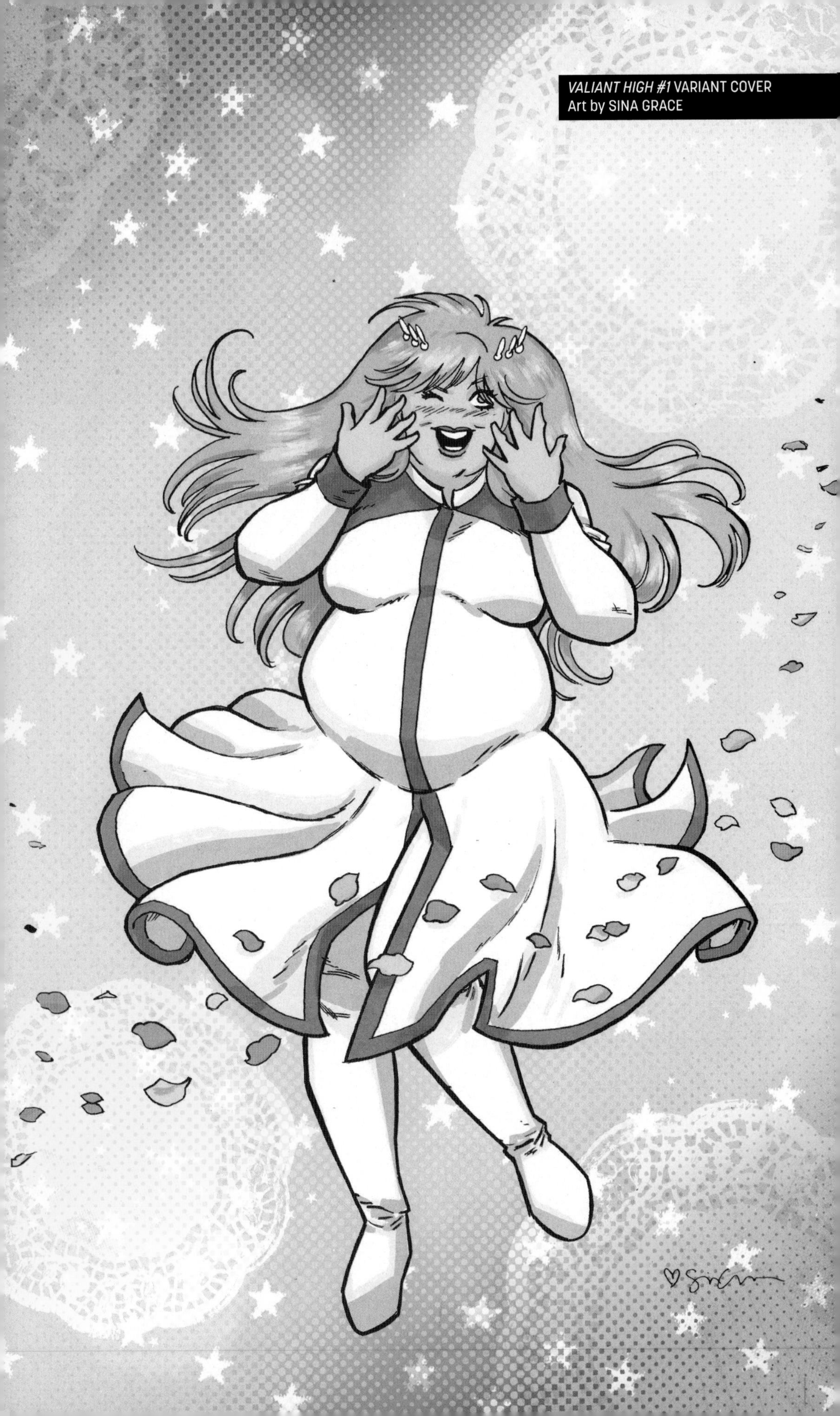

VALIANT HIGH #1 VARIANT COVER
Art by SINA GRACE

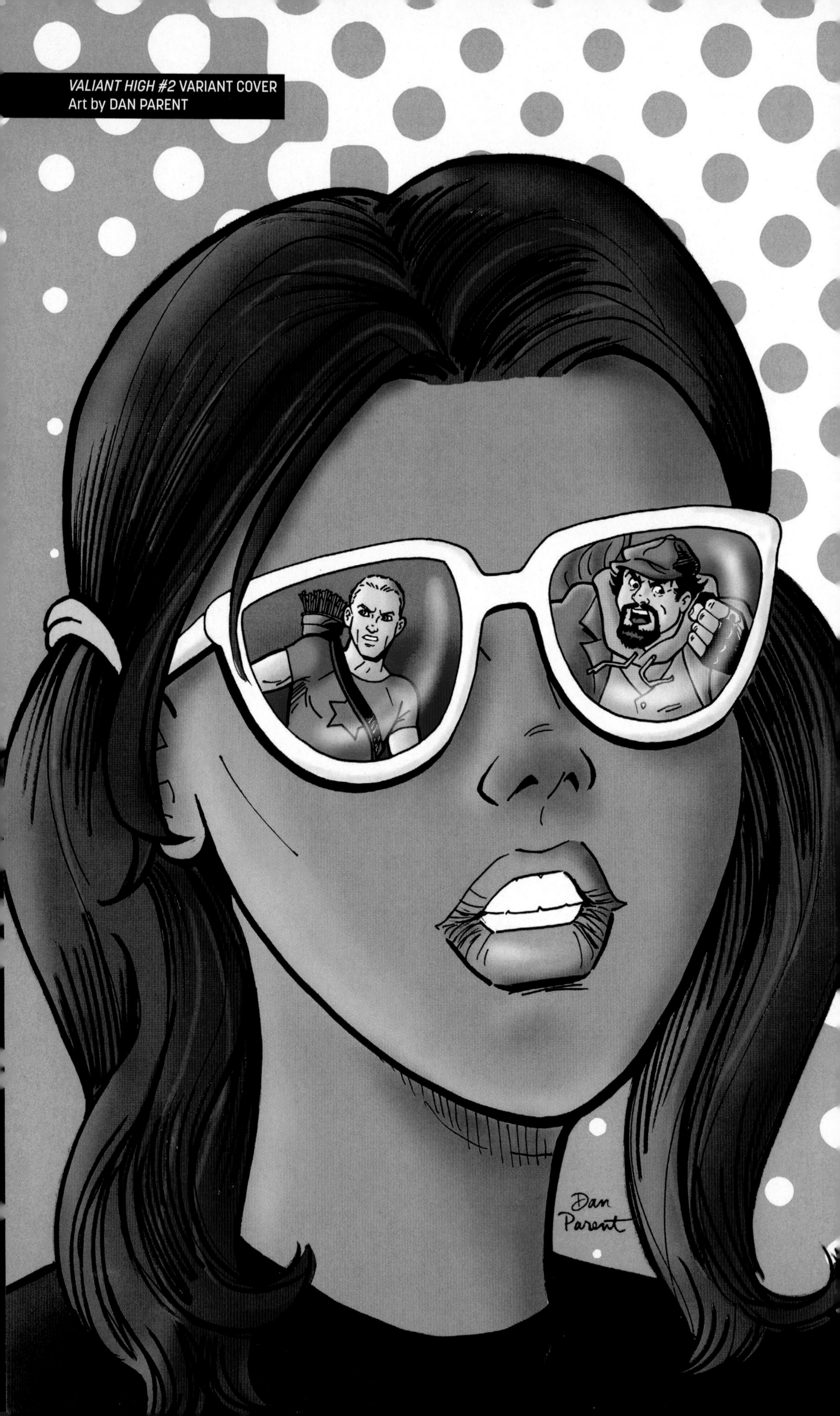
Dan
Parent

VALIANT HIGH #2 VARIANT COVER
Art by DAN PARENT

VALIANT HIGH #3 VARIANT COVER
Art by IRENE LEE

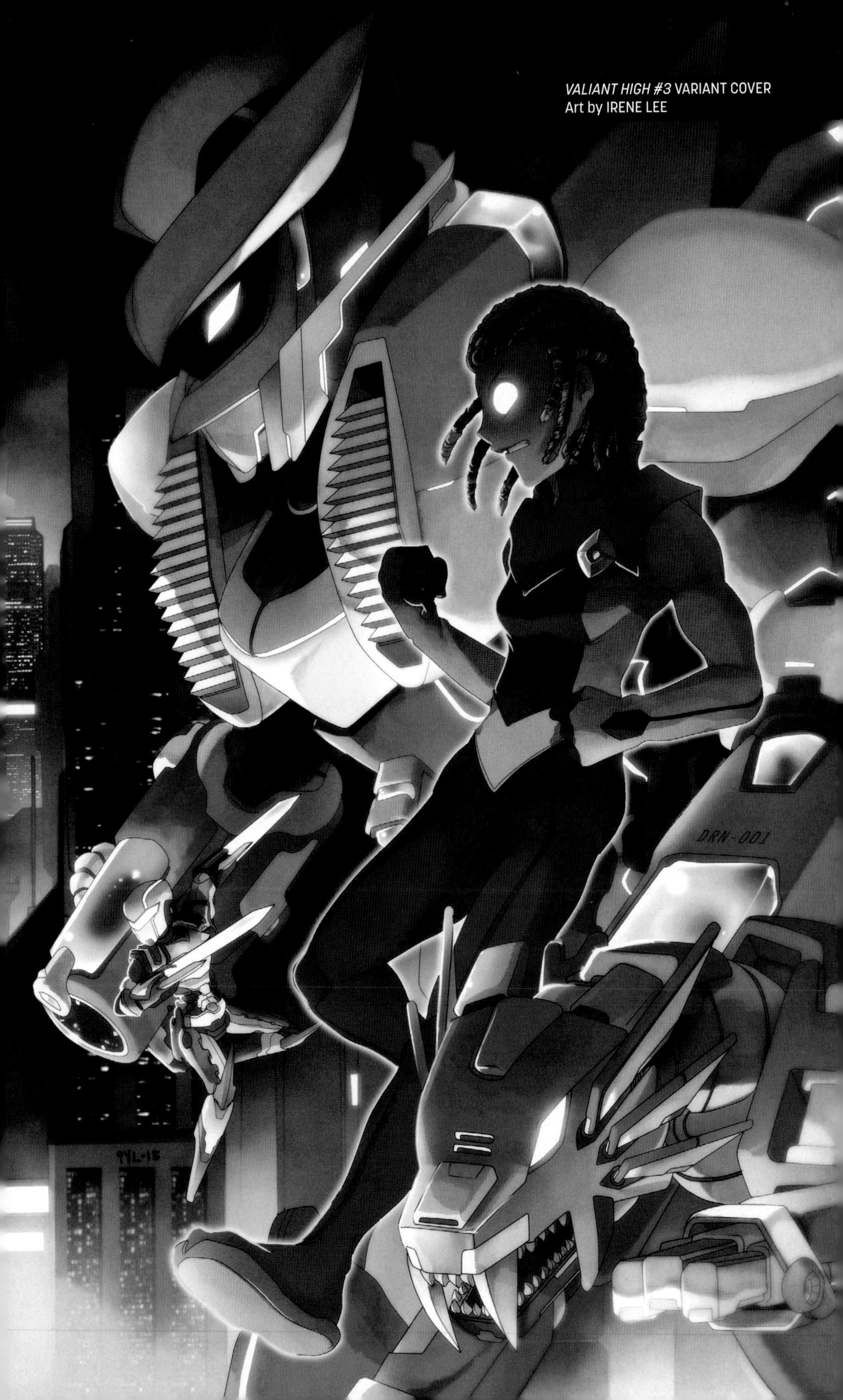
DRN-001

VALIANT HIGH #1, pages 16, 17, and 18 (facing)
Art by DEREK CHARM

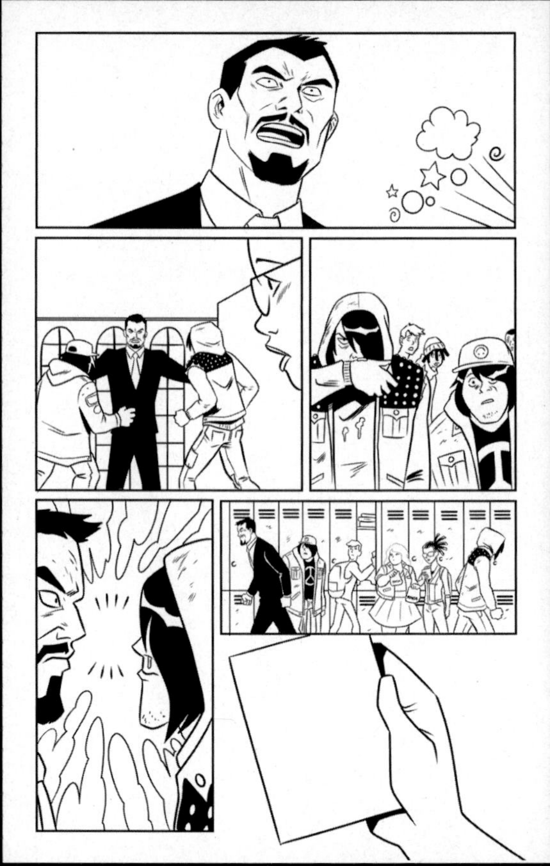

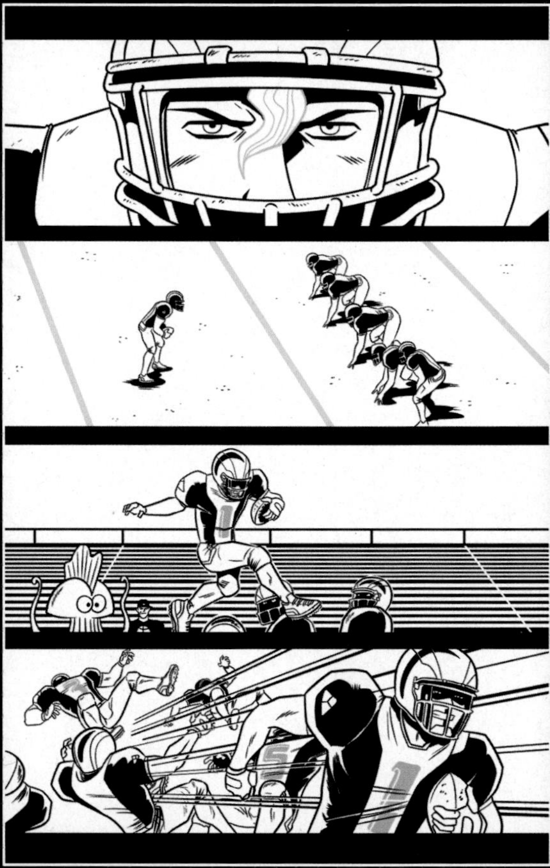

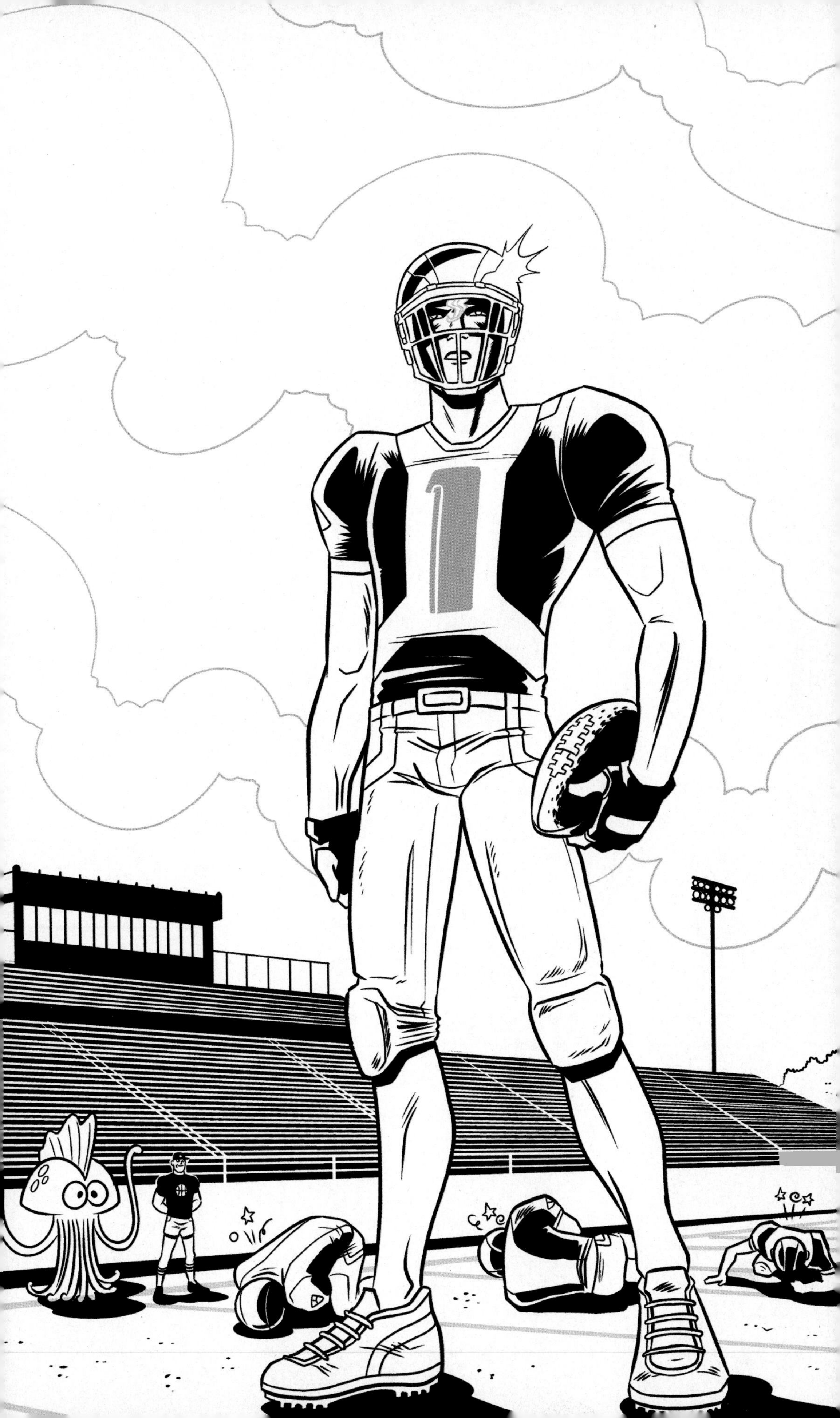

VALIANT HIGH #1, pages 20, 21, and 22 (facing)
Art by DEREK CHARM

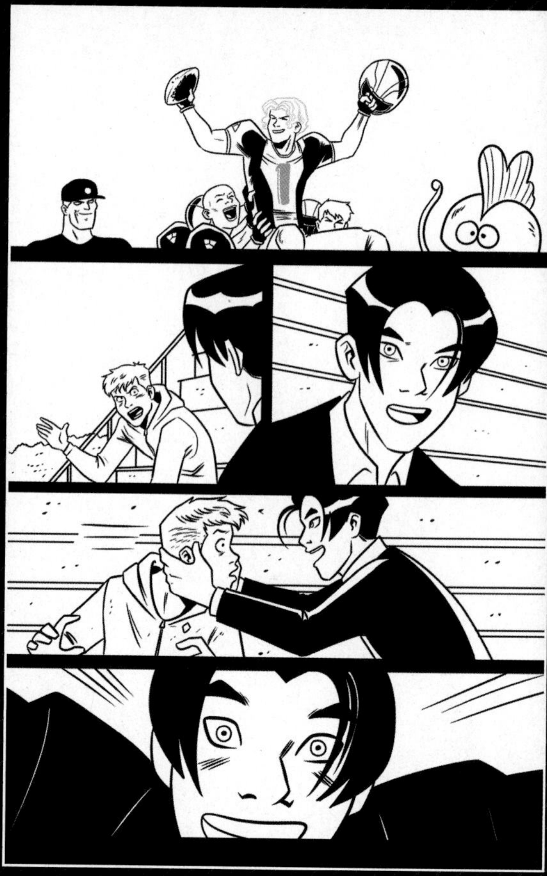

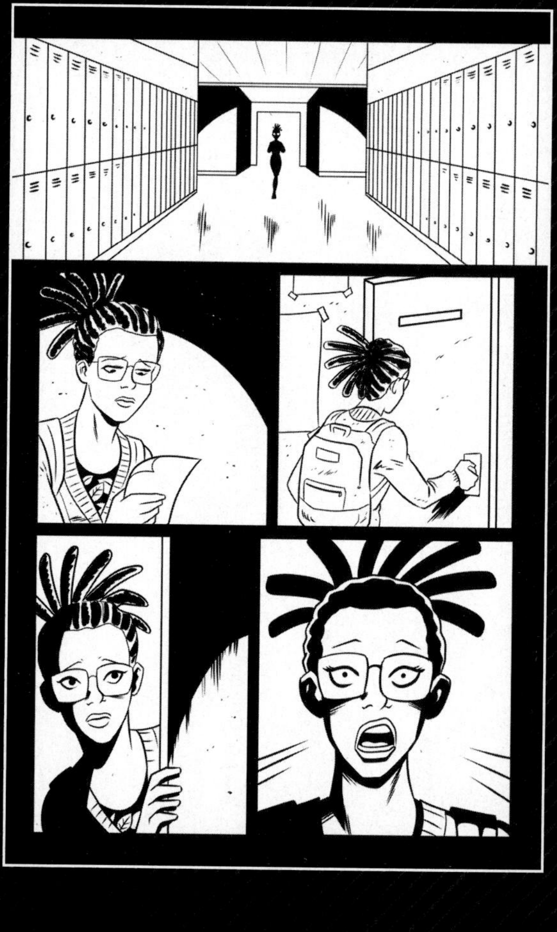

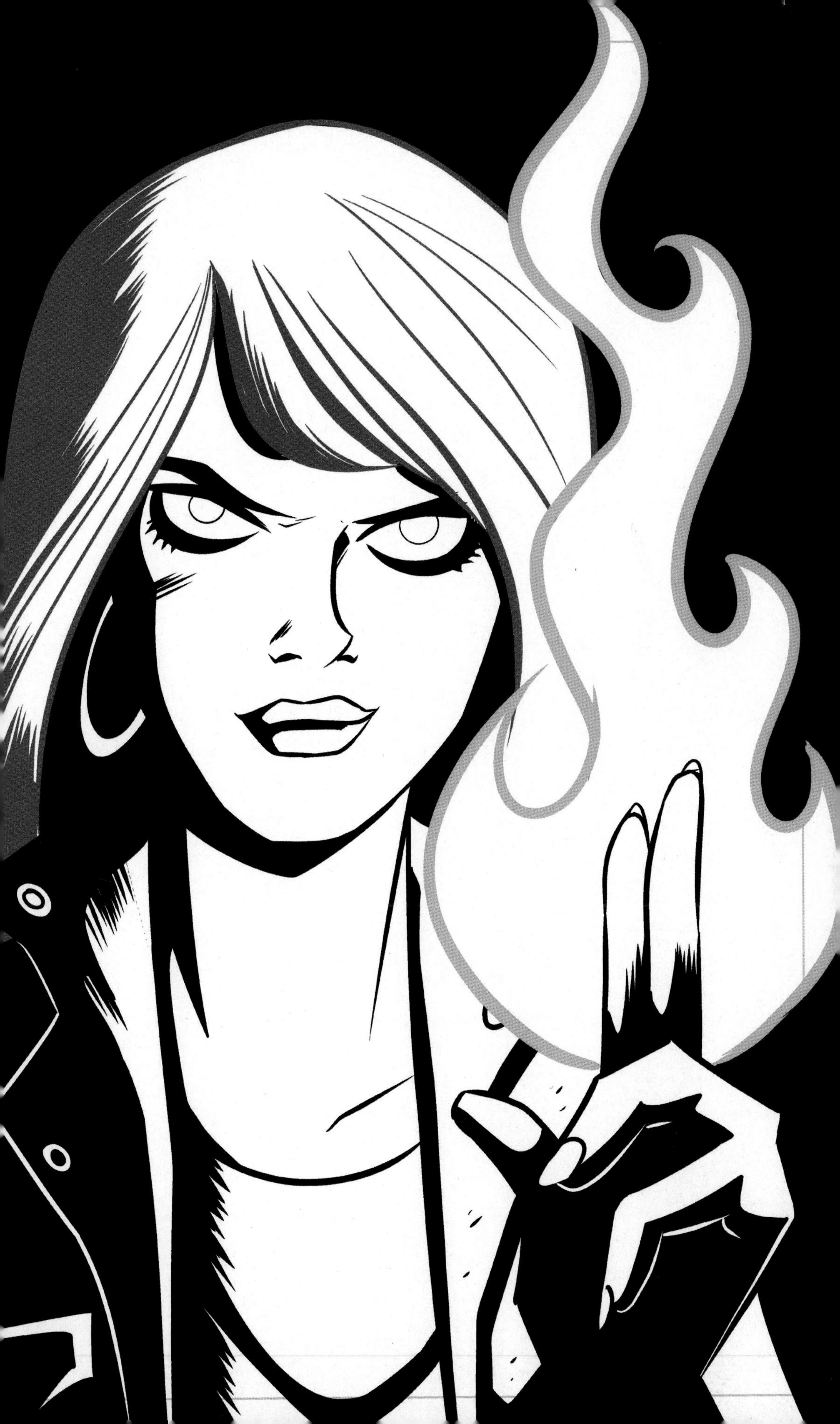

VALIANT HIGH #2, pages 6, 7, and 8 (facing)
Art by DEREK CHARM

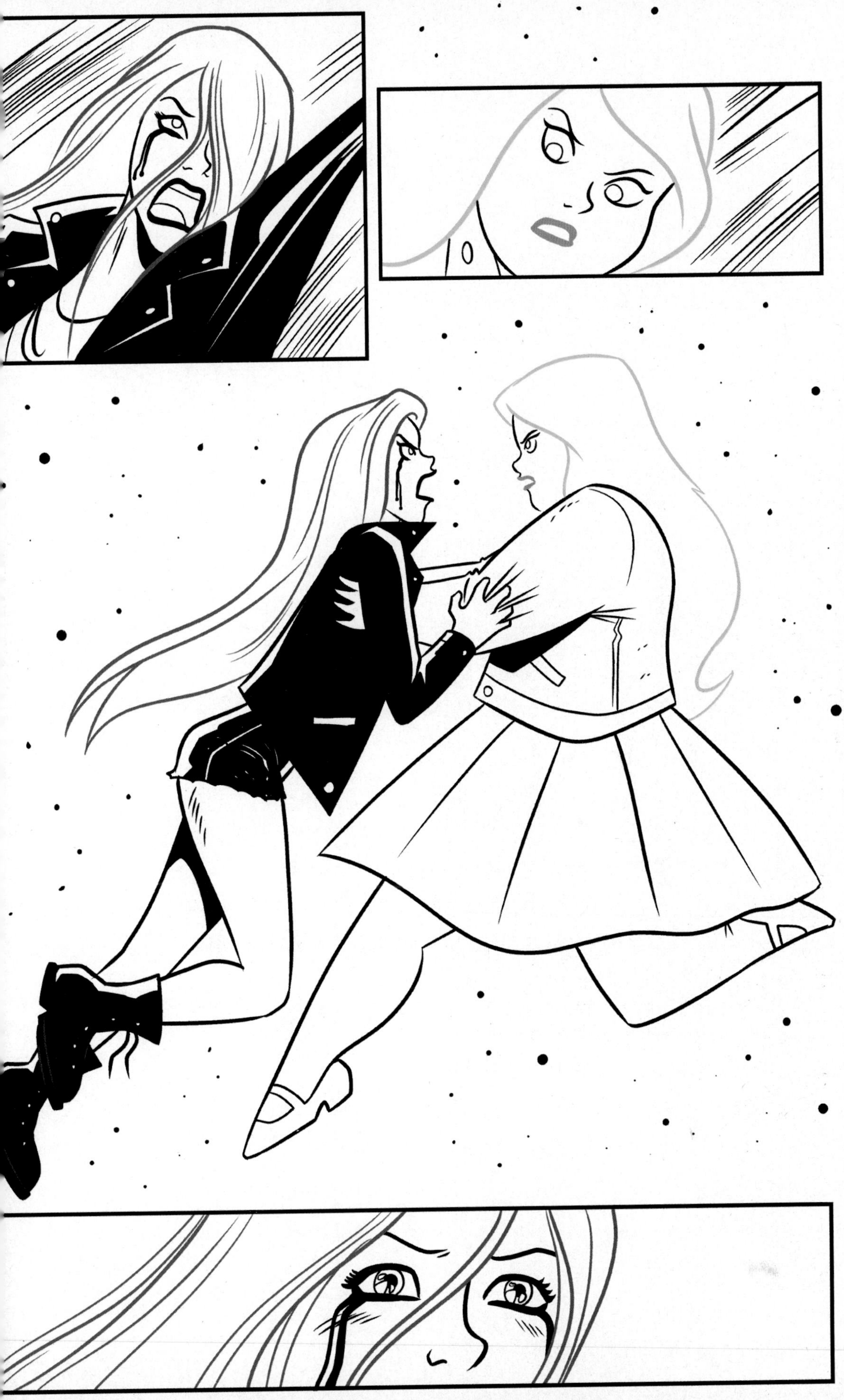

VALIANT HIGH #2, pages 11, 12, and 13 (facing)
Art by DEREK CHARM

V
V

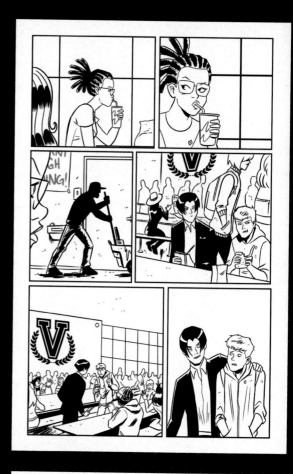

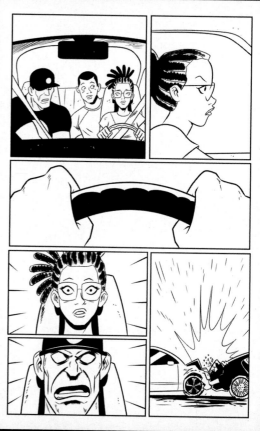

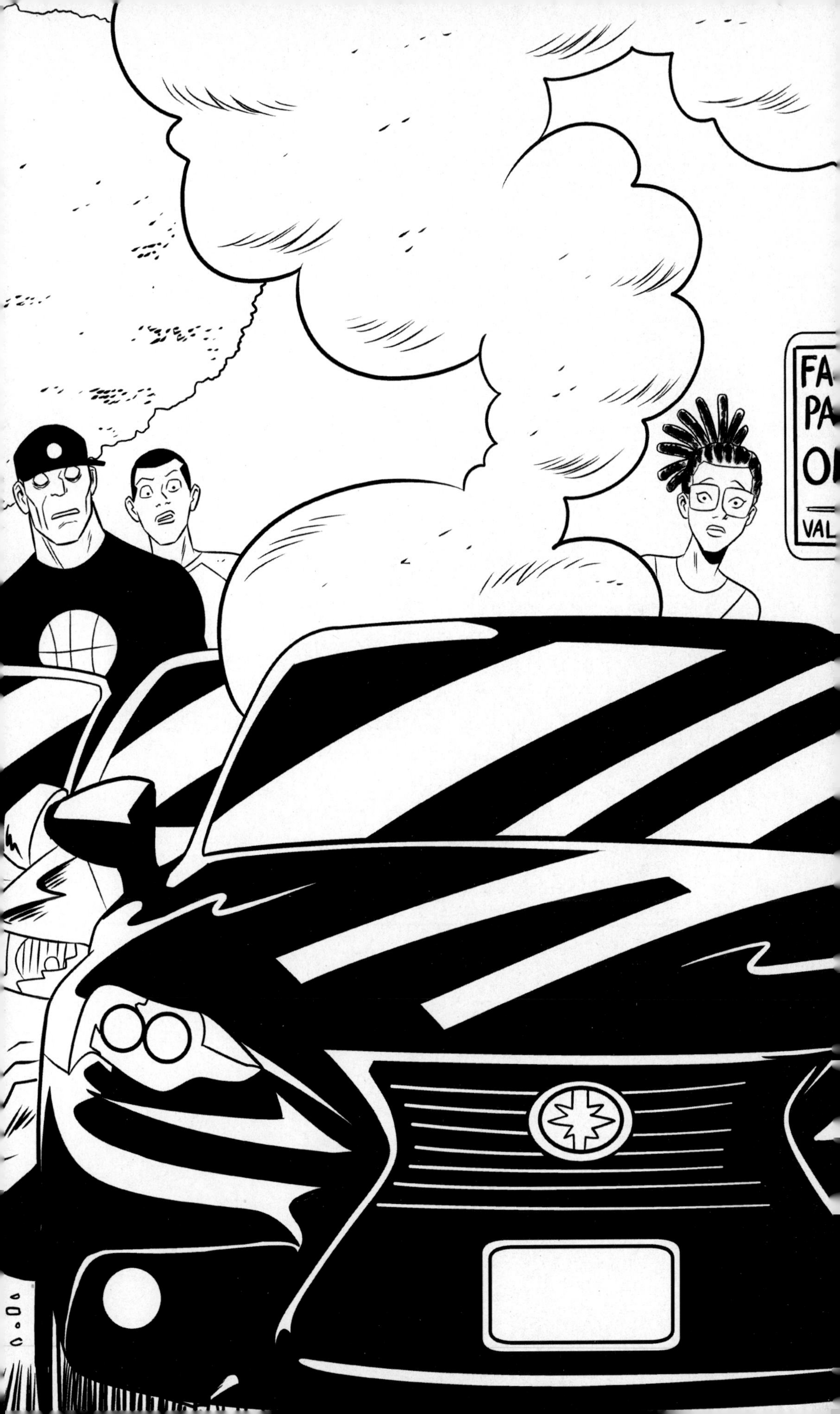

VALIANT HIGH #3, pages 1, 2, and 3 (facing)
Art by DEREK CHARM

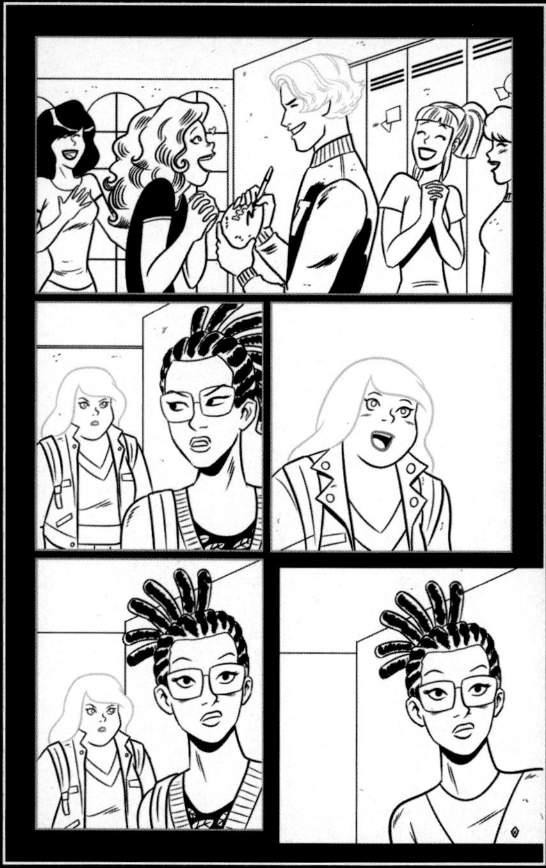

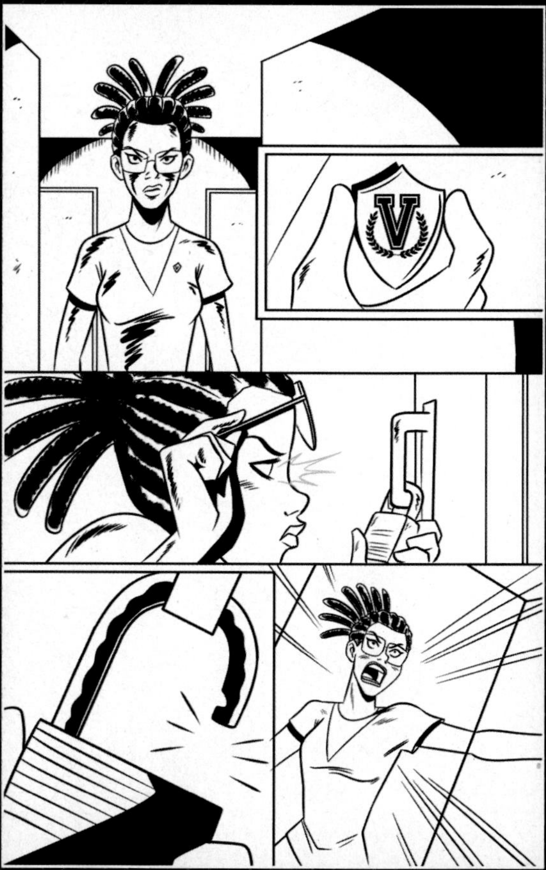

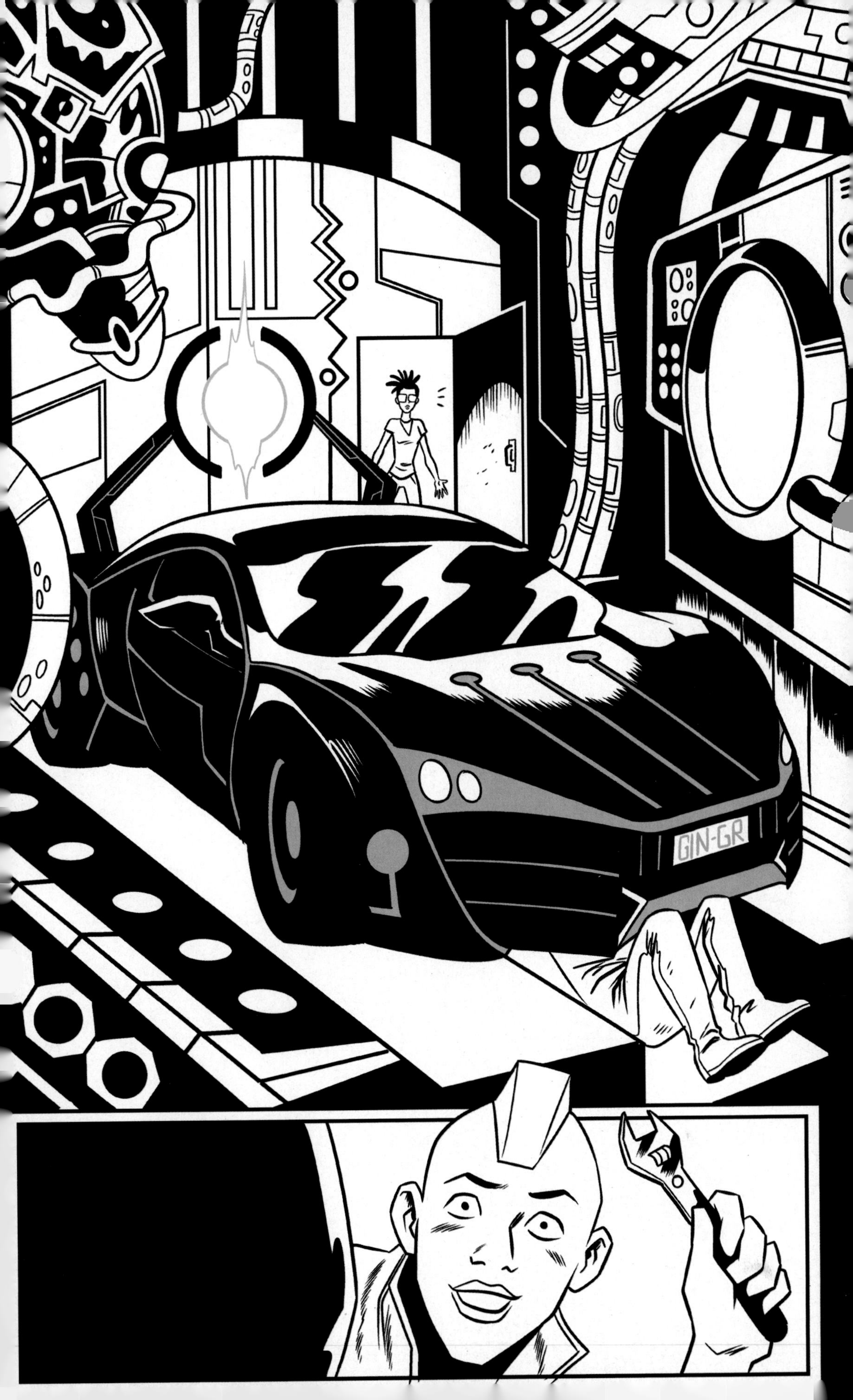
GIN-GR

VALIANT HIGH #3, pages 10, 11, and 12 (facing)
Art by DEREK CHARM

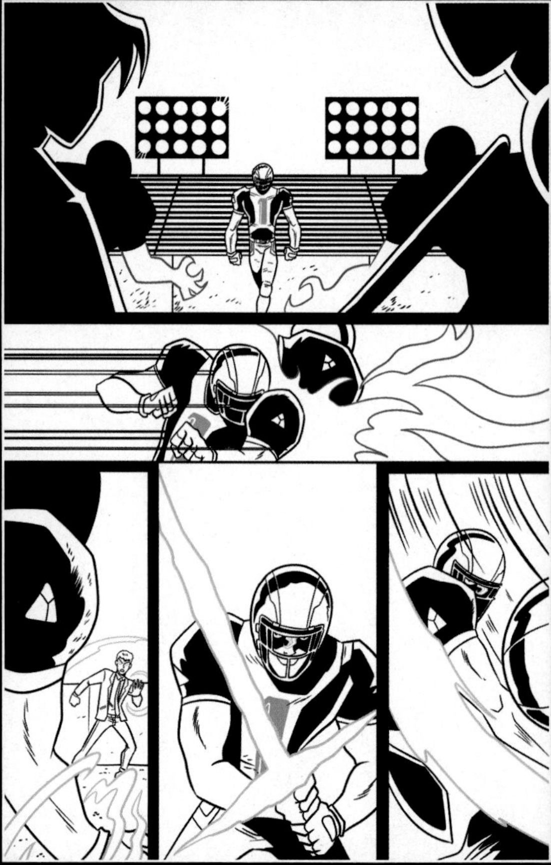

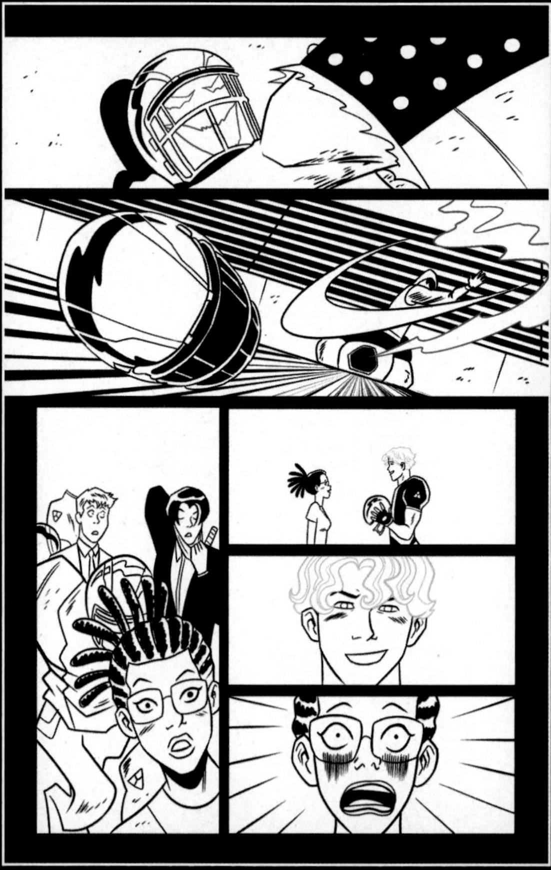

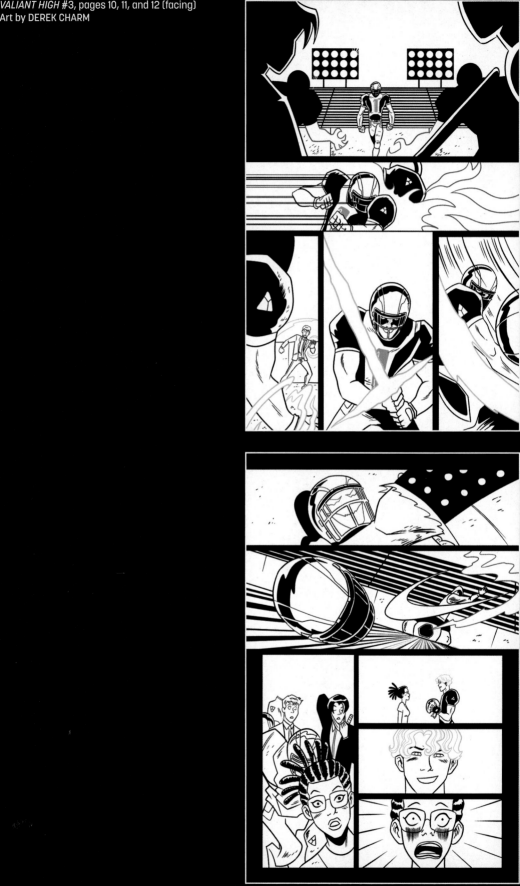

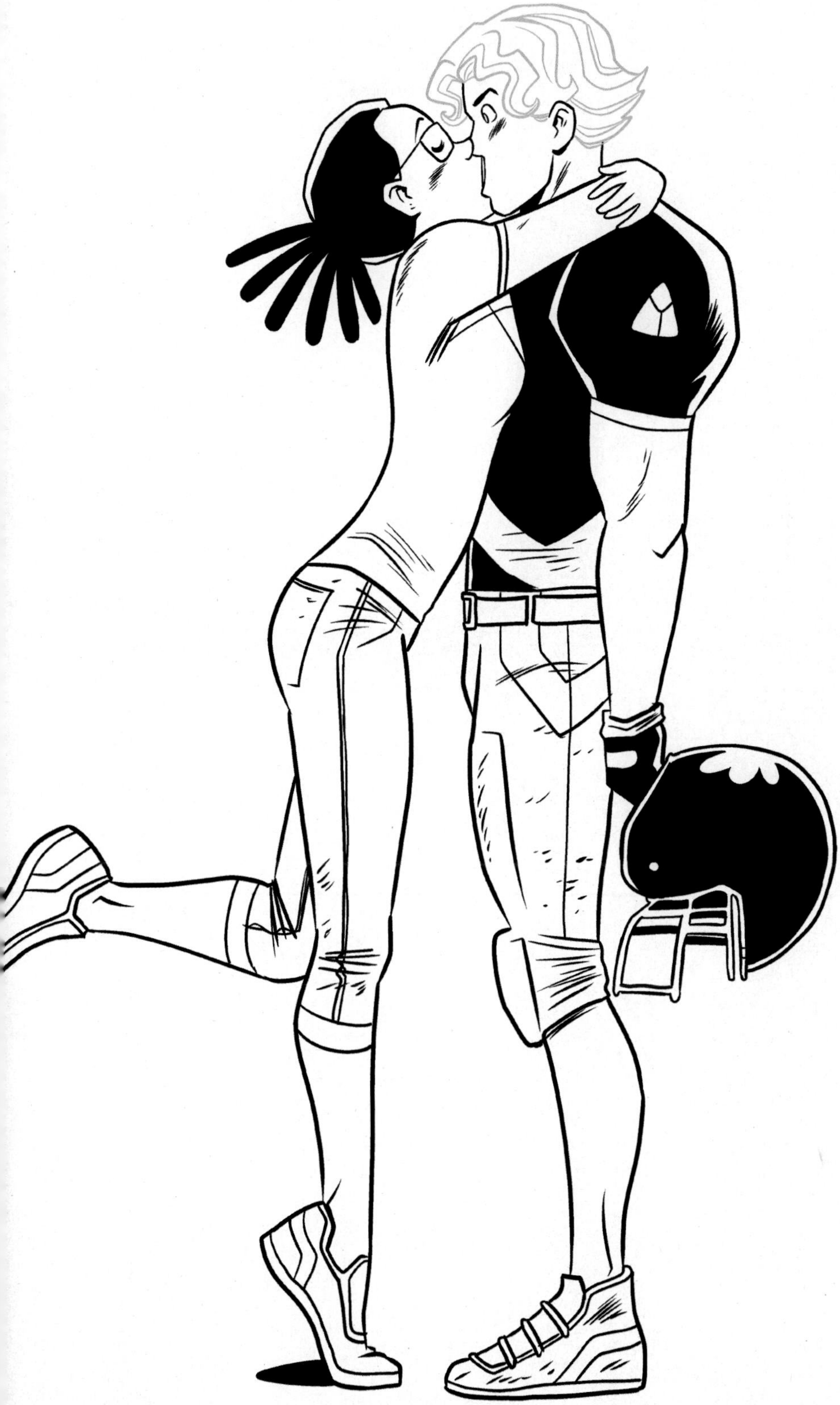

VALIANT HIGH #4, pages 2, 3, and 4 (facing)
Art by DEREK CHARM

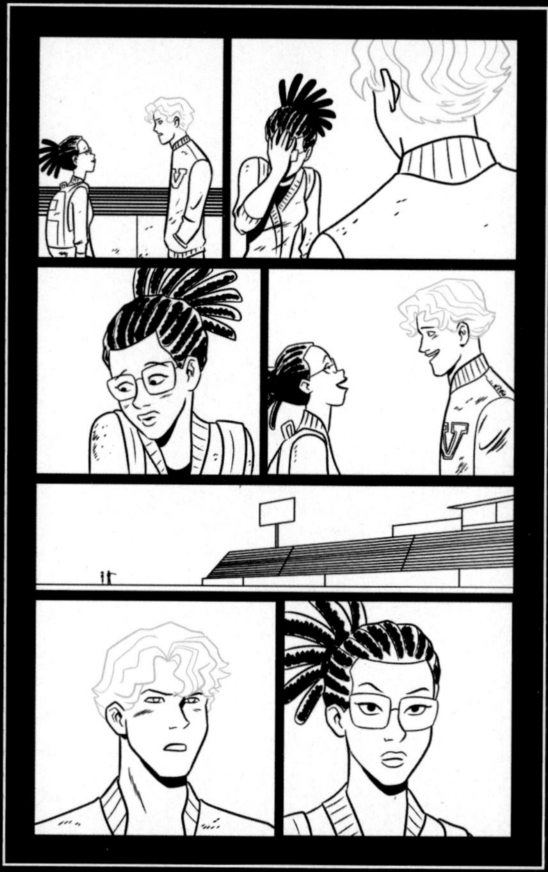

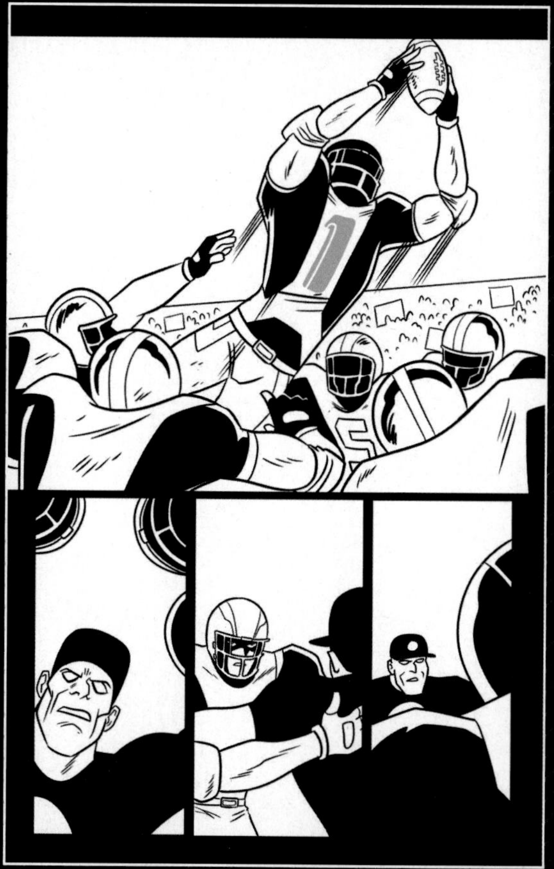

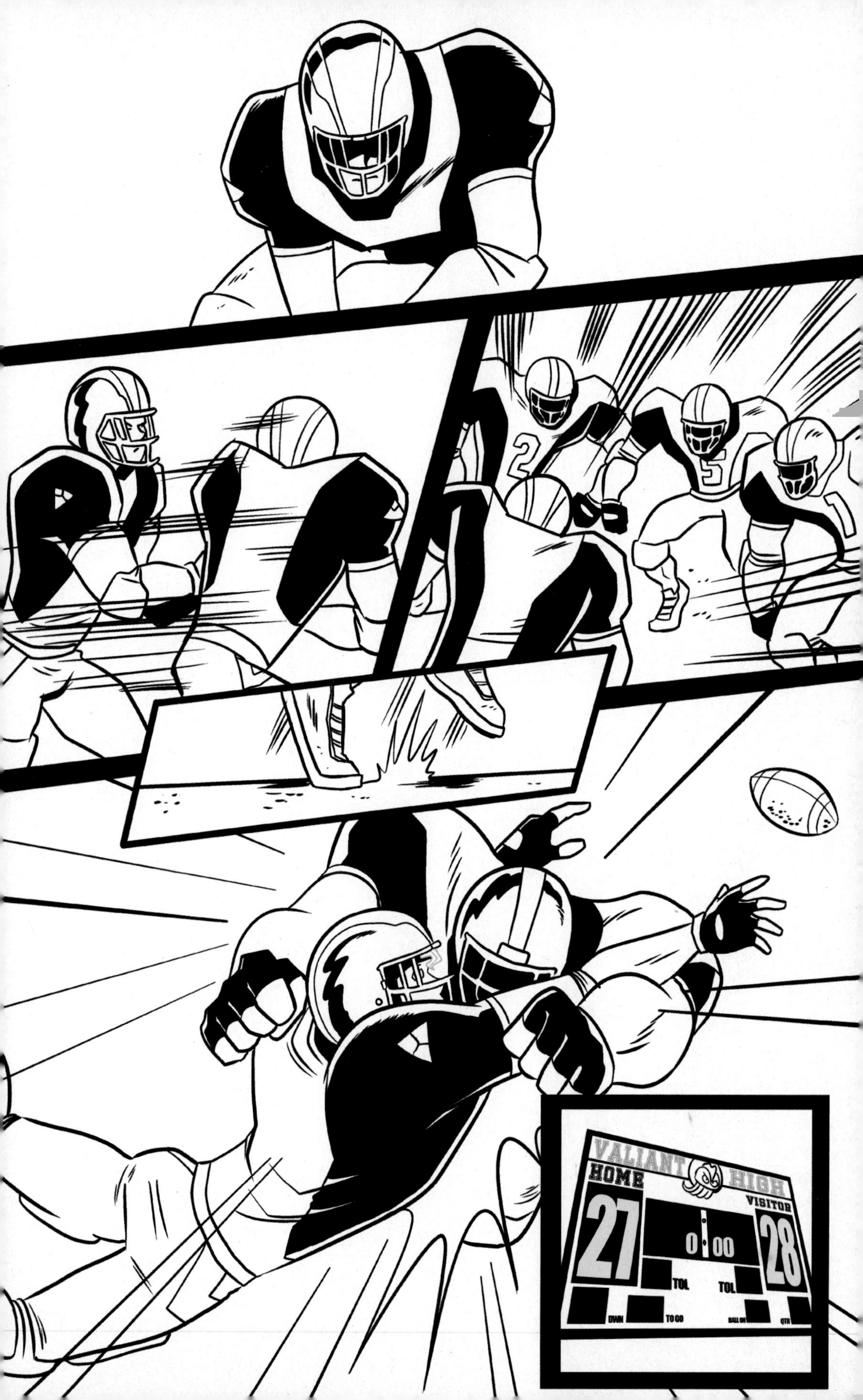
VALIANT HIGH
HOME
VISITOR
27
0:00
28
TOL
TOL
DWN
TO GO
BALL ON
QTR

VALIANT HIGH #4, pages 14, 15, and 16 (facing)
Art by DEREK CHARM

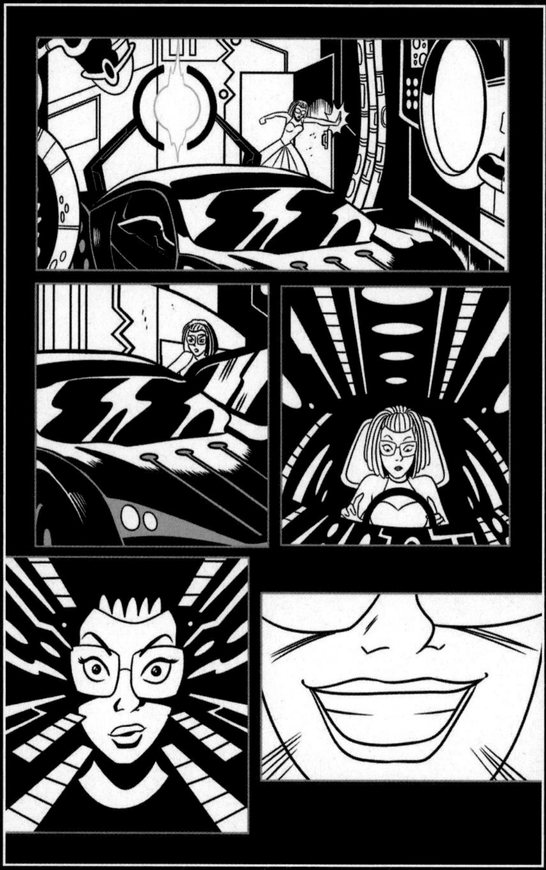

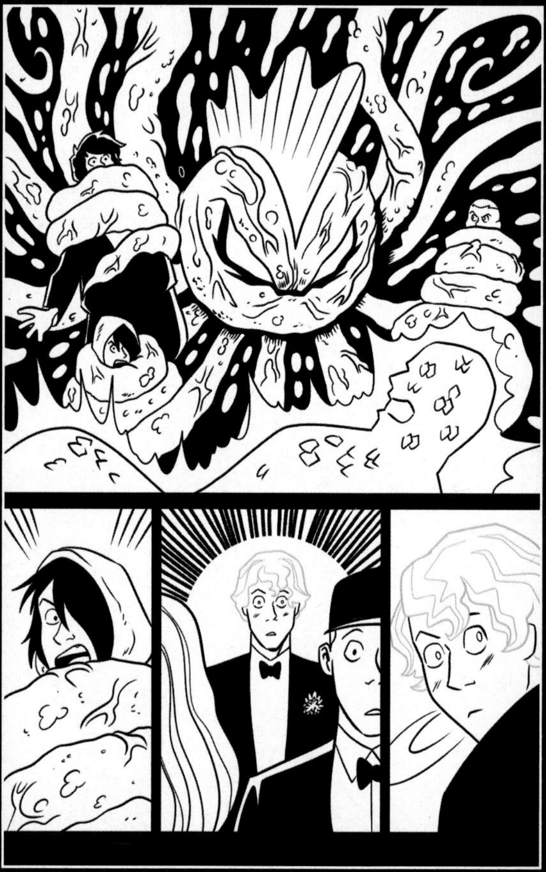

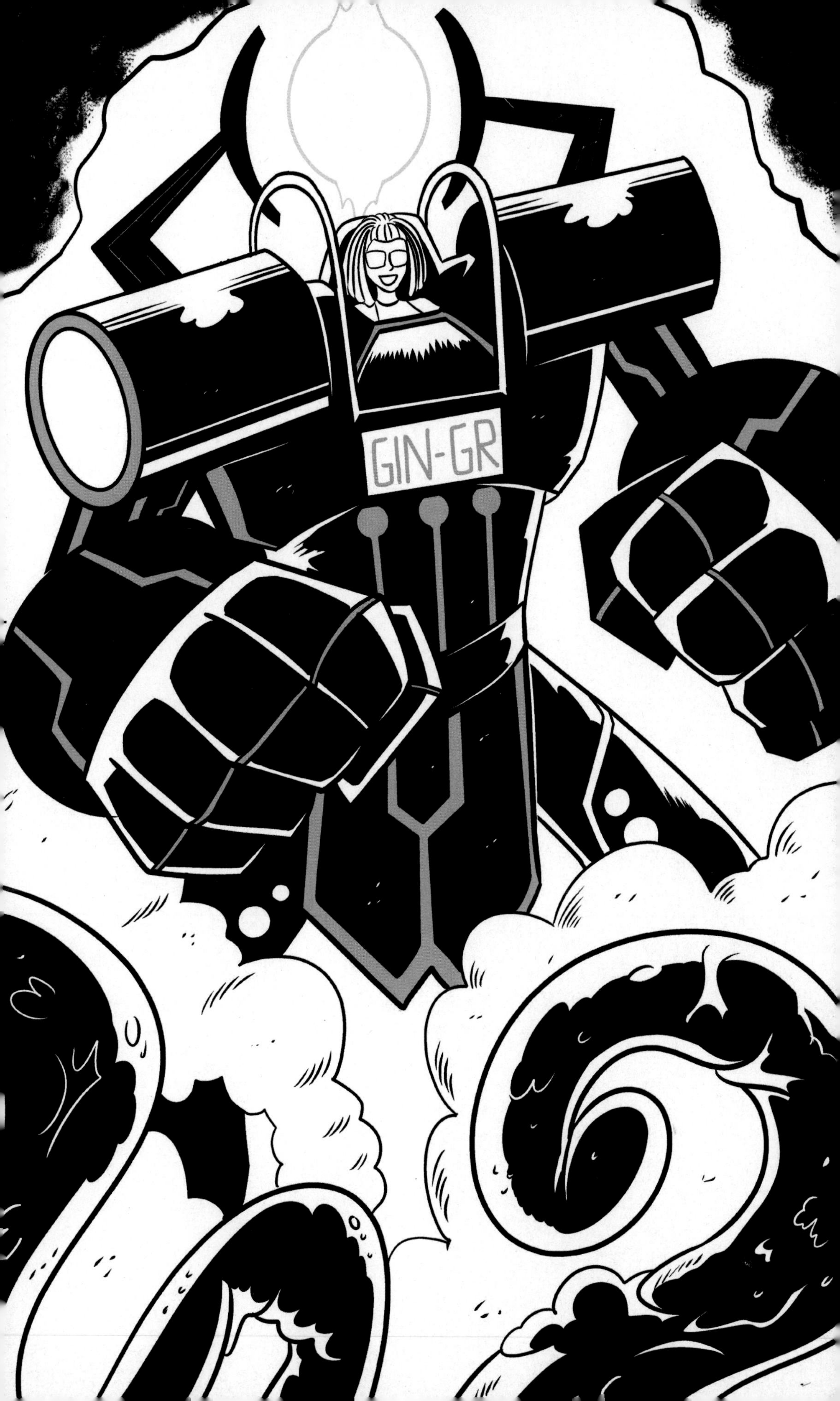
GIN-GR

VALIANT HIGH #4, pages 17, 18, and 22 (facing)
Art by DEREK CHARM

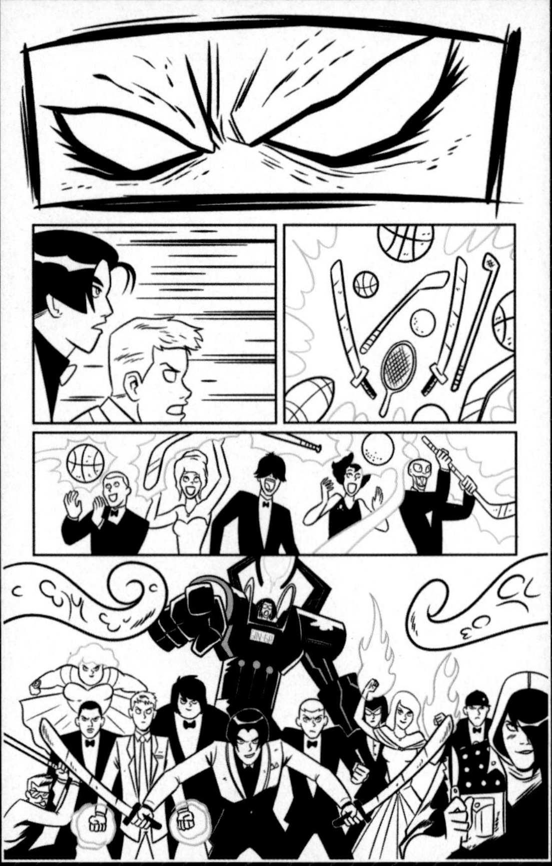

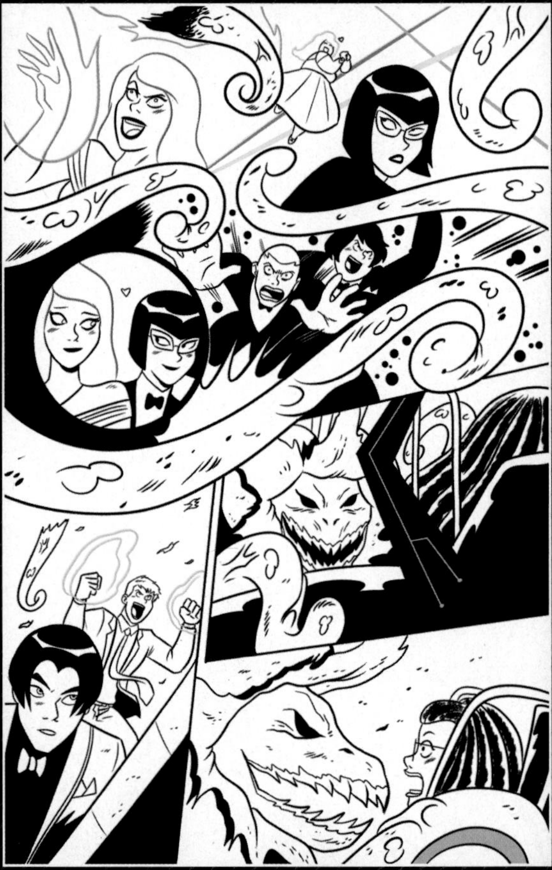

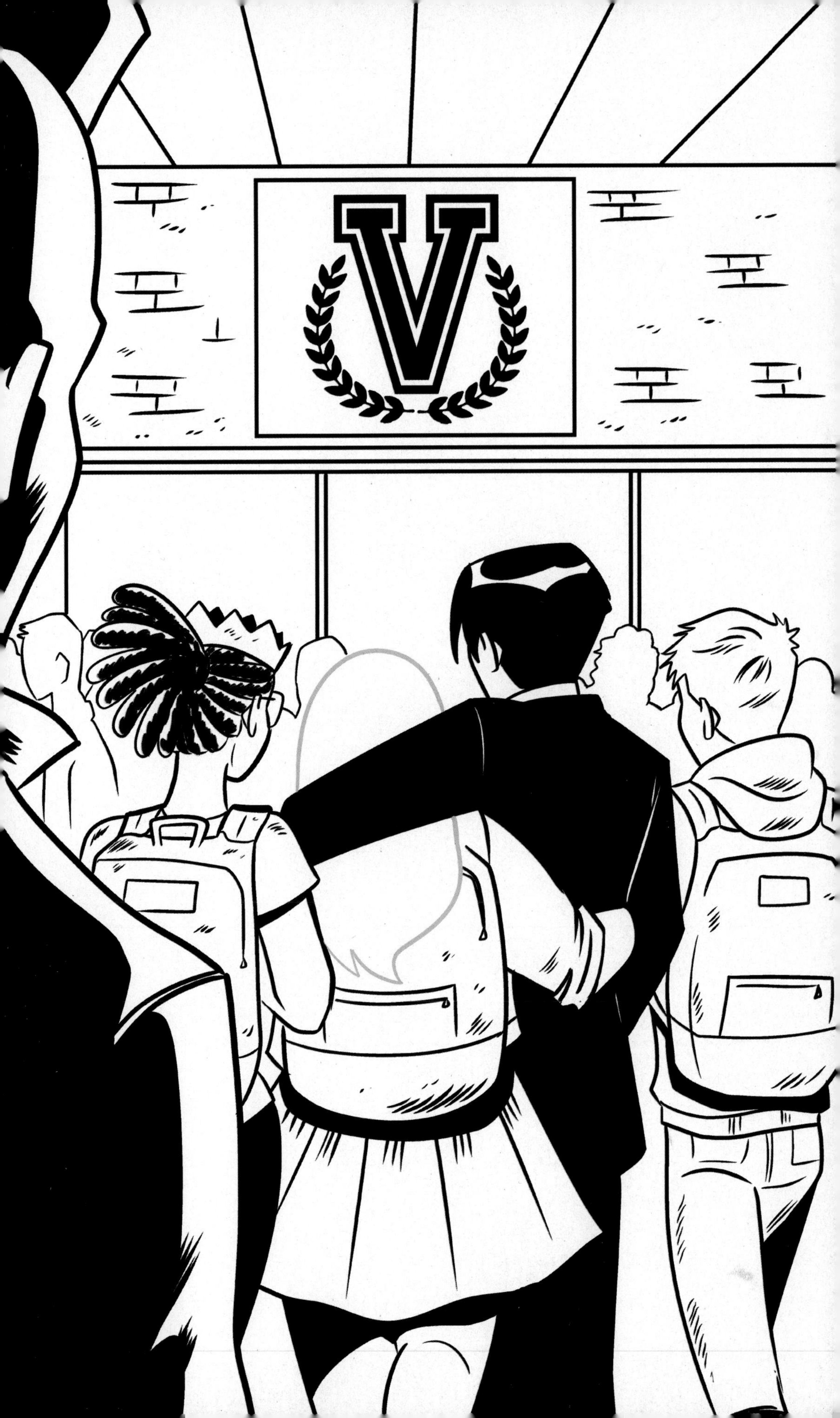

VALIANT
JODY HOUSER | PERE PÉREZ | MARGUERITE SAUVAGE
CALIFORNIA SCHEMING
Faith

VOL. 2: **CALIFORNIA SCHEMING**
TRADE PAPERBACK

VALIANT
JODY HOUSER | LOUISE SIMONSON | MEGHAN HETRICK | JOE EISMA | COLLEEN DORAN
SUPERSTAR
Faith
NAMED ONE OF THE YEAR'S BEST SERIES!
DOZENS OF AWARDS AND NOMINATIONS FROM THE A.V. CLUB, NERDIST, VOX, AND MANY MORE!

VOL. 3: **SUPERSTAR**
TRADE PAPERBACK

VALIANT
JODY HOUSER | JOE EISMA | KATE NIEMCZYK | MARGUERITE SAUVAGE
THE FAITHLESS
Faith
NOMINATED FOR
BEST NEW SERIES!

VOL. 3: **FAITHLESS**
TRADE PAPERBACK

VALIANT
FAITH
AND THE
FUTURE FORCE
JODY HOUSER
STEPHEN SEGOVIA
BARRY KITSON

FAITH AND THE FUTURE FORCE
TRADE PAPERBACK

EXPERIENCE THE LONG-AWAITED SOLO DEBUT

"★★★★★"
THE NERDIST
•
"★★★★★"
FIRST COMICS NEWS
•
"★★★★★"
COMIC BASTARDS
•
"★★★★★"
SPARTANTOWN
•
"★★★★½"
BIG COMIC PAGE
•
"★★★★½"
COMICOSITY
•
"★★★★½"
OUTRIGHT GEEKERY
•
"★★★★½"
AiPT!
•
"★★★★"
COMIC BOOK RESOURCES
•
"★★★★"
NEWSARAMA
•
"★★★★"
IGN
•
"★★★★"
DOOM ROCKET
•
"★★★★"
COMICWOW!

WRITTEN BY
JODY HOUSER
ART BY
FRANCIS PORTELA
MARGUERITE SAUVAGE
PERE PÉREZ
MEGHAN HETRICK
JOE EISMA
AND MORE

VALIANTUNIVERSE.COM
FB.COM/VALIANTCOMICS
TWITTER.COM/VALIANTCOMICS
#VALIANT

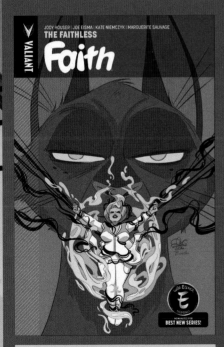

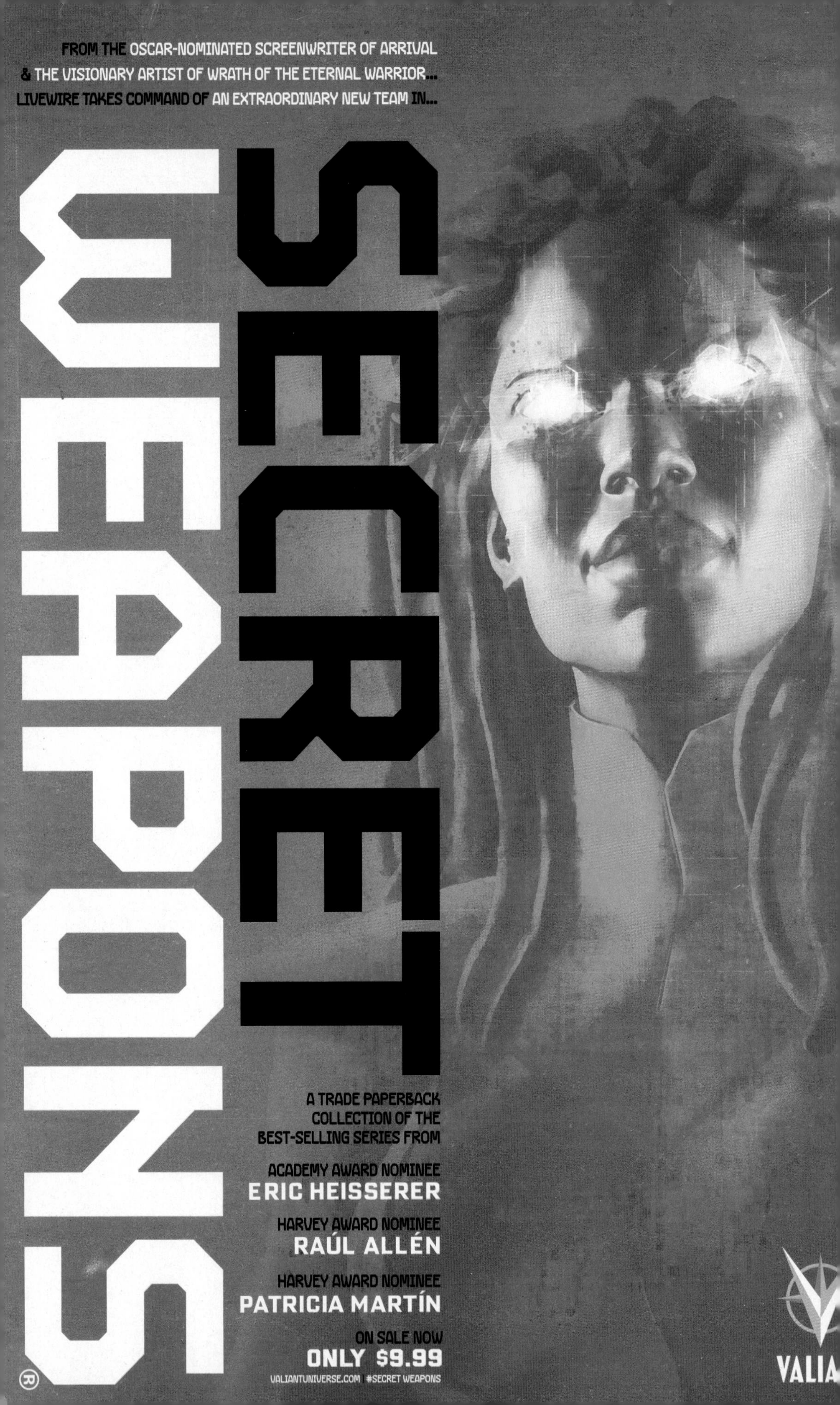
FROM THE OSCAR-NOMINATED SCREENWRITER OF ARRIVAL
& THE VISIONARY ARTIST OF WRATH OF THE ETERNAL WARRIOR...
LIVEWIRE TAKES COMMAND OF AN EXTRAORDINARY NEW TEAM IN...
SECRET WEAPONS®
A TRADE PAPERBACK COLLECTION OF THE BEST-SELLING SERIES FROM
ACADEMY AWARD NOMINEE
ERIC HEISSERER
HARVEY AWARD NOMINEE
RAÚL ALLÉN
HARVEY AWARD NOMINEE
PATRICIA MARTÍN
ON SALE NOW
ONLY $9.99
VALIANTUNIVERSE.COM | #SECRET WEAPONS
VALIA